MISTAKES OF NATURE

a novel

M R Cates

ISBN-13:
978-0615841014 (M R Cates)

ISBN-10:
0615841015

This is a work of fiction. All people, places, and events are either fictional or used in a fictional manner. Any similarity to real events or people is unintentional and coincidental. That said, the events in this book, or something very much like them, could indeed happen.

Dedicated to Sarah, who speaks with a voice of care and reason in my life, and in the lives of many others.

Prologue

IT WAS AFTER NINE IN THE EVENING when she left Hess Hall and walked briskly down off "the Hill" and across the university campus toward the library. Entering the expansive structure, fully lit and filled with busy students, she went to the desk and spoke to the clerk on duty, a young woman several years her senior.

"I have an order in for a book. Bea de Winter. Has it arrived?"

What the library clerk heard was a quiet, oddly childlike voice. And what she saw was a young woman who was a little smaller than average, with a nicely proportioned face but with eyes that were disturbing in their aspect. Only a single glance was given to those eyes, then the clerk looked away.

"I'll check," the clerk said, and strode through a doorway behind the counter.

Bea didn't look around, seemingly without curiosity for the people or the setting around her. She ran a hand through her short hair, standing with what appeared to be absolute patience.

The clerk returned, smiled politely and handed over a bound textbook. Bea signed the card, said thank you, and left with the book tucked into her backpack. Still in self-contained isolation she walked quietly to the dormitory a few blocks farther, near the western edge of the campus. Her room was on the third floor, at the end of the hall, occupying a corner. It was one of the premium rooms, equipped with a small kitchenette and a sitting area. The bed was screened from the sitting area by a high bookcase, built into the room. In effect, she had a small apartment, a luxury few dormitory students, graduate or undergraduate, were afforded.

With the backpack emptied and stowed, Bea spent a few minutes preparing a small meal for herself. She ate without fuss or fanfare. Actually, she cared little for food. Nor drink, with the exception of a good cup of coffee. She'd never drunk any alcoholic beverage, nor had any interest in them. This was in part because she wasn't legally old enough to imbibe such drinks, despite the fact that age restrictions had never applied to her in other areas of life. Bea finished eating, then cleaned up her few dishes and changed into well-worn pajamas, slippers, and a warm-but-frayed bathrobe, tossing the khakis, shirt and underwear into a hamper to be laundered, as always, every other weekend. The tasks of her day now done, she went to the mirror beside her bed and stood looking at her image. This was no examination of her appearance; she was looking herself directly in the eye. Then she sat down at her desk, tapped a combination into a lock on the drawer and withdrew a laptop computer. When it was booted up she took the memory stick she'd brought home and plugged it into one of the ports. She went to a file folder in the hard disk and started a program by clicking on "isolate.exe." When it was ready Bea set it to work on a data array from the memory stick.

"Five hours and ten minutes, Magdalene, more of less," she announced aloud to herself. Standing, she walked again over to the mirror and spoke to her image, "Tomorrow, with luck, we'll finish the structure. Do you have any questions?"

After a brief pause, Bea continued, in a different, stranger voice. "Yes, I have a question. Are the appropriate self-assembly conditions for the viral precursors in all genetic strains of males?"

"Hmm," she replied. "We get into that next week. But Magdalene, we certainly won't make that mistake. Any further questions?"

"No," she answered. Bea stepped away from the mirror, went over and poured herself a glass of water, then turned toward the mirror, and from about fifteen feet away, added, "So we'll be ready to release soon."

At this comment her face looked suddenly sad, and she spoke in a murmur, "Yes, soon. Very soon."

Chapter 1. Reflections

PROFESSOR WILLIAM CHARLES HAD LEFT a note in Bea de Winter's student mailbox. The note said simply, "Yes, I agree." He had dropped it off after locking up for the evening and making his way upstairs and out the front door of Hess Hall, located on the back slope of "The Hill" of the University of Tennessee. Professor Charles was en route to his car, located just outside, since he had the status to be the proud owner of a parking place along the circular road that connected the array of university buildings clustered on this landmark rise just above the huge Neyland Stadium, itself perched essentially on the bank of the Tennessee River.

It was mid September, moving toward fall. East Tennessee in autumn is rightly said to be one of the most beautiful places on earth. The air was crisp and cool, with the maple, oak, and gingko trees beginning to think about turning color. The fall term was in full swing and students were everywhere, moving in swarms, grouped together by twos, threes and fours. Charles loved the time of year, loved the campus, and loved his new job at UT. He had been hired just months before, forsaking his alma mater, Harvard, for an opportunity that was too marvelous to turn down. In a few minutes he'd pulled onto Cumberland Avenue and turned left, proceeding along the "strip" of university-related businesses until the street name changed to Kingston Pike. Once on Kingston Pike the route continued past churches and old mansions till he reached the turn-in to Sequoia Hills, Knoxville's expansive residential area on the shore of the river and only a few miles from both the university and the city center. His home was elegant but not large, about fifty years old, on a lot full of ancient oaks, hemlocks, and fully mature dogwoods that gave promise of a spectacular spring ahead. It would be his first spring there.

William Charles considered Bea de Winter the brightest student he'd ever had. And this was no casual belief from a man who was himself at the pinnacle of regard in his field. Bea was very quiet of temperament, enigmatic in a certain way, but astonishing in her intellectual abilities, insights, and laboratory skills. He'd brought her with him from Harvard, where she'd begun her graduate work at eighteen, passing the qualifying examinations with flying colors less than a year later. Tennessee had accepted her credits and examination scores, moving her directly into a fellowship program.

Professor Charles, as he did with everyone, especially females, kept Bea emotionally at arm's length. His interactions with her were strictly business and strictly formal. Further, he treated her with utmost and unwavering respect. Never would he walk in on her during her work or call her laboratory phone while she worked. His communication was almost entirely by hand written message, left in her student mailbox. And her responses and inquiries were made the same way: messages left in his faculty mailbox. Thus it was that Charles had left the note, replying to her earlier message: "Professor Charles, would you agree to my presenting a paper at the American Physical Society meeting in Albuquerque next month? I intend to present on the neural receptor distortion study. My fellowship will cover the travel costs."

Bea read his positive reply with no surprise. After reading the note she walked briskly back downstairs two flights to the biophysics laboratory, passing several students on the route, paying no attention to any of them. Had they been visitors passing through Hess Hall they'd not have known who she was. Bea dressed in loose khaki pants and oxford cloth blue shirts - almost every day. She wore sneakers and kept her short brown hair simply combed out, neat but not given any additional flair. On occasions when she had to make a presentation Bea wore slightly neater and newer khaki pants and blue shirt, but never a dress or female business suit. Professor Charles, who was also her dissertation advisor, was fully convinced that Bea de Winter would one day walk across the stage in Stockholm wearing khakis and a blue shirt.

Biophysics was a new area of emphasis at UT. William Charles, of course, was the reason. Until he had arrived, research using physical principles to study biological problems had focused mostly on near-repetitions of work that had been going on for many years. Charles' team dealt with kinematic processes within the human brain. In particular, he had made breakthroughs in understanding how the electric impulses from neurons - in number, intensity and degree of overlap - were responsible for memory and other types of brain function. The brain, in a sense, was "written" on by the learning processes and the available connections encoded by the genes. When Bea de Winter came on the scene she began adding insights into how genetic "learning" occurred within the brain; that is, how nature had put the brain together, and how it functioned in common with other mammals, as well as those ways which were uniquely human. One of the young student's greatest strengths was her ability to generate computer algorithms that emulated genetic processes. This kind of programming simulated the trial-and-error learning that goes on in the brain. As the brain receives sensory inputs - sights, sounds, smells, and the like - those neuron electrical sequences that are beneficial in some way become more firmly imprinted, less beneficial firings are not repeated, and over many millions of repetitions pathways are created that comprise learning and memory. Bea had been simulating these activities since undergraduate days using computer programs of her own design, run on massively parallel programmable chips, all coordinated by her desktop computer.

The greatest strength of genetic programming lay in the possibility that extremely complicated sequences of simulated brain function could be implemented without actually having to know exactly what was going on in detail. The route from point A to point B didn't have to be known. The only critical thing would be to know when point B was reached. The random processes that took place activated sequences that were either successful or not in producing some defined final result. Each approximation of the desired result got better and better, but the route to getting there didn't have to be, nor could it be known - given the degree of randomness imposed on the process. Again, this was quite analogous to the human brain, where we produce thoughts and draw conclusions mostly unaware of what route our brain took to achieve the results. Bea de Winter was given free reign by Professor Charles to go any direction she wished in genetic programming. She, in effect, had designed her own dissertation project. He knew instinctively that she had insights in this area that he could not hope to guide, already far deeper than he could go or would be interested in trying to go. His own research - concentrating on specific types of neutron functions - would be helped immeasurably by her work but was unnecessary to make her work successful, since she was concentrating on speculative processes - processes that may or may not actually occur in real brains.

—

In Bea's room before her mirror, she looked once again into her own eyes. Then Bea as Magdalene said, "Will William Charles suspect your neural simulations have a natural tie to the virus and trigger mechanism?"

And she answered herself, "Ah, Magdalene, of course not. And the precursors are natural proteins with difficult-to-distinguish variant surfaces. Besides, he is preoccupied with other matters." After a hesitation, she modified her statement. "A very wise man, however. We will not underestimate him."

Bea stood for a full five minutes, contemplating her eyes in the mirror, then crossed over to the bed, pulled back the covers, hung her robe on a coat hook mounted on the back of the closet door, got into bed, slid under the covers, turned out the light, and fell asleep within five minutes.

2. Guinea Pigs

MELISSA THOMAS WAS A SOPHOMORE at UT. From the little town of Sweetwater to the southwest, she was tall, pretty, with a good figure. The young woman was twenty, and would be twenty-one before Thanksgiving, something for which she was grateful, because Melissa had a bit of a drinking problem. She also was a smoker. Fortunately, she had her dear Reggie to buy both booze and cigarettes for her. Reggie was actually Reginald Pendergast, a wonderful hunk that spent essentially every night in her dorm room. Melissa's room was two doors from Bea de Winter's room. Because both she and Reggie smoked heavily Melissa's door was often left open to help ventilate the room. This was something of a source of irritation to Bea and other students living in the dorm.

Melissa and Reggie had sex over and over again at all times of day and night. They did close the door, however, for that. Bea, in passing the room, often caught whiffs of cigarette smoke and, when the door was open, glimpses of Melissa. From time to time she'd chance upon Reggie as well, often as he entered or left the room. Reggie was tall, a senior, handsome, and totally oblivious of Bea. If he noticed her at all it was to see a plain, smallish girl who would not deserve a second look. Bea thought about him as little as possible, and mostly felt sorry for Melissa.

Thanks to an enterprising printer in Knoxville, the New York Times was delivered daily to Bea's door before six o'clock, giving rise to a ritual opening of her door, not long after six, to retrieve it. Bea indulged herself in a "real" subscription partly because she enjoyed doing the crossword puzzles. Crossword puzzles, in fact, and occasionally dawdling over a good cup of coffee were basically Bea de Winter's only diversions. Melissa, surprisingly awake at such an early hour, had come out into the hallway stark naked and giggling. Why she was so disposed Bea had no idea, nor tried to contemplate one. As Bea bent to reach for the paper lying just outside the door, she noticed Melissa there in all her naughty glory, and the two found themselves looking directly at each other.

Melissa, flushed from both excitement and apparent exertion, said, "Good morning!" Then she wiggled in a mocking, seductive way, swayed her hips, and ran a hand through her mass of provocatively unkempt hair.

Bea said nothing for a moment, but didn't drop her eyes. "Good morning, Melissa," she then said. Afterwards, she simply picked up her paper, by feel, eyes locked on Melissa's eyes. The look was not aggressive or hostile but was mostly a look of quizzical pity, and thereby - as far as the naked girl was concerned - carried with it a terrifying aura. Then Bea turned aside and went back into her room. Melissa's giggles stopped, and she suddenly felt embarrassed, crossing arms over her exposed chest and bending slightly, knees together, to shield her loins. Fortunately, Reggie hadn't locked her out. When she got back inside her room Melissa was trembling.

As her surprise at the exuberant Melissa subsided, Bea went to her computer and looked at the results of her last night's run. The program ran an optimized series of random tests - in imitation of multiple genetic generations - and eventually reached an anticipated result. The result, however, was not the same thing as an answer. In this case, the anticipated result was a group of protein structures that would combine, when the chemicals around them didn't interfere with the charges on their surfaces, to form a virus. What the actual viral structure turned out to be wasn't certain - and that structure was the real answer. Bea started nodding to herself as she examined the details that had been produced by the sequencing. She then took its structure and put it in as input data into another program she'd written, entitled "neuraltrig.exe." After a relatively short run time - about fifteen seconds - the code had done its job, displaying a pattern of line drawings she'd devised to represent brain connections of different types. Bea sighed. She leaned back and looked up at the ceiling. She sighed again, stood, and spoke to the mirror, "Magdalene, it's basically done. Soon, don't you think?"

Bea's voice shifted in timbre, to a softer, reflective tone. "Yes," she murmured. "And where?"

Then she said to herself. "Close by will do just fine."

–

Bea de Winter spent the next two full days and most of the evenings in her laboratory in Hess Hall. To say it was her laboratory was technically incorrect: it was under the control of Professor Charles, and could have been used by other students and faculty. But it was left to Bea exclusively. The lab was relatively small, about 300 square feet and isolated. Perfect for her. Her work these two days had concentrated on the virus she had designed digitally. It was a virus designed to form within the human body by the right kind of chemical triggers. The design worked in the computer. And she had human blood samples to use to make culture media for the synthesis. As far as Bea could determine - and she had an enormous range of resources, from the entire Internet to all of thirty research libraries she could access by computer - the virus she'd designed had never actually existed anywhere before. She also guessed - and had designed it accordingly - that the virus would replicate quickly and easily in the right kind of blood environment, but not reproduce in other blood environments. That distinction had been the hardest part of her work - work that had been going on in the background of her dissertation research for more than a year. By the evening of the first of those two days, her virus had been synthesized in an appropriate blood sample, triggering its formation exactly as her genetic algorithm had predicted. Late that evening and the entire next day she tested its growth patterns and showed conclusively - at least with this original strain - that it would not reproduce in any but the proper blood chemistry.

Nothing she had done in this area had been published, nor revealed to anyone but herself. The fact that she had actually synthesized a living virus was not a special point of pride to her. It was a mechanism she needed to employ, and little more. On the third morning after her eye-to-eye encounter with the au naturel version of Melissa, Bea went over to obtain a couple of test mice from the biomedical laboratory at the university where the mouse population was raised. In the required written request, she explained that she needed a male and female for neural scans to compare with predicted results from programming. Technically she was accurate in her request; it was a procedure she'd followed a number to times already, as part of her research.

The young man, a Master's Degree student, who cared for the mice was one of the few people on campus with whom Bea spoke. His name was Mike Baylor, a boy of mostly African American heritage, hailing from Detroit.

To provide the mice, Mike had to have Bea's signature. She wrote quickly, took the mice - already transferred to the little cage she'd brought with her - and said, "Thanks, Mike."

Mike looked at her with dark, generous eyes. "Hey, you're welcome, Bea. But listen, before you go, can I ask you a question?"

"If you wish." Bea turned to face him, her attention jerked away from introspection.

"Uh, I mean, I want you to be cool with this okay, but they say you're some kind of prodigy, you know. Are you really jus' twenty?"

Bea didn't answer immediately. "Who are *they*?" she asked.

"Y'know, jus' people. People who know you, like." He grinned.

"What people, Mike?"

"Maybe students, I donno."

"Curious," said Bea. "But why would you ask?" She seemed to be teasing him, but only slightly.

Mike, with his dark skin, wasn't really able to blush. But the blood did rush to the surface. He hadn't expected such a response. "Uh, Bea, don't worry about it. Doesn't matter."

"Then why would you ask, if it doesn't matter to you?"

"I was ... well, y'know, jus' curious. That's all." He smiled, looking very innocent.

Bea gave him a kind of return smile. As much of a smile as she could manage. "I see. Very well. I *am* twenty, and will be twenty-one in about a month. I can't speak about being a prodigy, however. I simply am who I am."

"Right, it's cool," said Mike, eyebrows wrinkling. "So, jus' twenty. Pretty impressive. You'll be Doctor de Winter before long, huh?"

"Yes," she said. "I need to be on my way, Mike. Thank you again."

"Sure. Bye." He was grinning again as she gave him a last glance.

Bea walked away with her mice. She pondered Mike Baylor. As one who prided herself on her objectivity, she admitted to herself he was in a different category than most males in her acquaintance. She liked him in a certain way. He was a very non-threatening person. Mike was so much unlike, say, Melissa's Reggie. She wasn't sure why she liked him, since he was easily as large and masculine as Reggie. It was his attitude, she knew, and his non-threatening eyes. What was going on in Mike Baylor's brain that put him in this different category? Or was he really different? She had been fooled before, and admitted there was always that risk.

For three full weeks Bea tested her virus. She returned to Mike Baylor for three more mice: two males and another female. The weather, during that time got colder, and the deciduous trees turned colorful. Tennessee was moving toward winter, but the fall weather was lovely and basically mild. It was heartening weather, and matched the mood of the young researcher. She was now convinced that the virus she had created digitally in a computer could actually come into being within living tissue. More importantly, it did indeed have the major characteristics she had designed into it. For fifteen months she'd been working for this moment. And, in parallel, Bea completed several more phases of her doctoral research program and prepared the presentation for the meeting she'd gotten permission to attend. During this entire period she did not see Melissa Thomas at all, though she did hear her several times while passing a partly opened door. The noises were sexual in nature, to Bea's disgust, but were not unexpected.

Along with her concentrated effort, Bea had to deal, for a few days, with a burden she was mostly irritated about. She was asthmatic, and occasionally had a bout of chronic congestion and breathing difficulties that required medication from an inhaler several times a day. The interruption always angered her, even though she wasn't seriously worried about her condition. It was, after all, under control. In the back of her mind she'd planned to take her asthma head-on eventually, and work toward designing a chemical to permanently take care of the problem she'd identified as a natural weakness in her immune system. Slowed by this necessity, she continued her design work doggedly, fuming occasionally at being required to live in a human body in the first place.

Two days before her planned departure for Albuquerque Bea was ready to run her "release," as she called it. To form the virus in the bloodstream required a combination of chemicals that would enter the bloodstream without being broken down. Bea soon determined that the best method would be to breathe in the chemicals. The lungs, then, would eventually introduce them to the bloodstream, which would eventually get the assembled virus to the brain. All she had to do was get the chemical precursors - the virus building blocks - into the bloodstream. The precursors would be difficult to identify among the myriad other molecules that were there naturally. Her approach to getting the necessary triggers - to start the virus building process - into the bloodstream was to use another group of viruses, with the precursor chemicals bound to them. The carrier viruses, benign in themselves - using methods and routes she couldn't actually identify or write down, but had modeled with her program - over a few hours time, got into the bloodstream with the chemical "riders" still in place. There the chemical riders became unstable and drifted off the virus vehicles, available to begin their assembling process as they encountered the right chemical building blocks. The benign carrier viruses would soon break down and be absorbed, disappearing in only a few hours, leaving only the assembly molecules. Bea's virus strains carrying the precursors were prepared in the lab and dried into a pale pink powder. This preparation step was a critical one, and required her to don protective gear and use a glove box, both of which she'd done from time to time for other dangerous procedures. When the powder was ready to use she double sealed it into a small plastic sample vial and put it into her backpack.

As part of her earlier preparation, three weeks earlier Bea had found Melissa's door unlocked one afternoon, opened it and looked around at the inside portion of the door latch to get the code and manufacturer's name on the lock. Then she went to the dormitory maintenance man - an older fellow named Murphy - and asked for a copy of the key to Melissa's room number, implying of course that it was her room, explaining that she had accidentally dropped her own key into a sewer grating along the street. Mr. Murphy, who had six dormitories to maintain, had no reason to suspect the petite, quiet, youngish student, and produced a key for her.

It was about four in the afternoon when Bea came out of her laboratory and walked across the campus to the dorm, getting home many hours earlier than usual. It was Friday, a day she knew that Melissa and Reggie would be together, probably first for sex in Melissa's room, then out to some bar or restaurant, then return for more sex. The routine was common, occurring virtually every Friday night. Everyone on their hallway knew about it and expected it. As Bea passed Melissa's room, the door was closed but the action inside was loud enough to hear. About six, Reggie and Melissa left. Bea, alert to their departure, stepped out into the hallway as they disappeared and went to Melissa's door.

With the duplicate key, Bea, wearing protective laboratory gloves and filtering nose plugs she'd inserted before leaving her own room, let herself into Melissa's room, finding it - as expected - in a state of chaos. Clothing - mostly female - was strewn around everywhere. Cigarette butts filled four or five different ashtrays. It took Bea a few minutes to find what she wanted: two opened packs of cigarettes. Reggie, she'd figured, smoked one brand and Melissa another. Using a toothpick, she pushed a hole into the tobacco fill of one cigarette in each pack. One pack had twelve cigarettes inside, the other, eight. Then she tried a kerchief over her nose for good measure, opened the little plastic vial, and carefully poured the dried viral powder into the holes in the cigarettes, putting half into each hole. Then with the toothpick she worked the tobacco back into place on the outside, leaving the cigarette as if untouched. The powder was about half an inch deep into the tobacco. That done, Bea rearranged the cigarette packs like she'd found them, made sure she had everything she'd brought in, and returned to her own room. There she flushed the emptied virus vial, toothpick, shed gloves and nose plugs.

After washing her hands, Bea went straight to her mirror. "Magdalene," she said quietly, "it has begun." Then she sighed, slowly expelling a breath.

Following a long inspection of her reflection, Bea answered in her other voice, "Yes, I suppose it has. You've done well."

Bea closed her eyes, opening them only after a full fifteen seconds. There was a touch of moisture in each. "Have I? I truly hope so."

3. Reception

SOMETIME DURING THE NIGHT that followed, Melissa and Reggie smoked the doctored cigarettes. The viral particles entrained within the smoke had no taste at all. Bea had surmised that a sizable fraction of the dried powder might be destroyed by the heat of the burning tobacco, but only a trace was necessary to do the job. Some of the dried mass, carried by smoke, would enter the lungs as tiny particles, reactivate in the moist environment, and distribute itself as discrete viruses, going into the blood there in the walls of the lungs.

Bea, long before the lovers were awake, had walked through the cool fall air to her lab, resolved about what she had done, telling herself to be patient with the process. Her best estimate was that whatever effects she had stimulated in Reggie's brain would begin to accumulate enough to evidence themselves after about ten days, or a little longer. If, in fact, anything happened at all. Bea was realistic about her release. There was always a chance she would have to try again. Whatever happened, when and if it did, she would have gone and returned from Albuquerque.

During the passing days, Bea - as she always did - kept busy. Her ability to concentrate was astonishing. She had a child's single-minded focus on whatever fascination she had chosen for the moment. Yet in another sense Bea was extraordinarily adult.

Because she was so obviously young and so petite, the graduate student Bea de Winter was already whispered about around the UT campus. She had quickly developed a reputation as a prodigy, and was therefore - despite her own irritation at it - considered odd. As a girl, her remarkable intellect had been noticed by her father, Luke. Luke hired private instructors for her, and Bea's early formal education was conducted at home. When she was thirteen years old she received a high-school diploma and began study at Stanford University, with a major in biophysics. Now here she was, well over half a continent away, nearing her twenty-first birthday, well on her way to a doctorate.

—

Two weeks had passed, and Bea had been back from Albuquerque several days already, before she saw Melissa Thomas again. It was mid afternoon, an unusual time for the graduate student to be in the dorm, and Melissa's door was partly open, cigarette smoke ventilating into the hall. Forcing herself into a disposition she really didn't have, Bea stopped, peeped in and saw the young woman reclined on her bed, back to the door. The sophomore was in her underwear, skimpy items that were barely sufficient to their design function. She had her head on a pillow and was watching a small television, mounted in bookshelves against the far wall. Some kind of daytime soap was playing.

Bea tapped on Melissa's door.

"Huh?" the girl muttered and rolled back to glance toward the door.

The girl's mostly bare skin seemed to glow in profile against the window light. Bea said politely, "Hello, Melissa."

"Hi," came the surprisingly gracious reply. "What's up?" It was reasonable for Melissa to consider that Bea de Winter would not simply be passing the time of day with her, especially since it required getting her attention.

"Haven't seen you in a while," Bea said, sounding more awkward than she wanted to. "I'm surprised not to see your friend."

Melissa sat up, seemingly unaware that she was so thoroughly exposed, then got to her feet. The taller young women instantly gained a position of advantage over the peculiar girl at her door. As she stood, the fact of her thong panties became abundantly clear. Melissa said, cocking her head just a little to illustrate her amazement at having the conversation, "Really? I didn't know you wondered about Reggie." It was a thinly veiled poke at Bea's perceived nature. Bea knew, but promptly ignored it.

"Well," said the khaki-clad visitor, undeterred, "It's just that I've been out of town for a while and - pardon me for acting curiously." Bea put a touch of self remonstration into her tone.

"Reggie's coming over today," Melissa said, with a tinge of arrogance in her smile. "Want me to let you know when he gets here?"

Bea surprised her with, "Thank you. That would be nice. Sorry to have disturbed you." Then she promptly walked away from the door toward her own.

Melissa sprang forward and out into the hall, loosely bound breasts gyrating from the exertion. Brow furrowed, she stared at Bea's retreating back for a moment. Had she actually said she wanted to know when Reggie came? Melissa shook her head in something akin to amazement.

And as Bea turned the key, the other called out tersely, "I'll bring him by when he gets here, Bea, to get your approval. Okay?" Then she wrinkled her nose, but not so that Bea could see.

Bea opened her door, started through it and looked back. "Thank you, Melissa. I'd appreciate that." She added a pleasant look and disappeared into her own room.

–

An hour later, halfway across campus, Bea saw her professor, William Charles, walking her direction. He was as surprised to run into her as she to him.

"Hello, Bea," he greeted her in his pleasant way. "How are things going?"

Bea stopped and made eye contact with the man. He, like most people, towered over her, but she seemed not to notice the disparity in their heights. "Hello, Professor Charles," she replied, maintaining her formality as usual. "Didn't expect to encounter you on campus this evening."

"A reception at the Faculty Club, Bea," Charles said, with a sigh. "Can't get out of it."

"I see." Bea glanced ahead as if she were about to continue on her way.

Charles then suddenly asked, "Why don't you go over there with me, Bea?"

"To this reception, sir?"

"Yes."

"But I have no idea of what it is."

"Sorry, Bea," Charles replied, shifting his tone a little to try not to sound dominant over the young student he faced. "It's a gathering to greet UT's new senior fellow. I think she might like to meet you."

"You mean Dr. Cortland, I suppose?" She knew the Department of Microbiology had obtained this famous scientist, a kind of matching pearl to William Charles in Biophysics.

"Yes, Virginia Cortland. Naturally you would have heard. Anyway, since she's to be a colleague, I suspect she'd love to meet you, and I'm sure you'd enjoy meeting her."

Bea had turned sideways in her progress, and had stepped off the sidewalk back a few steps onto the grass. "But, sir, will there be students at this reception?"

He shrugged. "Who cares? Join me. It won't take much of your time. I doubt that you are behind on any of your work."

"I'm always behind, sir," she said, "but yes, I'll go if you wish."

The silence between them was palpable as they walked together to the Faculty Club. Neither broke it, though Professor Charles considered asking Bea a few mundane questions about her work. He reconsidered, however, knowing Bea would hear the words for what they were. She always kept him up to date on her efforts, unfailingly sending brief reports by email or handwritten notes to inform him of some recent result. So, the only sounds during their walking were the slight scrapes of shoes, the chirping of birds that were always in abundance around the campus, and distant background conversations that came and faded quickly.

The Faculty Club was a beautiful old mansion, modified from its original design, near the southern boundary of the campus. It was used regularly for functions of that sort, and offered a quiet, very charming informal setting for professors and other university staff who wanted to stop by for a drink and conversation. Bea had never been in the Faculty Club, and never had considered it a place she'd like to go, but there she was, coming up the front steps with her professor. The student looked young enough to be mistaken for William Charles' niece or daughter. She certainly did not give the external impression of the mind and disposition she actually had - unless you looked into her eyes.

The group of university faculty and administration was, to Bea's relief, only a handful. The gathering had been going already for over an hour, and most of those who'd simply come to be polite had already gone. Bea recognized the university president, Jefferson Gregory, who'd been brought in by Governor Wilkins shortly after her election. Dr. Gregory was a man Bea respected, and had been the implementer of the governor's aggressive makeover of the University of Tennessee system. Next to Gregory, carrying a half drunk goblet of white wine was a woman Bea didn't recognize, therefore she guessed to be Virginia Cortland. Cortland was not much taller than Bea, slightly plump, and looked very much like a grandmother - which in fact she was - but carried herself with an air of confidence that could be picked up on at quite a distance. Three others were in the conversation group, male professors that Bea vaguely recognized. The meeting room's fireplace was burning cheerily, and several student servers in white aprons were busy removing hors d'oeuvres plates and glasses and straightening up. Two other smaller clusters of people were talking quietly, thought often animatedly.

William Charles, after getting a glass of wine for himself and some sparkling water that Bea chose, led her over to the guest of honor. One of the three professors had left the circle by this time. Bea was introduced to all four, and graciously took each hand in turn. None of the adults questioned Dr. Charles' presumption of bringing a student to the reception. And, of course, all of them knew about Bea de Winter.

Virginia Cortland said to Bea, "I hear wonderful things about your work, Miss de Winter. UT is very fortunate to have you." The new senior fellow had a rich, unaccented voice, comparable in its commanding tone to that of Dr. Gregory across from her, but without any trace of arrogance.

"And you, too, doctor," Bea replied. "I read your paper on immune responses to mutating virile strains. Very interesting, and very helpful."

Cortland glanced around, aware that a technical conversation would quickly exclude the others there except Dr. Charles, but responded anyway, "I understand you're using genetic algorithms to predict neuron sequencing in short term memory."

Bea nodded. "We have a grant from the Alzheimer Foundation."

"Makes sense," smiled Dr. Cortland. "We're only a breakthrough or two away, aren't we?"

Bea glanced at Charles, then nodded again. "I'd say yes, doctor. Stem cells have already done most of the hard work. Thanks to microbiology." The compliment had been both honest and calculating.

If the middle aged scientist-physician considered the youngster's comments unusual or out of place, she didn't show it. Charles, however, realized that going on this way much longer would smack of impoliteness, so he said, "Virginia, why don't you come over to Biophysics soon and you and Bea can do all the shop talking you wish?" He added a smile that both women took as a gentle reproach.

"I'll do that Bill," Cortland nodded. "Pardon me for my excitement about this young lady's remarkable work." She glanced around at the others, showing by her look that she was now back at their disposal.

Bea picked up the cue quickly and said, "Thank you, doctor. You're being too generous. But I'd be happy to discuss our work with you, at your convenience, of course."

–

Bea was back in her room before nine, and considered meeting Virginia Cortland to have been worth the effort. After putting on pajamas she stood at the mirror and considered her visage. "Magdalene," she said quietly, "how nice that Cortland is here. Wouldn't you agree?"

"In part," came her reply in that different voice. "It is better to have the clever ones nearby, of course, but ..."

She shifted to her first voice. "You're saying, we should be careful of Cortland, then?"

And in the second voice, after a knowing look at herself, with a wrinkling of worry, "Exactly."

4. Conversations

THE NEXT DAY BEA MADE HER WAY to the biomedical mouse lab around ten in the morning. Mike Baylor greeted her pleasantly. He was in his usual bright mood.

"Hey, Bea, you're looking cool as usual. You okay?"

"Fine, Mike," she answered, mind distant. His friendliness didn't seem to register. She signed an order for two test mice and handed it to him.

"Research goin' well?" he asked, undaunted, always friendly to her despite consistent coolness.

"Yes, it is," she said, and looked up at him. He seemed very much the same as always. That day he was in jeans and a tee shirt bearing the logo of the Detroit Tigers. He was a strong young man, she could see.

"Bet we'll all know about you some of these days." Mike took the form and turned to go back to retrieve the mice.

"Probably so," she shrugged.

When he returned with the two white creatures, he continued as if he hadn't left the room. "These mice are important, huh? You've used quite a few of them. But don't tell me what happens to 'em." He grinned.

"Yes, Mike. They substitute for humans. Very useful."

"Hey, they tell me that," he said. "But I don't really see how a little wiggly thing like a mouse can be anything like a ... a person."

Bea, who suddenly seemed very patient, gave him a thin smile. "Mice genes are a lot like ours, Mike."

"Yeah, I hear that. I know that's the reason, but ... it's hard to understand. Doesn't seem right – at least to me."

"What's your major, Mike, if you don't mind my asking?

"I'm in botany."

"Are you a graduate student?"

He nodded.

"But working in the mouse house?"

"It was ... the job was available," Mike said. "I didn't mind messin' with the little guys. And I get to meet geniuses, too." Another grin.

She nodded similarly to the way he had. "I see."

As Bea started to leave, Mike added, "Hey, Bea, I guess you're twenty-one now, huh?"

The girl turned. Her eyes flashed a warning at his familiarity, but she knew it was unintentional; so she responded pleasantly enough. "I suppose I am. Is that important to you?"

He shrugged. "Damn straight. You can buy beer."

Bea's eyes rolled. "Right. Goodbye, Mike."

He watched her as she strode away. She was so young, yet acted so old. Mike didn't smile, but he did shake his head. He always felt good after she'd come by.

–

Bea worked in the campus laboratory well into the night. It was approaching midnight when she left the lab and started toward the dorm. The weather had turned rainy, forcing her to slip into a couple of intervening buildings during showery periods. Despite the well lit sidewalks, she was anxious about being out so late. Only her logical mind and determination made it possible for her to walk quietly instead of running toward her destination. When she finally entered the dorm - having avoided most of the rain - she was agitated and a little angry. She started down toward her room, suddenly thinking again about Melissa and her Reggie. She liked Melissa and certainly didn't hate Reggie. Melissa was a pleasant, non-threatening person, really. Reggie was someone not to be thought about much.

She stopped at Melissa's door and listened intently for a moment. There was music playing - ridiculous stuff, in Bea's mind - but no conversation or noise that might be associated with their usual animal rutting. Probably Reggie wasn't there. Bea raised her hand and knocked. She had carefully composed herself. When she heard no response she knocked louder. Immediately, the music stopped.

"What?" Melissa asked, opening the door. The young woman was wearing a tee shirt. It extended down like an extremely short dress. Her torso moved under the cloth, leaving distinct shapes for the observer, darker at the tips. She added, "What's going on?"

Bea asked, almost casually, "How are you, Melissa?"

"Damn, Bea, what do you want?"

"I expected you to introduce me to Reggie last night."

"What?" Melissa's pretty face formed a scowl of disgust.

"Remember, we had discussed it earlier." Bea's tone was very calm but her heart was racing. Conversation took strong self control.

"Hell, Bea, you're weird, you know that?"

"I suppose I am. Did Reggie not come over then?"

Melissa leaned out and looked up and down the hall, then stepped back, her actions indicating that Bea should come in and close the door. And Bea did so.

Melissa went back across her room and sat down in the chair by her desk. The tee shirt rode up on long shapely legs, showing the visitor more skin than many would consider proper. After looking at Bea a couple of seconds, she asked, "You want to sit down?"

"Is this a conversation, then?" Bea replied, moving toward the other chair in the room, an armchair similar to a pair that Bea's larger space held.

"Why not?" Melissa said. "Is that okay?" The question was presented with a definite bitter tone but without perceivable malice.

"Of course," Bea said, and sat, bringing her knees together. The loose khakis and carefully buttoned shirt were a marked contrast to the near nudity of her hostess.

"Do you mind telling me why are you suddenly so interested in Reggie?" Melissa blurted out.

Bea's eyebrows raised, then her shoulders in a shrug. "He's around here a lot."

"So?"

"Are you suggesting I not be interested in him, then?"

Melissa blew out some breath. "Why are you, anyway? Didn't think you cared about men."

"Why did you think that, Melissa?"

A petite, very young looking girl was facing a buxom, obviously sexy creature and speaking to her very much like a mother would speak to a daughter or a sister to a younger sister. The buxom one answered, "From what I hear, anyway."

Bea's eyes hardened. "Who speaks about my opinion of men?"

Melissa shrugged, "Hey cool it, Bea. It's just what I hear. But ... coming in here and talking about Reggie seems pretty weird, considering."

"Considering what?"

Melissa used both hands to rub her eyes. "He's ... gone home." She wasn't crying but did have a somber look.

A thrill went through Bea, but she waited a moment before saying, "Really? That's peculiar. His professors will be difficult to explain that to."

"Hell," Melissa muttered, "he's ..." She shook her head. "He's ... oh, forget it!"

"He's what, Melissa?"

"Why do you care?"

Bea shrugged again. "I was curious about him, and about you."

"About me?"

Melissa's knees opened a little as she relaxed, revealing a darkness between them, left in shadow by the overhead light. She shifted those legs a little to the side, ran a hand through messy hair, straightened it a little, then waited for Bea to answer.

Bea said simply, "Yes."

"How so?" The words were more a retort than a question. When Bea didn't respond immediately, Melissa added, "You don't like men, huh?" The tone sounded almost friendly, even though the young woman was totally astounded at what was going on in her room.

"I admire some men, Melissa, but only as human beings, not as males of the species."

"What does *that* mean?" There was a friendly smile attached to the comment

"It means that men have the ability to overcome their nature."

"You really mean this, don't you?" Melissa shook her head slightly, but had lost her antagonism completely.

Bea continued, almost as if Melissa were not there. "Males with too much testosterone are very dangerous. We have no need for them any more. Not even for sexual or procreative purposes. In fact, we are better off without them."

"Too much testosterone? You mean the really horny ...?"

"By middle age, men have become human again, with their unbound testosterone down to manageable levels. But before that the worst of them have done terrible things to all of us, in many ways. They have created a culture of violence, of cruelty, of emphasis on strength, intense competition, dominance, and possessiveness – instead of nobler values."

"This is really kooky, Bea, you know that?" Melissa's brow furrowed again. "And you think Reggie is ... what do you think exactly about Reggie?"

Bea didn't answer directly, instead saying, "As long as we remained in hunter-gatherer tribes, the behavior of males was advantageous for our survival. And those males with more testosterone became more dominant; therefore, their offspring tended to have more testosterone, too."

Bea's "lecture" sounded very academic to Melissa, and was made all the more strange by the circumstances, the setting, and the child-like voice of the lecturer. The listener, however, had overcome any temptation to be flippant. "So what can we do about this, anyway, Bea? Assuming it's true."

"We have to decide, Melissa, whether we want to be civilized or not."

"We do? I thought we already had decided. Why wouldn't we want to be civilized?"

"The worst of our males don't want to be civilized," Bea replied. "They don't want to be bound by the rules of civilization. They want to dominate. They will use violence as needed, or other destructive behaviors. Only the efforts of the rest of us have kept us - in some places, for some period of time - from reverting to our primitive past."

"The rest of us?"

"Women and older males. And males with discipline against their base drives. Or males without too much testosterone."

"You mean some guys don't have as much as others?"

"Correct. There's a distribution of levels among young men. Some have levels that are far less destructive."

"You sure about all this, Bea. Never heard of such a thing."

"Young men with reasonable amounts of free testosterone are less likely to be violent, or to be controlled by their sex drive, and better able to concentrate on learning or doing useful tasks. It's no more complicated than that, Melissa."

"What's *free* testosterone?"

"The amount unbound in the bloodstream. Not involved in any particular function in the body. Everyone - male and female - has some amount of it. We need it for various autonomic and endocrine functions."

The shirt-clad one shifted, tucking her legs under, careless in her display of bare hip. "I'll take your word for it. But why do we need it if it's free or whatever? It's not doing anything."

Bea released a gentle smile. Melissa's perception impressed her. "We use levels of various chemicals to provide a kind of reservoir of that chemical," she said. If enough is not available the chemical reactions won't get started or will produce different results. In the bloodstream or other bodily fluids chemicals are moving about more or less randomly. They need to encounter other chemicals to interact with them. If enough are not there the probability is low that anything will happen. Or if it does, it won't continue to happen very long."

Melissa nodded. "I see. I think so anyway." The pretty young woman pondered a moment. "Explain again how this has anything to do with Reggie," she added.

"My guess is that Reggie is one of those males with too much free testosterone," Bea continued, in a matter-of-fact tone. Did he speak with you before he left?"

Melissa cocked her head as if listening for someone else. Then she sighed. "He ... damned thing about it, Bea ... he didn't say anything to me. Just left. I called his apartment buddies and asked about him. They ..." She stopped speaking.

"What did they say, Melissa?"

"That he was ... well, kind of out of it. Was acting funny. Somebody called his family - don't know who - and his dad came and ... well ..." She shrugged dramatically. "He took him home."

"Did he?" Bea asked. "What do you mean by 'out of it?'"

Melissa shrugged as she had several times. "They thought he was on pot or something. But ... we didn't do much of that."

Bea stood up. "I should go now, Melissa. Sorry to have barged in on you."

"Hey, it's okay." The other one got to her feet, too. "I ... well, I thought it was weird of you to come by - like I said - but it was ... let's talk about this stuff some more. If you don't care."

Bea nodded as she opened the door. "If you like, Melissa. And would you let me know how things are with Reggie?"

"If I find out anything, sure." She followed the visitor out into the hallway. "The whole thing is pretty crazy - with Reggie, I mean. Look, Bea, I'm sorry I acted like a bitch - earlier."

"And I apologize for being weird," Bea answered, looking over her shoulder and tacking on a smile.

A moment later Bea was at her mirror. "Magdalene," she said, "I believe we've done it."

"Yes," answered Madeline, in the strange tone, "I believe we have."

5. Medical Discussion

REGGIE PENDERGAST SAT NEXT TO his father and mother in the waiting room of the Foothills Clinic. The clinic was located in an upscale neighborhood of Maryville, Tennessee, a half hour drive south of Knoxville. Maryville was only a dozen miles north of the Great Smoky Mountains National Park. The town was bustling and attractive, with a pretty setting, a good place to live. And the Pendergasts had lived there a long time. Their moods on that afternoon were difficult to describe. But, in the simplest terms, Horace was confused, Marjorie was worried., and Reggie was somewhere else.

The young man was dressed in dark slacks and light shirt, and looked amazingly like a younger version of the man beside him. Reggie was not speaking as they sat. In fact, Reggie was staring idly around the waiting room. His eyes didn't focus on either parent and he seemed not to know they were there. They had been in this seated trio for a half hour when a nurse opened a door and called their name.

Doctor Raymond Singh was, as his name implies, a person of Indian descent, but had grown up in Tennessee and had never been to India. He did carry a trace of the classic lilt to his English, but only because of his parents, both émigrés. Singh was an internist and functioned basically as the Pendergast family physician. He'd known and treated Reggie since his teen years. The doctor asked the family to sit down in his office and spent a few minutes going over the file in front of him. During that time Marjorie got Reggie settled, though not without some difficulty. The young man seemed more anxious to look out the window at the mountains in the distance than pay attention to the process of sitting.

Doctor Singh finally said, looking at Horace, then Marjorie, "We have the results of the MRI, and the EEG. But I'm afraid they tell us only a little, if anything definitive at all." Though Reggie looked occasionally the doctor's way, he showed no interest in the physician's words. The fact that the young man was in the room was effectively being ignored at the moment by the three others.

Mrs. Pendergast asked, "Do you see normal brain ... what is it, patterns or whatever in the EEG?"

Singh replied, eyes on the sheets before him, "For the most part, yes, but there are some anomalies. The MRI, however, appears quite normal. There is no visible degeneration in the brain tissue, as you would expect from neuro-degenerative diseases."

"Like Alzheimers?" Horace ventured.

"Yes." Singh turned a page. "I called the UT Hospital yesterday afternoon and set up an appointment next Tuesday. I hope that will work out for you." He directed these words at Marjorie first, then Horace.

"Thank you, doctor," the woman said. "We will ..."

Reggie suddenly stood, made a kind of squeaking sound and looked down at his pants. A darker shade had appeared on the front of his trousers and was spreading fast. All three others immediately saw it, and indeed smelled it. Reggie, however, was fascinated and began to examine his warm wetness. With help from the summoned nurse, they tied a towel around the young man's waist. He was ushered out, without resistance, then the two shaken parents resumed their seats.

"Tell me," Singh said, "when Reggie's friend called you."

Marjorie sighed. "Three days ago," she said.

The doctor asked, "What did the young man say about Reggie?" He poised with his pen to write notes.

"He said that he thought Reggie was sick. He had - Reggie, that is - had started mumbling in his sleep, but had not spoken to them in the morning. He seemed in a kind of trance - as he does now."

"So the problem occurred quickly?"

"I suppose so," Marjorie nodded.

"Probably, we should speak with your son's friends," Singh ventured. "Pardon me for asking, but did Reggie have a drug problem?"

It was Horace's turn to respond. "I think he's smoked some pot, doctor. At least it seems so. But I confess to having taken a few tokes myself at his age. But I don't believe he's done any of the hard stuff. And we did talk to his friends about that."

"Hard drug users may not be forthcoming, Mr. Pendergast. As you might guess."

The man nodded. "I guess not. But I still think he stayed away from anything but booze and marijuana.

"Does Reggie have a steady girlfriend?" asked the doctor.

Marjorie nodded. "A nice girl named Melissa. Melissa Thomas. From Sweetwater. They are ... were ... pretty serious."

"Have you heard from her?"

"No, we haven't. I suppose it would be good to speak with her."

"Yes," Singh nodded. "She may have some clue about the onset of his condition. Assuming they spent a lot of time together."

"I believe they did," Horace said.

"One other thing," Doctor Singh said, going back to his notes for a moment. "I sent blood samples to UT Hospital and requested an evaluation by the Infection Committee."

"What's that?" Marjorie wanted to know.

"A team of physicians and scientists who evaluate samples that might be associated with infections of some sort."

"Infections?" Both parents looked at each other. Horace said, "Could this be some kind of infection?"

"I don't know," Singh admitted. "But we have no definite clue yet as to what could have happened."

Marjorie asked, "How could an infection affect his behavior?"

"It's not clear, but the committee looks at rare conditions and tries to determine if some kind of infection is present."

"You mean germs of some kind?"

"Possibly. But possibly it's not an infection, of course, are there are also other causes."

"You mean other causes for ... whatever it is?"

"Exactly. Most diseases these days, in fact, result from viruses."

"So this committee looks for viruses, for example?"

"Yes, or, as I said, bacteria perhaps. Some foreign body in blood samples, for example, that interferes with the normal processes in the body."

"Well," Horace said firmly, "if this committee can help, let's get their opinion by all means."

"Thank you, sir," said Dr. Singh. "We will get their report in a few days. Their weekly meeting is tomorrow.

"Thank you so much, doctor," Marjorie added. Her face seemed even more worried than when the conversation had begun.

6. Questions Without Answers

MELISSA THOMAS WORE A BLUE TAILORED SUIT, stockings and medium height heels. Her hair was pinned up and she went light on the makeup. The young woman looked very businesslike. Only the ceaseless gentle tapping of her right foot as she sat gave away her nervousness. She was in one of three chairs along the outside wall of the office of the Department of Microbiology at the University of Tennessee. Across from her was another female student, dark haired and slightly obese, who was at a desk behind a low counter, busy typing something into a computer keyboard. The student secretary looked up at Melissa and gave her an encouraging smile. It had been a rather long wait: fifteen minutes earlier the visitor had entered, given her name, and said that she was to see Dr. Cortland.

"She'll be out soon," the girl assured the visitor. "She's in a meeting that's supposed to already be over."

Melissa nodded. She was impatient, yes, but didn't want to appear so. The right foot continued its tapping, a little more overtly now.

A couple of minutes later, two men exited the door to the left of the secretary's desk, giving Melissa only a passing glance. The waiting girl didn't know either of them, but figured they were important. Then Dr. Virginia Cortland came out, saw the visitor and walked over to greet her.

"I'm sorry, Miss Thomas, for your wait," the professor said. "Thank you so much for coming. Won't you please come into my office?"

Melissa stood, took the proffered hand and followed. She saw that the professor was about the age and shape of her own mother. There was, in fact, a motherly way about her that made Melissa relax a little.

Inside the small office, crowded with books and files full of papers, Melissa was indicated a chair under the single window, facing the desk opposite.

"Miss Thomas," said Cortland pleasantly, seating herself in the process, "I understand you are a friend of Mr. Reginald Pendergast."

"Yes, that's right, Dr. Cortland," Melissa answered, feeling a little blush arise as she adjusted herself on the seat. "He and I were ... have been dating for a while."

"I'm told you are aware that Mr. Pendergast is ill at the moment."

"Mr. Pender ... oh, you mean Reggie. Yes, I know he is." The pretty girl's face was in a frown.

"We are trying to understand his illness," Cortland said, moving along quickly to her point but with a sympathetic tone. "Thank you for being willing to help us today."

"Are you ... I mean, Dr. Cortland, I didn't know you were ... are you a doctor, then? I mean a ... you know."

"A physician? Yes, I am, Miss Thomas. And I serve on a committee that meets at UT hospital. We are interested in new or unusual diseases that turn up in patients from time to time. Our goal is to work with state and federal medical people, so we can all monitor potential outbreaks of disease."

"Does Reggie have a ... is this like part of an epidemic?"

"Not that we know of, Miss Thomas, but he does have a condition that seems to have arisen quickly. We'd like to have a better idea of what has happened to him. We asked you here to help us trace Mr. Pendergast's - Reggie's, that is - activities in the few days before he took ill."

"Activities?" Melissa blushed again, deeper this time. "Do you mean ... like the things he did?"

"To be more specific, Miss Thomas, we talked with the young men that Mr. Pendergast - Reggie - shared an apartment with. They did not see him during the two days prior to his being admitted to the hospital. We understand you saw Reggie during that time and before, and would like to get your description of how he was and how he behaved - if you would be so kind as to help us out."

Melissa expelled some breath and nodded. "I ... yes, I was with Reggie. We ..." She blushed again, this time heavily. "He ... was ... what do you mean by how he was, Dr. Cortland?"

Virginia Cortland had heard, of course, that this young woman had been intimate with Reginald Pendergast, and was sympathetic with the obvious embarrassment that was revealed. "I mean," Cortland said gently, "was his behavior or conversation similar to what it was days or weeks earlier? We'd like to have an idea of when the illness began to manifest itself."

"Oh?" Melissa seemed a little relieved. "Uh, well, he ..."

"We're interested in changes about him that you may have noted. We're certainly not trying to pry into your private life, Miss Thomas. I hope you understand."

Melissa of course blushed again, but said, "Oh, yes, I see. Thank you ... uh, maybe I ..."

"For example," Cortland continued, "did he talk more or less than he had days earlier, or speak more quickly or slowly, or possibly show evidence of forgetfulness? That sort of thing."

Melissa said, "Well, let's see. On the day ... before ... he was pretty quiet. Actually, I thought he was ... like beginning to be ... I thought he was losing interest in being with me, actually. It was ..." Her face clouded up, nearly to the point of tears.

"Did he stare off into space, for example, during that time?"

"I guess maybe he did. I thought he was ... well, thinking about something else."

"And earlier, before that, was there anything different about him?"

Melissa was now going through her memories in a different way. Till this point she had been avoiding them for the most part, but now realized things were not as she'd supposed. "I ... let me think a minute," she said. "It was maybe two days before that - before the last day I saw him - that he came to my ... well, my dorm room and seemed funny ... or odd. It was ... well he had his shirt buttoned wrong, for one thing. And when I ... told him he gave me a ... kind of a look that I hadn't seen before. Is that the kind of thing you mean?"

"Exactly, Miss Thomas. You say this was two days earlier, then?"

The young woman nodded. "He said strange things about sports - you know, the Vols' teams. Like ... it wasn't real odd or anything like that, but Reggie was always so sharp about the teams, what they needed to be doing to win more games - that kind of thing. But that time he was mostly just weird. It's hard to explain."

Dr. Cortland was taking notes. She looked up and nodded. "And, his posture, or the way he carried himself, Miss Thomas. Was there any change you noted?"

Melissa rubbed her forehead a moment. "He was ... like moved slower. Yes, and that last night ... er, day ... the one before, he did walk differently."

"I understand Reggie was a serious boyfriend, Miss Thomas. You and he were close. Is that correct?"

The student shifted away a little, not looking directly at Cortland. "Well, yes, we were pretty serious, I guess. We didn't date anybody else."

Cortland straightened her note pad for a few seconds, then said, "This is a little sensitive I know, Miss Thomas. And I'll also understand if you don't want to get into it. But, are you willing to say if your intimacy with Reggie had any changes during this time?"

Melissa turned beet red, bit at her lower lip. "Well, I guess it's important to ... it's not easy to talk about things like that, you know."

"Yes, I know very well, Miss Thomas."

"He ... you won't, I mean, this is between you and me, okay?"

Cortland nodded. "Of course."

"He ... Reggie was at my dorm the night before ... but left pretty early. It was ... I mean we didn't have sex then." She paused.

"But you had sex with him before that?"

Melissa nodded. "We ... well, yes we had sex sometimes. It was ..." Again she paused.

"Regularly, Miss Thomas? You had sex on a regular basis earlier? I'm sorry to ask so bluntly."

"Melissa nodded once more. "Yes, we ... yes, it was regular."

"At your dormitory, then?"

"Yes. He sometimes stayed over. Like the night before the last night. He stayed then."

"Go on. Was he his usual self that night? That last night you had sex."

"This is ... pretty hard to talk about, Dr. Cortland. But, well no. He was different." She hesitated. Her questioner simply waited, not speaking. Melissa continued, saying, "He couldn't ... well, he (she blushed again, heavily) couldn't ... you know."

"Couldn't get an erection?"

"That's right, yes. Reggie had never had that problem before."

"Did it disturb him, Miss Thomas? Was he upset that he'd not been potent."

"Maybe a little, but he ... he said odd things and I tried to, you know, get him ... well, going better, but it didn't happen."

"I see. Thank you for being so candid." Cortland had not written notes about this latest revelation. She continued, "The next night, the last night, I suppose there was no attempt to have sex?"

Melissa looked a little forlorn. "I thought he'd want to," she said. "But when he got there, he was – there was no real chance for any sex. Then he just left. He was gone without saying anything to me. And I didn't see he was mad or anything. Just ... well, just weird."

"So, for at least two days, then, Reggie was not his normal self. Is that fair to say, Miss Thomas?"

She nodded. "The day before that ... well, thinking about it, he wasn't exactly the same then, either. Little things about him weren't right. But, well, he was mostly the same."

"Sexually, and otherwise, right?"

Melissa nodded. "What's ... what's wrong with him? Don't you have any idea?"

"Only conjectures," Cortland said. "Nothing worth worrying you with. And you seem not to have any symptoms similar to the ones you described."

"Could something happen ... to me, I mean ... later?"

"Honestly, we can't say, but there's no evidence you've had anything similar happen to you. But I should ask, is there anything about yourself that has changed, as far as you can tell?"

Melissa shook her head, but was obviously searching her brain. "I hadn't thought about it till just now, but ... but, no, I don't think so. I think I'm the same."

"No weakness, mood swings, no change in how you feel?"

The girl shook her head. "No."

"Is there anyone else who might know anything about Reggie, Miss Thomas? Someone we should talk to?"

"I guess not. I have some friends that know Reggie, but they haven't been around when he's been with me in a long time."

Cortland had her notes together and looked about to stand, a signal that the interview would end. "And there's no one else you can think of that might know something?"

"No, not really."

"Okay, Miss Thomas," said the professor, now standing. "Thank you so much for your candor. And thank you in advance for going to the infirmary to leave those samples. I hope you'll do so right away. Just tell them who you are and that the samples are for me. But I don't think you should be concerned about your own health. And thank you so much."

"I hope Reggie is going to be okay," Melissa said, standing as indicated. She brushed at her skirt reflexively and turned to go.

"We hope so, too, Miss Thomas."

"Will someone tell me how he's doing?"

"Do you know his parents well?"

Melissa hesitated, then nodded. "Not too well, but I can ask them."

"That would be best," Cortland said, walking her toward the door.

7. Brain Drain

THE CREATURE WHO HAD ONCE BEEN Reginald Pendergast sat quietly on an examining table in the University of Tennessee hospital, in the complex of rooms isolated from the rest of the hospital - including the air and water systems - for evaluation of patients with potentially infectious diseases. Reggie, swathed in a head bandage, wore - in some loose definition of the term - a paper examining gown that lay draped around him in a halfhearted manner. Outside, trees and bushes were swaying in a sudden slight wind that was introducing a rainstorm. A touch of ozone was in the air.

Across from him, in two straight backed chairs, were Reggie's parents, Horace and Marjorie. Both wore shoe covers, light cotton gloves, and paper jackets over their clothing. Reggie gave no indication he noticed them or that they, in fact, were even there. One other person - also of no import to Reggie, and clad in doctor's scrubs, with shoe covers - sat at an angle from the couple, able to see them to her right and Reggie to her left. That person was Virginia Cortland. They were in the middle of a conversation.

Cortland was saying, "His limbic system is functional - for the most part - so, yes he probably does have memory. But let me continue in this area for a moment. I'll get to speech later." She added a polite smile. "Your son's hippocampus, in the limbic area, seems to be working normally. It is responsible for laying down memories into permanent storage and for regulating emotions. His thalamus, which regulates incoming nerve impulses, lets the brain know about input from outside the body, is quite functional as well. His hypothalamus, which manages body temperature, hunger, thirst - that kind of thing - is also doing its job. This region also controls hormone release from the pituitary gland, and seems to still be functional in this way. The pituitary controls all kinds of glands in the body and is working reasonably well with Reggie."

"Go on, doctor," Reggie's father said.

"The pineal gland," continued Cortland, "is normal, as well. That's the gland that manages the sleep-wake cycle. Finally, there is the amygdale. This is the part of the limbic system that deals with emotions. It is working at a very low level, if at all. It may be, however, that Reginald's amygdale itself is fine, but the inputs it uses are cut off."

"You mean he doesn't ... uh, feel anything, emotionally, I mean?" asked Marjorie Pendergast.

"I'm afraid so," was the reply, accompanied by a sympathetic look.

There was silence for a moment, then Cortland continued. "The limbic system is basically in the center of your brain. And the cerebellum is around the brain stem, just under the limbic region, approximately. The cerebellum regulates muscle movement, posture, balance, and such. Your son's is totally normal. But the important area is the cerebrum."

Mr. Pendergast said, "That's the frontal part, right?"

"Yes, but the cerebrum is more than that. The cerebrum is the largest portion of the brain and sits on top of everything else, kind of like a mushroom cap over the stem below. It extends all the way back to the occipital lobe, on the back of your head. That area, the occipital, for example, processes visual data. Reginald's occipital seems unaffected. And, coming forward in the cerebrum, we find the parietal lobe and sensory cortex, both involved with touch, pain, skin sensitivity, and the like. These areas, too, are normal. Continuing forward, above the ears - approximately - is the temporal lobe. This is the speech center. We're not certain but we think there is some loss of function here. Reginald probably doesn't understand or process speech, or not very well, in any case. That is why he doesn't respond to words. Only to gestures or physical urging."

Both parents nodded, but said nothing.

Dr. Cortland took a breath and went on. Of course there is the motor cortex - controlling nerve signals to make muscles move. That's also normal, but our biggest problem is in the frontal lobe, the most important part of this largest part of the brain."

"That's where we think, right?" asked Mr. Pendergast.

"Yes. That's where our consciousness is, in a sense. Where we are self aware. Where we formulate speech. Where we tie ideas together, where we come up with original ideas of our own. This is where we get our social behavior and where we express our emotions. As you can see ..." Cortland paused to sigh. "Reginalds's frontal lobe is ... well, is basically non-functional. The neurons there seem dormant."

Marjorie Pendergast dabbed at her eyes, finding herself now in tears. "Will ... can ... he's a vegetable, isn't he, doctor? Isn't that what you are saying?"

"For the moment, Mrs. Pendergast, his frontal lobe is not functioning. That's all we can say."

Mr. Pendergast, whose own eyes were a little misty, said, "What tests or measurements have you done, then? Isn't there something else you can do?"

"We've done brain scans, functional MRIs, CT scans, and we have several samples of brain fluid - thanks to your permissions - that are now being studied. Basically, we've done about all we can until we've finished those fluid samples. Fortunately, your son is not a real problem for us ..."

Marjorie Pendergast shook her head. She had controlled her tears, but her eyes were damp and red. "What could cause a thing like this?"

"Something that disrupts or weakens the neural processes in the frontal lobe, basically. That's all we can really say, so far."

"You mean the neurons, those things?"

"Exactly, Mrs. Pendergast. "The neurons in Reginald's frontal lobe are, for the most part, non-functional. We've tried several drugs that have had some success in stimulating neural function, but with no effect. The fluid samples we now have should help us understand this part of the problem."

He asked, "When will you finish these samples?"

"Two or three days. I'm working on them myself, and have asked a couple of colleagues to do independent looks."

"Thank you, doctor," Mrs. Pendergast said softly. "You have been very kind and ... and very diligent."

"I have been very frustrated, as a matter of fact," Cortland replied. "But we'll figure it out."

"Then can he be treated?"

"When we find out what caused it, we'll know better about what can be done."

"That's all we can ask, doctor," Horace Pendergast said, standing.

When the Pendergasts had gone, Virginia Cortland went back to the room where Reggie was held. The young man was asleep, a state induced by an injection. He lay on the hospital bed, covered by a sheet and thin blanket. His bandaged head was like a distorted white halo. She stood silently by him for some minutes. Then she crossed to the phone on the table and called the university switchboard. "Could you connect me to the office of Dr. William Charles?"

After less than a minute, Charles answered.

"Bill," she said, "this is Virginia Cortland. Do you have a moment to talk?"

After a pause during which he gave an affirmation, she continued, "I'm studying this Pendergast boy's case. Do you know about it?"

"Yes," Charles replied. "A very sad situation."

"I'm interested in brain electronics, Bill. Can you help me?"

"I hope so, Virginia. But why?"

"The boy's frontal lobe is turned off, nothing else. It has to be - or maybe has to be - that the frontal neurons have quit firing, or weakened considerably."

"Really?" After a few seconds, he added. "I've never heard of such a thing."

"Me neither. How about consulting on this one? I can get you some payment, to make it worth your while."

"Where will you get the money, Virginia?" There was humorous curiosity in the question.

"I have my ways, Bill. Don't ask." She smiled as she said it, and he picked it up from her tone.

"Okay, I'll do what I can."

"Listen," Virginia Cortland went on quickly, "I'll come over this afternoon, if you don't mind, and brief you."

"Sure. Make it three and I'm done for the day."

"That's a good time."

"Okay. Listen, I think I'll ask Bea to join us."

"Bea?" It took a moment but Cortland remembered. "Oh, yes, your student. The one I met. You must think highly of her."

"Don't tell anyone, Virginia, but she already knows more than I do about neurons."

"Then include her, by all means. I'll see you at three."

"Okay," he said. "Should be interesting."

"Very much so," she answered, assuredly.

8. Meetings

BEA DE WINTER, IN HER USUAL KHAKIS and loose shirt, sat in a corner of the Student Center, reading. Beside her was a shed light jacket. It was unusual for her to hang out there, but the morning had been cool and she decided on a cup of coffee. The Student Center had good coffee and was close, so she took advantage of it. Around her were clusters of students in conversation and others passing to and fro within the low but steady background noise. Naturally, all of this was fully tuned out.

Bea's mind was in high gear. Having heard that Melissa Thomas had been interviewed by physicians had to mean that Reggie's condition was being studied. They would find dysfunctional neurons, she knew. However, fluid samples - and they must have taken them - might show the mutated neurolgia, the cells that support the action of the neurons. Her guess was that a careful chemical analysis of brain fluid would reveal some suspect dead neurolgia and neurons, and possibly some viral component particles. Probably they'd see that some viruses didn't get into the neurolgia or didn't fully form. Both situations were statistically near certainty. The specific concern she had was that the free testosterone level itself might not be the only necessary marker. Had she made her release too early? If so, there was little she could do about it. Was it true that Mike Baylor - as an example - had a value similar to Reggie's? And what about his other hormone balances - for example, estrogen or related chemicals? She wanted to know more, that was sure. A sample of Mike's blood would be excellent to have. Better yet would be to have both his blood and a sample from Reggie. Was there any way of getting such things? As she started a second cup of coffee, Bea was stymied.

Tuned out to the student world around her, Bea was suddenly brought back into it by a touch on her shoulder. She literally jerked in her chair, looking around - momentarily dumbfounded - into the face of Mike Baylor himself.

"Hey, Bea, how're you doin'?" His grin was almost silly.

Bea expelled a breath, but managed a pleasant look. "Oh, hello, Mike. You startled me."

"Noticed. Sorry. Hey, can I sit a minute?"

"I'm about to leave, actually."

"Just a minute."

"Alright."

Bea slid a little to the side, slightly farther away from the nearest chair. Mike dropped into it. He was in black cords, with a gray shirt, and was wearing a light jacket, unbuttoned. The young man was always well groomed, but never seemed to make any obvious statement. That was something else Bea liked about him.

"Genius stuff goin' okay?" he asked.

"Are you referring to my work?" Bea asked, indicating a trace of coyness – incredibly rare.

He didn't answer directly. "Still goin' through the mice, I hope. So you'll drop by. Don't get much good conversation with mice." He smiled.

"Mike," she said, suddenly changing tack, "speaking of my research, are you willing to do me a favor?" Bea didn't smile at him but did show an earnest face.

"Sure," was his prompt reply. "But what does a genius need from me? I'm in botany, remember?"

Bea said, "Blood, Mike. Even botanists have blood."

"Who says? Maybe we have sap. At least, some people think I *am* a sap."

If she got the humor she didn't show it. "All I need is a blood sample. To build up some statistics. Will you provide me with one?"

"You mean it, don't you, Bea?" He grinned. "First you come get mice. Now it's blood."

"That's right," she replied, putting the slightest tinge of humor into her words.

"You have to fill out papers to get blood?" he continued, still light in tone.

"I can take the sample myself, if you'll allow me," she said, again not really answering his question. "It could be a little pinch, but honestly, it's no ..."

"An ouch, huh? Okay, if a genius wants blood, better give it to her."

"I take samples of my own blood quite often, Mike, if that will make you more comfortable with the prospect."

"You scientists are damn serious about your work, I have to say that."

"Of course. But you're a scientist, too, Mike. Aren't you serious about your work?"

The young man scratched idly at his neck a moment before answering. "Prob'ly not like you, Bea. But I'm not a genius either."

"Don't be silly, Mike," she retorted – as familiar in tone as he'd ever heard her. "I'm sure you're very capable, indeed. And remember, hard work is what is most required."

"Yes, ma'am," he smiled. "Can't forget that."

"May I come over to the rat lab tomorrow, then, and take that sample?"

"Funniest date I've ever had," he said, shaking his head pleasantly.

Bea almost snapped back that this was no date, but decided – rationally – that it was. Not a romantic date, to be sure, but an appointment with someone of the opposite sex. She had to fight off a blush, angry with herself. "I'll be there around five. You'll be on shift then, won't you?" She knew he would be.

"Yep. Bloodletting at five tomorrow. It's a date." He grinned once more in that totally non-threatening way. She nearly smiled back.

–

William Charles stood at a small conference table in the room adjacent to his office in Hess Hall. He was dressed very much like a professor, in slacks and cardigan sweater. He had on wire rimmed glasses and sported a carefully trimmed beard – something he'd started a few weeks earlier, for the winter. In a former age he'd have had a curved briar pipe to complete the effect. Bea, beside him and looking very small and young in khakis and long-sleeved shirt, had just stood, both attending the entrance of Virginia Cortland. Dr. Cortland wore a pant suit that fit her middle-aged body a little too tightly, a white lab smock, and sensible laced shoes. She did not wear glasses.

Charles said, "Dr. Cortland, you remember Bea de Winter, I believe."

"Yes. Hello Miss de Winter. Thank you for joining us."

Bea glanced at Charles and returned to her seat, in accord with his actions. There were only three of them in the small room, a room that had a permanent musty smell arising from constant presence of books and papers. There were several stacks of journals on the floor near corners and the table surface was almost completely obliterated by piled objects, mostly made of paper in one form or another, from loose sheets to open cardboard boxes containing stacks of documents. An easel stood by the table, holding a large pad of white newsprint and several ink markers. Bea looked over at the woman settling herself on the opposite side of the table and said, "Hello, Dr. Cortland. Nice to see you again."

Charles and Cortland chatted briefly about the weather, then he got them into the business of the day, saying, "Now, Virginia, tell us why we are here."

Virginia Cortland gave a small smile to both across from her and answered. "It's a case from the Infection Committee. Would like you to help me with it, if you will."

"The Pendergast boy," Charles said, for Bea's benefit.

"Yes," Cortland continued, "he's contracted a neuro-degenerative condition that is very bewildering. I have copies of the lab results. Would like to discuss them with you both and try to determine a recommendation to the committee."

Bea leaned forward slightly and asked, "I suppose, Dr. Cortland, that you think neural electrochemistry may have something to do with the problem."

"Yes, that's a real possibility," Cortland nodded. "We know where in the brain this patient's problems arise, but we don't know much else."

William Charles said, "You said, Virginia, that possibly the circuits in the frontal lobe were malfunctioning. Is that still the probable cause?"

"As much as anything could be said to be the cause. We don't really know the cause and effect relationships, even in our best understanding of neural function."

"Why," asked Bea, "do you think you've isolated the problem areas, doctor?" It was a mild, even naïve question, a good way for the student to insinuate herself into the discussion without revealing anything she already knew.

"Three things, Bea," Cortland replied. She stood to write on the paper mounted on the easel. First, the nature of the boy's symptoms. His autonomic functions seem basically unmodified, yet he doesn't speak and doesn't seem to know who he or anyone else is. Second, functional MRI results show low activity in the frontal lobe and some evidence of deterioration. Finally, the first looks at fluid samples show larger concentrations of dead neurons and neurolgia in the frontal lobe."

"Yes, it could be electrical," Bea nodded. "Or at least it could be manifested electrically." She turned her intense eyes on Dr. Cortland, but seemed to look right through her. "If the frontal lobe cells are dying at an increased rate, there might be a disease agent at work, of course; but if they are simply misfiring or failing to fire, that would imply some sort of localized electrochemical effect. If so, the neurolgia might, in the latter case, decide to turn off or purge the ineffectual neurons."

Cortland nodded, glancing briefly at Charles. "Mr. Pendergast's system is purging out the dead or non-operative cells. And there are a few other damaged regions - as you can see from the report." She passed forward two copies of a summary lab report.

Bea took and began studying the report carefully, taking the time to move to the blood chemistry data. She was immediately caught up in her study, oblivious for the moment of the other two in the room. Cortland glanced again at her colleague, caught his eye, smiled slightly at Bea. Charles saw his student's concentration and smiled back. For several minutes Bea read and memorized data. Finally, she returned - in a sense - to reality and looked up again at Cortland.

Bea said, "Something made those frontal neurons stop firing, Dr. Cortland. My first guess would be that the neurolgia are influencing the localized chemistry. Notice these three levels, especially the calcium." She pointed to several adjacent numbers.

Dr. Charles looked at the indicated data and turned to his student. "So, Bea, you think the neurolgia are functioning abnormally?"

"Sir," came the measured response, "it is only a conjecture, of course, but since the neurons are forced to function in the environment supervised by the neurolgia, if the neurolgia are somehow interfering with the chemistry at the dendrite-soma boundaries, the electric potentials could either fall below the threshold or the threshold might be elevated."

Virginia Cortland sat back down across from the others. "Could an infectious agent of some sort cause the perturbation you indicate?" She asked the student but included Charles with her eyes.

Charles answered, "Possibly, but it would have to be very specialized only to corrupt the frontal lobe region."

Again Bea was staring beyond the walls. She said, "A mutated cell might have triggered a localized chemistry shift."

Cortland said, "How, may I ask?"

"I'm speaking of the neurolgia, you understand," Bea continued. "If one released the wrong proteins - mutated in some way - they could corrupt a number of structures, including several types of enzymes. A chain reaction could occur if the enzymes themselves were modified in some inappropriate way. But I am not certain how that modification could take place."

"Unless," Charles said, picking up the idea, "the particular mutation produced a group of proteins that were accidental precursors to a DNA replication sequence producing more of the bizarre proteins. Then the chain reaction would go quickly."

Bea looked at her mentor and nodded, even smiling a little. "Yes, sir, that could do it. But seems very improbable, wouldn't you say?"

Cortland asked, "What about a prion or virus? Could we be talking about an true infectious agent, not a mutation?"

Bea rubbed her nose, seemingly in concentration. She was in fact considering exactly what she wanted to say. "An agent would have to infect either the neurolgia or the neurons themselves, and somehow corrupt the electrochemistry. It seems to me that a mutation - as unlikely as that is - is more likely than a specialized infectious agent that has such a narrow and focused action."

After a short pause, Cortland said, "Why would the probability for one be lower than the other, Bea?"

"Because, Dr. Cortland, a mutation would occur randomly and have a localized effect that wouldn't require the existence of a disease agent. Even prions - certainly viruses - are rather complex structures, that would have to come into existence in some way."

"Couldn't they form, however," Cortland persisted, "from a mutation as well, say, to an existing virus or prion?"

"Yes they could," Bea responded. "But there are hundreds of millions of neurolgia, for example, in any region of the brain. There is nowhere near the same number of prion or viral structures."

"Good point," Cortland admitted.

William Charles looked proudly at his prize student. "Virginia," he asked, "I haven't seen it here in the lab report. Did you find any chemical traces that might be associated with infectious agents of any sort?"

"Naturally, we did," Cortland said. "There is always a number of suspicious radicals and other structures in the brain fluid. Some of them we've isolated for further study. But I don't know for sure there was any foreign matter in there that can't be explained."

"Do you have blood samples, too, Dr. Cortland?" Bea asked.

"Yes, Bea, we have."

"With Dr. Charles' permission, I would like to look at the blood and the brain fluid samples."

"You have my permission," Charles nodded in agreement.

Bea nodded, "I would like to use the SEM first." She referred to the scanning electron microscope, with its high magnification." Then she added, "But in particular, I'd like to run some ion distributions on polarized samples."

"Good idea, Bea," Dr. Charles said. He looked at his colleague. "Virginia, we might be able - using a polarized sample holder - to show an ion map around various chemicals, especially damaged neurons left in brain fluid or protein structures - in blood, say - that are linked to enzymes we haven't seen before."

"We can arrange that. Will you have the time, Bea? I know Bill keeps you very busy on your own work."

Bea didn't smile but was pleasant enough in her response. "I'll find time, Dr. Cortland."

"Excellent." Cortland stood. "We'll have samples delivered over here then."

Bea spoke to her advisor. "Sir, may I work on them in my regular space. It will be more convenient."

"Of course," Charles said. "Just get the samples to me, Virginia, and I'll take care of it."

—

The graduate student remained with the senior researchers a few more minutes, then excused herself, citing the need to get back to her other work. Charles and Cortland continued in conference for another hour, discussing various details of the test data. Bea went back to the dorm to leave off some books and the copy of the test data available so far on Reggie Pendergast. That done, she spent a few minutes in thought and freshening up. She already had the syringe and blood sample kit in her bag for the meeting with Mike Baylor.

Passing the mirror above her sink she spoke to Magdalene. "Magdalene, they are close to discovering the virus."

"Yes, perhaps," came the voice-shifted reply

Bea reached the mouse house a few minutes before five. Mike Baylor was there, but away from the counter at a computer on a nearby desk, typing away. He didn't see her enter and was humming a happy tune as he typed.

Bea stopped a few steps from the counter and listened to him a while. She didn't recognize the tune, but it was nice enough. Mike wore a dark green, light-weight sweater and new-looking cords, looking his usual spiffy-but-not-overstated self. Bea finally spoke to his back.

"Mike, hello."

Surprised, the young man jumped and turned to see Bea. "Hey, Bea. You're early. Must be anxious to draw blood, am I right?"

"Very much so," she said, coming as close to teasing as he'd ever heard from her. "Is this a good time?"

"A good time to get stuck? Good as any. Sure. How you doing anyway?"

"I'm fine, Mike." She crossed to the counter and put her sample kit down on it. "If you'll give me an upper arm I'll take care of it right now."

"Most folks want a hand, Bea. You want an arm." His eyes twinkled.

"It won't hurt. Maybe a pinch."

"So you said." He smiled broadly at her, regarding the petite one in an open, friendly way. But with no discernible indiscretion.

He took off his sweater to reveal a strong upper torso covered by a light tee shirt. Bea noticed his muscles and richly colored skin, but convinced herself she was noticing these things in her usual analytical way. She took his left arm and lowered it to the counter, so the arm was bent at the elbow.

"Here's a good vein. Make a fist, please."

He complied, then she stuck him, as efficient in this as in everything else she did.

"Hey! What's this little pinch stuff?" he said, but without anger.

"Did it hurt?"

"Naw, you were right."

"Stay still, Mike. It takes a few seconds." She drew back the plunger and filled the small plastic sample reservoir. It had about half the volume of a small test tube.

"There," Bea said, and pushed a little wad of cotton onto the stick point at the instant she withdrew the syringe. "Just keep your arm bent a minute. You'll clot over quickly."

"Clot over? How 'bout that?" he said, shaking his head. "Ben stuck by a genius and now I get to clot over."

"Lucky you," she ventured and give him a near approximation to a smile.

"So, what are you going to do with the blood, Bea?"

"Some standard tests, to find concentrations of different chemicals." Her side was to him as she put things back in her sample case.

"An' you chose me for a good reason, I guess?"

She turned. "As a baseline person of a certain type, actually."

"So, now I'm a baseline person, huh?"

"Exactly." This time she actually gave him a little smile. Such an expression - partly because it was so rare for Bea de Winter - turned the plain girl into a luminous and very attractive one, at least for the few second span of the smile.

"Guess it's not cool to ask a genius why she does stuff, right?"

"Exactly," Bea repeated. "Thanks, Mike, for the sample. It's been very helpful."

"O-kay," he said. "Hey, what type am I?"

"Type?" She had been about to go, but stopped.

"Yeah, you said I was a certain type." His eyes were benign, but she instantly picked up the racial implication. It both irked and impressed her.

"Male, first of all," Bea said. "Oh, yes, your age, Mike. I need that. I guess you're twenty-three. Is that correct?"

"Twenty-four. Got you there, genius, huh?"

She didn't respond to the tease. "Fine. So the type you are is twenty-four year old male."

"Makes a guy feel pretty proud, I have to admit." He laughed out loud.

"Not many like you in the whole population," Bea continued, unfazed. "Thanks again."

"Hey, I should thank *you*, Bea," Mike said, shaking his head at her like he often found himself doing. "Now I'm male, twenty-four, a baseline person, a blood donor, and have gotten to clot over. Hard to beat that."

Bea raised her brows at him, though not unpleasantly. "I have to be going," she said. "But I certainly do appreciate this, Mike."

"Hey, I did you a favor, Bea. You game to do me one?"

She'd already taken a couple of steps, so she stopped and turned around again. "What favor?"

"Let me buy you a cup of coffee sometime."

Bea's eyes clouded briefly and she said nothing. "Mike, I'm ... like you, pretty busy with my work. Thanks, though." A blush had worked its way over her countenance.

"Sure," he nodded. "Guess geniuses don't have much time to spend with certain types." Then he smiled.

"No more talk about geniuses, Mike. I'll see you. Bye." Bea carefully draped her bag over her shoulder and started away, without looking back.

Mike Baylor watched her depart, shaking his head again.

10. Discoveries, Planned and Accidental

JUST AFTER FOUR O'CLOCK THE NEXT AFTERNOON, William Charles found a note from Bea de Winter in his mailbox. In her usual short-but-sweet style, it said, "Isolated new virion in Pendergast blood sample. Am continuing analysis." The professor looked at the note for a moment, pleased, but wasn't sure whether the information was something of note. He went straightaway to her lab and found her there, looking into an optical microscope.

"Yes, sir," she said, after returning his greeting and turning aside from her work, "it's a new virus. I have a SEM image over here. I'll show it to you."

It had a characteristic symmetrical shape, basically spherical with regular projections of protein structures above the surface, and was around 35 billionths of a meter in diameter, small enough that many thousands of its fellows could find plenty of room to rest on the head of a pin. There was a touch of irony here that would be necessarily lost on Charles. Knowing it would happen eventually, Bea had decided she'd just as soon be the "discoverer" herself.

"It's new, you say?" Charles repeated.

"Yes, sir. Its function, however, is not certain. We need to find it associated with neurons or neurolgia in order to know anything more relevant."

"I gather you're working on that line of approach now?"

"Yes, sir." Bea moved in a way that communicated her interest in getting back to the microscope she'd been using.

"How many of these new structures in the blood samples?" Charles asked.

Bea hesitated, then shook her head. "Not certain, sir. So far, I have only isolated this single one." It was a calculated lie, but she felt it was an important one. She had in fact measured the number density with good precision. But too much should not be revealed too soon.

—

Night had fallen by the time Bea finished for the evening. She found herself unusually tired. With a long sigh, she plopped onto her bed, not having even glanced at Melissa's door upon passing it. Within a few dozen heart beats, the girl was sound asleep.

At around four in the morning, Bea came awake suddenly. There was a noise at her door. She was still completely dressed, having chosen only to kick off her shoes before lying down. Sitting up, the roused one listened, clearing the cobwebs quickly from her brain. It was a kind of shuffling sound out there, more like someone rummaging around than knocking. Why the relatively soft disturbance had awakened her she couldn't decide. And she waited, hoping whoever was out there would go away. Bea had no interest whatsoever in getting up and seeing who was at her door - possibly rubbing up and down on it, as the sounds indicated. But the noise persisted, and she soon realized the person was not simply going to go away. Very strange, she thought. Reluctantly then, Bea leaned forward and stood, taking steps to bring her close to the door. Yes, someone was rubbing on it, or scratching on it, possibly. So she went to the peephole and looked out. Nothing but an empty and dimly lit hallway. Whoever or whatever was there was below her field of sight.

Bea spoke softly, cupping her hands around her mouth to project the words directly into the back of the door. "Who's there?"

The scratching stopped. Then a human voice spoke, or more accurately, muttered something. Bea waited some number of seconds, then the scratching began again.

"Who's there?" she repeated.

Once more the noise stopped. Then the barely audible voice said something in a raspy whisper. The something included a word that sounded like, "May."

"Is someone out there?" Bea said, a little louder.

Again the low inarticulate whisper.

Bea knelt and looked at the line of light below the door. Sure enough, it was interrupted by a length of shadow.

Someone was out there. She considered opening the door, but not for long. Heart rate ramped up now, all sleepiness gone, Bea went back to her phone and called the university police.

"This is Bea de Winter," she said, quickly giving her dorm address. "Someone is at my door and has given no identity. Please send an officer quickly." The urgency in her voice was clear, as well as the cool deliberation of her words.

After hanging up, she listened again. The noise was still there, and still very low and persistent. And the shadow remained. Returning to her bed, Bea put on her shoes, left the lights off, sat in a chair facing the door, and waited.

It took eleven minutes by Bea's watch before the campus police arrived. Their presence in the hall was immediately obvious. She arose and went to the door peeking through. Then she opened up to a strange scene. On the floor, huddled against her door, was young man. He was wearing a torn tee shirt, similarly frayed boxer-style undershorts, and nothing else. Not even shoes. And on a very chilly night. His dark brown hair was in catastrophic disarray, and he was looking away from her toward the arriving pair of uniformed police. The young man didn't get up, but got to his knees watching the officers. After a few seconds Bea realized he was muttered something incoherent under his breath. He was saying, "You're not ... not May ..."

One of the policemen had drawn a gun and proceeded to lead the other up to the door. Bea wasn't sure what to say, but chose, "Sirs, this ... person has been scratching at my door."

"Hold it there, fellow! You alright, miss?" asked the older - gun drawn - officer.

"Yes, sir. The noise awakened me, but nothing else happened."

The young man on his knees had turned toward her at the first sound of her voice, then toward the officers as they spoke, then back to Bea. She looked at him, head not that far below hers, and wondered who he was. He had a several day growth of beard and a generally very unkempt look. His features were regular, and Bea supposed he might be attractive to some eyes, under much better conditions. There was a look of some alarm on his face, but also confusion. He slowly lifted his hands, responding to the gun. At that instant the policeman asked, "Do you know this guy, miss?"

Bea shook her head, said, "No," and stepped back another step into her room. The young man looked to be in his twenties - probably a student - and had a vacant look in his eyes, very much like someone completely stoned on narcotics. There was no alcohol reek in the air.

"Get up, son!" the officer with the gun said. The boy did so, looking a little outrageous in his underwear. The officer continued, "Who are you? What's your name?"

The boy looked bewildered by the question. "Ah, I ... I ..." he muttered, then said nothing more.

"Did he try to get through your door?" was the next question, directed to Bea. The second, younger, policeman went to the strange figure and roughly put hands on his shoulders to turn him. The young man whimpered and seemed to struggle for balance, but didn't exactly resist.

"No, sir," Bea answered. "I just heard him out here making odd, but not loud sounds. Not knowing what to think I didn't want to take any chances, so I called you."

"Wise decision," said the second cop, speaking for the first time. "This one is stoned, I'd say." Then to the young man, he added, "You, there, what's your name?"

There was no immediate response. Both policemen then turned him around, attaching a pair of cuffs on his wrists. As they were doing so the boy said, "Ah ... ah Jah ..." He worked his mouth as if trying to clear away an obstruction and said, "Jah ... Kuh!"

The older policeman said, ""What are you doing here, fellow?" The two had turned the young man back to face them, with him now more or less leaning against the wall.

The shackled one looked at them with those stoned eyes. "She's ... nah May!"

"Will, get him out of here," said the older man.

The younger one gave assent and began herding the cuffed young man down the hall. At that moment, a door between Bea's and Melissa's opened, revealing a red-haired girl with sleepy but worried eyes.

"Is something wrong?" the girl asked, taking in the scene.

"Just a disturbance, miss," replied the senior cop. "Nothing to worry about. But if you don't mind, do you know this young man?"

The redhead was barefooted and wore a long silk robe. She came out a couple of steps, then shook her head. "Don't think so. Is he drunk?"

"Drugged, I'd say," Bea volunteered from her doorway. She recognized this Gloria something, but had barely spoken to her before.

"I'll say," muttered Gloria, eyeing the young man in question. "What's he doing here?"

"We don't know, miss," answered the spokesman cop.

Then Bea, who was the only one of the group facing that direction, saw Melissa Thomas open her door and look out. Immediately Melissa's eyes opened wider in amazement, then she moved quickly outside and called out, "Hey, that's ... what are you doing, Jack?"

The pretty sophomore had on a short robe that had been quickly tied around her. Bea could tell at a glance that was all Melissa had on. The policemen would notice it soon enough.

The stoned looking boy turned to the voice, and muttered, louder now, "May ... May!"

"Do you know this fellow, miss?" That question was now turned on Melissa.

"Sure. What's wrong with you ... with him, anyway?" Melissa was about ten feet from the one in custody, whose eyes were round now, looking at her.

Bea caught Melissa's eyes. "Drugs, I'd say, Melissa."

The two female students exchanged glances, not an unfriendly one on Melissa's part and at least an accepting one from Bea.

"Oh, my God, he's ... really ..." Melissa came up to the group of males. Her very noticeable female attributes quivered under the robe as she walked. "I don't understand what's going on," she muttered, mostly to herself but ostensibly to the investigating officers. In front of the boy, she said, "Why are you here, Jack?"

Jack's mouth gaped open a minute, he struggled uselessly against the policeman's grip, then he seemed to struggle for words. "Ah ... ah came ... see. Hi!" Something approximating a smile formed on his lips.

"He was trying to get in this young lady's door," the younger cop explained to Melissa.

"I'm actually not sure he was, officer," Bea said, now three or four steps out into the hall. Melissa's presence was a kind of odd comfort to her. "I simply heard him out there, didn't know what was going on, and called you."

Melissa came a step closer and Jack looked at her, carefully it seemed.

"He's ..." She looked away, to signify she wasn't talking to the boy. "... Jack Brady. I know him. But ..." Melissa shook her head in a mixture of amazement and dismay. "I can't imagine why he'd be here ... and at Bea's door." She looked at Bea, almost apologetically for implying that a male would be considered peculiar if he wanted to see Bea.

Jack Brady muttered out, "Ah ... to see May! Thought ..."

Bea said, "He must have been trying to find Melissa, since he apparently knew her."

Jack moved his head up and down in a peculiar expression of agreement.

Melissa stepped back a step. "Jack, you're ... hey, you're stoned, aren't you?"

Jack shook his head clumsily, but only said, "See ... May ..." before stumbling and dropping to his knees, only to be lifted again by the younger cop.

"We'll need you to sign a statement, ladies," said the spokesman, referring to Bea and Melissa. Then to Gloria, he said, "You, miss, we won't bother, if you don't know the guy."

Gloria the redhead shook her head and shrugged her shoulders. "Don't know him."

"Thank you, miss," the policeman said in a clear tone that suggested she go back into her room. After a quick look at Bea and Melissa, Gloria did just that.

The younger cop led Jack Brady down the hall and out. There was no resistance on Jack's part, though he did look back once and mutter something that contained the word "May." No one else appeared at any door along the hallway. The older cop produced a notebook. Bea, with growing presence of mind, said, "Come in, officer and Melissa, let's get out of the hall." Then she turned and led them toward her open door.

Inside, Bea closed the door, but didn't offer anyone a seat. Melissa took the time to adjust her robe's sash, coming close to accidentally flashing in the process.

The officer asked, "You both are tenants here, correct?"

"Yes, sir," Bea answered for them. "I'm a graduate student and Melissa is a sophomore."

The officer gave them a surprised look, then looked down to write. He asked Bea the particulars of why she called, got them repeated verbatim, then turned to Melissa. By this time the robe-clad girl knew she was not properly attired and had brought her arms up to cover her chest.

"And this fellow's name is Jack Brady, miss?"

Melissa nodded. "I ... yes, it is."

"How do you know him, if I may ask? Is he a friend of yours?"

"Uh huh, yes sir. Well, I have only just met him."

"But not *your* friend, miss?" he asked Bea.

"I haven't seen him before, officer."

"Why would he be at your door, if I may ask?"

"As I surmised, officer, he was probably looking for Melissa."

"Bea wouldn't know him," Melissa said, glancing at her dorm mate. "I only saw him once before. But maybe he was ... I don't know."

"And where was that?" continued the policeman. "Where have you seen this Jack Brady before?"

"At a ... like a party. A group of students, y'know."

"What kind of party, Miss Thomas? Were there drugs involved?"

Melissa blushed. "No ... no, sir!"

"When was this, Miss Thomas? This party."

"Oh, over a week ago. Don't remember exactly."

"And where was the party?"

"It wasn't really a party. Just some kids ... y'know, getting together. Over in the Fort, at some guy's apartment." Melissa was referring to a district of old rental houses near the campus called "The Fort" as shorthand for Fort Sanders, the site of an actual former fort from Civil War days.

"What's this guy's name, Miss Thomas? The guy's place where the party was."

"I don't know. Reggie would ..." She suddenly stopped and looked away, pretty face clouding up.

"Reggie?" prodded the officer.

Bea stepped in quickly. "Officer, Melissa's boyfriend Reggie is seriously ill right now, and will not be able to help you. And if she knew the name of the apartment owner, she'd happily tell you." These were strangely adult words coming from this slip of a girl, making them all the more compelling, and odd.

"And you don't know anything about this apartment or party, do you, Miss ..." He consulted his notes. "... de Winter."

"Nothing, officer. I suggest this Jack Brady person is in need of medical attention and counseling. Melissa and I know nothing about any of this."

"Is that so, Miss Thomas?" asked the officer, turning toward the girl who still hugged her chest protectively.

"I suppose he might have been trying to see me," Melissa said, forlornly. "I didn't mean anything ... I mean, we just met that one time."

The policeman eyed her a moment, but seemed to have run out of ideas. "Okay, ladies," he said, I'll need your signatures."

Each of the girls in turn complied, then the investigator folded his notebook and stuffed it in a back pocket. "We may want to talk to you both later," he said, being polite enough not to stare at Melissa's chest.

"We understand, officer," Bea answered for them.

After a half dozen awkward seconds, the campus cop reminded them to keep their doors locked, turned and left. Melissa and Bea watched him exit in complete silence.

Bea closed and locked her door and, without a word, led Melissa to a chair.

"God damn," came a mutter during the process of sitting.

"Who is Jack Brady, Melissa?" Bea asked, though without harshness.

"A guy." She had let her hands down, and looked visibly more relaxed. "But why the hell was he here to see me?"

"He looked very high on something," Bea answered, not choosing to respond to the direct question, considering it ludicrous to have been repeated.

"Sure did," Melissa admitted. "I ... this is pretty fucked up, this whole situation."

"What situation, Melissa?" Bea had taken it upon herself to get a glass of water for her unexpected visitor and carried it to her.

"Thanks." There was a long exhalation from the sophomore before she answered. "I mean, like y'know, Reggie's ... how he is, and now this weird thing!" Melissa gulped down a big drink of water.

"Who is Jack Brady?" Bea repeated, as if she'd not asked before. "He must have thought he knew you well enough to come here?"

"He's ..." Melissa blushed again. "Just someone at the party, like I said. I ..."

"And?" Bea prompted, though not knowing where the question would lead. She was still puzzled by all that had happened.

"And Reggie was ... real mad at me about him."

"Was he? So this was before Reggie got ill?"

Melissa nodded. "It was – I don't remember exactly, like I said."

"Why was Reggie angry about Jack?"

"Because I ..." Melissa put her arms up behind her head, shaking her hair into some better semblance of order. "If you must know, Bea, because I kissed him."

"Oh?" Bea looked away. It took a couple of seconds to control herself, but she did so and continued, "And kissing is what you do with boys you just met, right, Melissa?"

"Sometimes." Melissa suddenly grinned. "Well, not really. But ..."

"Forget it, Melissa. Was this party, where you kissed Jack, before or after Reggie left?"

Melissa thought a second. "Before. But why?"

"How long before?"

The girl shrugged. "Don't know. Few days, maybe. But why?"

"Because I'm curious."

Melissa's mind was also shifting into high gear. And her eyes were now alarmed. "Because ... are you saying that ... y'know Reggie got sick pretty soon after that. But not that same day or anything. Are you ... is that what you're saying, Bea?"

"I'm just trying to understand, Melissa. That's all."

"But are you saying that ..."

"No, I'm not saying that Reggie's condition has anything to do with this fellow Jack."

"Then what the hell *are* you saying?" Melissa's anger flared, but not exactly directed at Bea.

"Were there a lot of people at that party, Melissa?" Bea had turned her back, getting herself some water.

"Eight or ten, why?"

"Did you kiss anyone else?"

"Bea, shut up! You sound like a ..."

"Well, did you?"

Melissa's eyes narrowed. "Maybe. I'm not sure. But you do sound like ..."

"Like someone who is interested in you, Melissa. That's all."

"What does it have to do with me?" Then it hit her, and Melissa threw a hand to her forehead. "Oh, God! Are you saying that I ...?"

"I'm not saying anything."

"But ... well Jack ... he's drugged out. That's what he looked like, didn't you think?"

"Seemed that way to me. Quit worrying, Melissa."

Suddenly Melissa began to cry. Bea went and took the water glass from her. On Bea's way back to the sink, the distraught girl said, "Did I make Reggie sick, then, Bea? Is that ... is that what I did? And ... maybe Jack?"

"If Jack is stoned on something, Melissa, how could it be your fault?"

The tears had amplified her already-large eyes. "Bea, you didn't ... didn't see, Reggie, but I did! It was ..." She bit her lip. "Jack is ... Jack is just zonked, but Reggie ... Reggie is gone!"

"When did you see Reggie, Melissa? I thought he had suddenly left."

"Later. After they ... when they took him to the hospital. The doctors thought I might ... well, might help or something. And his parents said okay, so I ..."

"I see," Bea nodded. She crossed over to Melissa and put a hand on her shoulder. It was an action she'd never had thought - especially on that morning when she'd retrieved her New York Times - she would ever take. "Don't blame yourself, Melissa. It's not something you have control of." These words were meant to be consoling. But to Melissa, they were not heard for the exact truth they were.

"But I ...!"

"But nothing. You should go to bed. I'll walk you back."

Bea urged Melissa to her feet and led her to the door. Checking to be sure the hall didn't contain any curiosity seekers, the two went down to Melissa's room. Once the sophomore was inside, Bea bade her goodnight and promptly returned to her own room.

At the mirror, five minutes later, Bea said aloud, "Magdalene, what is your assessment?"

Magdalene quickly responded in her voice. "I'm still concerned about the range of effects and transmission factors."

"Yes," came the softer reply. "There is more complexity here than anticipated."

11. Women and World Culture

BEA DE WINTER DID NOT TRY TO GET more sleep. There was no way to turn off her racing brain, even if she'd considered it important to try. She dug out some notes and data sheets from the official project she was doing on the Reggie Pendergast case for Drs. Charles and Cortland. She also pulled up the blood analysis she had already finished on Mike Baylor. Mike's blood worried her little. His free testosterone level was a little lower than Reggie's - a kind of relief to her - though in the normal range for males, and probably under her design threshold. But he did have a mix of other endocrine factors that varied considerably from those of the infected young man. Were those variations critical? Among the data available had been a routine blood study on Reggie done about a year earlier when he'd gone into the university medical facility suffering from a flu-like virile infection. Fortunate, indeed, they had those results, Bea thought, because comparing them with the recent data allowed some estimation of expected blood chemistry changes after the new virus had begun its action. Another hour passed before she finished evaluating the young men's blood data. Next, she turned to the urinalysis and blood tests of Melissa Thomas. She had only given these a cursory look since getting them among the stack Dr. Charles had handed over to her. Several items were of particular interest and she jotted down little notes to herself about them. By nine thirty, Bea was beginning to feel physically exhausted and decided to stop. She'd use her remaining energy that day, she decided, to make a little more progress on her dissertation work, recently badly neglected.

After a shower and change into fresh khakis, shirt, and light cardigan sweater, Bea locked up and went down to the entrance of the dorm and started to leave. Before doing so, however, she retrieved a copy of the university newspaper, The Volunteer from the dispenser by the door. Outside the weather was crisp, but comfortable already with plenty of fall sunlight everywhere. She walked over to Cumberland Avenue and entered The Sunspot. She settled into a booth by the front window, ordered a coffee and opened the college paper. After leafing through the front pages and finding nothing of real interest, Bea found the schedule of university events and looked it over. She glanced at her watch after noticing a luncheon seminar that looked interesting. It was set for the university center and sponsored by WILL, Women in Legislative Leadership, a women's political organization she'd heard of but knew nothing about. Bea didn't think WILL was strictly a student organization; rather that it was of a more general character, like the League of Women Voters, but with specific feminist goals. The seminar, entitled, "Women and World Culture," sounded fascinating, especially after such an eventful late night and early morning. All this had left her ready for a change of venue and topic. Well, not really a change in topic: women and world culture was always the topic, wasn't it?

Bea had time to make it, so she paid for her coffee and walked briskly over to the student center a few blocks away. The luncheon was held in a small private dining room associated with the cafeteria, labeled by a printed paper sign that read: "WILL Seminar." There was a small fee required - basically for the lunch - which Bea paid without comment to a young woman student she thought she recognized from some class or another. She got a box lunch from a stack on the floor beside the ticket table. Inside the private room - with seating for about fifty people around rectangular dining tables - she saw about twenty females and, interestingly, one male, an older looking gray-haired creature who could easily be a professor of something, but no one she knew. The females were comprised mostly of graduate students or faculty, Bea surmised. Only one girl there looked to be within five years of her age. Bea took a seat at the table nearest the podium, a table having several vacant places. Along the wall behind her was a coffee, tea, and water service, which she availed herself of, getting another cup of coffee, again without comment to the three others at the table she'd chosen.

The speaker for the occasion was a Dr. Barbara Greinert, a tall regal-looking woman in her forties. She was introduced by a female professor of sociology whom Bea had never seen before. Greinert was obviously from New England, having the characteristic Kennedy "ar" sound for each final "a." For the first sentence or two of her presentation Bea was distracted by the woman's tone, but soon the subject matter began to sink in. Not far into her discourse Dr. Greinert had a very rapt listener in Bea de Winter, there not ten feet away.

"Women, and indeed the human race as a whole," Greinert said, now well into her presentation, "have suffered doubly from the male of our species. First, women have been systematically abused, raped, insulted, enslaved, and reduced to secondary value. And possibly worse, we have been ignored despite the fact that we have been the sex capable of making our race and our planet something other than a cesspool of ignorance, stupidity, and violence. Why, you may ask, are women alone capable of producing a race that is not simply millions of intelligent apes in constant turmoil? Because only females of the species have evolved properly to achieve certain critical interrelationships necessary for development of civilization. Females have necessarily taken on the burden of bearing and caring for the young, with emphasis on teaching their children as well as protecting them. Males have always been consumed with struggle for supremacy, concentrating their energies outwardly instead of within the family nest. Those behaviors males have taught their offspring have typically been those necessary to struggle for supremacy. Males consequently are poorly adapted to administer a society that functions by non-violent compromise and cooperation."

Bea found herself agreeing, naturally, and jotting down notes on a nearby napkin, focusing all her attention on the speaker.

Greinert continued. "But you may also ask, what are we to do about it? Isn't our society completely locked up by male control? Don't all our social institutions revolve around male interests and protocols? Worse, perhaps, isn't it true that when women reach positions of leadership they do so primarily by appropriating, even co-opting, male values, approaches, and attitudes?"

Greinert then began to talk about specific social programs, and how women could influence them. She led from there to political action, with particular emphasis on organizing to vote in blocks for candidates and ballot initiatives that stressed women's values and approaches. The gist of her talk, in fact, was a concentration on the details of what could be done. Bea, however, began to lose interest as these points were - as she saw them - belabored. By the time the thirty minute speech was concluded, Bea had ceased taking notes and was doodling protein structure patterns on her napkin. There was vigorous applause, which Bea supported appropriately, then the sociology professor acting as moderator stood and asked for questions from the floor.

Several women asked clarifying questions about certain specifics mentioned in the discourse. Bea listened with some interest but with growing frustration. The core issues, in her mind, were simply not being given proper attention. Finally, six or eight minutes into the questions, she raised her hand.

The moderator saw the petite girl's request and nodded. Yes? You, here?"

Bea looked straight at the speaker, eyes keen and locked onto the other's. "Dr. Greinert," she said politely, "what relevant data can you cite that male behavior on our planet is ever going to change for the better?"

The speaker regarded the questioner a moment, and like everyone was, was taken aback a little by the incongruity of the words and eyes of this slip of a girl. "Well, yes, an excellent question," she said. "But would you not agree that the world is a more civilized place today than, say, two or three thousand years ago?"

Bea responded with no hesitation. "Yes, of course, doctor, but not because the male of the species has changed. Simply because society has gradually evolved to have more influence - small though it may be - from females."

"Well, I certainly see your point," Greidert nodded. "But that is consistent with what I ..."

Bea interrupted. "Dr. Greidert, I certainly agree with your premise, but I feel it is naive to believe that fundamental changes in male behavior are possible, at least male behavior in the critical reproductive years."

It was a twist in her theme that the speaker had never heard before, and said so. "That is a very interesting perspective you have. May I ask your name?"

"Bea de Winter. It seems to me ..."

"Is this your first year at UT, Bea?"

"Yes, doctor. I'm in the biophysics graduate program. It seems to me that the social revolution you mentioned, noble as it is in concept, is only achievable by eliminating the influence of males during their physically strongest and most sexually active phases. Males have evolved, as you implied, doctor, to abuse, rape, dominate, and destroy, for the purpose of passing their genes forward to the next generation. Conditions on this planet, by cruel accident, were such that this behavior was successful. Again, as you indicated, doctor, male traits during their reproductive years left their negative marks on the evolving society. But I suggest you need to consider the specific chemical indicator of this entire problem. We human beings, after all, are basically biochemical machines that have been fashioned by nature's random processes to accommodate a specific group of environmental conditions on our planet."

All eyes in the room were on Bea, who still remained calmly in her seat. A low murmur grew up around her when she'd stopped speaking for the moment.

Dr. Greinert, amazed but trying not to show it, said, "A specific chemical indicator? Would you care to elaborate?"

"Testosterone," Bea said. "Testosterone evolved to produce the aggressive tendencies necessary for male behavior to succeed in our primitive development. What nature - being mindless - couldn't know was that testosterone is the unique chemical that stands in the way of allowing us to continue our evolution from survival to true civilization."

The murmur in the room rose up again. If anyone had been tempted earlier to doze or lose focus those temptations had instantly vanished.

The moderator, feeling like she should get into the action, asked Bea, "It's very interesting to bring a chemical into this discussion, Miss ... I'm sorry, I didn't get your name."

"Bea de Winter." Since more than just the speaker were now involved, Bea turned a little to encompass the entire room. "Testosterone, of course, is a necessary hormone for all human beings. Its excess, however, is the source of our major difficulty. That excess was programmed by nature to exist in males of reproductive age. It is easy to see, if we simply look at history, that males in that category are the source of essentially all of our destructive and uncivilized tendencies."

Dr. Greinert, who now found herself in an odd position of perceiving that she was defending the opposite of her original thesis, said, "Can it be as simple, then, Miss de Winter, as one chemical?"

"In a nutshell," Bea answered immediately, "yes. Admittedly, there are other chemicals involved in comprising the attitudes and dispositions of all human beings, and different kinds of chemical balance may achieve similar traits, yet testosterone is uniquely determinant for aggressive male behavior. We have ample data to support this assertion, and ample data to show that males, with lowered testosterone levels, lose most of their destructive and dangerous traits."

The gray haired man - the single male in the room - stood with hand lifted, interestingly looking at Bea for permission to speak. When she looked his way and paused he said, "Young lady, are you saying perhaps that we men are mistakes on Mother Nature's part?"

Laughter followed his question, partly in response to his humorous tone and partly as a kind of relief from the tension that Bea had generated so effectively.

"Sir," Bea responded, in a kind of patronizing tenderness, "some of you, and I'm sure you are a fine representative of these, have endured nature's insult with great dignity.

Unfortunately, many of you have not and have been permanently scarred, after your reproductive years, with destructive traits you were not wise enough to outgrow."

"So," the gray head said, maintaining his humor, "your answer, I take it, is yes. We are a mistake."

Again the laughter.

Bea nodded. "In a word, sir, if such is required, the answer has to be yes." Then she gave him a slight smile.

Again the laughter, with something more of an edge to it.

The moderator, at this point, chose to change the direction of the discussion, a relief to everyone except Bea. There were a few other questions, all either inane or politely supportive of the speaker, then the time was up. The attendees gathered their possessions, and in small groups, began to leave. Several came to where Bea had remained seating to tell her how provocative her comments had been. The gray haired man had been one of these, introducing himself as Dr. Josiah Zorn, from the Department of Physics. Bea was one of the last to leave, having taken time to finish the sandwich from the box lunch.

"You have a remarkable theory, Miss de Winter," said Dr. Greinert, approaching her as the student finally stood to go. "Thank you for sharing it with us."

"Thank you for an excellent presentation, Dr. Greinert," Bea responded. "And best of luck in your efforts to stimulate positive social change."

"But you seem to think I am doomed to failure, if I read you correctly." Greinert added a light smile to take the edge off her comment.

"We must each work in our own area of experience and interest, doctor," Bea said. "All of us contribute either positively or negatively."

Bea had started walking out of the room. The speaker's attention was called for by the moderator and a couple of other authoritative women nearby, so she had to let Bea go. She said, "Goodbye, Miss de Winter. It's been a pleasure."

"And for me, as well," Bea said.

After the graduate student had left the room, Dr. Greinert spoke to the several women remaining, including the moderator. "That young lady is something, don't you think?"

"That's Bill Charles' pet grad student," pointed out one of the group. "She's supposedly a genius in biophysics."

"I shouldn't doubt it," nodded Greinert. "And reducing all our social problems to testosterone is a clever stroke indeed. If in fact it were only true."

"But isn't it, possibly?" asked another. "That's the big difference between males and females, after all."

"Well, there's estrogen," said one.

"Yes, there's always estrogen," Greinert nodded, then smiled.

12. Melissa's Second Meeting with Cortland

MELISSA THOMAS WAS ONCE MORE in a formal business suit. This one was gray and fit her a little too tightly, she thought, something which made her promise herself to lose a few pounds. With Reggie gone and with so much else on her mind, she'd been drinking too much and eating too much. It was a reality she forced herself to admit.

"Thank you, Miss Thomas, for coming over," Cortland said, entering. Melissa's mind had been wandering, so the words startled her slightly.

"Oh, yes, ma'am," the student said, hesitant about standing, and didn't manage to do so before her hostess seated herself opposite, across the cluttered desk. "I don't know if I can help, but ..." With a shrug, Melissa stopped speaking, not sure how to end her sentence.

"You can understand that we are concerned about Mr. Jack Brady, especially after the developments related to your friend Mr. Pendergast."

Melissa nodded.

"And," Cortland continued, "we are also concerned about you as well, as you must expect, since you are the only person we know who has had any contact with both young men."

Again Melissa nodded. "I feel okay," she said quietly, "but I worry, too."

"As would anyone." The professor began looking through a thin sheaf of papers before speaking further. "Anything you can tell us about Mr. Brady could be very useful, Miss Thomas. I understand you had only been around him on that one occasion, the party I believe you mentioned."

"Uh, yes," Melissa said. "I mean, that was the only time I really did anything with him. I'd seen him before, though."

"How did you happen to see him at this party?"

Melissa shifted herself around a little, appearing uncomfortable. The skirt to her suit was short - in the style of the young, Cortland supposed - so the young woman's knees were clearly visible.

"It was sort of on the spur of the moment, I guess. The party I mean. We do that some."

"As did I and most people during college years," Cortland said, encouragingly, and added a smile. "And you just happened to see Jack Brady?"

"I didn't know he would be there, if that's what you mean. Jack was there and some others."

"How many were there, approximately?"

"A dozen maybe. I gave the ... the police all the names I knew, but I didn't know but two people. Reggie knew most of them, but he ..." She looked away. The young woman felt a discomfort in the pit of her stomach.

"I understand, Miss Thomas. Did you spend some time with Mr. Brady at the party?"

"Yes, some. And with other people too."

"Of course. Did you have any ... well, like did you dance with Mr. Brady, for example?"

Melissa colored a little. "Yes. Reggie wasn't all that happy about it ... well, you know."

"I know." Cortland smiled again. "And did you dance with other young men perhaps?"

Melissa's color grew again, and she had to make herself make eye contact. "Just Jack. And Reggie, of course. Jack came over and ... and asked me. So I danced with him."

Cortland nodded, looked at her papers another few seconds, and said, "So that was it then? You just danced with him."

"There – Dr. Cortland – it wasn't that kind of a party! I mean, we didn't screw around or anything!"

"I'm sorry if I implied that, Miss Thomas. But I ..."

"Well, I did kiss Jack, but that's all." Melissa blew out a long breath, as if the confession had taken something out of her.

"Kissed him? Well, I suppose that's pretty natural at a party." Again the smile.

"Sure." Melissa looked down briefly and controlled her blush. "It was mostly to rag Reggie, actually." She shrugged. "It was too much of a kiss, I know."

"Too much of a kiss?"

"Yes, ma'am."

"I don't know exactly what that means, Miss Thomas."

"I ... well, I Frenched him, actually. I know, it's pretty slutty, but I ..." She shrugged again. "But you wanted to know."

"I did. And thank you for your honesty."

Melissa's eyes took on a sudden look of concern and fear. "Did I ... do you think I gave Jack *and* Reggie something? Is that why you're asking about stuff like this?"

Cortland shook her head. "We don't really know, Miss Thomas. That's the problem. Any information we get might be useful. But you should know that we've looked at the blood and urine workups we did on you, and haven't seen any problems. You don't have any medical condition that we've been able to find."

Melissa sighed again. "Thank God for that, but I feel ... I really do feel pretty guilty, you know. It's ... I've been worried a lot lately."

"As would any of us be. That's why we've asked you to undergo a more complete physical. I hope you don't mind."

"No ma'am. I'm already scared." The pretty face clouded over, on the verge of tears. "And I feel so sorry for Jack, really. What if I ... if I did this to him? He ... I was just using him really, that's the damn truth of it. I'm so sorry!" And she looked like she truly meant it.

"Don't blame yourself, dear," Cortland said. "I've been to a few parties myself."

"But ..." Melissa caught herself, and asked something she obviously had been thinking about. "Is Jack going to be okay? I mean, I don't know how he's doing or anything."

Cortland hesitated, then answered. "He's not doing very well, sad to say. But not nearly so bad as Mr. Pendergast."

"Is he - I mean Jack seemed mostly like he was drunk or something."

"Mr. Brady knows who he is, yes, and knows other people. But he has problems with keeping track of the world around him. Yes, like he's drunk I'd say. He remembers things but not exactly correctly. And he forgets to do normal, routine things."

"Yeah," Melissa muttered, "like putting on his pants."

"Yes, like that," Cortland nodded, trying not to grin. It was, after all, a very serious situation.

"Is he any better, Dr. Cortland?"

"He's about the same, I'm afraid."

"Oh." Melissa shifted again, obviously uncomfortable. "I wish I could ... could just do something! I feel so horrible about this!"

"You're doing all you can, Miss Thomas. I'd say you're a very brave young woman."

"Thanks, but I'm not really. I'm pretty fucked up right now ... er, sorry, messed up."

Cortland allowed herself a little smile. "I would feel the same and would probably say 'fucked up,' too." Again she looked at her papers. "Another thing, Miss Thomas, if you can help me understand. This fellow Mr. Brady was actually found at Miss de Winter's door, is that right?"

Melissa nodded. "It was Bea that heard him. And she was the one who called the police."

Cortland also nodded. "But Miss de Winter didn't know him, as I understand."

Melissa laughed lightly, thinking about the unlikelihood of Bea de Winter having any contact whatsoever with someone like Jack Brady. "No. And he didn't say who he was, I guess."

"That's what I understand, Miss Thomas. I'm asking this because I'm concerned about Miss de Winter, too. She does live close to you, as I understand."

"There are two rooms between us, actually."

"But you've spent a little time with her lately, haven't you?"

Melissa nodded. "I guess so. Sure."

Virginia Cortland shoved her papers aside symbolically and leaned back. "What do you think of Miss de Winter, if I may ask? Is she your friend?"

Melissa's brow furrowed. "Not exactly, no. But, well I hardly knew her until - you know, recently. She's really smart! Didn't know you knew her."

"I know her through a colleague, Dr. Charles. Dr. Charles has gotten her involved in the analysis of samples associated with Mr. Pendergast and Mr. Brady."

"Really? I didn't know that. That's weird, kind of. Wow, she must be smart."

"Quite a remarkable student. But what do you think of her, as a person, I mean?"

Melissa pursed her lips. She suddenly looked much younger, overriding the effect of her business suit. "Maybe I'm not being, you know, fair and all, but she's pretty funny - I mean, like weird. At least to me. Because she's so smart, I guess. But she's nice. I mean, I crashed at her place a while that night. Was a little ... you know, pretty spaced out from all this stuff." Melissa wasn't about to confess she'd been drunk.

"I'm glad you've gotten to know her, Miss Thomas. Professor Charles says Miss de Winter is pretty much a loner."

"She sure is. She mostly never talked to me for a long time."

"It's good she knows you, Miss Thomas. I actually think it makes her more interested in helping us with the case."

"You think so? She has been nice, like I said. Nice in a funny way. She's so ... so formal, you know."

Cortland thought she understood, but really didn't know Bea de Winter very well at all. "Do you like her? I mean, is there something about her that would draw you to her as a friend?"

"I like her, sure." Melissa pondered the question seriously. "But I don't know what she thinks about me, really. Even though she is nice to me."

"Kind of a mystery person, huh?"

"For sure. You think I may have ... I mean, could I have, you know, infected Bea, too? This whole thing is a real bummer!"

"We'll check Miss de Winter as a precaution. But don't worry about it. After all, you didn't kiss her." Cortland smiled, trying to force some of the seriousness out of the atmosphere.

Melissa blushed. "No, not that," the girl said. "But I was at her place."

"Right. But like I say, it's not something to be overly concerned over. We're just now beginning to get some idea of what this whole situation is about."

Melissa shifted again, knees toward Cortland. Worry showed on her face. "I'm really ... but thanks for being so nice to me. I am such a mess right now!"

"It's very normal to be concerned, Miss Thomas. Putting myself in your place I'd have reacted very much like you have. But we want to make sure we don't neglect anything that might be helpful, to you as well as to Mr. Pendergast and Mr. Brady."

"Thanks." She wasn't sure what else to say.

"I think it might help you, Miss Thomas, to talk to a counselor, if you're willing. The university will take care of any expense."

The young woman looked at the other. "I ... do you think so? I've never done anything like that before. It's weird, kind of."

"It's nothing to be ashamed of, let me tell you that. Any of us can benefit from talking with an interested but unbiased listener. If you want I can set it all up for you."

Again that heavy sigh. "I guess so, Dr. Cortland. If you think it's good."

"I can get you an appointment if you wish."

"I can ... I can do it. My mom has a ... well, she sees someone."

"Fine. Just let me know if you want any help from me."

"Okay." Melissa ran a hand through her wealth of hair.

"Please don't worry, Miss Thomas," Cortland said earnestly. "If there's anything you can think of that would make you feel better about the situation, please let us know."

"I just want to ... to want all this stuff to be over. Especially for Reggie. Is there ... I mean, can he get better, do you think? It's so terrible, what's happened."

"We aren't sure about his prognosis. But we're working hard on it."

The pretty but worried girl nodded. “Okay,” she said, and stood, then added, “Thank you.”

13. More Conversations

BEA DE WINTER FOUND A NOTE in her student mailbox from William Charles. "Bea, can you meet with Dr. Cortland this PM? She's worried about you maybe getting exposed from Melissa Thomas. Thanks."

Bea looked at the note. She wasn't concerned, of course, for her own health, but was angry at herself for not taking such things into consideration. Details were everything in life, she knew very well indeed. Bea scribbled an answer, saying she'd go see Cortland later in the afternoon, then walked out, deep in thought. She didn't notice that Mike Baylor had been hanging around outside Hess hall, waiting for her, and had followed her at a distance until he had a chance to cut across an expanse of grass, get ahead of her, and wait again near the edge of campus. This time she did see him, sitting on the grass, leaning back against a tree, apparently reading.

"Hello, Mike," Bea said.

"Hey genius! How's it hangin'?"

"By a thread as usual, Mike. What are you doing over here? Never seen you here before."

"Just hopin' a brilliant girl old enough to drink would come by and brighten up my day."

Bea turned her head a little, blushing. But she regained composure quickly. "You and your thing for brilliance, Mike! Let me tell you, brains aren't any good if you don't use them. And I need to use mine – believe it or not. Got to go, sorry."

"Can I walk you over to your place?"

The young man was on his feet. Today he wore a pretty navy blue sweater and perfectly fitting black denim jeans.

"Don't bother, Mike. Thanks, though."

"Jus' want to talk a little longer, that's all. Don't want to cause any wear and tear on your brain, though. Okay?"

"Okay." Bea sighed a little, both in exasperation at having to be with someone, and a little bit from embarrassment that someone would want to be with her. She began walking immediately, and didn't slow for Mike to join her stride. He did so, however, and very quickly.

They were in sight of The Strip. Bea had to cross Cumberland Avenue to get to her dorm, passing by and behind the businesses along the main drag.

"Want a cup of coffee first, Bea, before you got off and generate all those prize winning thoughts?" Mike was pointing toward The Sunspot.

Bea stopped herself from saying the automatic "no." She slowed her pace and thought a minute. Something associated with Mike Baylor had come into her mind. "Coffee, you say?" she said instead. "I guess I could be talked into it. But only a few minutes, alright?"

"Deal, Bea." Mike grinned cheerfully. He was a very large presence beside the petite girl, but seemed so amazingly gentle. It was the thing she admired most about him. And the thing which most confused her. She didn't like being confused.

They changed course and crossed over to The Sunspot. Bea led him inside and they settled in the same window seat she'd been in earlier in the day. Settling into the booth was awkward for Bea. It dawned on her both that she had never done this sort of thing before, ever, and that doing it was not as disgusting as she'd have guessed. The difference, of course - and Bea was certain of it - was this fellow Mike Baylor. Who could ever be disgusted by him? But why was that so? Never had she thought about anyone else in those terms. When that realization struck her, she blushed again.

"So, Bea, how'd you get to be so smart?" Mike asked when the waitress had brought their coffees and left.

Bea was concentrating on her cup, then looked at him. She saw an open face with dark, intelligent eyes. Never before had she seen eyes like that. It worried her. She answered, "What makes you think I'm smart, Mike? Just because I'm young." Her manner was plain, with no accompanying smile.

He grinned. "That has to be part of it, you know. Never heard of anyone twenty-one and workin' on a PhD. Pretty cool,

I'd say." He sipped, keeping eye contact but not staring – another remarkable trait she'd noticed.

"Well, I don't really know," she continued. "I'm who I am and that's it."

"That's plenty. Have you always liked biology, stuff like that?"

She nodded. "For a very long time anyway. Ten years or so."

"Like when you were ten or eleven. Cool. How'd you start gettin' interested? Hey, I don't mean to be nosy, but if you don't mind sayin'."

Bea looked away from him, dealing with a potential blush. She didn't like to talk about herself, especially her history. But she didn't want to be impolite. Nor did she want to simply lie. "I'm not sure, Mike. How'd you get interested in botany?"

His solid wide-eyed face frowned briefly. "Hard to say all the things that caused it, really. Maybe that's what you're sayin', too, huh? I guess I always liked trees, especially, and flowers and gardens. Grew up in Detroit where there weren't many of those. But there was a ... kind of a vacant lot a couple of blocks from my house. When I was a kid. Had a bunch of trees on it. Sort of growing wild. And weeds, too." He grinned. "Used to go down there and think about those growin' things. Finally went to the library and got books to learn more about them. That's how it went. I would tell my Aunt Jacie – that's who raised me – and she thought it was great. I suppose all of us get interested in things because of something that happens to us or maybe something we see and are comfortable with."

Bea considered his comment. "So you were raised by your aunt, then?"

"Yep. My mom – oh, you don't want to hear all this stuff, Bea!"

"Sure I do. Tell me about your mother."

"She was ... well, a crack head. Sorry to say. Died when I was about two, I think. Don't remember her at all."

Bea's brow furrowed. You never know what things have happened to people. "I'm sorry to hear that," she said.

"No big thing, really. Since I don't remember. Aunt Jacie was my mom's sister, and she's really my mom, when you think about it. She's a great lady."

"Sounds like she is. Was there a man, too, like an uncle, who helped raise you?"

Mike scowled a little. "No. Aunt Jacie had trouble with men, and kind of gave up on 'em, I'd say. She said the only man she ever looked up to was Jesus Christ." Then he smiled.

Bea cocked her head a little, sipped, then said, trying to be reasonably casual, "Jesus Christ? Are you a religious family, then, Mike?"

"Aunt Jacie always took me to church, yes," he nodded. "But she was never ... well, exactly orthodox, if you know what I mean."

"I suppose I don't," she admitted. "What do you mean?"

"Oh, she thinks most churches and most people in 'em were phony. But she still goes."

"Do you go, Mike? To church, I mean."

"Sometimes I do. I kind of believe in a God, Bea, but not like most people believe."

She was interested despite herself. She knew she really should cut this short. "What kind of God do you believe in Mike, if you don't mind saying?"

Mike looked at his coffee. Not making eye contact with Bea he said, "I have a little trouble with God, Bea. I guess I do think that ... well, the universe has some kind of meaning and some kind of ... what would you call it - an organizing principle."

Bea thought about his words. "It sounds like we're alike that way, Mike," she said.

"I can't be much like you, Bea," he smiled suddenly. "I'm just a guy that takes care of mice and wonders how certain girls can be so damned smart."

"Don't be silly," she scolded gently.

"What do you mean we're alike in thinking about God, Bea?" His light mood had shifted suddenly.

"That there is an organizing principle in the universe. But I don't exactly know what it is. I suppose we could call it God."

"Do you believe God will continue to make things better, then. More organized, maybe."

Bea sipped and deliberately sat the coffee down, looking at the mug before responding. "I think this organizing principle, this God, has helped organize our brains, Mike. And that we have to do the real work - beyond what the organizing principle allows through evolution."

"Hmm," he muttered, scowling a little. "And we men, did we get organized wrong, then? As you've said before."

"An interesting way of putting it," she said. "Most men are less than useful to our culture, though, if you don't mind my being honest about it."

"Maybe, Bea." He smiled. "But we're the best other sex you ladies have."

"That's a valid point," she replied, not sharing his humor. "Did the kids you grow up with think you were a nerd, Mike?"

"Did they ever!" He grinned even more broadly. "I would be down there at the empty lot staring at some dumb lookin' weed and wondering how in the world it got to be like it was. My friends would come by and just shake their heads at me. I was a lost cause to them." Again the grin.

"But you are a male, Mike, at least. You didn't suffer physically for your difference." The words came out more powerfully than she had planned, but she couldn't take them back.

Mike looked at her a moment. "Don't tell me," he said quietly, "somebody hassled you for being so smart, and probably so different."

Bea looked away briefly, but forced her eyes back on his. "It's never been easy to ... well, you have to understand, since you were the weed watcher while the others were probably playing ball or something." She imposed lightness on her tone and even smiled a little.

He wouldn't be deterred from his concern. "I can't believe anyone would want to give you a hard time, Bea. But I know some folks are total assholes. Sorry, I shouldn't have been so ... you know."

"You're right about some folks, Mike. But you know those folks you call assholes are mostly male folk, don't you?" Her tone was not acerbic, almost clinical.

"Guys are like that, Bea. Sorry to say. Wish you girls didn't have to deal with us. Like I said, you're stuck with us." He didn't grin.

"Do you really mean that, Mike, or are you just trying to be nice?"

"Mean what?"

"That males are not trustworthy, or that you wished females didn't have to deal with them."

"Both, Bea. Hey, but you know it's not easy being a male, either. Did you ever think about that?" He punctuated with another grin.

That was an angle she'd never considered. Males might not consider their sexual condition easy. She certainly had seen very little evidence of it. But neither had she detected any guile in Mike Baylor. Bea was uneasy and didn't like it one bit.

"Listen, Mike, I have to get on back, but I have enjoyed the conversation."

"Well, we sure didn't talk about the weather, did we? Guess that's what comes of chattin' with a genius." The grin again.

"Guess so, Mike," she said back and stood. She'd finished her coffee.

His cup was still half full, but he stood, too. "I can walk you on over to your place, Bea."

"No thanks, Mike. Don't want to send you out of your way. I'm fine. It's just a couple of blocks."

"Don't mind really. It's nice to be around someone who doesn't ever say anything about 'those Vols'" He rolled his eyes.

"The sports teams, you mean?"

"Yep. See, you even had a hard time knowin' what I was talkin' about."

"Stay and finish you coffee, Mike. I'm paying, okay."

"Can't let you do that," he protested.

"Yes you can." She gave him a pleasant but not teasing look. "I didn't grow up in Detroit, Mike. You had a lot more to deal with, I bet. It's my pleasure to buy the coffee."

Mike didn't sit down but gave her a curious look before he smiled. "Damn, I don't guess I'm supposed to understand the really smart ones, am I?"

"No you're not," she nodded. "Sit down now. Don't let that good coffee go to waste. They do brew a good cup here."

"So you really mean it, don't you?"

"Absolutely. And thanks again."

Mike shrugged, glanced a couple of tables away to notice a couple noticing them. Then he settled back into the booth. "No, my turn to thank you, Bea. You be careful, now."

"See you later, Mike." She waved slightly and went over to the cashier to pay the tab. Before going out she waved once more, then simply left.

Mike did finish his coffee. He was drinking as he watched the petite and mysterious girl disappear down the street.

–

Bea walked into Dr. Cortland's office exactly on time, arriving at 4 o'clock, and looked exactly like she always seemed to. At least in Cortland's short experience with her.

"Hello, Bea," was the warm greeting. "Thanks for coming."

"I understand you're worried, Dr. Cortland, about my possible contact with Melissa Thomas." Bea took the indicated seat across from the professor.

Cortland replied, "Yes, exactly. We're going to do a full work-up on her and I thought maybe - for completeness, and since we don't really understand much yet - we should do the same for you."

Bea said, "I did draw some of my blood and kept a urine sample, thinking the same kind of thing. Is there anything else you'd like to evaluate?"

"That's a good start. Have you had them analyzed yet?" She was referring to automatic blood and urine sample analyzers available either in the University Hospital or in Hess Hall on the campus.

"I turned them in yesterday. But haven't seen the results yet. I suspect they're ready, though. I've been rather busy."

"I'm sure you have." Cortland smiled at the peculiar and remarkable young lady. "And congratulations on finding the un-cataloged virus. Any further information on it?"

Bea nodded. "Thank you. Not much more on it. We've been trying to make it replicate. No luck yet. Fortunately - or possibly unfortunately - we did find other viral specimens. Pendergast's blood turns out to have lot of the virus. Pretty good chance, I'd say, that it's the culprit. Or at least part of the culprit."

Cortland looked thoughtful. "So no idea yet as to its action. It must have something to do with neurotransmitters."

"That's naturally our working hypothesis, doctor. We'll figure it out." Bea gave a wan smile.

"I suspect you will. Thank you, Bea."

"Is there anything else, Dr. Cortland?"

"Not that I can think of at the moment. Please let me know about those tests on your personal specimens. I'm concerned that we may have gotten you involved in something that has put you at risk."

"We're all at risk, doctor. The world is full of viruses, prions, and bacteria, as you know."

"Nice of you to philosophical about it, Bea, but I'd hate to have to call your parents with news that we'd done something to make you ill."

Bea stiffened a little, and the professor picked up on it. Then Bea said, "My parents are dead, doctor. I suppose you didn't know."

"Oh, I'm so sorry!" Virginia Cortland stood, leaned over and put a hand on Bea's. "No, I didn't know. Was it ... I mean were their deaths recent?"

Bea felt awkward being comforted but struggled through it. "My father died six years ago. My mother died two years ago."

"How tragic for you. Do you mind telling me what happened?"

"No, of course not, doctor. My father had a massive heart attack. My mother had suffered all her life from Lupus. She had a severe recurrence and didn't pull out of it."

"Were you home when your mother passed on?" Cortland had realized that Bea would have been in the university at the time.

"No. I was called and told of her death." Bea showed no sadness in her words, but her tone was subdued.

"I'm really so very sorry. Do you have siblings, Bea?"

"No, doctor."

"Are you completely on your own then? How difficult for you."

"Not difficult at all, doctor, but yes I'm on my own. My Aunt - my mother's sister - is my closest relative. She ... her home became my official residence after my mother's death. You see, I was not of legal age yet."

"Yes, I knew. You are very brave about such misfortune, Bea."

"I confess to not being very close to my parents, Dr. Cortland. Their loss was not pleasant, certainly, but not a great misfortune. I don't want to sound callous, but am simply stating the truth."

"Well, I know you are a person of great intellectual gifts, Bea, but perhaps you miss your parents more than you understand."

"I'm aware of all the psychological implications of my situation, doctor, but I assure you I am perfectly fine."

"Were you closer to your mother or your father, Bea?"

Bea leaned back, and almost refused to answer. But she found herself saying, "My father was seriously flawed, doctor, and my mother was emotionally ill, I would say. Living with my father could easily have been one cause of her problem. I was not close to either. Yet I could trust my mother."

The middle aged professor considered the small girl-woman seated across from her. "I should not have dragged you back through such unpleasant memories, Bea. Please pardon me."

"You had no way of knowing, doctor. No forgiveness is necessary."

Cortland offered a pleasant smile. "I think I understand much better now, certainly. And please, do let me know about the test results on your samples."

"I will, doctor. Thank you."

Bea stood, shook the other's hand, and left, moving deliberately and not seeming to rush.

Virginia Cortland sat for a few minutes, thinking about the graduate student. She'd never come across anyone like her. Bea had an impenetrable wall around herself, and was so supremely confident. What, besides her brilliance, could be the source? But maybe brilliance and single-minded devotion was source enough.

14. Two More Names

AT TEN O'CLOCK THAT EVENING, Bea de Winter tapped on Melissa Thomas' door. It was a full minute before the door opened. Melissa was wearing a pale blue cotton robe, and looked thoroughly disheveled. Her puffy eyes betrayed an excess of alcohol in her system.

"Bea, what's going on?" she muttered, stepping back a little.

"May I come in for a few minutes, Melissa?"

"Sure, come on." The buxom young woman stumbled a little as she moved. An empty wine bottle and a half full one sat side by side on the bedside table. There was a water glass there, too, a quarter full of wine. The bed itself was a confused mass of sheet and blanket mixed with scattered pillow.

"Melissa you're drinking too much," Bea said simply as she pushed some panties and stockings onto the floor from the chair she wanted to sit in.

"Maybe you're not drinking enough, Bea. That's what I'd say."

"I suppose you would. Listen, are you rational enough to talk a little?"

"Sure, Bea." Melissa plopped onto her bed, exposing herself unknowingly because the robe fabric shifted under the loose tie, but Bea ignored it.

"Did you kiss any of the other guys at the party, Melissa?"

The question caused a hesitation. Melissa was worried that she in fact had done just that. "I ... it was a party, Bea. Well, maybe you don't know about parties, huh - bein' a fuckin' genius 'n all. Maybe I kissed some other guys. Who knows?"

"You should know, Melissa, unless you were stinking drunk then, too."

"I wasn't ..." Melissa's eyes narrowed and she suddenly began to sob. "I didn't ... have that much. Oh God, Bea! We had some coke that night. I didn't want my ass thrown in jail, so I ... well, you wouldn't have told either, would you?" The poor thing looked absolutely forlorn.

"Cocaine, Melissa? You idiot!"

"See, I'm fucked up! That's why."

"Did you take this cocaine early in the evening, Melissa? Tell me."

"Maybe. Well, yes, sure. It was ... well, it gets you pretty hot. You see, I ..."

"I'm sure it does! Makes you want to fuck everyone there, doesn't it? Melissa, you are such a fool!"

"Well, you asked. What am I supposed to say?"

"Think about it. Did you kiss or get close to any other people at that party?"

"I ... stop it, Bea! Quit ragging at me."

"I will not. Answer my question."

"I have to pee."

"Great, Melissa. Be my guest. Then answer my question."

Melissa got to her feet and, much to Bea's surprise and disgust, untied and dropped her robe on the bed as she stepped away from it. She swayed across the room, very womanly and very nude, and into the adjoining bath. While she was in there, Bea took the partial bottle of wine and the glass and poured them down the sink located on the wall just outside the bathroom.

Melissa returned, still weaving a little, and sat on the bed again, apparently unaware or unconcerned that she didn't have a stitch on. She actually began to sit on her robe, completely ignoring it, as Bea snatched it from under her and imposed it on Melissa, helping her back into it. Bea then sat and asked again, "Okay, who else did you kiss or get close to at the party?"

Apparently Melissa, drunk or not, had been thinking. She said, "Probably Casey. I think that was his name."

"Casey who, and what did you do with him?"

"I didn't fuck him. But I ... I think I Frenched him, too."

"Casey who?"

Melissa shrugged, but seemed to be trying to come up with the name. "Maria would know. I can't remember what his last name is. Maybe I never heard. Hell, I don't know!"

"Maria who?"

"Santos. You going to ask her?"

"Absolutely, I'm going to ask her, Melissa. Now think. Anyone else? Did you kiss any of the girls?"

"Bea, are you saying I'm a lez? You are ... are real piece of work, you know. Stop ..."

"Did you kiss any of the girls?"

Melissa blushed beet red, a total surprise to Bea. "God, probably! And I ... God I Frenched Maria. Oh fuck!"

"Maria Santos, then. I'll talk to her."

"Where's my wine?" the drunk one asked, looking around.

"Poured out. You certainly don't need any more right now."

"Damn you, Bea! Why don't you leave me alone?"

"Because you can't take care of yourself. Did you tell Dr. Cortland about all your fun at the party?"

Melissa lifted her arms, fooling with her hopeless hair. She said, "I told her about Jack. Why, are you mad that I did?"

"Of course not. But did you mention Maria or, what was his name, Casey whoever?"

After a pout, Melissa admitted, "No, I didn't ... just now remembered."

"I'll tell her, Melissa. You need to sleep it off. Now be honest with me, have you had any coke since that party?"

Melissa didn't answer. She brought her knees up and suddenly hugged her bent legs. "I ... maybe," she muttered.

"Not maybe, yes. Am I right?"

"Yes. But ..."

"Where is it?"

"Where is what?" Melissa looked away.

"The coke. Where is it and who gave it to you?"

"It's ... none of your business."

"The coke. Where is it and who gave it to you?"

"It's not here. I didn't ... it was at Maria's."

"So she's into coke, too?"

"It's probably all gone now. She just had a little. We ... I thought, after Reggie's problem, you know, that it was a good thing to just ... to just forget for a while."

Bea sighed. "Do you forget what you do when you're on coke?"

"Bea, stop it! You keep asking ..."

"Do you forget what you do when you're on coke?"

"Not exactly. But ... maybe it's real and maybe it's not. That kind of thing."

Bea stood. "You need to go to bed, Melissa."

"Why?"

"Now lie down. I'll cover you up and turn out the light when I leave."

"Okay." Melissa stood and let Bea straighten the bedclothes enough that it was possible to get under the covers. Without another word, the graduate student put the undergrad to bed, making no suggestion about a nightgown, or anything else. She covered Melissa and stepped back.

"Good night, Melissa. Sleep. Understand?"

"Yes, mother dear!" The reclined one pulled down the sheet off her robe-clad body and looked at Bea. "Do I get a goodnight kiss?"

Bea acted as if she'd heard nothing, walked to the door, opened it, then turned off the light. In the slant of yellow illumination coming in from the hallway Melissa could be seen staring out toward Bea with odd, inebriated eyes. Then the visitor left, closing the door softly behind her.

Inside her own room, Bea considered sending an email message to Dr. Cortland to relate the new names Melissa had told her. These students, and the others at the party, would have to be contacted. She decided not to, thinking she'd make the contacts herself. Then she opened a can of fruit drink, turned and began speaking to Magdalene before reaching the mirror. "What are we going to do with Melissa, anyway?"

The reply, sounding more exasperated than angry, was, "Learn from her, of course. Start using your brain and stop letting your emotions cripple you!"

Bea sighed, and spoke again, more quietly. "Oh shut up, Magdalene!"

Chapter 15. Surprises

AFTER GENETICS CLASS, BEA WENT to Hess Hall to get her blood and urine test results. The report was dumped automatically into a secure file in the server associated with the group of machines used for the standard analyses. Bea had been given the password when Professor Charles had arranged for her to work on the Pendergast Project, as it was now being called. Her procedure to isolate the new virus was not a part of the automated protocol, so she had reserved one vial of her own blood, knowing she would be wise to see if she, too, were a carrier. It was that analysis she would do next, and would be including blood from Melissa Thomas and Jack Brady - assuming the Brady blood had been left for her in her lab. The blood and urine analyses done by these operator-free machines, however, were extensive, and included several detailed chemistry studies that had not been in their sequence before the Pendergast evaluations had begun. Most important of these, as far as Bea was concerned, was the free testosterone determination and several other hormone levels, including estrogen and three or four fairly rare compounds whose functions were still not well understood.

Bea was sitting in the analysis lab and looking at her own body chemistry report when William Charles entered and greeted her.

"Hello, Bea. How are things?" he asked, though he seemed, as always, preoccupied.

"Fine, sir."

"Whose analysis are you looking at there?"

"My own, Dr. Charles."

"No surprises, I hope."

Bea had been making various check marks on the printout. She didn't answer promptly and looked up as if still registering the question. "Well, actually yes, sir. I didn't expect such a big white cell count - since I'm not dealing with a cold or allergies, that sort of thing."

He came over to her, looking over her shoulder. The page she was looking at was one of three, and contained a number of results relating to immune system response. "I don't want to alarm you, but could it be," he asked, "that resisting some kind of infectious agent has stimulated your white cells?"

"Possible, yes. But I do suffer from asthma. Always have some abnormality in my white cells. But I'm going to include my blood in the viral study this afternoon. Do you know, sir, if the sample of Mr. Brady's blood has been delivered to my lab?"

"I think it has, yes," he answered. "Anything else besides the white count?"

"I'll let you know if anything else is abnormal, when I finish going through it, sir," she replied.

"Appreciate it. I have to get to class. Talk to you later."

"Goodbye, Dr. Charles."

Bea finished making notes on the sheets, identifying all the values she considered curious, and left the analysis lab, headed for her own lab. There she settled in, starting the complicated process of looking for and extracting the new virus and some of the associated carriers. She had her own blood, Mike Baylor's - as a kind of control - Reggie's, to re-examine, Melissa's, and now Jack Brady's. The procedure was detailed and involved the use of the electron microscope next door, so Bea still working busily at six o'clock. Outside, the sun had set and darkness was settling in.

These results were less of a surprise. Her own blood and Mike's were free of the virus. Melissa's was teeming with the marker precursors she'd selected. Reggie's was similarly teeming, and Jack Brady's system had significant numbers. She isolated individual viruses from each sample that had contained them and did a detailed structural analysis. This had been the most time-consuming aspect of the work. The structures were consistent and hadn't mutated. She'd expected slight variants to show up quickly, but they hadn't yet. As long as the virus structure remained stable there was no mechanism she could imagine that would weaken its virulence. And by the time the virus is identified in the blood stream it was too late. It'll mutate, though, she thought, eventually. And the first strains will eventually become weaker, but she could add variants as time went by - assuming she was not found out. Bea felt her heart rate go up a little. She was tempted to speak out loud to herself but fought off the urge.

The haggard grad student was worn out when she left the lab and started home. It was after seven and dark. The evening had turned out a little chilly and she had only a sweater to put on over khakis and shirt. Even her sneakers seemed a little thin for the occasion. It was not wise to push herself like this, Bea well knew. That white cell count in her own blood reminded her of the weakness in her own immune system. Not related to the virus, no: it was something she was born with. Someday she would deal with that. Again she almost spoke out loud to Magdalene as she walked, wanting to tell herself to become more reasonable. This was no time to get ill.

Bea crossed the campus noticing how few students seemed to be around. Probably having dinner, she guessed. She usually went to her dorm either earlier - before dark - or later, nearer midnight. On those later transits she would naturally not expect to see many students, but there were always a fairly large number around. Especially near and in the various businesses along The Strip. The exhausted girl walked slower than usual, and mostly with her head down, thinking of one thing or another. She wasn't even remotely aware that she was being followed.

Crossing Cumberland Avenue, Bea saw that The Sunspot at least was busy. People were standing outside waiting to be seated. She had considered stopping there for an unusual dinner out, but changed her mind when she saw the crowd. Turning the next corner she began the climb up two blocks and over two to get to her dorm. Now she was quickly alone again. Or so she thought. Half way up the second block a car pulled out of a street behind her and began to approach. The lights came on and Bea glanced around, not wanting to cross the street into the path of the vehicle. She had left the sidewalk and was walking along the edge of the roadway intent on crossing over in a kind of long diagonal. As the car approached she stepped back onto the sidewalk. Coming from the vehicle she heard a very noisy stereo system inside pounding out some harsh heavy beated pop music - if such noise could be called music. She winced a little, anxious for the car to get on past her. But it didn't pass. Rather it went ahead only about twenty feet, then stopped. The pounding music from the car suddenly cut off. Someone on the passenger side - nearest her - lowered the window and looked out at her.

"Hey babe, wanna party? You look like a party doll."

The speaker was an East Tennessean - or so his accent seemed. And maybe African American in descent. He was shrouded in shadows like the others in the car. There seemed to be three of them, maybe. Bea wasn't sure whether they were all male.

"No thanks," she answered. "Have to study." She tried to make her tone calm and pleasant, but couldn't keep from giving away her youth, sounding as always more like a girl than a woman.

The young man opened the door and stepped across in front of her. The car now was to her left, blocking any graceful going around, and this person was directly in front of her. A twinge of fear materialized in the pit of her stomach. This was something she really didn't need right now!

"Come on, don't be a snob, girl. Don't tell us you don't want a good time." He took a step toward her.

Bea stopped. "Really, I have to study," she said, glancing to her left. Another young man was getting out of the back seat. He was swarthy in appearance but not black. Probably Latino. She also caught a glimpse of the third passenger, the driver. It was another male. She couldn't identify anything else about him.

The second male suddenly reached out and grabbed Bea's left wrist, totally taking her by surprise. "Listen," he snapped, in a tone more ominous than that of the first, "it's party time, honey. Git in the car!" Again the local dialect.

"Let go of me!" Bea shrieked, knowing she was in trouble and needed to make some noise.

"Cut the crap, girl!" the one holding her wrist said, and jerked her toward him. Bea stumbled and came down hard on her knees, striking the sidewalk.

She yelped in pain, then shrieked again, "Let me go!" The first fellow was approaching now. She managed to yell out "help!" before he got to her.

The two quickly disabled the petite young woman. The young black man grabbed Bea's legs and lifted her by the ankles, jerking her up from the pavement, preventing her kicking by clamping those ankles together. The Latino had her waist. They were intent on throwing her into the back seat of the car. That back door had been left wide open. The car's engine was still running, of course, and the driver was at the wheel. It would only take seconds before she was whisked away. Bea's mind understood this bitter truth essentially instantly. Unfortunately, that same mind assessed her probability of avoiding disaster to be near zero. She let out another scream just before a hand was clamped over her mouth. She smelled the presence of the two and was sickened by the odor of sweat and stench. Squirming was all she could do, and she squirmed, for all she was worth. The backpack was jerked away from her in the process and slung aside, one of the straps torn loose.

Bea felt herself being moved toward the car. She got her hands out and grabbed for the door frame around the opening, resisting the process of tossing her inside. The hand over her mouth was so large most of her vision was also cut off. Trying to scream was worth doing but produced no sound. The fear in her stomach was overwhelming, sweeping over her entire body. A hand came across and roughly tore her right hand away from the door. Bea gasped, struggling to even breathe. Tears were streaming out of her eyes and her eyes were wide in abject horror. She looked across at the driver, who turned and looked at her. He was a stubble-faced white guy, about the same age as the other two and had a terrible leer on his face.

A voice behind her yelled out, "You pieces of shit!" Something about it registered with her, but Bea was so awash in pure terror that she sensed little more than another dimension to the commotion. There followed a sudden "whomp!" a powerful impact that caused the car to shake, the vibration passing through the one hand she still had on the door frame. Bea supposed someone had struck her, but she was numb to pain. Her mind suggested this was possible because her rational self knew what distress she was in. The impact was followed by a yelp of pain. It was too low in pitch, not her! Then another "whomp!" and another crying out. Then the grip around her mouth and waist vanished! Both Bea's hands were free and she caught herself on the curb, screaming loudly, "Help!" Then the third shuddering "whomp!" and Bea's legs were dropped. She came down again on her knees, now numb to the pain. Turning she took in a scene that was beyond belief.

Bea's two assailants were down on the ground, struggling to regain balance and stability, and there, swinging a four-foot long tree limb about three inches in diameter, was none other than Mike Baylor! She watched him bring it down on the Afro American's back, just missing the dodging head. Then with lightning speed Mike swung the limb sideways at the Latino, catching the side of the head and knocking him three or four feet to the side. "You scumbag bastard pieces of shit!" Mike yelled out, absolutely enraged. He was an unbelievable and awesome sight. Bea had never seen such rage, or such strength. The knocked aside Latino, yelping in pain and showing blood on his face and right arm, stumbled forward and flung himself into the car. Before the door that they'd tried to push Bea through could be closed the car lurched forward, wheels burning rubber, and hurdled away from the curb. Bea rolled to a sitting position, overwhelmed still, but now feeling an indescribable surge of relief flood through her.

Mike, glancing at the departing vehicle, swung once again with his makeshift weapon, blasting bark loose as he caught the remaining assailant in the right thigh, essentially knocking him off his feet. The man caught himself, scraping his hands terribly, got up somehow and began to run, careening against the brick building on the right with his shoulder and spinning off, shrieking in agony. Bea could see that Mike could have easily caught the man, and probably could have killed him if the next blow were to the head, but Mike stopped. He was breathing hard, eyes still focused away from Bea at the man he had just beat to within an inch of his life. Some kind of inner control held him back. The assailant stumbled away, too beaten and in too much pain to cry out any more. In less than ten seconds he'd rounded the corner ahead and disappeared to the right. She could hear her own and Mike's heavy breathing. He was only two steps away when he turned, finally, to look at her. Bea gasped at the sight. Mike Baylor was looking directly at her and weeping!

"Oh God, Bea, I'm so, so sorry!" he said, quietly and in that same ingenuous voice she had come to admire. He took a step forward and she rose to hug him to her, enveloped quickly and totally in his powerful arms. They neither spoke again for some seconds. She actually felt his tears fall on the back of her neck. It was a moment beyond her understanding. All she could do was cry and hang on. The reality of herself as a fragile, physical being was too massive a truth to get her mind around. There was no way to know how long they'd have remained in that altered state had the first of several running students not arrived a few seconds later.

"Hey, what happened?" called out a young man, about Mike's age, someone who could have been an athlete. Behind him two more youths were running. They had raced up from The Strip, probably hearing her screams, the fight, and the squealing car exit.

Mike released Bea and stood. He was trembling now, but forced a level of calm into his voice, calling to the arriving help, "She's okay! She's okay!"

"What happened?" the onrusher repeated, the two behind him were in earshot now.

"Some bastards tried to grab Bea," Mike said, rubbing a hand through his eyes, banishing tears. "They're gone."

The three young men were now with them. The first one said, "Where did they go?"

Mike pointed up the street. "Drove off," he said. "Two did. A third ran. We won't catch him probably."

Two more students were hustling toward them, a young man and woman who'd come out of the back of a restaurant and heard the noise. Bea, like Mike, was busy composing herself. She straightened her rumpled clothes quickly, tucking in her shirt. Both knees, however, were badly scraped, the khakis torn, and blood stained. Swallowing before she spoke, Bea said to the gathering group, "I'm alright, really. Thanks to all of you."

"Are you hurt?" the girl from the couple called out.

"Just my knees," Bea said. "I'll be alright."

"Those bastards!" muttered one of the guys. "We should call the cops."

"We did," said the girl, holding up her cell phone.

Bea's heart was still racing, and she continued to struggle inwardly. She tried to blank her agitated mind of the terror that had so rapidly descended upon her. Mike stood next to her as they were surrounded by the others.

By the time the Knoxville police - not the campus police - arrived, three additional students had joined the group, including two more girls. One of the girls offered to tend to Bea's knees, but was turned down. Bea explained that she was near her dorm and would go there to clean up. Fortunately, Mike handled most of the swelling discussion, and cautioned people not to bother Bea at this difficult time. When the police cruiser about five minutes later pulled up the crowd was still jabbering steadily and Bea was very weak in those damaged knees. She wanted desperately to be rid of all these people, but knew she'd have to talk to the police, and that others there would be asked about what they'd heard and seen.

After finding out the rough facts of the attempted kidnapping, the two policemen were wise enough to send the crowd, except for Mike and Bea, away some distance to speak with one officer while the second - the superior officer -

remained to interview the two directly involved. He took down notes and told both young people they needed to come the next day to police headquarters to give a formal deposition. Finally, after what seemed an inordinately long time, they were released. The police officer offered to drive Bea to her dorm, an offer she turned down since Mike said he would walk her home. The other well wishers had been interviewed by this time and sent on their way. When the police car drove off, Bea and Mike were standing only a few feet away from the still-smelling tire skid marks of the attempted kidnappers' car.

"Mike," Bea said quietly, "how did you happen to be here?"

He knew her implication, but answered directly. "I followed you. Was tryin' to come up with an excuse to, you know, run into you on campus."

She nodded. "I can't thank you enough. You took a serious risk for me."

He looked down, almost shyly. "I'm ... still sick inside to think people would do such things."

Bea made herself not mention males of the human species. "Where did you find that ... was it a tree limb?"

"Yeah. That tree back there." He pointed down the sidewalk to where several trees were growing along the inside of a fence. The area looked to be the back of some business or possibly an old apartment house. "There was a dead limb sticking out over the sidewalk. I always notice trees."

Bea, for the first time in this awful encounter, smiled. "Thank God for that nerd habit."

He nodded, smiled back at her, then they started the two and half block walk to her dorm. Bea found herself walking a little closer to him than ever before. If Mike noticed it, however, he made no mention of it. When she left him at the stairway up to her floor, Bea put out a hand and took his.

"You're a fine human being, Mike," she said, and meant it.

"Comin' from a genius," he answered, "I'll take that as a big time compliment."

16. Deposition Morning

BEA DE WINTER ENTERED HER ROOM just before nine. The last two hours had been the longest of her short life. She was thoroughly shaken, emotionally and physically near the point of collapse. Both knees were throbbing painfully and her heart continued to beat faster than normal. With hands trembling from fatigue she got out of her khakis and put them in the hamper, sat in panties and shirt to wash her knees with soapy water, then treat them with antiseptic cream. Though this took only five minutes, Bea was exhausted by the process. With the light still on above the desk, she got the bedspread pulled back and dropped down on the top sheet, hugging the cover to her, giving in to a sleep that would be deep at first, evolving in a few hours to a series of fitful nightmares and vaguely focused soul searching. Bea didn't actually leave her bed until after six the next morning, but she'd lain awake much of the previous four hours.

As it began to lighten outside, Bea's rationality returned to a semblance of normal. She'd escaped certain rape and possible death. As she brought the image of Mike Baylor into her head the eyes of her assailants continued to appear unbidden from time to time, looking directly at her; and she knew a very long time would pass before they left her forever – if indeed that ever occurred. She stood for half an hour in a hot shower, trying symbolically to purge herself from the stench of evil that had brushed so rudely against her the previous evening. Bea spoke quietly to Magdalene during part of this time, answering that she must try to regain control. There was still so much to do, and now, so much new to understand. But even as she spoke to herself, Bea realized that the paradigm of her life had changed. There was no honest, realistic hope of living in a future that was not tinged by the past evening.

After dressing, Bea considered the day looming before her. The required deposition for the police dangled above her like a Damoclean sword. And there were other, more significant, things on her mind. It was important, first of all, to try to find and speak with Maria Santos. It was probably even more important to set up a new series of programmatic test cases to send her computer into, cases that reflected the latest realities in the virus research. Neither should she neglect her dissertation work, and possibly it would also be the easiest thing to concentrate on at this particular moment. None of these four activities, however, could Bea generate any immediate enthusiasm for. She kept turning her mind to the most bewildering things, those things she'd thought she understood so well before, and now didn't understand at all. How could she factor Mike Baylor into her global equation? His interaction in her life made him forever a non-ignorable factor. And - in a thought that totally amazed her she should think it - how did Melissa Thomas factor in? What was there about her that was so disturbing? And there was Reggie, and this fellow she didn't know, Jack Brady. They had imposed themselves on her as actual individuals, not as - despite the fact that in all fairness and for the greater good they should have been - important test cases. She knew that many physicians thought of their patients as cases, not people, and that to consider them otherwise would involve them so emotionally as to limit any ability to actually do the most good for them. Bea's mind drifted to Professor Charles, someone whose place and role she'd been so absolutely certain of before. Now she sensed she was underestimating him in some way. She was more realistic about Dr. Cortland, but that didn't ameliorate her confusion about the woman.

Bea was a mess! She told Magdalene that and received a completely agreeing response. The only consolation she allowed herself was the realization that she'd gone through a trauma of the first magnitude, something which occurred outside the bounds not only of normalcy but of order and logic. Combing her hair without looking in the mirror, Bea went over to the room phone. It was an instrument she rarely used. And rarely had anyone called her. She dialed the number she'd memorized and waited, sitting down in the nearby chair as she did so.

"Hello," said Mike Baylor. He sounded like he always did.

"Hello, Mike. It's Bea. How are you today?"

"The question is how are you, Bea?" There was a background noise implying he was adjusting himself or possibly sitting down.

"I'm okay," she answered, but not without a slight delay.

"I'm not," Mike said. "I'm still very angry, tell you the truth. This world is not right, Bea, you know that?"

"I know that," she said. "Where shall I meet you to go down to the police station?"

"I'll drive over and pick you up there, Bea. It's a green Civic. Not much of a car, but ... well, it works."

"I certainly appreciate your driving, Mike. Thank you. We're supposed to be there at ten."

"I remembered. So how about I come early so we can have breakfast first? Or is that a bad idea?"

Bea sighed, holding her head away from the phone to do so. She had powerfully mixed emotions about the meeting with the police. And even more mixed emotions about being in the presence of Mike Baylor. How she hated owing him so much. Yet, how little he seemed to expect. And she had so much else to do! As she began her answer Bea didn't actually know what she would say. She was a little surprised to hear her own words, "Alright. I'm ready. Where do you suggest we go?"

"There's a café not far away from the station. It's called something like ... uh, Coffee something. I know how much you like good coffee."

Bea nodded. "Coffee Corner," she said, not sure why she knew. She'd never been there.

"Right. How'd you know?"

"Not sure. Maybe the verbal alliteration."

Mike's smile transmitted itself through his tone. "I forgot, it's a genius thing, right?"

"Right, Mike. I'll be down at the door. Is five minutes too soon?"

"Give me ten, okay."

"Alright. See you then. And thank you so much."

"Bye." He was gone.

Bea went to her mirror. "Magdalene," she said, "what do you make of this?"

The harsher tone came back to her. "I think you should be very, very careful."

With another sigh, Bea nodded at her reflection, not speaking further.

When getting into the car a few minutes later, Bea was in her newest khakis and Oxford cloth blue shirt. She wore a lightweight dark blue nylon jacket. Her shoes were suede sneakers with leather ties, a pair she had not worn since arriving in Tennessee. The weather outside was bright and cool, a near perfect fall day.

"You look very nice, Bea," he said from the driver's seat. She'd hurried to get in on the passenger side, worried that he might get out and hold the door for her. That would be more than she could handle well.

She settled in and put on the seat belt before answering. "And you look nice, too, Mike."

He did, of course, in gray corduroys, a cream-colored shirt and a lightweight charcoal gray leather jacket, unbuttoned. Mike's short dark hair was glistening in the sunlight and his strong jaw line was set without any hint of machismo.

"Thanks," he answered, watching ahead as he pulled out. "I'm a little nervous about this deposition thing."

Bea nodded. "Have you been to the Coffee Corner before, Mike?" she asked, determined to lighten the mood.

"Several times. I jus' don't have the memory some people have." He glanced warmly her way.

"I practice memorizing, Mike. It's not magic."

"You don't expect me to believe that, Bea, do you?"

"Why do you like this café?" She would not fall into any complimenting trap.

"Well, good coffee, for one thing. And they don't gouge you for it like Starbucks. And – I don't know what you like for breakfast, but they make omelets that are pretty good. Remind me of ... well, my Aunt Jacie actually."

"Tell me a little more about her, Mike, if you will." Bea's hands were folded neatly in her lap. She was looking forward steadfastly.

He glanced briefly her way before answering. "She's ... well, she's a true lady, Bea. Lives in the middle of a terrible place, a ghetto, and she's ... I think of her as a miracle."

"She has certainly inspired you to make something significant of yourself, it seems to me."

"I've always wanted her to move away from there, but she won't. She says they're her people. And they need her."

"She does seem remarkable."

"I wish you could meet her, Bea, but ... well, you might be a little disappointed."

"Why would you think that?" Bea ventured a quick look at him.

"'Cause she's ... well, just a black mammy type, you know. Do you understand what I'm tryin' to say?"

"A black mammy type?"

"Like ..." He grinned suddenly. "Like Aunt Jemima on a pancake mix box, for example. She doesn't look like much at all. Wears one of those kerchiefs even. Pretty round, too. Not the least bit cool."

"I'm not sure I like 'cool', Mike, to tell you the truth."

"But you are cool, Bea. The coolest girl I ever saw."

"I wasn't cool last night, Mike. I was ..." Her voice broke, much to her dismay. "... was terrified."

His voice was quieter and had a serious edge when he said, "No more than anyone would be. Those bastards were really bad news. I know that type. I grew up around them."

"But you didn't come to be like them, Mike. Was it your Aunt Jacie then?"

"It was," he nodded. "She's the greatest person I've ever known, or ever expect to know."

"You are fortunate indeed, then. My parents were ... well, I wouldn't speak so highly of them."

"What are they like, Bea?"

"They're dead."

Mike looked abashed. "I'm sorry. That was ..."

"It's not your fault they're dead, Mike, nor anyone else's either. But they weren't great people."

"They had you, Bea. That means something."

They were in downtown Knoxville by this time, only a short drive from the university. Mike had driven past the Coffee Corner - on a corner as its name implied - and was turning into the next side street, looking for a parking place.

Bea shook her head. "It means nothing, Mike. I'm just their genes' creation. They hardly ever noticed me, nor did I want them to. Mostly we stayed out of each other's way."

"Did you like that, Bea? I mean growing up like that?"

"I didn't consider any alternatives. But then I didn't have an Aunt Jacie." She turned and smiled at him. A smile on Bea de Winter's face was a transforming creation, and something she had rarely seen herself.

"There's a spot," he said, dazzled by the amazing sight.

They walked a block back to coffee shop. "I insist on buying the breakfast, Mike," Bea said.

"Why should you?" he answered. "You bought the last coffee. It's my turn."

"No arguments, Mike. It's something I need to do. For you and for me."

He didn't respond immediately. Bea's stride kept her about half a step ahead, and he left it that way, sensing she'd be more comfortable. His physical strength, so evident to anyone who looked at him, was, for the first time to Bea, a comforting resource for her, allowing her to look the world around her directly in the eye. Mike finally said, "If it's something you need, then I have to respect it."

"I appreciate that."

They entered the place. It was small but beautifully furnished, more like a British Pub than an American eating establishment. They were seated at a table for two near a window, allowing them to look out on Gay Street, Knoxville's old main street. In sight was the Bijou Theater, venue of music concerts, plays, and even an occasional opera. It was the one place in downtown Knoxville that Bea had actually gone to, attending a Knoxville Chamber Orchestra concert there the first week of the term. Their waitress, a girl of college age, wore an ankle length dress and a frilly white apron. Even Bea noticed the attention to detail the owners had paid, from the style of apron on the waitresses to the style of furniture. For a while they talked only about food and coffee, with Mike ordering a Spanish Omelet and Bea French toast. Mike teased her about their different choices in food from foreign countries, adding that the French were cool and the Spanish not so much, like Bea and himself.

The meal was good, and the coffee, as Mike had said, was exceptional. As they ate, Bea steered the conversation away from herself, the ordeal of the night before, and anything associated with the University of Tennessee. When they were done, she put cash on the check, left it in the center of the table, and they got up to leave. The waitress would have no way of knowing the petite girl had paid the bill. Mike did not miss the gesture.

Instead of driving to the police station, they walked the few blocks necessary to get there. Inside, Mike spoke to a dispatcher who sent them down a hall to an interview room. Five or six minutes later, one of the policemen from the night before and another, older cop tapped on the door and came in. After greetings, the older policeman got their permission and turned on a small tape recorder, placed in the center of an old table they occupied the four sides of, and began the deposition. Normally, each would have had her or his account taken separately; but, probably because of the nature of Bea's involvement, it was agreed they would be deposed together. The entire procedure was done in about forty minutes. The two young people signed the printed deposition, prepared in less than another half hour, during which time they had sipped cups of far worse coffee than they'd had at breakfast. Then they were back on the street.

Bea was more subdued now, having just relived the previous night. Mike didn't pester her with his usual banter, walking quietly the established half step behind. He also seemed to have his thoughts in other places. They could have been taken for strangers who happened to be walking together. The car was only a couple of blocks away before Bea said, "Will you be telling Aunt Jacie about last night, Mike?"

"Unless you tell me not to, Bea. I told her about you."

"What did you tell her?"

"That you were a genius, and pretty, and now able to buy beer." He smiled down at her.

"At least the third is true," she said, almost sounding like a quip.

"I stand by my statement," he said, "and if Aunt Jacie were here, she'd know I was right."

"Hush, Mike. You've already done more for me than I could ever deserve. I'm simply who I am."

"Not simply, Bea. Nothing simple at all. That's the thing. You're ... you've always got something on your mind. Something ... well, profound. You probably don't want to tell me about it, but I know it's there."

Bea stopped walking and turned to look up at him. "That's right, Mike. I do. And I don't want to tell you about it. But you're the only person who ever realized that. There are things in life I have to do. Not that I really want to do them. But I must."

"More than just genius stuff, right?"

She nodded. "More than that. I don't think you'd be saying nice things about me to Aunt Jacie if you knew what I have to do. But I have to."

"And you don't want my help, do you?"

Bea was still looking up at him. "You've already helped me, Mike, more than I ever expected."

"I was just the right place at the right time, Bea. It's no big deal."

She shook her head. "Not that, Mike. You saved my life last night. You saved my sanity. You gave me a new chance. I could never find words or actions or anything that could express enough gratitude for that. But – strange as it seems, possibly –

I'm speaking of something else far more important. You've helped me understand something of what I thought I understood but didn't. And every time I encounter you I learn more. Thank you. And I believe I should thank Aunt Jacie, too." Again, that radiant smile. Its luminosity almost brought tears back into Mike Baylor's eyes. But it vanished soon after it came into being. That was Bea's way.

The drive back was quiet, but neither needed words when they were together as much as they had just a day earlier.

17. Discussing Associations

DR. JOSIAH ZORN, HIS GRAY HAIR LOOKING very white against the deep red of the chair cushion, sat down his glass of Zinfandel, and formed a triangle with his fingers, resting its apex against his nose a moment, listening to Virginia Cortland's words carefully. The two sat across from each other in front of the flickering fireplace in the back room of the Faculty Lodge. It was the same room where Cortland had met Bea de Winter. The occasion was an informal one. A small group of faculty members at the university had common ties in their educational and professional experience and had formed an informal club they called "The New Englanders." Each had spent some time in New England, either as students or in their professions, and each had a particular fondness for the area's influence on their own lives. Zorn's tie to New England had been a little different than Cortland's, or William Charles' - who both had worked there for a number of years. Zorn had grown up in Maine, the son of a lobster fisherman.

William Charles was also in the room for the bi-monthly late afternoon gathering, as were six others that particular time, including three women professors from widely diverse disciplines. Charles was talking to two of these women out of earshot of Zorn and Cortland. Several members had already excused themselves for the evening. It was dark outside, cloudy and chilly, but still only 8:30. The typical meeting began with a catered supper at 5:30 and concluded with open ended conversation of a totally spontaneous type, often centered on small, sometimes shifting groups of participants. Cortland and Zorn, however, had not been a part of any other conversation that evening. They'd begun across the dining table from each other, then moved naturally to the fireplace, where they'd remained.

"Everything about this case is peculiar and frightening," Virginia Cortland was saying. "It makes me wonder if we are not regularly experiencing virulent forms all over the world but rarely realizing it. And by good luck, most of the time they follow their natural courses, mutating to something benign eventually, and leaving no trace that is ever found."

"How did you come to discover this one?" he asked.

"Only because of Bill's student," Cortland answered. "The student isolated a new virus from this young man's bloodstream. We're still evaluating it, but it's almost certainly the culprit."

"A student, is that right? Well, I suppose students do all the real work nowadays, Virginia. Wouldn't you say?"

She smiled. "Not only nowadays, Josiah. I well remember being a student myself."

"Do I know him?" Zorn asked.

"Who?" Cortland was slightly confused.

"The student."

This led to an open laugh, loud enough to catch the brief attention of the other conversation groups in the room. "You are such a Chauvinist, Josiah. And to think you've lived everywhere. The student is not a male. Shame on you."

"Mea culpa," Zorn said, properly chastised, and took up his red wine again. "Then we should drink a toast to her, whoever she is. To her and to hope that I return to your good graces, Virginia."

"Here, here!" she smiled, raising her own glass of Chardonnay. "Her name is de Winter. Bea de Winter."

"How intriguing!" exclaimed the now wide-eyed gentleman. "Bea de Winter. You don't say?"

"So you know Bea, then?"

"'Know' is too strong a term. But I did meet the young lady."

"Oh? And what do you think?"

Zorn proceeded, at that point, to tell Cortland about the WILL luncheon, the talk given by Barbara Greinert on Women and World Culture, and made an attempt to summarize Bea's energetic and crowd-stirring comments. Cortland listened intently, setting aside her wine as she did so.

"She contended that males have been of more negative than positive value to humanity? Is that it?" Cortland smiled a little. "Sounds like she's up to date on the latest facts, Josiah."

"Touché, Virginia. Her argument, however, did agree that some of us – she was gracious enough to suggest I would be among these – are not totally corrupted by testosterone and do get over it."

"Testosterone?" Cortland smiled again. "She really does understand, doesn't she? The girl is only twenty-one. Did you know that?"

"Really? That's incredible. She totally swamped Barbara Greinert, leaving her without much to say."

"I had no idea Bea had such strong feelings. Actually, on any subject. The girl seems totally focused on her study. And when we got her into the effort of the Pendergast case, she jumped in with both feet. But it didn't seem to me that she had any real interest except the related biophysics."

"She went so far as to say that nothing can be done about us males except to chemically alter us, or something like that."

"You mean like chemical castration?" Cortland laughed again, but not too loudly this time.

"In a manner of speaking. Fortunately, since I'm now in my dotage my testosterone level is manageable. And she was nice enough to say that I seem to have dealt with the poison reasonably well."

Cortland grinned at the older man. "Because she doesn't know your history, Josiah. Count yourself fortunate."

"Oh, I do, I do. But tell me more about this wunderkind, Virginia."

"Bill's student. Brain biophysics. He says she knows more about the brain than he does. He's probably being too modest – if you can imagine that from Bill Charles – but I'd say that's quite a compliment."

"I'd say. And you say she's a young workaholic, then?"

"Without doubt. She keeps up with her research – I don't know the details of it, since Bill hasn't really mentioned it – and this Pendergast work, which – considering she tracked down a new virus and completely characterized it - should be a full time job for most people, even if they knew what to do."

"Miss de Winter does seem a bit icy, I'd say," Zorn quipped. "Matching her name."

"She's serious, that's for sure. Always polite and businesslike. I've not tried to socialize with her, and neither has Bill. But he's always hands off with students, girl students especially."

"Yes, that's the word on Bill. Probably wise. Well, at least till you get my age, it's wise. Now, of course, no female could feel threatened by this old codger. I could probably get by with coming on to a young lady because she'd only laugh, thinking I could not be serious."

"Clever ploy, Josiah, low-balling yourself. So did you speak to Bea at the meeting?"

"I did. I asked her if she considered males a mistake Mother Nature made."

"And she said?"

"Yes."

They both laughed. Cortland said, "A succinct summary. I think now I like her better than I did."

"Did you not like this wunderkind earlier then?"

"Well," Cortland said, musing into her wine, having just picked it up again, "it's not exactly dislike. It's more that I think she's patronizing me a little. Always polite, always to the point, but never seeming to need anything from me. Am I getting insecure in my old age, Josiah, you think?"

"Probably, Virginia. It's inevitable for the best educated, most diverse, and most competent people to grow more insecure as they advance in life. One of the great jokes the purported Creator has played on us."

"Nasty of her, wasn't it?" Cortland said, smiling.

18. Reporting In

ENTERING HER ROOM AFTER RETURNING FROM the deposition, Bea saw the phone message light blinking. When had she ever received a phone message? It was so rare as to be frightening. When she heard the voice of her major professor, she was slightly relieved. But Professor Charles had never left her a phone message before.

"Bea, sorry to disturb you at home, but am curious about your findings on this new virus. Do you mind coming by and giving me an update? Thanks. Let me know."

Charles' voice didn't give away any variation from his normal tone, but Bea didn't like it that he'd called instead of leaving a note. She prized her privacy greatly, and simply didn't want to be called at home about anything. But she also knew that he couldn't very well leave a note at her dorm and fuming over it was not useful, so she glanced at the time and decided to go over to his office. This meant crossing the campus, and even though it was broad daylight, she hesitated. Should she call for one of those available escorts - often guys from one of the sports teams - to walk her over, or not? Bea shuddered. She could not let herself get into this kind of situation. Crossing to the mirror, she was about to ask Magdalene about it, then stopped herself. For a long moment she stood standing and regarding the image before her. Then she reached up and adjusted her hair a little, experimented with a smile, turned away and walked over to the phone. First, she called Dr. Charles' office, got his student secretary, gave a time she'd be there, and hung up. Then without letting herself consider further, she called Mike Baylor. He was home, and when he answered she felt a wave of relief mixed with embarrassment.

"Mike, would you do me a favor?"

"Sure, Bea."

"I'm concerned about walking over to the campus this afternoon. I know it's irrational, but ..."

"It's not irrational, Bea. Damn, I'd be petrified myself. Want me to walk you over, then?"

"If you would."

"Hey, escorting a genius is pretty good work when you can get it. Right now?"

"Yes, please."

"Gimme ten minutes, alright?"

"Fine."

–

Virginia Cortland was talking to one of her daughters, long distance, when a call waiting bleep came into her phone. The scientist-physician was at home, working from her personal computer, as she often did during the afternoon. She said goodbye to her child and switched to the incoming caller.

"Yes, this is Virginia Cortland."

"Hello, Dr. Cortland. This is Brent Leichter over at UT Hospital. You probably don't know me but I've been told to contact you on a patient."

"Brent Leichter, is it? Are you on the teaching staff?"

"No, I'm in private practice, an internist, over at Fort Sanders." He was speaking of a hospital near the university campus and the suite of private physician offices in the same complex of buildings. "I have a new patient that the people here tell me you should know about."

Cortland sat up a little at her desk. A sheaf of papers associated with the Pendergast case was stacked there. She'd been looking at the latest summary of lab results pertaining to it. She said, "Tell me about your patient, Brent. And please call me Virginia."

"Thanks, Virginia. The patient's a UT student, named Harold Atkinson. Came in to my office yesterday afternoon, brought in by friends. I thought he was in drug withdrawal or some such problem, at first. He had trouble avoiding things while walking, was unable to speak clearly - though occasionally I figured out what he was saying - and seemed to be forcing himself to concentrate, but without a great deal of success."

Cortland sighed. She knew what was coming next. "Did his friends tell you anything about his situation?"

"Yes, they said he'd begun to act strangely a day or two earlier. They – one shared his apartment and the other was a close friend, it seemed – they swore it wasn't drugs or alcohol and didn't have any idea what was going on. The two had called his mother, in Memphis, and found out I was his doctor. Harold's dad is a colleague of mine, from med school days, and I'd promised to look out for his boy over here in Knoxville. I'd treated him a month ago for a bad sinus infection. The dad, Arthur Atkinson, called my office and said they were bringing in his son."

"And you couldn't imagine what was happening to the boy, and sent him over to UT, is that right?"

"Exactly. I talked to some of the Fort Sanders staff, and they suggested UT. They admitted him last night and ran the usual checks. When I got over here today to check on him, I was given your name as the contact for the Infection Committee."

"Brent," Cortland said, her voice quality carrying the gravitas she felt at the moment, "it sounds like your Harold Atkinson is the third case we've seen of something very mysterious. Thank you for calling me."

"Case of what, Virginia? And why mysterious?"

"Do you have the time to wait for me there at the hospital?"

"I ... well, I did have to postpone several appointments today. Is it important?"

"Very. I can be there in ten minutes, fifteen at most."

"Then I'll wait."

"I suppose you're in the infections wing."

"That's right."

"Wait in the physician lounge there. And thank you very much, Brent."

"Okay."

–

Bea, wearing her backpack, met Mike outside. He was his usual neat, easy-going self, dressed in new-looking jeans, gray shirt and light denim jacket. Bea could detect no difference in his nature, despite his heroics the night before.

"Where are we going?" he asked.

"I have a meeting with Dr. Charles."

"That's at Hess?"

"That's right. I really appreciate this, Mike."

"I'm flattered you called me, Bea. Makes me know I'm good for something." He grinned.

"Don't be ridiculous!" she snapped back, but not too viciously. "Your Aunt Jacie would scold you for such foolishness." Then Bea smiled.

Mike basked in the amazing event for the few seconds it lasted and stepped into rhythm with her walk, one half step behind. Not unexpectedly, she didn't converse. She seemed to be somewhere else most of the time, but did occasionally look over and give him a look that yes, she was still with him. At the entrance to Hess Hall, after they'd climbed up the steep slope leading up the cluster of university buildings atop the Hill at an impressive pace, Bea stopped.

"Thanks, Mike," she said. "I'll arrange to get back to the dorm later, so you don't need to stay."

"Don't mind, Bea," he said. "Done for the day, anyway. Really."

"But I don't know how long the meeting will last."

"I'm cool. Brought along my botany book. See?" He had carried the textbook unobtrusively the whole time.

"Are you sure?" Bea glanced around. It was uncomfortable for her to be carrying on such a conversation out there in front of the building.

"Absolutely sure, Bea. You go do your brilliant stuff, okay?"

"Mike, cut that out!" She shook her head at him. "Alright, but if I'm going to be long I'll get word to you."

"Whatever. I'll be here reading."

"It's pretty cool outside."

"Really, it's perfect. Have a jacket. Notice?"

Bea sighed. "Alright. Thanks again. Bye." Then she turned and went inside.

Inside, she went to her mailbox to check messages. None. Then she swung by her lab and printed out a few sheets she'd need at the meeting. There, she shed her backpack and took out a few other sheets from it, along with a thumb drive she'd loaded with some parts of her data compilation. Then, in Bea de Winter fashion, she walked into William Charles' office precisely on time. She was somewhat taken aback to find Virginia Cortland there, too.

"Hello Bea," Charles said. "I took the liberty of inviting Dr. Cortland. Hope you don't mind."

"Not at all," Bea replied, composing herself quickly. "How are you, Dr. Cortland?"

"Fine, Bea," the woman responded. She sat across from Charles at his table, not too cluttered at the moment. Between them, at the end of the table facing the door, was a place for Bea. Bea took it, settling herself without looking at the others.

Cortland continued, "I understand you've been a busy little bee lately." She smiled at her pun.

"I have, doctor. But I'm here to be busy, after all."

William Charles said, "Dr. Cortland has discovered another case of the Pendergast type."

The petite young woman looked up and made eye contact with her professor. "Really? Was it someone known to Reggie Pendergast?"

"Someone at the party that Mr. Pendergast and Ms Thomas attended a couple of weeks ago," Cortland added, watching Bea's face as she did so.

Charles said, "I spoke with Maria Santos today. There are two other girls and three other boys who were at this party." Bea winced a little. She'd not followed up with Maria as she'd planned. Charles continued, "The boys are Harold Atkinson, Stan Harvester and Lamarc Johnson. The girls are Martha Jane Rogers and Cynthia van Landingham."

Cortland nodded. "Unfortunately, Harold Atkinson is the new case we've found."

"Are the symptoms like Reggie's then?" Bea asked, curiosity written plainly on her face.

"More like Jack Brady's actually," Cortland said. "I saw the young man just an hour ago. Over at UT Hospital."

Bea's brow furrowed. "Has your committee, Dr. Cortland, contacted the others?"

"We've left them messages," Cortland said. "It was through Harold Atkinson's friends that we got their names. Neither young man was at home when we called."

Bea nodded.

Charles interrupted gently. "Bea, would you please give me that summary we discussed. I'm still a little unclear about what you two are discussing."

Again Bea nodded, glanced at Cortland for approval, and began to describe her efforts. She related her discoveries of virus particles in Jack Brady's samples and lack of virus particles in Melissa's blood. Then she put the recorded thumb drive into the laptop available and showed more details of the virus structure. She didn't mention the viral precursors, not only because she didn't want to alert the others to any clue about the process that unfolded but also because she didn't want to make them think she had discovered so much so fast.

Cortland asked, "Bea, have you replicated this virus you've found?"

"Not yet, doctor. But I have begun the process, using several different growth media, and with both variants of the virus."

"So there are two variants?" Charles said.

Bea nodded. "We expect mutations, of course. We have found just the one so far."

"How much variation?" he asked.

"Hard to say. At least as far as its function is concerned.

"Good that you're making the effort to replicate it," Cortland said. "When we have enough, maybe we can try to discover more of its effects. Obviously a cerebral environment would be most important."

"Yes, doctor," Bea continued. "I have lab mice reserved for the tests."

Cortland looked over at her colleague. "Bill, is anyone else working on this, from your group?"

He shook his head. "I put my best brain on it." He smiled at Bea, but she gave no response to the compliment.

"Our UT group has begun to work with Bea's results," Cortland said, for both their information. "Thank you again, Bea, for giving us something to work with."

"Has your group made further progress?" Bea asked, but didn't show unusual interest in her eyes.

"Not much. We did try to grow the virus and have not been able to. We need to coordinate our work, Bea. That's one reason I wanted to be here today."

Bea nodded. "Here are the media I'll be trying first." She handed over a sheet with recipes for five different culture media.

"Fine," Cortland said. "I think it will be important to meet regularly on this, Bill." She glanced at him. "Can we use your office and get together in two days, unless something comes up?"

He agreed. "And I think Bea should be here, too."

"Absolutely," Cortland smiled. "Without her we wouldn't be where we are now."

19. Speaking of Goals and Concerns

AFTER THE MEETING, BEA WENT BY her lab to pick up a few important printouts and load a few files onto a memory stick. Normally she'd have remained there to work a few hours, but her routine was now broken. She'd not mentioned the attempted assault to either professor and wondered if she should have done so. Eventually, she supposed, word of the attack would get through to them. It had been kept out of the Knoxville paper - following a policy the university had established - but various university officials certainly knew about it. Very likely William Charles would be notified. Bea was a little surprised he'd not been as yet, or at least he hadn't mentioned it as yet.

The grad student came out of Hess Hall looking much like she had as she had entered it. And Mike Baylor was there, sitting on the steps reading his botany text.

"Go well, Bea?" he asked, looking up.

"Fine, Mike. Thank you for waiting. It was very kind."

"Got caught up on this course. Good for me, too." He got to his feet, even a step below her standing slightly taller than she. "Where to now?"

"I need to work at the dorm, Mike. Do you mind?"

"Not coffee at the Spot?" He grinned at her.

Bea looked at him. "One cup then. And my treat."

"Deal. But I sure am draining your funds."

She didn't answer, starting into her stride. Halfway down the Hill, after half a minute or so, Bea glanced toward him and said, "Are you doing well in your botany course, Mike?"

"Yeah, I suppose."

"Are you being modest again?"

He raised his eyebrows at her, then smiled. "Can't be modest if you don't have that much to brag about, can you?"

"I know better than that. So, what is your area of specialization?"

"What do you guess, Bea?"

"Plant physiology, of course."

"Of course. But more specifically."

"Trees, naturally."

"Naturally. Are you interested in trees, Bea?"

She shrugged. "Not like you are, Mike. But yes. I'm interested in any living being."

"But you don't talk to trees like some of us do."

"I suppose not. What aspect of the physiology of trees?"

"I'm worried about losing trees, like we lost the American Chestnut."

"So you're involved with diseases that affect trees?"

"Or pests, which is more often the problem."

Bea nodded, having never broken stride as they spoke until they had come to a stop at Volunteer Boulevard, waiting for a break in the traffic. When it came they proceeded quickly across, passing by the Student Center and turning west toward the nearby Strip. Negotiating their way through traffic and around the flow of other students interrupted the conversation for a few minutes. Once back in their former rhythm, Bea continued as if they'd not been interrupted. "Tell me about your work in protecting tree species, Mike."

"Well, I haven't done much so far. But in the Spring I'm going to start my research – in the Smokies looking at four or five species in particular. You know, finding what's infecting them and seeing how certain kinds of things can be done to lessen the damage. Actually, as I said, most problems are bugs of some kind."

"Are you looking forward to the field work?"

"I'm going to love it, Bea." He beamed at her. "That's why I stayed in school. And the Smokies is the best place in the world to do that study."

"I suppose because of its enormous biodiversity within the Temperate Zone."

"As a genius would put it, exactly." Again the beaming smile.

Bea became quiet again as they walked. But she felt at ease around Mike and felt no compulsion to speak. As she considered it, some part of her thought there was something wrong about feeling that way, and another part was pleased that she did. When they entered The Sunspot the place was not crowded. Once more they were lucky enough to get a table by the window and settled in quickly, facing each other. The waitress, dark haired and bearing a certain wary look, festooned with five rings in each ear, arrived and took their coffee order, then left.

"How are you doing, Bea?" Mike asked, his tone indicating a change in emphasis, referring clearly to her emotional state after the harrowing events of the night before last.

"I'm not sure," she admitted. "But thank you for asking."

"Anything I can do to help?"

"No. I have to deal with it myself."

"I have a feeling," he said, a little brighter in mood, "you figure you have to handle everything yourself. But what are friends for, anyway?"

Bea's eyes flashed, a little ire rising then subsiding. "It's not a subject I can continue at the moment, Mike. If you don't mind."

He raised his hands in symbolic submission. "I dig, Bea. Enough said. Tell me about what you want to do for the world. I know that's on your mind. What else could make you so driven?"

The young woman's eyes narrowed introspectively. "I want to make the world a better place, Mike. Just like you do. I suppose I'm just coming from a different direction than you."

"We can each make our little dent, I guess," he nodded.

"Dents won't do it, Mike, unfortunately. We have to crack the structure and put it back together better."

"That's a tall order. What structure are you talkin' about?"

"Human nature."

He laughed lightly, but with no hint of rancor. "Do we have one? Nature, I mean? I thought we were all different."

Bea looked at Mike, suddenly concentrating on his face. "Interesting comment. Thank you."

The young man shrugged, looking oddly helpless despite his obvious strength. "You're welcome, I guess." Then he smiled.

–

Forty minutes later Bea told Mike goodbye at the door of her dorm, then watched as he walked away. For his part, Mike noticed that she – for the first time since he'd known her – didn't simply turn and make a no-nonsense departure. Their conversation over coffee had been sparse and had veered away from any further serious veins, but pleasant enough. Bea had not seemed unusually anxious to finish and go, though she'd not dallied either. He couldn't really assess their friendship and knew it was not worth trying very hard to do so, and contented himself with the time he had. Bea didn't linger at the door long, but did regard the young man for a moment. Her mind was in a multi-layered turmoil and she knew it, so she did much as Mike did, contented herself with what amounted to the possibility of a real friendship in the making – a luxury she had not afforded herself before in all her twenty-one years.

The day was mostly used up as Bea mounted the stairs. She was a little tired but determined to get to work immediately. There was so much to do, so many avenues to explore that she'd not expected and a number of others that she'd known about but simply hadn't gotten to yet. Walking briskly past Melissa's door, Bea thought about her neighbor briefly, but felt no temptation to check in on her. After unlocking her own door and pushing it in, the grad student was surprised to see a handwritten note on the floor, a note she nearly stepped on. It had been slipped under the door.

It was from Melissa: "Bea, stop in tonight. Maria's coming over. Whenever, okay?" It was signed with a long slurred "M," leaving no doubt as to its authorship. Bea's heart quickened a little when she looked at the note. Socializing was not something she wanted or had time for. She thought about going back down the hall and telling Melissa she didn't have time, but settled on simply ignoring the request, since she could later explain how busy she'd gotten.

Bea did take the time for a long shower. Once again the hot water had a purging quality, scouring away a little more of the terror she'd endured. She wouldn't let herself consider how fortunate she'd been to escape the fate planned for her, but she couldn't escape wordless feelings and formless visions in her imagination. Work, Bea decided, was not only the best therapy for herself but now bore a certain extra value, in that what she would achieve might lower the probability of outrages of that sort in the future. Or at least, so she was determined.

Bea put on her pajamas, ate a few bites from the refrigerator, and passed her mirror before sitting down at the computer.

"Magdalene," she said to the image, "our concentration is needed more now than ever. I hope you understand."

Magdalene answered sharply, "Our concentration will be moot if you don't stay motivated. And you know it!"

Bea sighed. "I know it. Keep reminding me."

The clock reached ten-thirty before Bea even paused in her efforts, taking a brief break to run to the bathroom, then open a can of caffeinated soda. She stayed on her feet as she drank just to exercise her legs a little. While in that posture Bea heard a knock on her door. She muttered an inaudible curse and started forward, supposing it had to be Melissa. She heard the sophomore's voice before she got to the door, sounding insistent. Bea looked through the viewer and, sure enough, saw her neighbor's bright, pretty, but agitated face.

"Hello, Melissa," Bea said politely as she opened the door. Melissa stood there in a ridiculous red indecently short silk nightgown.

"Bea! Hey, you're supposed to come over, remember?" Melissa's eyes had that getting-drunk look. "Maria's here. Come on!"

"Melissa, I'm studying. But thanks for asking."

"Come on, Bea, you need to lighten up sometime, you know!" Melissa grabbed Bea's wrist and pulled her forward, encouragingly.

"I need to study, Melissa, and you probably do, too."

"We want you to come over, Bea. Please!"

"Why, Melissa?" Bea extricated her wrist from the other's grip, but didn't step back or make an effort to close her door. "You can party without me. I'm not the partying type."

"We're frazzed, Bea. Come on!"

"Frazzed?"

"Look, you know. The weird stuff about Reggie, and being ... we're poison or something!" Despite her tipsiness, Melissa managed to look rather crestfallen. Bea closed her eyes a minute, not sure of what to say.

"I not going to get drunk with you, Melissa."

"Just come over. We need somebody smart."

"And why is that?"

"Maria's losing it, Bea. Please!"

"Okay, Melissa. But dammit, just for a little while." Bea wasn't sure why she agreed.

"Just a while, sure. Come on!"

"Let me put on a robe and get my key."

"You don't need a robe. Hey, it's just us girls." Melissa posed briefly in her nightie, turning slightly both directions as if being viewed by an audience.

"My key anyway. Just a minute."

Bea turned and went for her key, leaving the door open. When she started to return she could see Melissa's body outlined in shadow, backlit from the hall. The girl was practically nude. And in that absurd red! What is with her?

Melissa's door was standing open as they approached. Bea caught a glimpse of what must have been Maria's bare feet to the right.

"Hello, Maria," Bea said, entering, and before she could see anything but the brunette's feet and legs. There Ms Santos was, sitting on the rug, leaning back against a big pillow, eyes a little puffy, a tipsy look on her face.

"This is Bea," Melissa said from behind.

"Hi Bea. Hell of a bitchin' time, isn't it?"

Bea crossed over and sat on an available chair, noticing underwear on the floor. She supposed it was Melissa's. Strewn clothing was a Melissa distinctive. The room smelled of smoke, but Bea couldn't see any alcohol bottle anywhere.

"You two should stop worrying," Bea said, in a tone nearing exasperation. "This is a waste of time, you know. There are better things you could be doing."

"Like what?" Melissa said, bouncing onto her bed, legs disregarded so much that Bea had to look away to avoid seeing her exposed crotch.

"Like studying, for one thing. You can deal with worry a lot better by doing something than by sitting around drinking and pouting at each other."

"I knew you'd ... say something like that, Bea!" Melissa said grouchily. "Why can't you tell us something to make us feel better, anyway?"

Maria nodded in exaggerated agreement. She raised her knees a little and leaned forward on them. Maria's words were beginning to slur as she said, "We're fucked up, Bea!"

Bea looked at them both. "What are you two drinking?"

Melissa laughed. "It's grass, silly! Want a hit?"

Then Bea saw the ashtray and partially burned cigarette. Its rough shape - hand rolled - then became evident. The sweetness in the smoke aroma now made sense.

"No, thank you, Melissa. Do you think this stuff is doing either one of you any good?"

"Hell yes!" Maria answered for them, leaning forward, coming to her knees and reaching across to grab the stub, bringing it back dramatically to her mouth and sucking in the smoke. "Damn, this is really good!" She exhaled slowly through her nose, replaced the cigarette, and leaned back again into her former position, brown legs prominent.

Melissa said, "Might help you to get that stick out of your butt, Bea."

Bea chaffed a little at the comment, but said, "I'm not the one messing up my head."

"We have sodas," Melissa said, not reacting to the scolding, eyes poorly focused on their visitor. "Or booze. But you won't drink booze, no not you!"

"Nothing to drink, thanks. Talk to me, Melissa and Maria," Bea said, insistently. "Why are you two willing to mess yourselves up like this?" As she spoke Bea sat primly in her pajamas, knees together and hands in her lap. She seemed totally at ease, if a little too prissy.

"You wouldn't undersh ... understand, Bea," Melissa said, a little sadly. "You never understand."

"I can't understand unless you say something. Say something."

"We're fucked!" Maria said, logically.

"You're not," Bea replied, just as logically.

"We are," Melissa agreed. "Unless somebody figures out how we can ... what this whatever is we are carriers of. Damn, we can't get near a guy until we ... see, we're fucked big time!"

Bea understood. She was now irked at herself for being so heedless. Both these young women realized they might be carrying a dread disease. And indeed they were. How long it might be true Bea didn't know. The precursors, in their dried state, could be taken in breathing, and in their activated state in the blood, would stay in the bloodstream more or less indefinitely. But some of the active organisms would be present in the lungs, too. Bea knew that but didn't believe the number was large. Yes, coughing or maybe even regular breathing could release a few of these viral forms, but their survival outside the blood nourishment would be very short indeed, only seconds. Technically, yes, the viral forms could be transmitted as aerosols but that would be a rare event after the dried components had activated. And the threat was reduced because several species of precursors had to be present together, and in the right chemical solution, to form the virus. No, Melissa and Maria weren't as poisonous as they thought - or probably weren't - and she should tell them. But she had to be careful.

"Listen, you two," Bea said, as gently as she could manage. "I've been working on this problem, as you know. We've found a virus that probably has caused Reggie's and Jack's condition. Can you understand me, or am I wasting my time talking to a couple of zombies?"

"Fucked up zombies!" Maria corrected, sounding oddly upbeat for a moment.

"There's no virus in your blood, Melissa, and probably not in yours, either, Maria. The blood tests will show it. So you ..."

"Not with my luck!" Maria protested. "They'll find it in me, you can bet on it."

"No they won't," Bea insisted. "At first, back at your party, you might have been communicative, but not now."

"How do you know?" Melissa asked.

"It's the way this kind of virus behaves. Now relax, okay? You're messing yourselves up. Time to start acting like human beings again."

"You're not just telling us that to ... to shut us up?" Melissa asked.

Bea stood. "No. Stop worrying unnecessarily."

Maria looked at her a little peculiarly. "That's easy for you to say."

"I'm sorry," Bea said, becoming as earnest as possible. "I wasn't being fair to you. I know you've been worrying. But I'm not telling you a lie."

"You mean ... there's no way we ... we can get somebody sick?" Melissa asked, matching Bea's earnestness.

Bea rubbed her nose. That was a harder question. There was a way they could get someone sick and that way would be there for a long time. Each young woman had viral precursors circulating in her bloodstream. These precursors, borne by benign viruses, could live a long time in that environment, even after their virus transports were gone and absorbed. Her best guess was several years, a time comparable to the cell lifetime in a typical human body. Cells would eventually die after replicating, but these protein structures would not replicate - so they would eventually vanish. But even when ninety percent or more of the precursor structures were gone enough might remain to form the virus when conditions were right. If a little of Melissa's - and probably Maria's - blood were transfused into a male bloodstream with enough testosterone, the virus could form. Bea wasn't sure whether sexual intercourse would cause such a transfusion, but guessed it might occasionally, analogously to the spread of HIV. When these young women have sex again – and realistically, Bea knew at least Melissa was not one to go without sex for very long – they could spell doom for their partners. But that was just the point, Bea reminded herself.

She was surprised to hear herself say, "You should be careful not to have blood contact with anyone else."

Maria cocked her head at the standing one. "What dush .... does that mean?"

"Let me put it this way," Bea said, not making eye contact with either of them. "Make the guys use condoms, okay?"

"What guys?" Melissa sputtered, not making the connection.

"When you decide to have sex," Bea said. "If there's any problem at all, it would be in your blood."

Maria muttered, "God, we have poisoned blood?"

"Go on to bed," Bea said, starting toward the door. "And stop worrying. I have to go now."

"So you won't shtay ... stay and play with us, huh?" Melissa asked, suddenly grinning.

"No,"Bea said, opening the door to go out.

"But it's okay if we play with each other?" Melissa persisted, looking over at Maria. "We're already both poisoned." Maria laughed.

"Do what you want with each other," Bea muttered. "I have to study."

"Bye, Bea," Melissa said. "Stick in the mud."

"Right," Bea said. "Good night." She closed the door softly behind her.

20. Victim Four?

HAROLD ATKINSON WAS A SHORT YOUNG MAN, only about five feet six, but stockily built and seemed to be in good aerobic condition. He was in an isolation ward in the section of the UT Hospital maintained for patients suffering from dangerous infectious diseases, or - as in this case - from diseases of unknown or rare type. Harold was asleep, sedated by the medical staff, and receiving a slow drip of an antibiotic cocktail through an intravenous port taped off on his left arm. Unlike for Reggie Pendergast during the first days of his illness, isolation for this sleeping patient was complete. His parents, now in Knoxville, had been allowed to see him only through the viewing window into the room. There was an unfathomable sadness in the couple's eyes.

After the Atkinsons left, Virginia Cortland joined Brent Leichter, the young man's physician, in the doctor's lounge at the end of the hall. It was her second meeting with him, about five hours after he'd called her the first time.

"Tell me more about this young man," she asked him. "We have a good picture of his medical background and the time leading up to his infection, but I'm curious about what sort of fellow he is."

Leichter, who looked to be about fifty, said, "I guess you're referring to his lifestyle. Is that right?"

"Yes," she nodded. "It seems there was a party a couple of weeks ago. All three young men infected were at that party. I understand we've just located one of the two other boys there that night. There were four girls and five boys, as best we can determine."

"And three of the five boys are ill, then. The girls?"

"No sign of this virus we spoke of earlier in their blood. At least for two of the young women. The test for the virus is not straightforward as yet, so it takes time to make the determination. The other two young women should be going to the university infirmary tomorrow to give samples. We considered quarantining them but are worried about the publicity. We did find the virus in Atkinson's blood – or at least we think so. Our staff here found the strain isolated by the grad student who did the analysis on the other samples. But we don't actually know for certain this virus is our culprit. "

Leichter nodded, then asked, "I suppose there's nothing else to report on Harold?"

"The symptoms you reported are still current. He is asleep at the moment. We're trying an antibiotic drip, hoping to prevent any collateral infection, though his blood count gives no indication of any damage to his immune system."

"Has he spoken any more?"

"Yes, but not during the brief visit of his parents. The young man seems to perseverate on various themes, one of them being Melissa Thomas. She's the girlfriend of the first patient."

"The Pendergast boy, right?"

Cortland nodded. "Miss Thomas is quite attractive and probably got a lot of attention at this party. Was Harold, as far as you know, Brent, the type to be attracted to someone else's girlfriend?"

Leichter smiled. "Harold's always been something of a party animal, though I wouldn't tell his dad. Art – actually Arthur. I've known Art for years. But Harold seems to have had a way with the girls. Maybe his being an athlete helped. He's – or was, I suppose – the catcher on the Vols baseball team. One of the best college baseball players in the country, actually."

"It would make sense then," she said, "that he might get close to Melissa Thomas during this party?"

"I'd say so, yes," Leichter said. "College parties have a way of getting frisky, as most of us remember."

Cortland smiled at him. "Yes, it was even so in my day."

"Your day, Virginia, I doubt is much different from mine."

"Thanks for the compliment," she answered, "but I can tell you we were taking notes in Latin when I was in college."

Both laughed. Leichter then said, "Harold's parents have asked me to sit down with them and talk about their son's case. I need to know what I can say."

Cortland nodded. "Not much I'm afraid. We can't afford to let anyone know there are three similar cases among students who were together a couple of weeks ago. The odds are that we can't suppress this much longer, but any time we have before word gets out to the general public is precious time. You can tell them we don't know what the malady is, because we don't, and that we're doing everything we can to find out about it, which we are."

"Anything about how long he might be sick?"

She shook her head. "We can't say and we don't know. But please don't mention that we suspect permanent brain damage. It would be nice to be wrong about it."

He nodded soberly.

—

The next morning Bea de Winter was out of bed and working hard at her computer by nine o'clock. The first thing she'd done was to dial into the data base in her lab, something she'd rarely done before. There she'd obtained the preliminary test results on Harold Atkinson. Now that she was working with Cortland's team Bea was routed copies of the data compilations as they came in. That routing went into her lab computer, and through the phone link, to her home equipment. The UT Hospital medical team had found the virus - following Bea's methods from the other two cases - and showed their data, including a micrograph. The image was not exactly what she wanted, but she was able to work out the details fairly well. Bea got up and walked around the room for a few minutes, stretching leg muscles and letting her mind wander off the concentrated focus of the morning. She avoided walking by her mirror. At the moment she didn't want to confront Magdalene. Or more accurately, she didn't want Magdalene to remind her of any foolishness on her part. She needed to purge her mind of the clutter of work, quit thinking about all the details that had been so important for the last few weeks - indeed, for most of the last few months. Two ideas needed a fresh look, an analysis unburdened by the prejudices of the approaches she'd been taking. The first was the potential mutation of her virus. Her guess was that any expected variants - and there had been one - would arise from differences in the way the precursor viruses released structural components into the bloodstream. Small changes in chemical levels were the likely causes. This was both a frustrating and encouraging fact, were it found to be true. Frustrating because of the additional factors that would have to be taken into account in an already hellishly complex process, but encouraging because subtle chemical differences might be useful in future modifications she might make of the virus. She bit at her lower lip a moment. Would there be any opportunity for her to do any modifications? And what about the rate of transmission from the first release?

These thoughts brought Bea to the second idea that needed attention: that very thing, the transmission of the virus. How the virus would spread from person to person had been a second order concern when she was designing it, and necessarily so because the nature of the viral effect was very specific - therefore its encoding molecules had to be specific - and the process of assembling components into the virus was very specific. These specifics - despite the complex, basically unknown routes between them determined by the genetic learning processes - dictated the structural issues. Now she could begin to think more about how the virus might get from one bloodstream to the next. But again, would she have a chance to use this information?

Obviously blood transmission would be effective. That would most likely come from sexual intercourse, but not always. If no capillaries were broken none of the precursors could leave the host bloodstream. Nevertheless, this obvious method had some appeal. The type of male she wanted to infect would be the type most likely to engage in sexual activities that might release blood. The nature of the virus and its precursors were such that the blood transmission possibility could not easily be eliminated.

As for aerosol transmission, there remained a possibility that viral precursors moving into the lungs from the bloodstream could be transmitted by a cough or expelling of breath - assuming they were breathed in promptly by the receiver, within seconds. Bea had not tried to model this transmission route as yet, and considered how she might do it. Her guess was that some of the precursors would be more difficult to release from the blood into the lung membrane than others, but she wanted some quantification. The most important people now were those four girls. Very likely each would have the precursors in her blood. Bea would soon be in a position to know that. And aerosol transmission had its appeal. Should she make more, with some of the tweaking of properties she was planning? She wasn't ready yet, she decided. The potential variant forms of the virus had to be evaluated. But, whatever she did, it would be a race against time.

Bea's conflicted mind returned to nag at her. She should get away for a while. Go somewhere to clear her head. This was one of those rare times she wished she had a car. But she was being depended on to do work for Cortland's team studying the three cases. Not only was she the best student to do that work - something Bea was completely rational about - but being involved was important to her. There was no way to know the infecting virus was not a natural structure unless people began finding and assembling information on chemicals other than the actual virus, and Bea was in a reasonable position to know if such effort were undertaken. Even if the link from precursors to virus were found few would suspect any researcher could have actually made these materials. The precursors would be assumed to arise naturally. Hmm. Bea pondered the idea of releasing the precursor information. That might in fact cause Cortland's team to go off in many directions. But finding corresponding new chemicals in the girls' blood would certainly make ties among the various people at the party, but might also lead them to wonder why the girls didn't have the infectious virus themselves. No, she'd hold off on the precursor idea for the moment.

Nourishment. Bea realized she was hungry. She hadn't eaten anything that day. The still barefoot girl went to the refrigerator and rummaged, finding nothing of interest. Then she looked through the shelves in her little kitchenette. There was some cereal and canned goods, but nothing that had much appeal. Curious why she even considered it, Bea decided to go down to Melissa's room and see if the girl were there. Maybe they could go down to the Sunspot for some real food. Melissa and she - in broad daylight - should certainly be safe together. And maybe she could learn some more from the sophomore. What exactly she might learn she didn't know, but Bea had to have a rationale for any action, especially any that might be construed as social.

Melissa was there. She answered the knock after Bea added a little more force to her knuckles. Even though it was early afternoon the young woman was basically sleeping off the effects of the night before. Maria, however, had gone, and Melissa came to the door in jeans and tee shirt, looking through the peep hole to see Bea outside.

"Hi, Bea," she said through the door. "What's going on?"

"Melissa, are you interested in going over to the Sunspot for some lunch?"

"Huh?" muttered the now-yawning one. She took a moment to get over the yawn, then said, "What time is it anyway?" Then she opened the door. "Come on in, Bea."

"One forty-five, Melissa."

Melissa turned, snuggly clad round pretty rump moving in characteristic female rhythm, and started toward her closet. "Sure I'll go. I'll get a jacket."

"Shoes would be good, too" Bea said, shaking her head slightly.

Melissa rummaged for shoes, bent over at the waist in her open closet. "Maria went home already," she said. "'Bout ten. Then I fell asleep again. We really hit it hard last night, didn't we?"

"I suppose so," Bea said, standing and looking around at the typical chaos of Melissa's room. The visitor had to fight back a compunction to pick up the strewn clothes and toss them into a laundry hamper she saw near the closet door. Why can't she just take the time to put her dirty clothes in the hamper? It must take all of ten seconds.

"Didn't know you liked eating out, Bea," Melissa continued. "Maria thinks you're scary, you know."

"Does she? Why should she do that?" As Bea spoke she was still looking around, assessing the room.

Melissa came over. "Ready," she said. "We walking?"

"We'll walk, yes," Bea affirmed. "It's only a few blocks, after all." She'd forgotten that Melissa had a car, like so many students did.

"Okay," Melissa repeated and started toward the door.

The walk to The Sunspot was basically a one-sided conversation, with the sophomore going on about how strange her head still felt after last night, how "fucked up"- and in another sentence, "frazzed" - she and Maria still were about Reggie and Jack. She also went on about how she was "screwed" in her classes and might as well just go home. And as they were about to enter the restaurant, Melissa restated her concern that she was "poison."

"Guys won't touch me, Bea, if they find out."

"And that's a problem for you, I suppose," Bea commented, pointing to a booth farther into the restaurant. None of the tables by the windows were available. They slid in, facing each other.

"You don't like guys, do you, Bea?" Melissa suggested.

"Not all guys, Melissa." The tone was an indication that she thought maybe Melissa did like all guys.

Around them there were numerous others, mostly students, but - except for the boys who'd noticed Melissa enter - in their own worlds of conversation and eating. A bespectacled Asian-looking girl in a long sack dress was their waitress and came up promptly. Bea ordered a grilled chicken salad and Melissa a hamburger and fries. Both chose water to drink. The meals were delivered to them only five minutes later. They talked a little longer, Melissa commenting on various clothing, hairstyles, and behaviors she was aware of among the females in the room, and Bea, mostly working on her food, occasionally threw in a brief remark that let Melissa know she was listening. Finally, Bea got around to asking questions she was actually interested in the answers to.

"Do you mind if I ask you about Harold Atkinson?"

"Harold? What about him?" Melissa was blushing a little.

"Have you seen him since the party?" By this point using the word "party" always meant the particular gathering two weeks earlier that was identified with Reggie's and Jack's illness.

"What if I have? Bea, God damn it! You're like my mother or something."

"Did you have a date with anyone, Melissa, since the party?" Bea repeated.

"Yeah, I did, sure. I didn't ... didn't know I was poison." The pretty thing suddenly looked forlorn.

"Who?" Bea persisted, bringing out a little note pad from her khakis pocket.

"A guy named Rick."

"Rick who?"

Melissa shifted her voice downward in volume. "Bea, fuck you! I know I have to tell you, but this is ... is so weird!"

"Rick who?"

"Rick Forrest."

"What class is he in? Junior, senior, what?"

Melissa blushed again. "He's ... he's not a student."

"Not a student? Come on, Melissa, who is he?"

"He's a ..." Melissa looked around to ascertain whether anyone might be eavesdropping. "He's a professor. In the Double E department."

"A professor?" Bea's disdain was obvious.

"Well, an assistant professor or something. He's not old or anything."

"How do you know him?"

"I ... well, I met him out at Cotton Eyed Joe's. After Reggie had ... you know."

Bea sighed inwardly. Melissa had probably thought Reggie was avoiding her before she found out about his illness. Bea said, "A Double E professor out at a dance hall? Sounds strange to me."

"He's not that much older than Reggie."

Bea said with open sarcasm, "And of course Reggie is now a thing of the past, right?"

"Fuck you, Bea!" Melissa repeated, but not loudly enough to be overheard. "I'm not joining a convent, just because Reggie got sick."

"And he really didn't mean that much to you, right.."

"It's not like that, Bea," she said plaintively. "I did like Reggie, but I ... oh, you wouldn't understand."

"Try me."

"When he ... when he left I didn't know what was going on. The next day I thought ... well I thought maybe he'd walked out on me. I didn't know he was ... you know, that he was sick. So I ... I went out to Cottoneyed Joe's with some people."

"And met this Rick Forrest then?" Bea was looking at the name she'd written down.

"Yeah, and he was real nice, you know."

"I have to know, Melissa," Bea said, shifting her own voice to dead seriousness. "Did you and this Rick Forrest have sex?"

Melissa this time turned crimson. She rubbed her eyes, holding fingers over the eyelids as she spoke. "What if we did?"

"I think you know what, Melissa."

"But I ..."

"I know you didn't know you were doing anything dangerous. I'm not blaming you, Melissa. Did you tell Dr. Cortland?"

"Damn me, no." The pretty girl was clearly distraught.

"I guess I don't understand you, Melissa," Bea continued. "Do you have sex with every male you date?"

"Not every one. What do you think I am?"

"Let's not go there," Bea said. "How about you and Jack Brady, or other guys who were at the party?"

Melissa whispered indignantly, "I didn't fuck Jack. Just kissed him. Come on, Bea!"

"So only this Professor Forrest? He's the only sex you've had since Reggie?"

Melissa nodded, looking away for a minute to glance around the room. Bea wasn't sure she was telling the truth. She was pouting as she added, "Don't you see?"

Bea did something surprising, both to her and Melissa. She reached out and patted the pretty girl's shoulder. "I do see, Melissa," she said in a comforting tone. "I know you didn't understand and thought you'd been jilted. Thanks for telling me."

"I didn't think I'd ever like you, Bea," Melissa said, rubbing her eyes a moment. "but really ... you're somebody I can trust. Really. I hope you're not mad."

"I'm not mad. I'm going to order coffee. How about you?"

21. Interview with Mrs. Forrest

A COUPLE OF HOURS LATER BEA PULLED UP the UT directory on her laptop, found the Department of Electrical Engineering, then the entry for Richard I. Forrest, PhD. He was an assistant professor, probably meaning he'd been at UT only a few years at most. His home phone number wasn't there, but with his full name she switched to the city directory and found it. Forrest lived in Fox Den, a middle class neighborhood out in west Knoxville. She couldn't tell if he were married since only his name was in the listing. Bea then walked over to her phone and dialed the number. After four rings someone answered. A female.

"Hello?"

"Hello," she replied, pleasantly. "I wonder if I could speak to Dr. Forrest."

"Who is this calling?" The woman didn't sound especially polite. But she didn't sound upset either.

"This Bea de Winter. I'm a graduate student at UT. I don't actually know Dr. Forrest. May I ask if you are his wife?"

"You may ask," said the woman, "but first tell me why you're calling."

Bea was unfazed by the comment, but registered the mood transmitted as having some importance. "I'm working with Dr. Virginia Cortland, here at the university, on a problem. A problem in biophysics, actually. I understand Dr. Forrest might be of help."

"He's not here."

"Do you expect him in later in the evening, if I were to call back then ...?"

"I don't know when or if to expect him back?"

"Oh, I'm sorry." Bea maintained her aplomb, sounding as earnest as possible. "Then has he left town?"

"Probably. And yes I'm his wife."

"I suppose he didn't tell you, then. I truly apologize, Mrs. Forrest. You must be very upset."

There was a moment of hesitation, then Mrs Forrest said, "Listen, I'm sorry to go off on you like that. It's just that I ..." She hesitated.

"Did your husband leave recently, then?"

"Two days ago."

"And you've heard nothing from him?"

"Not a peep."

"You must be quite concerned."

"Concerned? Do you think I should be?"

Bea hesitated. "Do you mind if I ask whether your husband was behaving strangely before he left?"

Again a quiet moment. The woman's tone was clearly less harsh, but with renewed suspicion. "Strangely in what sense?"

"Was he different from his usual self?"

"Am I missing something, here," Mrs. Forrest suddenly asked. "I don't think I understand where you're coming from."

"Mrs. Forrest. Listen, perhaps it would be better if I spoke to you in person. Do you ..."

"I believe that's right, young lady."

"Is it too late to come this evening?"

"Damn, is it that urgent?" Her expletive showed a mixture of recurrent anger and worry.

"Possibly. I believe I can arrange to be there in about forty-five minutes, if that's not too late."

"If it's important, sure. Do you know how to get here?"

"Is your address the same as in the phone book?"

"Yes."

"Then I'll get the route. And, Mrs. Forrest, if I can't come I'll call you back in a few minutes."

"Fine." Her tone, however, belied the comment.

When Bea hung up she thought a moment. Melissa would be the wrong person to ask for a ride. It would not do to have Rick Forrest's student trick taking her out to visit his wife. So - with some reluctance - she called Mike Baylor. Would he be home?"

He was. "Hello?"

"Mike, it's Bea. Sorry to disturb you in the evening, but ..."

"Bea, it's okay. What's up?" He knew her better than she might have supposed, and knew very well that she wouldn't call him on a whim.

"I need a ride out to Fox Den."

"What?"

Bea actually laughed a little. Like her smile, her laugh was a personality changer. "I am really quite presumptuous, am I not?"

"Who understands the mind of a genius, Bea? So to Fox Den, huh?"

"Yes. It's out west."

"I know about where it is. But why there? Oops, sorry, I mis-spoke. Can't ask why, can I?"

"No," Bea confirmed, but with friendliness in the word.

Mike said, "I guess you're talking about right now, aren't you? You usually are." There was a gentle chiding in his words, something Bea picked up easily.

She suddenly felt angry with herself and irked with him. Then she fought back her latter feeling, knowing it was unfair. "Sorry," she said. "I will certainly try to make it up to you. But, yes, right now."

"See you in ten, Bea," he said. "Out front, huh?"

"Yes, thanks."

Mike was as good as his word, arriving in exactly ten minutes. Bea, who lived a life of precise timing, took his promptness as something natural. She was waiting, in her usual khakis, blue oxford cloth shirt, leather tie shoes with blue socks, and a lined tan nylon jacket against the cooling air of early evening. Her hair had been given some attention and looked neat.

He wore gray cords, a green sweater, light-weight hiking boots, and a black nylon jacket similar in weight to hers. He'd also taken the time to shave.

"Your taxi, ma'am," he said, waiting for her to get in. Mike knew it would be the wrong thing to get out, come around and hold the car door for her entry.

"Mike, it's kind of you to help out," she replied, after closing the door and buckling her seat belt.

"So, off to Fox Den. That's a pretty fancy neighborhood, you know."

"Is it?" She didn't really know or really care. "I have the route from the net, Mike. If you'll get on I-40 and go west, I'll navigate." She had taken a sheet of paper from the single zipped plastic folder she was carrying.

"Fair enough. I suppose this must be someone's house."

It was a few seconds before Bea answered. She'd been looking out the window, though not at anything in particular. "Yes, it's the home of Dr. Richard Forrest, an assistant professor of electrical engineering."

Mike was amazed at the wealth of information in the response. "But you're not telling me why you want to see this professor, right?"

Bea looked over at him, seemed to ponder a minute, then said, "It relates to something I'm working on for Dr. Cortland."

"Okay," he nodded, going through a turn. "Something hush hush, I suppose."

"You're curious, aren't you?" Bea sounded almost teasing. It made him suddenly feel better. She added, "Actually, if you don't mind, Mike, I'll like to ask you to come in with me."

"Because you're worried about this professor in some way?"

"No, I'll be speaking to his wife. It's just that ..." She was temporarily at a loss for words. "Mike, you'll be eventually finding out why I need to speak to this woman. I think it's better to give you factual information. Possibly you can be of help."

"Really?" He took a quick look at her. "Now I'm really curious."

Bea spoke succinctly, looking straight out the car windshield as she did so. "There are three cases of an illness of unknown origin that has struck students at UT. Dr. Cortland has a team investigating these illnesses. I'm on the team. There's an association among these cases with an undergraduate student in my dorm. This professor Forrest has also been associated with her."

Mike's face went from relaxed and bantering to serious. "A bad disease?"

"Yes. Probably a permanent - or very long lasting - brain function loss."

"Damn, that is bad."

"I think you'll understand, from my questions to Mrs. Forrest, the kind of association I'm speaking of."

"Sex, right?"

"Right."

"So maybe Mrs. Professor whatever will be a little sensitive about her husband."

"Right again." Bea adjusted herself a little, looking at the route, and gave him more driving instructions. Then she said, "Dr. Forrest has left home. His wife doesn't know where he is. It's perfectly possible that he's gotten the disease. She doesn't know about the illness."

They reached the Forrest home eight minutes later, with little further conversation. The house was one of many residences in a row that were boxy in style, close together, and each contained at least six thousand square feet of finished space. The front door was reached by four concrete steps. There was a two-story high front porch held up by two fake white pillars, colonial style. The rest of the house was nondescript, with some kind of painted siding. The front yard was small and covered with mown grass. There were narrow flower beds up against the house with some fall blooms still visible here and there.

Bea rang the bell and waited. Mike remained a long step behind her. The door opened after forty-five seconds.

"Hello, Mrs. Forrest, I'm Bea de Winter," Bea said, offering a hand. "This is a colleague, Mike Baylor, also a graduate student."

"Hello," the woman said. After his returned greeting, she looked at the petite young woman and the dark young man a moment, her face unreadable, then said, "Come in, please."

The two were ushered into a high-ceilinged foyer where a curved staircase came down from higher floors. They entered a little sitting room, a place that would have been called a parlor in an earlier generation. The hostess seated them, together on a couch opposite a matching upholstered chair, where she would sit. There was a nice coffee table in between.

"May I get you some coffee or anything?" she asked the visitors.

"No, thank you," Bea said, speaking for them both, it seemed. "We're sorry to disturb your evening, Mrs. Forrest, so we'll just get directly into our purpose here, if you don't object."

"Please do," the woman said, and sat. She was probably thirty, Bea guessed, was attractive enough, nicely groomed, a natural brunette with pale skin, and maybe twenty pounds too heavy. The hostess wore a dark skirt and light blouse, looking very businesslike except for some slip-on shoes. Bea guessed, based on Richard Forrest's graduation dates in the faculty listing, that he would be about thirty-four or five. To all outside appearances the Forrests would be a typical couple living in a typical upscale neighborhood.

Bea said, "Our reason for coming in person, Mrs. Forrest, is both to emphasize the seriousness of the conversation and to ask you to keep its subject matter in your confidence."

The woman looked suddenly more worried. "This has something to do with my husband's disappearance, then?"

"Possibly," Bea responded. "You see, there's reason to believe he might have contracted a newly-discovered disease from his association with a female student."

"Oh God! You mean something like AIDS?" Mrs. Forrest rubbed her eyes with thumb and forefinger.

"Nothing like AIDS," Bea said. "The immune system is not involved. But there are possible brain effects."

The woman found herself looking at the young man, so far silent after his opening greeting. She expelled a breath, then turned her attention back to Bea and said, "You asked me about him being different or something, before he left."

"Yes, did you notice any change or difference in him?"

"Actually, yes. He was ... was morose, and didn't say much for a couple of days. Then he left, without saying anything or even leaving me a note. And he hasn't called since."

Mike asked, "Did he drive, Mrs. Forrest?" It was a good question and Bea appreciated it.

"Yes, he took his car. It's a Toyota hybrid."

"Where might he have gone?" Bea asked.

The brunette woman shook her head. "We're not from Tennessee originally, and don't have relatives around here. I can't think of where he might have gone. Actually, I didn't think about it at all."

Bea said, "Because you were angry at him." She wasn't asking a question.

The woman looked at the small, girl-like woman, curiously so much in control of herself and the strong fellow with her, and started to reply, but thought better of it. She said, instead, "What about this disease? I haven't heard about anything like that."

"No, we're trying to keep the information from the general public. While Dr. Cortland's team studies the situation."

"Who's Dr. Cortland?" Mrs. Forrest asked.

"Dr. Virginia Cortland," Bea replied. "She is both a physician and professor, and heads up the team studying the disease I mentioned. I work on the team, as a graduate student."

Mrs. Forrest, looking more and more disturbed, asked, "What do you do for them, Bea?"

"I do basic diagnostic studies of lab samples."

"And you, I'm sorry I haven't remembered your name?"

"That's okay," Mike said to her. "I'm Mike Baylor. Actually I'm not on this team. But I take care of the test mice that Bea uses."

"Test mice?" The situation seemed to get more and more worrisome. "I'm not really sure what to do next," she said candidly, getting to the root of her concern.

"What else," Bea asked, "can you tell us about your husband's behavior before he left?"

"I'm not sure what you want."

"For example, you said he was morose. How did that manifest itself?"

"Oh." Mrs. Forrest gave the clear appearance of thinking hard. "Well, he ..."

Mike spoke up gently. "You see, Mrs. Forrest, we don't know your husband, so we aren't sure what his usual behavior would be, so when it changed we'd be even more uncertain."

Bea glanced at her companion with eyes briefly flashing gratitude, then turned them back to their hostess. Mrs. Forrest bit at her lower lip a couple of seconds, then nodded. "Rick is ... he always makes jokes about everything. Doesn't take anything serious. And ... when I said he was morose I meant he was, well, too serious. Sometimes I got mad at him for taking everything so lightly, but ..." She looked away. There were tears in her eyes now.

"And you knew about his association with this college student?" Bea continued.

Another long breath was expelled before she answered. "I ... I got a call from a mother."

Mike looked over at Bea, then decided to ask, "The mother of a student, is that what you mean, Mrs. Forrest?"

She nodded. "Yes, and it took me very much by surprise." The tears amplified her eyes' appearance, then were brushed away with a hand.

"When did you receive the call from this mother?" Bea asked her.

"It was the day before he left. It was a Mrs. Thomas, from somewhere near Knoxville. I've forgotten the town."

Mike looked at Bea to see if the name rang a bell. He saw that it did. Bea shifted her posture before speaking again, then said, "Her daughter's name is Melissa."

"That's it," affirmed Mrs. Forrester, bitterly.

Mike gave the woman an encouraging look, "Maybe he has some friends in the area that he might contact, ma'am."

Mrs. Forrest thought about it. "Oh, maybe. He ... his best friend around here is a man named Tory McAnn. Someone he knew in college who lives in Oak Ridge. The guy's an engineer out at the national lab."

. "Do you have Mr. McAnn's number?" Mike asked politely.

"I don't but ... it's probably in the book."

Mike gave her a soft look, then asked, "Do you have your husband's license number, Mrs. Forrest? And what color is his hybrid?"

"I can get the number," she answered. "It's red."

Bea smiled to herself. She'd have guessed red. "Thank you," she put in. "Is there anything else you think might help us?"

"I don't think so. Are you going to try to find Rick, then?"

"Yes," Bea said.

"This disease," the woman persisted, "is it ... you know, very contagious?"

Bea stood up, indicating they were about done. "There's no reason for you to be concerned about yourself, Mrs. Forrest. We're still trying to understand its transmission, but very probably it came from the student we mentioned, and you had no contact with her."

"No. I just can't understand Rick!" She had suddenly exploded in her anger and frustration. "Is there anything I can do?"

Mike had also stood. Bea spoke gently. "Nothing at all, Mrs. Forrest. Please, however - and this is very important - don't speak of this situation to anyone at all. We cannot overemphasize the importance of confidentiality until we know more about the disease. I'm speaking of close relatives or friends, as well. Absolutely no one, please."

"Alright." The poor woman looked, at this point, like she'd been run through a wringer. She got to her feet, looking less than stable and went through the motion of walking them to her door.

22. Surprise in the Secret City

MIKE LOOKED OVER AT BEA, WHO WAS GAZING out her window. She'd said only a few words since they'd left the Forrest home. "I think I understand why you've been so caught up in this stuff," he said.

She turned her attention his way, making eye contact before he turned his eyes back to the road. "Yes, the disease has been a challenge."

"Are you sure you should have let me know about it?"

"It's something I've considered a while. I trust you."

"That's a real honor," he said, but without guile or facetiousness. "But now I'm worried."

"I'll keep you from any chance of infection," she said, something that would have sounded odd coming from anyone else.

"I'm sure you will. Bea, I didn't know biophysicists were into diseases and things."

"We're into physical processes. Diseases involve physical processes."

"Naturally. Ask a genius a question and you get an answer that makes you feel like a fool."

Bea shook her head at him. "Hush that up, Mike. You're certainly no fool. And don't think I don't know you're being self effacing. I don't trust you because I think you're stupid."

"Then why do you?"

"Because you're trustworthy. And I don't say such things lightly." She turned away, avoiding a blush.

Mike knew to stop pushing the subject. "Do you want me to help you track down this guy Forrest?"

"Can you take the time from your studies?" She spoke as if to the world outside her window.

"You're taking time from your studies, aren't you? I'll make the time."

"Are you sure?"

"Look, Bea, I'm a curious fool, you see. Having a mystery disease around UT is pretty cool, in a scary kind of way. Don't get chances like this every day."

"It would be very nice to have some transportation and, well ..." She didn't complete the thought.

"I wouldn't want you goin' around by yourself anyway, Bea. Genius or not."

Bea was back in full control. "Listen, since you're serious, I'm grateful for your help. And don't worry about the cost. I'm sure Cortland's budget will pay for your car expenses and the like."

"Bea, I'm doing it for you, not for any other reason."

"I know. Except that you're curious." She gave him that almost teasing look, evoking a grin.

"Damn, I can't ever fool you, Bea. I should keep my mouth shut."

She didn't react further. "Mike, I'd like to contact this friend Tory McAnn. Are you up for that right now? It's only eight o'clock."

"You mean, go to his house?"

"We'll call him first."

"Okay. So, give me some orders, Bea." He smiled at her.

"Do you have a cell phone with you?"

"In the glove box." He smiled again.

"Good. Why don't you pull over while I make a call?"

"Yes, ma'am." He pulled over. They had not gotten back to the interstate.

Bea seemed to instinctively know how to use his phone, though she'd never seen it before. She tapped in 1-4-1-1 and got Tory McAnn's number in Oak Ridge, then had the electronic operator ring it. As it rang she looked wordlessly at her new partner. After four rings she got McAnn's answering machine. The message came from a female voice. Bea's eyes widened as she listened.

The speaker's voice was openly sexy. "Hi there. Tory's not answering. Too bad. Don't you wonder what he's doing? Ask him after the beep." When the beep came, Bea hung up.

"Aren't you going to leave a message?" Mike asked, figuring there'd been no answer.

Bea rubbed her nose a moment. "This is remarkable," she muttered, partly to Mike and partly to herself. "I got his answering machine and guess who had recorded his message?"

"Got me."

"Melissa Thomas."

"The disease girl?"

"Yes."

"That is peculiar, Bea. Guess I don't know enough about what is goin' on."

"Mr. McAnn must know Melissa, Mike, and probably through his friend Rick."

"That much I figured out."

Bea gave him a wan smile of apology, then nodded. "Oak Ridge is close. Do you mind if we go out there?"

"You're the boss, Bea. I'm a junior member of this team."

"Mike, I know I'm taking advantage of your kindness. Be honest with me."

"I am. I told you I was curious and that I would make the time needed."

Bea favored him with a quick smile. "Mea culpa," she said. "Okay, let's drive into Oak Ridge. I'll get his address with your phone."

"Unless it's unlisted. With an answering machine like that, it may be."

Bea nodded. "You're right, but we'll take the chance, okay?"

"Okay."

A few minutes later they were driving along Pellissippi Parkway, going toward Oak Ridge. Mike, mostly concentrating on driving, suddenly said, "Hey Bea, ever been to Oak Ridge?"

"No, I haven't." She was working with the phone.

"Did you know it was called the Secret City?"

"No. I suppose because it was involved with the Manhattan Project."

"Yep, right on. But it really was secret, sort of. Nobody in East Tennessee knew what they were doin' there, even most of the people in Oak Ridge."

"Interesting," she said, sounding only slightly interested. "I've never glorified the making of war, Mike."

"I wouldn't expect you would."

"War creates more problems than it solves."

"Probably." He turned to her a couple of seconds and added, "But what about some wars? Like the Second World War, for example. Should we have stayed out of it and the let the Nazis and Fascists take over most of the world?"

"There are better ways to solve the problem of violence."

"Maybe, but once Hitler got in there, what could we have done except throw him out?"

Bea was silent for a moment. Mike thought it was because his question had put her into a conundrum. Then she answered. "Mike, with all due respect, the problem of violence is fundamentally a male problem."

"You mean girls are never violent?" he responded, trying not to sound defensive.

"No, I don't mean that," she answered, taking him literally and not reacting to his implication. "Females," she continued, "can be violent, yes, but in being that way, are falling for, even co-opting the male approach to solving problems. Most women who are violent can trace their violent impulses to male violence that they have perhaps experienced or have seen the destructive effects of."

"Could be," he admitted. "But maybe girls aren't as violent because they aren't as strong. Could it be as simple as that?"

"No," she said flatly. "We're talking about hundreds of thousands of years of evolution, Mike. Females have evolved to understand that solving problems is best done by working out compromises in relationships, by building teams that function without power-based hierarchies, and by avoiding conflicts when possible. It was vitally important for the survival of the primitive tribes. Every life was precious. Infants had to be taken care of for many years before they were self sufficient."

"Was there no God in this process, Bea? The organizing principle, maybe?"

She narrowed her eyes, thinking about his question. "I can't say," she admitted, with meticulous and slow pronunciation of the words. "God, or the organizing principle, may be at work, but in a different way than you imply. Because we have intelligence we can analyze our situation and do something about it, not having to rely on random evolutionary processes."

"But evolution still got us where we are? Today, that is."

"Right."

"So why did men evolve the way they did, Bea? Had to relate to survival, didn't it?"

"It did. Violence had its place as long as the group was primitive and small, and relatively weak."

"I don't follow, Bea, exactly."

"Small groups of early primates - our ancestors, Mike - committed violence approximately the same way that other animals did, in close contact, one on one. As tools were invented and used, however, males got better at killing. And at a distance. With rocks and spears and spear throwers, and eventually arrows. As long as the tribes stayed small and relatively far apart those violent capabilities had some survival benefits."

"What, for example?"

"There was competition for food and other basic resources. The tribes with the strongest and most effective males won out in the competition. Being reasonable and trying to work out a compromise wasn't always likely among those early brains because the competing tribes were not family, not seen as providing any security for children or help in gathering food. In fact the opposite. So killing them or driving them away was understood as necessary. And males raided tribes to steal females." She gave him a strange look, not scoldingly but as if she was sorry to have say such a thing to him. "They would kill the males and take their females, because they'd evolved to understand, in some primitive way, that inbreeding would eventually destroy their tribe. They needed fresh breeding stock, and violence - given the natural suspicion between tribes - was often an effective way to get it."

"What about trading, that sort of thing?"

"Trading is a female trait, Mike. Probably the females, trying to keep their children alive, understood that reciprocity in trade is better than reciprocity in violence. And certainly they wouldn't want their brothers and uncles and fathers killed by other males as they themselves were being stolen to be these brutal strangers' mates. Tribal life constantly was a mix of trade and violence. Each had its advantages over those long centuries before we started to build towns. But the violence depended on the males, not only because of their physical strength, but also their disposition."

Bea paused, looking out the window a moment. They had crossed the Clinch River in Solway, now in the last few miles before entering the Secret City. Mike glanced at her, seeing the introspection and feeling the intensity of her discourse.

He broke the silence with, "Our dispositions - our male dispositions, I mean - had to be optimized for violence, then? Is that what you mean? For us to be good at killing, we had to enjoy it, right?"

"Right. Can you see what a tragedy it became?"

"You're sayin' that when we got better and better at killing then killing got more and more important."

"Exactly." Bea turned partly toward him. Her eyes had a forlorn look that he'd never seen before. Then she gathered some inner resources and came out of it. "We have to get rid of that impetus for extreme, uncontrollable violence, Mike. And we don't seem to understand how important it is that we do so."

He turned his eyes her way a moment. "Do you have a plan, Bea?"

She closed her eyes, fighting back a visible reaction to his unerringly accurate question. "We each have to do what we can," she said. "I hope to do my part."

"What about my part? It seems that it's even more important for me, since I'm part of the problem already."

"You're already doing your part, Mike. And I will always be grateful to you for that."

He hesitated, before saying, "Maybe you'll explain that to me sometime, how I'm already doing my part."

"Maybe," she said, then inexplicably, she smiled.

Mike's car entered Oak Ridge along Illinois Avenue. They passed a long series of businesses. Mike looked around idly. The parallel ridges of the Cumberland hills were visible to the northwest and southwest from his vantage, and Black Oak Ridge, itself - for which the town was named - loomed a little farther northwest. It was a pretty spot for a town, he decided.

Bea began giving him directions. They reached their destination after a few more minutes. The McAnn home was an attractive duplex on the east side of Oak Ridge, in an area not far from the Clinch River and its famous rowing course. The development was a new one, probably less than five years old, and seemed as upscale - in a less boxy and oversized way - as the area of Fox Den where they'd visited with Mrs. Forrest. The route was easily followed because of good street lighting. There was a red Toyota hybrid in the driveway, something both Mike and Bea immediately noticed. A light burned brightly above the garage door, and dimly somewhere inside the home.

"He's here," Mike said. "How about that!"

"His car's here," Bea corrected. "McAnn's car must be in the garage." There was an attached two-car garage on each side of the duplex, part of which extended under the upper level of the dwelling.

They parked and started up the short walk to the door. McAnn's duplex was to the left. On the right they saw several children's toys on the small entrance porch, implying a young family next door. This other home was brightly lit, including a yellow porch light.

Mike rang the bell. They heard what they thought were noises from inside, but no one came to the door. He rang again, then a third time. No one came to the door.

"Hmm," Bea muttered. This time Mike knocked, rather loudly. And this time they heard a responsive sound of some kind in there, though probably not in the front room. They looked at each other but didn't speak. Mike knocked again.

The sound got closer. It was human, probably, and an utterance of some kind, but not spoken words. It was more like a humming, with something of a tune to it.

"Someone's coming, finally," Mike said. Bea nodded, eyes narrowed a little.

The humming sound reached the door and the person seemed to be trying to open it, scratching on the wooden surface. A peculiar sensation went through Bea's body. She knew what to expect, at least approximately. Mike didn't, and was quite confused by what he heard. As the scratching continued, he reached down and, on a whim, tried the door knob. It turned.

With a glance to get Bea's concurrence, Mike pushed the door partway open. He had not been sure what he expected to see, but this sight was well beyond any expectation. "Damn!" Mike muttered, wondering whether to close the door. But Bea pushed it wider.

They were greeted - if such is the right term - by a barefooted man dressed only in a dirty white tee shirt. His dangling penis was evident even in the low light from outside and the dimness within. Warm air from inside flowed around him, bringing a stench outdoors. The man had strange dull eyes, a face with several days growth of dark beard, messy dark hair, and stood unstably, looking at them. Or more accurately, through them. It was hard to guess his age by his appearance, but he was not an old man nor a very young man. He didn't voice any word of greeting, but continued his somewhat tuneful humming. After a second or two his right hand went to his penis, the other hand to his hair, scratching. As best they could interpret his look the man was trying to figure out who or what they were.

"Mr. McAnn?" Bea said firmly. She was close enough to touch him.

The man's eyes shifted appearance slightly but he remained standing and humming. Mike was dumbfounded and glanced at Bea, amazed that she seemed so in control.

"Mike," Bea said intensely but quietly, eyes remaining on the man at the door, "Don't touch him. No matter what, don't touch him!"

23. Fatal Complications

AN HOUR LATER TWO AMBULANCES FROM UT Hospital arrived at the McAnn duplex. There were no sirens, but the vehicles had moved quickly, exceeding all speed limits en route. Virginia Cortland was in the lead ambulance, along with the driver, a male nurse. In the other were a burly hospital orderly and a female nurse, chief nurse of the isolation wing. After a quick consultation with Bea, who was standing outside with Mike, the four entered the duplex garbed in masks and gloves. All already wore their hospital uniforms. A man found upstairs was certified as deceased and removed on a Gurney, covered by a sheet before they got him outside. The other man was clad in a robe, despite a slight protest on his part, then given a sedative injection. In a few minutes he was asleep, then laid out on the other Gurney, strapped down, and placed in the other ambulance.

Cortland returned to Mike, and Bea. Bea said, "Dr. Cortland, this is Mike Baylor."

The physician scientist shook the young man's hand. "Thank you for your help," she said to him. "I have an important favor to ask you both," she added, making brief eye contact with each.

Mike nodded. "I understand, Dr. Cortland," he said, his voice strong, although he was far from recovered from the whole ordeal. "This is not something we should talk about."

"That's right," Cortland said. "We need to find out more about what happened, and certainly don't want any neighborhood panic."She shifted a little, looked at the young man, then added, "I gather you're a friend of Bea's."

"Yes, I am," he said.

Bea interjected, "He drove me over to Oak Ridge, Dr. Cortland. And yes, he does know about the illness we're studying, and is completely trustworthy."

Cortland smiled. "So Bea vouches for you, Mr. Baylor. I do hope you understand why it's important not to speak about this illness to anyone."

"Yes, ma'am," Mike nodded, glancing at Bea. "It's very mysterious, isn't it?"

"Very," Cortland confirmed.

"Mike is a grad student in botany," Bea continued, sounding a little more plaintive than she intended, and angry at herself in consequence. "He also coordinates the lab mice we've been using."

"Ah, I see," Cortland said. "Well, thank you very much for helping out. As you must know, Bea is important to our efforts."

"I figured she would be," Mike said, proudly.

Bea, however, seemed not to even hear the compliments. She said, "Dr. Cortland, we don't know which of these men is which. But one is almost certainly Dr. Richard Forrest and the other Mr. Tory McAnn. The duplex is Mr. McAnn's."

"So I gathered," Cortland said. "The dead man is probably Dr. Forrest. There was a wallet on the floor upstairs, with his driver's license. We'll ask his wife to confirm it."

Mike rubbed his eyes and said, "It's tough to tell families, I bet."

"The worst part of a doctor's job," Cortland agreed. "Mr. Baylor, if you'll go with John – John Dory is one of our best nurses." She signaled the man who'd driven the ambulance she'd ridden in, who, in smock, gloves and mask, was just coming around the vehicle after finishing the details associated with getting the dead body secured for transport. "John, we need samples from this young man."

Mike went to join the nurse.

"We'll need your samples, too, Bea," Cortland said.

"If you don't mind, doctor," the young student replied, "I'll take care of that in the morning. That should be soon enough, I would imagine."

"I wish I were sure about that, Bea."

"The tie," the petite student continued, "must be with Melissa Thomas. We had no blood contact with these men."

"But you breathed their air," Cortland pointed out.

Bea started to say something else, but stopped herself. "You're right, doctor"

"In a moment, Bea, but first, what is this about Melissa Thomas?"

Bea hesitated, then replied, "I'll explain it to you, doctor, but if you don't mind, could it be tomorrow? It'll take a little time. I'll report first thing in the morning."

Virginia Cortland's tone suddenly softened. "Of course you can," she said, apologetically. "You've been through a lot this evening. I'm sorry. I'm so sorry you were forced to deal with this terrible situation. We didn't expect you to have to ... to manage such horrible things. It must have been very shocking to encounter the poor man."

Bea felt a short wave of uneasiness wash over her, but answered promptly. "Thank you, Dr. Cortland. I was ... well, intellectually prepared, but you're right. The real thing is ..." She blew out her breath, not finishing the sentence. "

Let me say that you handled it very well, Bea. Thank you for that."

"We did what was needed, that's all," Bea said, always insecure with compliments.

Cortland regarded the small young woman a moment. "I suppose we've done the necessary things, for now. And yes, let's get together in the morning. At Dr. Charles' office, if that's alright with you. But tonight, do you have any further comments about what you saw?"

Bea nodded assent to the morning meeting, then pulled out her notepad. "I wrote a few things down. You can add them to your data."

"Thanks, Bea. Anything else?"

"I'm wondering about the cause of death of Dr. Forrest."

Cortland looked at her intently, curious about the comment. "I don't quite understand," she said.

"Well, the autonomic systems seem to be continuing to function in the other patients. I'm curious as to what turned this one off."

"I'm curious, too," the doctor nodded. "But really, all things considered, Dr. Forrest and his family are, in many ways, probably far better off than the others."

"Yes," Bea nodded. "Perhaps so."

24. Late Night Conversations

WILLIAM CHARLES SAT DOWN AT THE TABLE in his office across from Virginia Cortland. The biophysicist looked tired. He had been working late, and on the verge of leaving for home when his colleague had called in route from Oak Ridge and asked to meet with him. Fifteen minutes later she had arrived. It was now after ten o'clock.

"We have a fatality from our mystery disease, Bill," Cortland said.

The man's face darkened. "Who is it?"

"It's a faculty member here at UT. Richard Forrest."

"Richard Forrest? Not been at UT long. Engineering school. Oh, no. What a shame! How was he ... I don't understand how he could be infected."

"We don't either. His body has just reached UT Hospital. I'll be going over to assist on the autopsy tomorrow. In a few minutes I'll have to call to deliver the sad news to his wife."

"She doesn't know? Where did he die?"

"At the home of a friend of his in Oak Ridge. The friend is Tory McAnn, and he is also infected, though still alive."

Charles was rubbing a hand on his cheek, obviously disturbed. "This is really so ... well, unexpected. I'm sorry you're the one who has to tell his wife."

"Me, too, but I was the attending physician." She paused, then looked at him more intently, adding, "Bea de Winter says the connection is Melissa Thomas."

" Bea says what? What connection?"

"I don't know for sure. It was Bea and a friend of hers who found the two. I'm not certain how she tracked them down, but I suppose - since she made the comment about the Thomas girl - that this association, in whatever way, led her to them."

"Could these two have been at the unfortunate party?"

"I would not have guessed so, except for their illness. I'll speak with Bea in the morning. I figured she'd gone through enough for one day. We took samples from her and her friend."

"Who's she?"

"She? The friend is a young man. His name is Baylor. A graduate student in botany. He handles the ..."

"Oh, Mike, yes. He takes care of our lab mice. Nice young man."

"That's probably where Bea knows him, I suppose," Cortland said.

"Probably. So, he was with Bea? That's rather surprising, I must say."

"And why is that, Bill?" She had lightened her tone. "Don't you expect your prize student to have a personal life?"

"Actually, no." He smiled. "Virginia, Bea is all business. You've had to notice. I can't imagine her having anything but a businesslike relationship with anyone."

She gave him a slightly scolding look. "You're probably being unfair, and you know it."

Charles shrugged. "Apparently I am. Can never tell about people, can you? Even students."

"You're assuming students are people. How generous of you, Bill."

"Getting soft in my old age."

"Sounds like it. Listen I wanted to let you know quickly, and was glad you were still here. I also wanted to ask you to join me when Bea comes in tomorrow morning."

"Thanks, Virginia. This is a worrisome twist."

"Very much so. I don't mind telling you I am extremely concerned. And we will need to consider when - and how - to release information beyond the UT and university team."

He nodded. "And just what information to release, as well."

"Yes." She looked directly at her colleague. "It's very possible this thing has gotten away from us."

He returned her look. "Let's hope not and keep our fingers crossed."

—

As she entered her room, Bea's mind and spirit were conflicted, strangely so. So, this fellow Forrest had died. She mulled it over. The next day they'd have samples from him and McAnn. The virus had either affected him differently because of something in his chemistry, or it had mutated. She pondered what she would do when she found out, for either circumstance. Could it be that something about her design was not stable? It was important to reconsider everything, work through all the presumed binding energy profiles and understand the differences between the calculated values and the real, in-vivo, structure.

Months before, as she'd planned the viral design, Bea had been careful to have it produce indirect effects, not direct action on neurons, dendrites or axons. The virus's target was actually the conductive zone in the cerebrospinal fluid around neurons. It was here that various types of chemicals caused the communication between brain cells. The virus ties up - binds itself to - certain structures that cut off the conduction, turning off that portion of the brain. The virus, in effect, doesn't alter the neurons themselves; rather it changes the behavior of the type of neuroglial cells - the "housekeepers" among the brain cells - that are associated with certain brain areas, especially in the cerebral cortex. In order to achieve the subtle effects involved, Bea had found that, with the design restriction of allowing the virus to form only when the free testosterone exceeded some threshold concentration, she could not create any arbitrary type of viral action. So, at first she had studied various forms of lethality and decided that those fatal results she could achieve would necessarily come about slowly, increasing as the virus multiplied. Fatality, therefore, would require some number of days and - if the personality of the victim were not altered - would cause discomfort, probably pain, and certainly an awareness that life was slipping away.

It would be inhumane to intentionally cause death, or death in this way, she had decided, and opted instead for a breakdown of personality. The affected person would not be aware of what had happened to him. She intentionally had not opted to cause an end to the depleted personality's life function. There was even a possibility, in fact, that functionality could return, though unlikely for many months, but only when two independent events had occurred. First, the virus had to be purged from the brain - by some yet-to-be-determined treatment - because otherwise the virus would continue to replicate. The second requirement was that the precursors still in the blood could no longer form the virus - that is, when the free testosterone level was too low. That would be the ultimate stable condition for all males. But there had to be the viral effect itself to produce willingness to lower free testosterone. There would be statistical variations, however, and she guessed the Forrest case had been one of those statistical fluctuations. Unless some mutation or some type of neural chemistry had changed the viral effects enough that death had become more probable.

Bea remained conflicted. The viral strain that had affected Richard Forrest had mercifully ended his life. And, apart from a treatment for the virus, death was certainly the best state for those affected. Well, to be more precise, death was the best state for them with respect to their families and friends. But these men, or their loved ones, didn't truly deserve to suffer, since their affliction was primarily an accident of nature, not some kind of chosen evil. She understood rationally why she was conflicted. It was something she'd expected to be. But not so strongly perhaps. Probably Mike was the major cause. That much she could recognize. He was nothing like most men of her acquaintance and that confounded her. She had come to realize she could not categorize so simply, even on the basis of testosterone levels. There was other chemistry - and physics - involved and she needed to find out what it was. Bea couldn't accept that human behavior was independent of body chemistry. She simply didn't believe that. Not that behavior within the species couldn't vary significantly, and not that experience and training were not important. Rather, she believed, natural impulses were driven by chemistry fundamentally - at an almost instinctive level - not by training or acts of will. Training and will were secondary processes. Natural impulses took control of people subconsciously and therefore had so much more power than deliberation. Even the most intelligent and gifted men in history had regularly fallen prey to their testosterone-driven tendencies. In those times when testosterone ruled them - no matter how rarely - men could be expected to respond in destructive ways. And so much damage could result from one reversion!

Before getting in bed Bea looked over her simulation runs of the day just past. She spent a half hour or so checking various factors and marking in corrected parameters for the next set of runs. Several new test sequences were encoded and set off to compute all night. When she hit "enter" Bea sighed openly, stood and faced herself in the mirror.

"Magdalene," she said quietly, "we have entered phase two, I would say. Do you agree?"

The answer came after a long pause and in Magdalene's usual forceful tone. "Not entirely, no. How do you define phase two?"

After an expelling of breath, she said, "Evaluation."

Magdalene was almost insulting in tone as she responded, "What makes you think you're in a position to evaluate anything? The virus eventually modifies itself, so don't be so foolish as to think you're really in control. You need to learn more, don't you understand?"

"Yes, right," came the contrite admission, then Bea looked away from the mirror. She walked to the bathroom, eyes not concentrating on anything, got herself ready for bed, returned to get under the covers and hoped for a good night's rest. She was destined to be disappointed in that hope.

About four in the morning, Bea got up, eyes red. She'd dropped off into a fitful sleep and had gone through a series of bizarre dreams. Mostly, the dreams were not well-defined events but feelings, disturbing feelings that pervaded her with a kind of cold confusion. Mixed among the shapeless sensations and fleeting feelings were glimpses of the badly brain damaged Tory McAnn, there half nude in his front door, eyes vacant. Melissa Thomas also showed up, exuding an altogether different persona, babbling on about useless things, always cheerful. Then came the terrible kaleidoscopic images of Mike. Even as she dreamed she shuddered. Mike was wandering around, with a dull look in his eyes, running into things and calling out her name. Those images faded into something even more frightening. There were those hands coming at her suddenly, grabbing her as she walked and pushing her toward the back seat of that car! Bea sensed she was writhing in the bed. She heard herself call out, then went wide awake!

The shaken youth sat on the side of the bed a moment, letting her breathing slow down. Were there tears in her eyes? After a long time, during which her breathing normalized, she stood and went to her kitchenette, avoiding the mirror. The still trembling young woman took some fruit juice out of the refrigerator and drank it in three or four long gulps. Then she put on khakis, shirt and shoes, deciding that - like it or not - she was up. Again, not looking at the mirror in the bathroom, she brushed her short hair, mostly by feel. Then she splashed water on her face, letting the soothing liquid run through closed eyes. After brushing her teeth, she came around the corner, unbolted her front door and stepped out into the long hallway. There on the right was Melissa's room, and a dim light shone under the door. Bea walked by it and down the hall to the stairs. She then retraced her steps, coming the other way. It was kind of an extended pacing. Back and forth she went, the leather surface of the shoes making light clipping sounds on the hard floor. She was in her sixth or seventh crossing of the space when Melissa's door cracked open.

"Bea," the girl whispered loudly, "what are you doing?"

Bea stopped. Her back was to Melissa, about ten feet past the other's door. She turned and sighed. "Can't sleep," she said simply.

"Me neither. Want to come in?"

The pacing student hesitated. "I'm not sure ..." she started.

"Oh, come on," Melissa encouraged. "Besides, you're gonna wake up somebody if you keep walking."

"Maybe so," Bea nodded. "Thank you, Melissa."

Melissa pulled her door back and waited as the other entered. Bea marched past her before turning around, discovering when she did that her neighbor was wearing a man's tee shirt for a nightgown. Her hair was messy, but even so it graced her face nicely. It would be difficult for Melissa Thomas not to look very pretty indeed.

There remained a slight staleness in the air from cigarette smoke, but Bea sensed that Melissa had not been smoking recently. Nor were there any cigarette butts in view. The one ashtray she noticed was empty.

"Want some wine, Bea?" Melissa asked, referring with her eyes to a half empty bottle on the little counter by her sink. There was only a single lamp burning on the bedside table, and on it there was also a book, turned over to mark the place. The young woman had been reading.

"Maybe so," Bea said, after taking a moment to consider. She'd never drunk wine in her life, or any other alcoholic drink.

"Really? I'll get you a glass." Melissa moved gracefully over to her more compact version of a kitchenette, hips swaying

"What's been keeping you awake, Melissa?" Bea asked.

The buxom girl's eyes were red, and she did look very tired indeed. "I'm a ... a real mess, Bea," came her reply while she poured a few ounces of the pale liquid into a clear crystal wineglass. Melissa finished pouring, sat down the bottle, and turned, giving the glass to her guest. "I ... I can't ... I keep thinking about Reggie, and Jack. They are ... it's a hell of a situation, and I feel so fucking guilty! It's so ... it's like a nightmare."

Bea said earnestly, "You couldn't have known you were possibly carrying a disease. Nothing you did was intentional."

Melissa wrinkled her pretty face and sat back down in the other chair with a thump. "The hell it wasn't!" She looked at Bea holding the wine and added, "That's still pretty cold, but if it's too warm, I can get you some ice."

Bea took a tentative sip. She wasn't sure what she expected, but the wine's lack of sweetness surprised her. She supposed it would be like juice. But it was okay.

"Is it alright?" Melissa asked.

"I suppose," Bea shrugged. "Don't know much about wine, actually."

"It's Chardonnay," the other explained.

"Is it?" Bea sipped again, feeling a little of the sensation she knew about but had never felt. Now was as good a time as any to find out about wine. Holding the glass out to the side, a little awkwardly, Bea said, "I heard your voice on Tory McAnn's answering machine."

Melissa blushed. "You did? Why'd you call him?"

"We were looking for your professor friend, Rick Forrest."

Melissa looked a little sheepish. She didn't say anything.

Bea continued. "Tell me about you and Tory McAnn." Then she took another sip. It tasted better than the first one.

"What do you mean?"

"Did you have sex with him?"

"Bea, damn it! You keep asking me these things!"

"And you know why."

The young woman rubbed her eyes, bringing both elbows up to rest on her breasts, flattening the soft tissue a little. "I ..." she started. "You don't have to remind me I'm nothing but a slut."

Bea took another drink. She'd consumed half of what had been poured for her. "I suppose," she said, but in a different, quieter voice, "that means you did have sex with him."

Melissa nodded and looked away.

"About the same time, I assume, that you were having sex with Professor Forrest?"

"It wasn't with both of them at the same time, or anything," Melissa said, defensively.

Bea's sarcasm came out unbidden. "Well, that's certainly a relief, Melissa!" Then more gently - catching herself - she said, "In both cases, before you heard about Reggie's condition."

Melissa nodded again. There was a tear in her left eye, and she wouldn't let either eye focus on Bea.

"You should have told me or Dr. Cortland about Tory McAnn, Melissa. You know that, don't you?"

"I know."

"Is there anyone else you've been having sex with?" Bea surprised the other by forming something close to a smile on her face. "You don't seem to have any trouble finding willing partners."

"I've been ... like in a convent since ... no, Bea, really!"

"I'm not saying it's bad that you had sex, Melissa. We just need to know if you had it and who with."

"Right." The pretty girl closed her eyes a moment, seemingly composing herself. "What kind of poison am I anyway?" Melissa snapped out, angry but not aiming it at Bea. "Will I ... always be like this?"

Bea sighed and drank another portion of her wine. But she didn't answer the question.

25. Viral Matters

AS SHE ENTERED WILLIAM CHARLES' OFFICE Bea's eyes were a little puffy and red, and her face showed evidence of fatigue. Her mind, however, was as resolved and focused as ever.

"Bea, you do look a little worn out from last night," Virginia Cortland said, pleasantly, and with no implication in her sound. The physician scientist was sitting on the opposite side of the little conference table from the door through which the student entered. "I hope you got some reasonable sleep."

Bea nodded assent at the greeting, gave a pleasant look to her professor sitting at the end of the table, and settled herself in before speaking. "I'm afraid I had a little problem of insomnia, doctor," she said to Cortland but deferring her glance toward Charles.

Dr. Charles said, sympathetically, "Dr. Cortland tells me you had a real ordeal, Bea. I hope you can get it out of your mind."

Cortland said, "I don't suppose it's something to get over quickly, Bill." Then, looking at Bea, added, "Had you called us, Bea, you know someone else could have gone out there." The tone was very slightly scolding.

Bea was not a person who was likely to go on the defensive. Her normal response was to do the opposite, and here she did exactly that. "Dr. Cortland," she said, "Melissa Thomas is apparently a key person in the spread of the virus to date. Apparently she was not strongly enough advised to be forthcoming about her sexual behavior."

Virginia Cortland found herself struggling to keep from smiling. The serious words coming forth from this slip of a girl, albeit this remarkable slip of a girl, were so out of character with the visual image she presented as to be humorous. "I daresay you're right, Bea," the woman acknowledged. "Apparently you got her to admit some indiscretions."

"Yes," Bea said, "and when we found out about Dr. Forrest we decided to go to Oak Ridge with the hope of finding him."

Dr. Charles asked, "Bea, didn't you think he might be infected? It might have been wise to take some precautions."

Bea felt the scolding in her advisor's tone, matching Cortland's attitude. But she was not about to apologize. On the other hand, she was not about to explain that she knew she was in no danger and didn't expect Mike to have significant risk either. She said, "We made an effort to touch nothing, and Mr. McAnn was quite docile."

"That he was," Cortland admitted.

"How is he now?" Charles asked.

Cortland answered, "About the same. Unfortunately, he - like Mr. Pendergast - has had a strong reaction. Mr. Harold Atkinson and Jack Brady have less virulent effects. They still have some awareness of themselves. They both can still speak, even though figuring out what to say seems very difficult for them. There are other problems, of course, but these two appear to know they are ill. They remind me of stroke victims who can understand but cannot speak."

"So you think these two have some awareness?" Charles asked.

"Yes, but I wouldn't go so far as to say how much. They're not exactly like stroke victims, of course. And their awareness does seem limited. But it is in striking contrast to the basic vegetative state of Mr. Pendergast, say."

Bea looked down, as if she were not listening at the moment. These were not words she wanted to hear.

Charles asked, "Do we have a summary of all the identified symptoms for all the victims?"

Cortland looked at several of the papers she had in two stacks in front of her. "Yes. I have it here, but well, these are the main ones. Pendergast and McAnn don't know who they are, as far as we can tell. People around them are responded to in the same way as objects. They are clumsy, and tend to lock their attentions on moving or bright scenes. They have to be reminded to eat and drink, but have no basic digestive problems. Elimination is random, since they apparently don't know what they are doing. There are no rashes or other skin conditions on any of the five. Blood counts on the four living ones are normal.

Bea, now listening, asked, "What about the blood count on Dr. Forrest? Do we have that?"

Cortland shrugged. "His body is set for autopsy in an hour. I'll be there. They will have drawn blood and urine already and sent them for analysis. We'll know before the day is over."

Charles commented, "It would stand to reason that Forrest's white count would be up, since he died."

"Not necessarily," Cortland pointed out. "If enough brain function went away."

Bea shifted a little in position, then said, "What will you look for in the autopsy, Dr. Cortland?"

"All the usual things," she replied, "with a concentration on the brain tissue. Sad as it is, it is our first opportunity to examine neurons and neuroglial cells in detail, particularly in the cerebral cortex."

Bea nodded. "That's where we'll find something about the mechanism, I suspect. I hope I'll be allowed to work with those cells."

"I'll see what I can do," Cortland said, agreeably, "but Bea, tell us more about Miss Thomas. How did you learn about her and Dr. Forrest? And I still don't understand Mr. McAnn's involvement with her."

Bea straightened up. "I asked her. She admitted to a sexual relationship with the professor. And last night I spoke to her again, and she mentioned Mr. McAnn."

"That she'd had sex with him, too?" Charles prompted.

"Yes."

"So," Cortland summed up, "she's had sex with Pendergast, Forrest, and McAnn. But what about Brady and Atkinson?"

"They were at the party," Charles pointed out. "It must have been transmitted there, too, wouldn't you suppose?"

Bea nodded, "Very likely. But we've seen no virus in Melissa's or Maria's blood."

"That's very curious," Cortland said. "Neither McAnn nor Forrest was at the earlier party, as far as we know. Any idea how Miss Thomas was passing on the disease?"

Bea fought back a rush of blood. She'd been too strong on her comments about Melissa. With no virus detected in her blood, the likelihood of her being a carrier would have to be speculative at best. "Dr. Cortland," the student said, with barely any hesitation, "that connection was not clear to me until last night's event. I simply drew the conclusion that because the two men were infected that it had to be through Melissa. I can see no other likely route."

"But how?" Cortland repeated. "Only if there is some indirect mechanism."

"Or," Bea suggested, "if the virus is not usually entrained in her blood, but maybe growing in the marrow or some other static location."

William Charles looked very thoughtful. He said, "Actually, we don't know that these last two are related to the others at all. It could be that the virus has appeared in the population and could have spread by some unknown mechanism."

Cortland looked at her colleague. "You might be right, Bill, but it's a nightmare scenario to think so. Hopefully - and from the data to date, most likely - there is a single source.

Charles said, "I'll grant that. But how would the virus get from the girl to the last two infected unless she carried it in her blood? If it were transmitted more casually, then we'd probably have more cases."

Bea promptly replied, "We don't know for sure that blood is the likely mechanism, sir." She then looked at Cortland and continued, "Possibly airborne virus, from respiration, is released only occasionally, from time to time. That would explain how the people at the party were infected without actual sexual intercourse. And could explain infection from intimate contact, because of proximity to exhalation."

Again Virginia Cortland worked to avoid a smile. Bea's speaking about sex so casually was humorous to her, whether it was fair or not to feel that way. But there was still something peculiar about their arguments so far. She said, "Look, folks, we have given Miss Thomas the onus of being a carrier without benefit of anything certain she is carrying. And why, given her intimate association with three men who've gotten ill, has she shown no physical change whatever."

"As far as we now know," Charles put in.

"Well, sure, Bill. Bea, you spoke with her recently. Did you notice any difference in her manner and looks?"

"No, doctor, I didn't. Melissa has no external symptoms."

"This is very strange indeed," Cortland said, almost in a mutter. "So, as I understand it, Bea, you and your friend were worried that Miss Thomas had possibly infected the two men you tracked down. Is that why you went out to Oak Ridge?"

Bea took her time answering. "Not exactly, doctor. I was trying to find out about Melissa's associations because of her attendance at the party and her known relationship with Reggie Pendergast. It was an effort to be complete. As far as I knew, the people at the party were the only ones infected. But I supposed that most any disease associated with a virus in the blood would be transmissible through blood contact. That meant sex, most likely, so that was why I probed into Melissa's associations. I admit, not being a physician myself, I was really only speculating. Possibly I was too presumptuous." The student appeared to be trying to apologize in her own way.

Dr. Charles rubbed his eyes in thought. "Is it at all likely," he asked, "that certain people will be infected and others left untouched?"

Cortland said, "Of course, Bill. That's true for any disease. The Great Plague only killed a third of the Europeans, after all. Is that what you mean?"

"No, Virginia, not exactly." His tone carried a little irritation that she'd think him so foolish. "What I meant was that the degree of exposure for, say, the Thomas girl was as great or greater than for any of the men, with the possible exception of Pendergast, yet something in her body kept the virus out, or at least kept it from reproducing in her system. She could be a living source of defense against this thing, you see."

Cortland's eyes narrowed as she considered the idea. "Maybe she is, in fact, Bill. A good thought! Maybe something in her blood prevents or kills out the virus before it can do harm. It would be nice to think so. I think we'll ask her to come in again. Possibly her chemistry has changed a little."

Bea listened intently to the basic line of discussion. It was pretty close to on target. "Doctors," she said, finding an opportunity to speak, "we've been assuming the virus we discovered is the cause of the disease. But what if it is not? Wouldn't it be wise to see if the virus is found in Dr. Forrest's brain?"

Cortland looked at the young person a moment. "Technically you're right, Bea. We don't know. But - and I hadn't told you this yet - we have started experiments with one sample of the virus so far. It does bind to mice brain tissue and it apparently cuts off neural circuits. Mice sometimes become moribund and some die."

"Really?" Bea's eyes lit up. She was both pleased and disturbed by the news. But she was a little angry at herself for being surprised. Obviously, mice would be tested with the virus. She had done that herself, extensively. And once the virus assembles it can, in principle, affect basically any mammal brain, male or female. If it lives long enough. These had been key elements in her computer simulations and later lab tests. It had been fairly straightforward to require the necessary testosterone level in order for the virus to form, taking advantage of binding sites on testosterone to pull apart the precursor structures so they could properly reassemble. But once formed the virus could live in lower testosterone concentration levels for a period of time. There were different sites on other molecules that were needed to pull apart or surround and kill the formed virus, and those sites had to be disabled by the presence of testosterone. Given the finite set of chemicals available in the blood, she was limited in what options she had for both forming and maintaining the viral structure. But since the route through the blood-brain barrier took some time, she had been able to design it so the virus, even if present in the blood, would die too soon to infect a female brain. That she'd been ninety-nine percent sure of, and Melissa's case was certainly indicative. She'd probably had blood contact with the men since they'd had blood contact with her. Unless she still retained sufficient precursors in her lungs, released close to the men during intimacy.

Bea went on, saying, "Was this done recently, doctor?"

"Yesterday actually."

Bea took a breath. They were going to find this out eventually, she knew. Now was the time not to react too strongly. "Did they inject the mice brains directly with the virus?"

"Yes, that's the approach. We weren't certain, however, the virus was alive in all the injections. It seems to be very unstable."

"My findings as well, doctor," Bea said, looking through her papers briefly in a show of looking for something she already knew perfectly well. "My findings, however, are based on trying different culture media for the virus. Very few were adequate to keep it alive and replicating."

Cortland nodded. "Yes, that was our problem from the beginning. We were forced to keep the virus in a human blood sample in order to keep it alive. We're not sure yet that some of the mice didn't die from receiving incompatible human blood."

Bea looked intently at the woman. "Yes, the formula I used was basically blood strained of most red cells and a few other types of molecules. You might want to try that instead of actual blood samples. Had I known about this I'd have spoken earlier." There was the tiniest hint of reproach in Bea's voice, something she figured the very capable scientist deserved.

"That we will do, Bea. Thank you!" But Cortland did not seem the least chastised. "Further, we can use your medium to prepare injections into the mouse bloodstream. That will most likely give us critically important information."

"I agree absolutely," Bea said.

William Charles was still thinking about his earlier suggestion. He brought them back to the subject when he suddenly said, "Why did Melissa Thomas not get ill? Or this other girl, what was her name?"

"Maria Santos," Bea said.

"Good question, Bill," Cortland admitted. "Maybe Miss Thomas was somehow the carrier and Miss Santos, not being intimate with her, would be spared."

"Or," Charles said, with a shrug, "females don't get sick and males do."

Bea winced but said nothing. She knew Cortland's team, with or without her help, would eventually find out that only males could get the disease. But she couldn't avoid her reaction. Not that finding out would make a lot of difference in what could be done. Or so she perceived so far. Bea reminded herself again to make no assumptions and stay focused. Since the physician-scientist didn't respond immediately, Bea decided to.

"That would make sense, sir," she said. "Or at least it's consistent with results so far. Dr. Charles, we also have preliminary tests from the other two females at the party. They also don't appear to have any of the virus in their blood." She changed her inflection a little, starting a new line of logic. "Let's say that females and males are equally susceptible and that chances of susceptible people getting the disease are not a hundred percent. So, given a finite probability that exposure does not necessarily lead to disease, but that all exposed are equally probable for getting the disease, since five males are affected and no females, this is simply a 'flip-of-the-coin' probability problem, approximately, at least."

The two older adults looked at Bea oddly. "I don't quite follow, Bea," Charles ventured.

Bea continued, "Let's say Reggie and Melissa were equally likely to contract the disease, but only Reggie did. That's one chance in two. Not surprising. But similarly, Jack and the other three males also got the disease, and Melissa didn't. Now we have a two to the fifth power probability to contend with. Thirty-two to one. It's very unlikely, therefore, that the sex of those exposed wouldn't enter into the process."

Cortland narrowed her brow to say, "So you are saying, Bea, that probably males are more likely to get the disease."

"That's what I'm saying, doctor. We can't say that females can't get infected, of course, but we can say that probabilities point to their being less likely, maybe far less likely, to get infected."

"It does make sense," Cortland said, almost to herself.

"I knew we males are more fragile in general," Charles said, a little lightness coming through, "but this can be bad news indeed."

Virginia Cortland looked at her colleague a moment. "Bill," she said, no humor in her voice, "whether this virus is sex specific or not, it is still very bad news! The fact that so many people we know of that have been exposed have become infected is extremely frightening."

"Sorry, Virginia," he muttered. "Yes, I understand. But on the other hand, I don't really understand. Where did this thing come from? The AIDS virus came from some African monkey. Is that what we're talking about here?"

Bea looked at her advisor. "In the case of AIDS, sir, the African monkeys were resistant to the virus. Only when it got into the human population did it become dangerous. Yet mice seem to react similarly to this one - or so the early work implies. Is that true, Dr. Cortland?"

"It's really too early to tell for sure, Bea," Cortland said. "But as far as we know now, yes, that's right."

There followed a few seconds of quiet. All three were in their individual thoughts for a moment. Virginia Cortland was the one to break the spell. "Bill and Bea, I'm ready to conclude that this virus is not something we ought to keep to ourselves any longer. Unless you can convince me to the contrary I'm going to call Atlanta after finishing the Forrest autopsy." She referred to the Centers for Disease Control, who, to their knowledge so far, had no information on the virus.

Charles nodded. "That's wise," he said. "But we still would be wise not to let the media know, don't you think."

Cortland nodded. "I agree. And Bea, be careful. Since you know Melissa Thomas well, and have met others involved, be careful what you say. I hope you understand."

"Certainly, doctor," the student said.

Charles looked a little grim as he added, "This is not a good time to be a man, I can tell you that."

26. Questions and Further Complications

LATER IN THE DAY, DR. VIRGINIA CORTLAND sat quietly in her office and looked at the telephone she had just hung up. The several conversations she'd had with the Centers for Disease Control had been a very sobering experience. As had the autopsy of Richard Forrest. Over the last two hours, she had spoken with four different people at the federal facility, two of whom she hadn't known before. Cortland sighed. Part of the effort, mercifully, was out of her hands, but that which remained was enormous. And there were four young women and two young men who would feel the immediate impact of what was required of her. The girls and remaining uninfected boys from the now infamous party would have to be put into a condition of isolation. She didn't relish such a thing, but knew it was a must. A part of her cursed herself for not having done it sooner - or possibly, not have having called CDC sooner. With CDC now on board, some heavy hitters in the realms of immunology, virology, and other branches of bio-medical science would soon be looking into their East Tennessee problem. In fact, they might discover - as Bill Charles had suggested - the particular disease that seemed so new might be found other places. She hoped, at one level in her mind, this were true, but really didn't believe it. No one - as her conversations and forwarded image files had proven - had ever seen this virus before. And where, of all places, for such a thing to occur but in her own backyard!

Mother Nature was a bitch! And in this case, she'd picked on the males of the human species, it seemed. Cortland remembered Bea's lesson in probability, and smiled a little bitterly at the thought. The enigmatic Miss Bea de Winter. And with a boyfriend, now. Well, boy friend, at least. Given what Josiah Zorn had told her, that was even more unexpected.

This virus was like Alzheimer's. What if a large number of people in the population got sudden cases of Alzheimers? The economic burden alone could overwhelm the whole society. These young men affected by the virus so far were representative of advanced levels of Alzheimers. And they were in their twenties! What if Reggie Pendergast and those like him lived on for twenty or more years? Cortland shook her head in consternation. They had to figure this thing out, and take care of it.

Scratching her head thoughtfully, Cortland felt a sudden onset of fatigue. The adrenalin was wearing off. What a day! What conclusions could she draw for the moment? Very little until more work was done. They'd been unlucky, yes, but also lucky. How often would she luck out and have a colleague like Bill Charles? And, of course, his remarkable student, Bea de Winter. Really, Cortland realized, she didn't know much about the girl. They were not about to remove the student from the case, though they would certainly try to keep her from any more possible contact with the virus. It would be good to understand that enigmatic mind better. That much she could do: she herself could spend more time with Bea, and convince Bill to work more closely with her. So far the student had been the pivot around which everything they knew had revolved.

The now-yawning scientist-physician picked up her phone again. She checked a note pad on which she'd written various phone numbers, found Bea's and dialed it. Four rings and no answer, but she left a message. "Bea, I know you're busy. It's Virginia Cortland. I wonder if you and I can meet before the end of the day. I'd like to pick your brain on a few subjects, if you don't mind. If you prefer, I can meet you at Hess Hall, or your dorm if you wish. Let me know a convenient time. Thanks a lot."

–

Bea had been busy. She'd spent almost all day in her laboratory on the campus. There she'd lost herself in intricate work, with two basic goals: understanding the secondary blood and brain chemistry coupled with testosterone levels, and, with the improved knowledge, modifying her virus structure. This latter goal also required extensive and in-depth characterization of the group of precursor molecules and their transporting viruses. She wanted to tailor the virus more carefully, to make its action even more specific. If she could. Bea couldn't be sure how long any virus structure would be effective. Would the precursors survive for months or more in various blood streams? She wasn't certain. Would the virus mutate enough to be ineffectual? Or could something in the immune or other body systems start to kill it? None of these possibilities was likely, she thought, but then neither was it likely that the virus would continue to function indefinitely. There would need to be further releases. Assuming she got another opportunity.

The afternoon was waning when Bea found the message from Cortland. She returned the call was asked to come right away. Cortland's campus office was nearby in another building, and Bea took only five minutes to get there. She tapped on the closed door.

"Come in, Bea!" Cortland called. "Thank you for being so prompt."

Bea entered as the other stood. The student had brought along a few papers in a manila folder.

Cortland said, cheerfully. "How about a cup of coffee?"

"That would be very nice, doctor," Bea said, seating herself at a small circular table a step or two out from the desk.

Cortland was back quickly with two cups of steaming black coffee. It smelled good.

The older woman said, "I believe you like it black, right?"

"Yes, thank you." Bea took the porcelain cup, with "UT Microbiology" embossed on it in orange, and drank a sip, savoring the taste.

Cortland seated herself directly across from the student. She had no paperwork with her, a fact Bea noticed immediately. After a sip of her own coffee, she spoke.

"Bea, I wanted to bring you up to date on some things, but mostly I just want to sit and chat. I know you're very busy, but with this disease crisis we're now in, I feel it's important to simply reflect a while. I'm curious about your thinking and I'm confused about my own. Does this make any sense to you?"

Bea supposed it was better to be a listener than a speaker, so she said, "You're conflicted, doctor? Is that what you're saying? May I ask about what?"

Cortland took another sip before responding. "Let me give you some background first, Bea, if I may. Today I talked to the CDC. Our disease problem is being taken very seriously. A team from Atlanta will be here in the morning, arriving this evening. The four girls and two un-infected young men from Miss Thomas's party will have to be put in isolation for a while. They've already been notified. All of us who have had some potential contact with the virus will be in for another round of detailed testing. Your friend Mr. Baylor will have to be included, as well. And your lab space, for example, will have to be examined minutely for any potential danger. You won't be able to use it till they're satisfied with it. We went ahead and let you work there today, because I really don't think there's any contamination. But all the same, when the CDC people take over, they won't cut us any slack."

Bea's brow wrinkled. This was a very unfortunate turn of events. But not unexpected. She made herself count to five before speaking.

"I hope there won't be long delays, doctor. We have a lot to do, as you know."

"Yes, I know. And we here at UT and the hospital will continue mostly as before. At least for a while. However, the CDC will have two van labs parked over at the hospital and will insist on taking charge of operations."

"Is that truly wise, Dr. Cortland?" Bea asked, the implication in her voice saying it wasn't.

"Maybe or maybe not, but inevitable. We do have a serious problem, as you certainly recognize."

Bea slumped a little in her seat, adjusted a moment, straightened up again, and said, "Yes, doctor, I think I understand the situation."

"Good," Cortland said, but didn't continue.

Bea said, "Do you mind explaining more about the nature of your confusion, doctor?"

Virginia Cortland looked even more haggard than her middle years would suggest. This tired look didn't surprise or disturb Bea, because she herself was tired. Events had dictated fatigue for all involved. But the woman bore another kind of look. Bea couldn't figure what it implied.

Cortland said, "Bea, you know more about this virus, probably, than anyone else. Tell me more about it. Where did it come from?"

Bea didn't hesitate. She replied, "Organisms of this type, doctor, generally form naturally, from mutation sequences affecting some older form. The genetic material in the older form is somehow changed."

"Yes, yes, I'm aware of that, Bea. But it seems so unlike Mother Nature to strike a group of young people at the healthiest time of their lives? Why wouldn't it be more selectively advantageous for a virus to form that affected a weakened portion of the population, like most disease organisms do?"

"Oh, I see your concern, doctor. The virus, as we understand it so far, is a very unstable structure and seems to require special conditions for survival. Possibly those conditions exist only in the particular part of the population we've seen affected."

Cortland nodded, regarding the young person thoughtfully. "Apparently that is the case, Bea. And that is upsetting to me. Part of the reason AIDS was so horrible when it came on the scene was the fact that very young people could be infected and die much too early. What is your guess about the parent virus that this thing mutated from?"

"Well, doctor, as you probably remember, most viruses have either cubic or helical symmetry. This virus is helical, consequently its structure can be longer or shorter without effecting the basic symmetry. When the virus assembled not all structures in the helix formed identically to the parent. But the parent virus would almost surely be helical, as well."

Bea paused a moment, and Cortland asked, "What do you mean by 'assembled,' Bea?"

The young woman shuddered internally, hoping it didn't show on her face. "I mean when it re-formed from the mutation process."

Cortland cocked her head a little. "Mutations, as I understand them in this context, rarely make anything but small changes in structure, but you seem to be saying the parent virus could be broken up in effect and re-form in a different way."

"I probably didn't speak clearly enough, doctor. Yes, of course you're correct about mutations." Bea's color had heightened a little, unavoidably, and she was angry with herself.

The older woman appeared suddenly very thoughtful. "Tell me, Bea," she said, "could a virus be assembled from disparate components? Have you come across such a thing in your research? Or has Professor Charles mentioned it?"

"I'm not certain, doctor," Bea said, but didn't make eye contact as she said it. "We may be speaking more about definitions, actually, than actual processes. Complex molecules are constantly assembling and disassembling, as you know. DNA and RNA are prime examples."

"Perhaps we *are* talking definitions, Bea. Sorry. But since, as you reminded me, viruses generally have a very symmetrical structure, it stands to reason that they, like your DNA and RNA examples, could come together piecemeal from smaller components, guided of course by the genetic material. If so, our mean little creature could have formed, not from mutation, but from a kind of assembly process, maybe in the bloodstream. That could explain its unique characteristics. After all, even in its standard helical symmetry it has very different components - or so your major professor explained recently - from other known viruses of similar shape."

Bea swallowed and kept her voice as steady as she could. "Doctor, I think you are probably on track with that analysis. Probably Professor Charles and I are too close to the problem to see it as clearly as you have." She added a complimentary look.

"If so," Cortland said, not reacting to the compliment, "the virus might form only under stringent conditions. That would explain why we had such difficulty in finding a replication medium for it."

Bea nodded. "Yes, that might in fact explain it."

Cortland continued, "This kind of assembly method might also explain something else, Bea." The older woman rubbed her eyes a moment before going on. Bea didn't speak, and Cortland added, "The potential for viral formation may be present, for example, in Melissa Thomas's system, but it didn't form. Even though she was exposed. Does that make sense to you, Bea?"

Bea couldn't think of a way to divert the flow of Cortland's logic. But she did say, "Clearly, there are wide variations in body chemistry. I suppose that's your implication."

"Following that line then," Cortland went on, talking a little faster, "What would be significantly different about Melissa's blood, compared to Reggie Pendergast's, say?"

"They are different blood types," Bea said, "but that is ..."

Cortland interrupted, "No, the blood type doesn't matter. The big difference is hormones, obviously." She looked at Bea keenly, as if examining some detail about the young face. "Maybe that's our clue, Bea. Sex hormones."

Bea expelled a breath. "We can certainly check that out, doctor."

"Yes, we can. Tell me, what blood did you use to make your first effective culture medium, Bea?"

Bea was taken a little by surprise. Cortland's mind was obviously working fast. The student could only afford to hesitate a little. She said, "It was ... actually it was from the Pendergast blood sample. As I said I strained the red cells out and several other types of molecules. The details are in my lab, I'm sorry."

"The young man's blood, yes." Cortland narrowed her eyes in thought. "Any hormones would still have been in there, right? Those weren't taken out?"

Bea nodded. "Yes, the hormone levels weren't changed."

"You're following my thought, aren't you, Bea? Let's check this out right away, before the CDC closes us down for a while."

"Yes, doctor, we should do that."

"Great!" Cortland stood up. "I want to talk more about this, Bea, but it looks like we both have work to do right away. Thank you for coming in."

"Thank you, doctor," Bea said, careful to be properly grateful. "This is a promising new direction in our study."

"We'll see." The older woman came around and put a hand on Bea's shoulder. "Let's get together tomorrow, if you don't mind. We can compare notes and, since we'll be put on hold for a while in the lab, can take the time to talk philosophy."

"Philosophy?" Bea asked, having stood and about to leave.

"I want to talk about something we seem to have similar opinions about." Cortland smiled at the bewildered face. "I heard you recently went to a WILL meeting and stirred up a bit of controversy."

Bea had her unopened folder under one arm. "Yes, I heard Dr. Greider speak. Do you know her?"

"No, actually I don't. But look, let's get into this tomorrow. Thank you again for coming by."

Bea knew she was being dismissed. "Thank you again, doctor," she said, went into the hall and strode toward the building entrance. When she was out of Cortland's sight, a worried look formed on her face.

27. Suspicions and Reactions

WILLIAM CHARLES WAS AT HOME IN HIS NEATLY decorated den looking out at trees busy shedding multicolored leaves. The sun had just set, ending a mild sunny afternoon, and he was sipping a gin and tonic, when his cell phone rang. The professor hesitated, then withdrew the instrument and checked the caller ID. Virginia Cortland.

"Hello Virginia," he said pleasantly. "Long time no speak." He'd spoken to her only two hours earlier, as it turned out, just before her conversation with Bea.

"Hi Bill," she returned. "Interested in having a drink with a grandmother?"

Charles sighed inwardly. He really was liking the process of ending the day. But he said, "You obviously want to talk."

"I do. I just had a conversation with your prize student."

"With Bea? What did you two decide? Will the CDC cramp your style a little?"

"Probably, but that's not what's on my mind. How about it?"

"Are you at home?"

"Not yet, just about to leave my office."

"Do you mind drinking with a bachelor in his den?" There was a smile evident in the phrase.

"If you can deal with a grandmother I can deal with a bachelor."

"Come on over then. Just come around back. The door's open. What'll you have?"

"Whiskey and soda."

"It'll be ready for you."

"Thanks, Bill. It should be no more than fifteen minutes."

It actually took her only fourteen. Sequoia Hills is in easy commuting distance from the campus, and Cortland, like him, had a convenient parking place, hers just outside the new microbiology building. She tapped lightly on her colleague's back door before pushing it open to see him moving toward her with a glass in hand.

"Fine service at this bar," Cortland smiled. "Thanks."

He led her over to a comfortable chair just across from his. It was darker outside but something of the splendor of Tennessee autumn still could be seen through the picture window.

After a first sip, Cortland said, "I'll get right into it, Bill, if you don't mind."

"Shoot."

"Tell me more about Bea."

"More about her in what sense, Virginia?"

She looked at him intently. "Is she capable of manipulating genetic material to make a new virus?"

William Charles widened his eyes, stunned by the question. "Are you suggesting that Bea could be responsible for what we're dealing with?"

"I'm not sure what I'm suggesting, but tell me, could she do it?"

"I don't know," he admitted, then stood up. "I think I need another G and T."

Cortland smiled, and spoke to his back as he went through the motions at his little bar. "Bill," she said, "you must have a good idea of what such an achievement would involve."

He turned, came back with his freshened drink, and nodded. "It would require detailed understanding of the binding conditions of the molecular components of the virus. And it would involve finding a way to modify genetic material according to some selected recipe. And remarkable care and precision in the laboratory. Not to mention structuring the result to match the parameters and factors whereby the virus would enter and breakdown various target structures. The task is enormous."

"Could Bea do it?" she asked again, watching his eyes.

"If anyone could, yes," he said, then sat down. "But, why do you ask?"

"Probably I'm paranoid, Bill, but after talking with her this afternoon, it seems like a possibility that we shouldn't ignore."

"Virginia, this is a very serious paranoia, if so."

"Very."

"Do you realize – you must, surely – that doing such a thing would be a scientific achievement of the first magnitude. Bea is just twenty-one, for God's sake! We're talking Nobel Prize here."

"Or life in prison."

William Charles looked suddenly very sober. "Yes."

"But is that true?" Cortland asked. "That she could be assembling a virus from dead matter?"

"Not exactly, no. Or at least probably not." He tilted his head back a little, thinking. "She'd probably adapt an existing virus, changing its genetic material appropriately. She's an expert at genetic programming, as you may remember. We would be talking about a starting point – the base virus – and an end point, a viral structure with the ability to break down the neuro-transmitter links. The process could be simulated – that's the way Bea would do it – and computed using her genetic learning models. Some complex route might be found, since the electronic fields are reasonably well understood for a lot of those molecular structures. And, with her codes, the degree of complexity could be very high, not even describable."

"Why not describable?"

He rubbed his nose in a characteristic way. "Because the genetic learning works it out by weighted random processes."

She nodded. "I thought that's what you meant. It's really amazing, if true."

"What did Bea say to you, Virginia, that made you suspicious of her?"

"Nothing very specific, except the mention of 'assembling' a virus. When I thought about the idea of *assembling* a virus, it seemed more like a construction than a mutation, if you get my meaning."

"I do, but she must have said more or other things to bring you to this concern."

Cortland nodded. "It was a combination of her easy facility in talking about the subject and something about her reaction. Bea seemed a little ill at ease, and I've never seen her that way before."

"That's a rare condition, I'll give you that. But she has been pretty much in the thick of things, getting that first hand look at poor Rick Forrest. This all may have upset even her cool."

"I know, and I may be completely off base. But what if I'm not?"

Charles pondered the question. "Then we're in serious trouble," he said.

"We're already in serious trouble, Bill," she countered. "We have a previously unknown and deadly disease with five known cases. What if this is only the beginning?"

He nodded, then sighed heavily. "Where is she now?"

"In her lab, I'd wager. I told her the CDC would be closing her down for a while in the morning. There are some things we discussed that she wanted to do."

"What, for instance?"

"I wondered if a culture medium containing the proper hormones might explain the fact that the virus has only infected males."

Charles rubbed his eyes in thought. "Oh, God," he muttered. "You mean that male hormone levels might be required to keep the damn thing alive?"

"Exactly."

"And she was going to look into that?"

"Yes. We both thought it would be good to get whatever possible done on it before they shut her down."

"Oh damn, damn, damn!" he said, closing his eyes as he did so. "But if she were responsible, she really wouldn't need to go through the motions."

"No, but can you imagine Bea simply going back her dorm after that conversation?"

"No, she'd go to the lab. Besides, there are other things she can do with the time."

"Yes," Cortland nodded. "If she has done something unthinkable, she would certainly want to cover her tracks."

He nodded. "But we can't really assume she did such a thing, Virginia. Surely not."

"No, we can't. But I wondered if you might want to join her in the lab this evening, Bill. It's presumptuous, yes, but ... well, I think you see my drift."

"And here I'm on my second G and T," he said with bitter smile.

"I started to stop you making that second one," she said, "but then I thought you might actually need it."

He smiled again, less bitter this time. "I guess I should 'drop in' on her. There's certainly a good reason, since CDC will be stopping her work tomorrow. I can offer to lend a hand."

"Would you?"

"Shall I call you at home later?"

"Would you please?"

"Absolutely. We should get on with it."

She arose and started toward the door. "Thanks, Bill," she said warmly.

"I hope you and I both are wrong," he said, following.

–

Bea de Winter was indeed working hard in her lab. On the way over there she'd considered what she should do. Dr. Cortland, Bea was certain, was suspicious. This had been a contingency she'd considered from the first, but hoped it would never have to be dealt with. Her critical files on the computer could be protected, however. She knew encryption would not be enough, because the authorities could demand access to these files, and refusing would be tantamount to admitting guilt. Bea's approach had been simply to hide her work. All the input and output files and the source codes were kept on memory sticks. When the computer was in use, they were read into memory or loaded from memory. Bea had written a managing code that did an overwrite of memory at the end of the day or whenever she needed. The overwrite was clever in that it was a copy of one of the major codes she used in her dissertation work, along with various results that could be seen as pertaining to her degree program. Further, the management code was also kept on a memory stick. Its presence, while not impossible to find traces of, would not be found by anyone not looking specifically for it. The memory sticks associated with her virus project were now tucked into her backpack.

The actual lab work was harder to hide. But she could do it, and did. Fortunately, she used her own shorthand for labels on test tubes, Petrie dishes and the like, making them difficult to decipher. The virile strains under test could be associated with the analysis work she was doing for Cortland's team. And she had always kept three separate notebooks. One was for her dissertation, the second for her 'legitimate' work on Cortland's team, the third was for her personal work. It was this third notebook she had to keep hidden. Even though its entries were cryptic, an expert from the CDC or Professor Charles would eventually figure out what she'd been doing. The notebook had more than two hundred pages of entries, a massive compendium outlining a biophysical and chemical achievement never before completed by any other researcher.

Bea took this third notebook out of the lab and went down the hall to another lab two doors away. Months ago, she had obtained a key for this lab by checking it out in the name of the regular user, another female graduate student. Bea, wearing vinyl gloves, opened the lab and opened a drawer full of tubing, dirty or chipped glassware, and several old lab notebooks. It looked to be a junk drawer, a collect-all to put unwanted things into, but things someone didn't want to throw away. Her notebook, she knew, would be full of her DNA traces, but if it were not discovered there would be no problem. When she tucked it away it looked like everything else in that drawer, neglected and nearly forgotten. Her name had never been on it, though she had put it on the other two notebooks.

That done, Bea retraced her steps and entered her lab. She was startled to see her major professor standing there, looking at her second notebook.

"Professor Charles, I didn't expect to see you tonight." She tried to keep the tension out of her tone, but knew some had remained.

He gave her a pleasant look, doing a better job in disguising his mood than she had done. "Hi, Bea," he said. "Sorry to surprise you, but I heard the CDC was going to close you down tomorrow, and wondered if you needed any last minute help to get to some stopping place or another."

Bea took a breath, calming herself. "I think I have everything in order, sir. You can see my notes there, and determine what I've done so far."

"Yes," he muttered, scanning through the pages. "I was surprised when I came in just now and you were out. Usually you lock the door."

"I was ... well, just down in the ladies' room. Didn't expect anyone to walk in. Sorry, sir."

"No problem, really," he said, still scanning her notes. "It's just that, well, you should be careful to keep this place locked, especially now."

"You're right, Dr. Charles. I apologize. It won't happen again."

"Are you sure there's nothing I can do to help?"

"Nothing, sir. I came back, finished up with that mouse, and put him in the freezer. That's all there was to do, short of starting something we don't have time for."

"Fine," he said. "Then I'll be heading home. Will you be around much longer?"

"Actually, no, sir. And could I ask you a favor?"

He stopped, having already started for the door. "Sure."

"Do you mind dropping me at the dorm. I'm a little reluctant to ... well, to walk across campus at night."

All of a sudden, Bea seemed to have turned from a confident young woman into an insecure girl.

"Of course, Bea! I should have offered, actually. You're wise to ... well, it's not always safe out there."

Bea looked at him. "Sir, did the campus police report any incident to you? An incident involving me?" Her eyes carried a mixture of earnestness and discomfort.

"Campus police? No, Bea. Involving you?"

"I'm sure they'll send you a report. I hope you don't mind that I listed you as a contact person, since I don't have parents."

His heart quickly went out to her. She seemed very small and defenseless at that moment. "What kind of incident, Bea? I hope it was not serious."

"It could have been, Dr. Charles. Three men tried to ..." She looked away. Bea was not acting at this point, and struggled for composure. "They tried to abduct me ... just a few blocks from the dorm."

"Oh, God, Bea!" He wanted to hug the girl but was afraid to attempt such a thing. He did take a step towards her. "Do you want to talk about it?"

She took a long breath. "You should know, sir. Because it has ... well, it's a little more awkward for me now to come and go from the lab. It's a ..."

"Of course it is," he said, consolingly. "Thank God it didn't happen."

"Mike Baylor saved me, Dr. Charles." Bea had straightened up, forcing as brave as face as possible. "He saw the attempt and ... and actually attacked the men, driving them away."

The professor, for the moment, had forgotten viruses and diseases, appalled at what could have happened to this most brilliant of graduate students. And more importantly, to this very fragile-seeming girl who surely had experienced very little of life's seamy side.

"I must say," he said, struggling for the right words, "it's a real shock to hear such a thing. You must be ... be going through hell worrying about your safety."

Bea was quickly returning to normal. She expelled a breath and said, "I try to stay busy, sir, and Mike has been kind enough to accompany me when I ask him."

"Is that why he was with you in Oak Ridge then?" Reality was beginning to dawn on him.

"Yes, sir."

There followed an awkward moment. Bea was offering no more information and her professor was not about to pry further.

"Well," Charles finally said, "I suppose we can be on our way then. Are you sure there's nothing else you need to do. The CDC will be here early tomorrow, as I understand."

Bea, who truly wanted to do much more, said, "No, sir. But thank you."

They left together, Bea a half step ahead, which seemed to be always where Bea was.

28. Firestorm

THE STORY WAS NOT BROKEN BY THE KNOXVILLE News Sentinel, nor any other local paper or television station. It first made its appearance in spoken words on CNN Nightly News, and was read by a stalwart of the CNN news bureau, known to most Americans and many around the world, Randall Jackson.

Mr. Jackson, as always, fatherly in aura and neatly dressed, in his soberest tone, read: "We have just received this: a breaking story out of Knoxville, Tennessee. Sources at the Centers for Disease Control in Atlanta confirm that a deadly virus of unknown origin has infected five young men associated with each other through a campus party at the University of Tennessee. We go now to Erica Rotherford, on site at the University of Tennessee hospital in Knoxville.

Ms Rotherford, pretty and blond, looking very serious indeed, appeared on screen with one of the CDC vans behind her, and behind that the imposing entrance facade of the hospital. She said, "The disease produces symptoms not unlike advanced Alzheimer's, quickly transforming healthy students and faculty members into a near vegetative state. Doctors here in the Infectious Disease unit and members of the CDC staff have declined comment for the moment. They have not given us any information on the potential for spread of the disease, but the presence of CDC gives a clear message of a possible epidemic. We'll continue to probe for information and will give updates as quickly as new information is obtained."

The story then shifted to brief interviews with two medical experts, a Dr. Lawrence Danforth from Harvard Medical College, and a Dr. Priscilla Gonzales of the Cleveland Clinic. Both were quick to urge for caution on the part of the general public, and not to blow the news of the virus out of proportion. In contrast, however, both stressed the possibility of a serious outbreak and that every precaution would need to be taken.

The CNN report, naturally, fanned the flames of the fulminating firestorm. And by the time Virginia Cortland reached UT Hospital that morning, for a meeting with her

Infection Committee and the CDC, she well knew the genie was out of the bottle. Reporters seemed to have come out of the veritable woodwork. They were lounging about everywhere, it seemed, but concentrated in the region around the two parked CDC vans. Four TV vans were there, too, kept back by strands of yellow ribbon cordoning off the main hospital entrance and the two official portable laboratories nearby. More than a few police were seen in the area. There were several video cameras on rolling mounts, some pointed toward the entrance, others scanning along the hospital structure, probably creating background shots for various reports. She found herself driving around the hospital and into the visitor's lot for the emergency room, luckily finding the last parking place, fortunate the media had not yet found and swarmed upon every available space. After entering through the emergency room she took the key-operated elevator to the locked wing where the four virus patients were now held in isolation. There, in the physician's lounge, she plopped down with a heavy sigh and retrieved the cell phone from her purse.

William Charles answered almost immediately. "Good morning, Virginia. I'm watching the news."

"I confess I didn't," she said, "but should've. I'm at UT Hospital. The place is swarming with media."

His voice carried clear agitation. "Someone in CDC ratted on you."

"How's that, Bill?"

"They knew about the party, that a member of the faculty was infected, and the basic symptoms. And they said they got it from the CDC."

Cortland joined him in agitation. "Damn those politicians! What did they expect to accomplish by leaking it?"

"Probably more funding," he said bitterly. "That's almost always the game. With them out in front and the public properly scared, the Congress is ripe for the picking."

"I suspect that's exactly it, Bill," she muttered. Then she composed herself a little and asked, "Tell me about Bea last night. Did you learn anything?"

"I learned she was nearly abducted recently. And her friend, the young man with her in Oak Ridge, saved her from it."

Virginia Cortland was taken aback. "Really? That's ... what a terrible thing!"

"You wouldn't have recognized Bea when she said it. She nearly broke down."

"Unbelievable! I knew there had been rapes around campus. All universities seem to be plagued with them, but ..."

"Three men, she said. I'm planning to call the campus police today. She said she'd given me as a contact, since she has no parents. For some reason they didn't contact me. Or maybe they'll do it in their sweet time."

"My God, Bill, that is ... how has she continued to work?"

"Because she's Bea de Winter, Virginia. Who knows what drives her?"

"Tell me, Bill. Am I paranoid about the girl, or not? Could you tell what she's been up to?"

Charles hesitated before speaking. "I didn't get very far in checking her out, I confess. She was about to leave, and asked me for a ride. Then she explained about the assault. I had planned to let her go, then go back in and rummage around some more, but ... well, I'm sorry."

"Completely understandable, under the circumstances. So, no impressions, even?"

"Her lab is neat as a pin, like always. I did go through her notebook on the virus work, looking at the last dozen pages or so. No obvious clue that she's doing anything other than what she says. But ..." Again he hesitated. "If Bea wanted to ... to disguise something, she'd do it."

"But surely you could track it down in her records, couldn't you?"

"Eventually, sure. But going through her lab notebooks is like studying a foreign language. She writes her own shorthand, everywhere. I noticed this back east. It's because she's thinking too fast for writing, I suppose, and needs her own symbols.

When she writes a report for me, however, it's in precise English with virtually no acronyms."

"She's an enigma, Bill. But I'm very sorry about the attempted assault. And I understand young Mr. Baylor's role now."

"Yes, she is an enigma. But Virginia, the CDC will be in there today - in her lab. They're already in Hess Hall. I'll suggest they go over her notes with a fine toothed comb."

"That's the best we can do, I suppose," Cortland responded. "Better to have you doing the combing, however."

"If they'll let me, I will. But the time involved will be ... well, major."

"They'll let you. If I know the CDC and the media, you'll not have time for anything normal anyway."

He muttered as he said, "Probably. Listen, I'm sorry I didn't do a more thorough job before the storm broke."

"Don't apologize, Bill. I'm just hoping they'll let us here at UT work in parallel with them. I'm going to stress that today in the meeting. As well as possible, we should keep on with what we've been doing."

"I certainly agree, Virginia. And I'm at your disposal. What's your thinking about Bea's role?"

It was Cortland's turn to hesitate. "If she did the unthinkable, Bill, it would have had to be in her laboratory. Is that the way you understand it?"

"Absolutely. The equipment to do gene spicing, electronic field patterns, not to mention the so-called standard things, is rare anywhere, but we have the best of it, as you know. And it's all within steps of Bea's lab. That's where she'd do it."

"Would there be traces?"

"Probably, but they'd be hard to find. Never underestimate her, Virginia."

"Oh, I don't."

"On the other hand, even if she is guilty," he said, "her days of unhindered lab work are over. The CDC will be everywhere, interviewing everyone. And if even a whiff of suspicion takes place, the law will soon follow."

"Yes, Bill. That leads me to another question. Should we leak any of this, say to the FBI? If there's a crime committed, they should be informed."

Charles was mulling over scenarios as he answered. "I'm worried that if she isn't guilty - and we certainly don't know she is! - then the incredible mound of ... of fecal matter we'll find ourselves in, from the media and everyone else, will drown any science or any hope for a rational future."

"Yes, I can see that," Cortland said, "but if the virus spreads, what do we do?"

He blew out an audible breath. "We stay out of the way and let the CDC have it. That's all we can do, Virginia. They won't have it any other way."

"So, it's really out of our hands already, you say?"

"Except for what we can do as researchers, assuming they let us alone except for daily briefings, or whatever."

"Hmm, I suspect you're exactly right," she admitted, sounding sorry to be doing so. "And I think maybe we should not cast any suspicion on our Miss de Winter just yet. It'll be up to you, Bill, to find out if she's up to hanky panky. Hate to be so direct, but you know I'm right, don't you?"

"I do, Virginia, but I'll need you for a sanity check."

"I can do that."

"Do you mind calling me again after your meeting?"

"Will do. Worse, Bill, I'm going to ask them to include you on the official team. They'll snap up the opportunity. Does that mean our friendship has now ended?" There was at least a touch of their usual repartee in her voice.

"Probably," he said, sounding friendly in doing so. "Listen, thanks for the call."

"Thank you, Bill. Talk to you soon."

—

Mike Baylor sat at the desk in the mouse lab typing entrees into the computer. The door was open into the back area where the mice were kept, allowing a trace of distinctive rodent odor to creep out. It was something, however, the young man didn't notice, having long since gotten used to the smell. He heard someone over his shoulder and turned. Mike recognized Dr. William Charles, well aware he was Bea's major professor.

"Hello, Dr. Charles," he said and got to his feet. "Can I help you with something?"

"Hello, Mike," came the parallel greeting. "No mice for me today, thanks. But I'd like to speak with you a few minutes, if you aren't too busy."

If Mike was put on guard by the request he didn't show it. "Sure," he responded with a smile. "Not a lot to talk about with the mice. Have lots of time."

Charles came around the counter and entered the little area, aiming toward the only other available chair. "Thanks, Mike," he said, affably, then sat down.

The student closed down the files he was working with and turned to face the professor. "I read and heard the news, Dr. Charles," he said. "Quite a to do, isn't it?"

"Quite," Charles nodded. "Mike," he continued, "have you been contacted yet by someone from the CDC?"

Mike's brow furrowed. "No, I haven't."

"It'll happen soon, I'm sorry." Charles examined the pleasant, richly animated face. "They'll want to do another series of studies on your blood, urine, and maybe even an MRI on your brain."

Mike sighed. "Not surprised, sir. Expected it actually. Bea told me it would happen."

"Have you seen her today?" Charles asked, as casually as possible.

"No, I haven't. Figured she'd be in a tizzy over the CDC."

"They'll be in her laboratory, maybe as we speak," the professor nodded. "I saw her there last night, getting ready for their arrival."

"Sounds like Bea," Mike answered. There was a distinct tinge of pride in his comment.

"Doesn't it?" Charles paused a moment before continuing, then said, "Mike, has Bea talked to you much about this virus? Since you were with her in Oak Ridge I supposed you were somewhat up to date on things."

"I did ask her about it," the student nodded. "Apparently it only has affected guys, so far."

Charles nodded. "Apparently so. Did she talk about it in any detail?"

Mike sensed the peculiarity of the question, since Dr. Charles was a well known scientist and would certainly know virtually everything about his student's work. But he answered ingenuously, "Not really. I'm not sharp enough to follow the details, and Bea knows it. She kept it at my level." He tacked on a self deprecating smile.

"Do you mind if I ask if you and she are close?" Charles said.

Mike blew out a breath. "Bea isn't really very close to anyone," he said. "She's really ... well, there's something about her, you know."

"There certainly is," the professor agreed. "So you and she haven't dated or anything?"

"I wish," Mike said honestly. "I don't mind sayin' I really like her. She's ... but she's always living somewhere else. In some different world that she's completely in charge of."

Charles let that interesting comment sink in as he said, "Is it her intelligence that attracts you, Mike?"

The young man didn't immediately respond. When he did it was something of a surprise to the questioner. "No, that's not it. Not that I don't know she's incredibly smart. It's ... you probably really know her better than I do, Dr. Charles, but ... and maybe you've seen it, but she's so amazingly determined. She's not pussy footin' around with life. She ... I really like that!" He seemed to be struggling, all of a sudden, with emotional control. "She's one of a kind. Can't help being attracted to her? Does that make sense?"

William Charles was touched by the response, and thoroughly impressed. He put a hand out on Mike's upper arm. "It makes sense to me," he said quietly. "I want you to know how much I appreciate what you did the other day, when Bea was attacked."

Mike came out of his reverie. "I was lucky to be there to help. It was ... the idea of anyone hurting Bea is so ... I don't like to even think about it. Just did what anybody would have done, you know. She ... " He looked directly at Dr. Charles as he continued, "She's handling the whole thing better than I am. Like this virus thing, too." He shook his head in expressed amazement at Bea de Winter.

"She's remarkable in many ways," Charles said. "And has put in a lot of effort on the virus problem."

"Bea said she was just tryin' to do her part. She also said I was doin' my part, too, but didn't tell me what it was." Mike grinned.

"Doing her part, is she?" Charles cocked his head pleasantly. "Did she say anything about the virus only affecting males?"

"Only that it did. Explained that we were genetically ... well, more vulnerable. Because we didn't have all the gene redundancy. Or something like that."

"Well that's true enough," Charles admitted. "If women were physically stronger we'd be in second place everywhere."

Mike shrugged. "Isn't that the truth, Dr. Charles?"

'29. Another Link in the Chain

THE CDC WAS THOROUGH, IF NOTHING ELSE. Their first priority, of course, had been those known to be infected by the virus. Virginia Cortland's team had already gotten them all into UT Hospital's isolation unit, and there the CDC's various experts were quickly swarming. The next level of priority was the group of people possibly exposed. These people included Bea de Winter, Mike Baylor, those on the response team that went to Oak Ridge, and - most importantly - the six thus-far-not-infected young men and women at "the party." What actually comprised exposure was not clear, however. If simple contact with someone infected became a definition, then already hundreds, if not thousands, of people would have been exposed. It was both impractical and impossible to find and seclude all these people, so the logical recourse was to do a repeat examination of those that could be clearly identified as possibly exposed. This meant that Melissa Thomas, Maria Santos, and others from the party would be given special study. But it also meant that Bea and Mike, Virginia Cortland herself, and Mrs. Rick Forrest) would also be examined in some additional detail.

These CDC responses were certainly not unexpected by Bea. She had steeled herself to the necessity. Further, she knew that any hope she had of getting any laboratory work done was dim, at best, for several weeks, maybe longer. She had sensed a certain suspicion from both Dr. Cortland and Dr. Charles, but fought back any feelings of paranoia. There was, in her awareness, no tangible evidence that she had anything to do with the virus except to discover its existence. But, whatever pall of suspicion cast over her, the student had been very careful to make sure nothing of her personal virus project would be visible to the investigators in her campus laboratory. No one would pry into her personal files at the dormitory without a warrant associated with some evidence of foul play. And there was no such evidence, as far as she could thus far determine.

It was after three in the afternoon before Bea completed the requested round of tests at UT Hospital. And, as far as she knew, there were officials still in her laboratory over at the university. Before leaving the complex, she got a request from Dr. Cortland to drop by her office. Thus it was that Bea knocked on the office door in the wing next to the isolation wards, was asked to come in, and discovered that Professor Charles was also there, the two already seated. Bea took the other available chair and sat down.

Charles smiled at his student and asked, "So, have you been probed and poked enough today, Bea?"

"I would say so, sir," she replied pleasantly, nodding also to Virginia Cortland.

Cortland said, "Thanks for dropping by, Bea. We thought we'd pick each other's brains awhile. We'll certainly have time, given the interruption of everyone's routine."

Bea said, "Yes. I just hope we'll be able to get back to work as soon as possible."

Charles plunged them directly into the planned discussion. He said, looking at Bea, "Dr. Cortland and I were talking about the viral action on the brain. We wanted to get your thoughts on it."

Bea seemed more petite than ever in this setting. Cortland was a middle aged woman who'd grown naturally more round and grandmotherly year by year, and Charles was a man of average build and height. Both, therefore, were much larger than the student in their midst. Bea considered the question a moment before responding.

"It's quite specific, Dr. Charles. Electrical pathways in certain areas of the cerebral cortex are interrupted. The virus makes proteins and other structures - we don't know how many yet - that distort the field contours. I wrote a summary and sent it ..."

Charles nodded as he interrupted. "I realize you sent it to me, Bea. And I apologize for not being more involved. But, yes, I saw the writeup this morning. And I promise (he looked over at Cortland as he said this) to give this situation all my attention from now on. But what we're looking for, Bea, is less what the effects are but more how the virus achieves them. Both Dr. Cortland and I had expected the virus to penetrate neurons or other structures in the electrical pathways to effect the disruptions."

"I presume you mean," Bea said, "the normal mechanism, where the virus takes over the cell for purposes of its self replication?"

"Yes," Charles said.

Cortland asked, "I admit to being less than up to date on biophysical processes, Bea, but do you have an idea of what this virus does – in terms I might understand?" She smiled graciously.

Bea wasn't about to be charmed into saying too much. She said, "The mechanism isn't clear, Dr. Cortland. But I have seen that the virus doesn't infect or destroy the neurotransmitter links. They continue to work. Or more precisely, they continue to be able to work, but the conditions for their firing are no longer correct."

Charles, scratching his head, added, "So the proteins and other structures released are changing the electronic fields around the neuro-transmission zones? That makes sense." He nodded, as if to himself. "But where is the virus getting nourishment, Bea? Where is it replicating?"

"My guess," the girl said, speaking more slowly than usual, "is in the neuroglia. It is the most logical place. There are so many more of them than any other cell type. When we get a chance to get back into the lab, I hope we can look specifically at that."

Eyes squinting as he thought, Bea's professor asked, "Have you seen any evidence of infected or killed neuroglial cells?"

"Evidence, yes," Bea nodded. "No proof yet. But that's my take on it."

"So," Cortland interrupted, "are you two saying that the virus grows or replicates in the neuroglia then does its damage in the cerebrospinal fluid?"

Bea looked at her professor, waiting for him to respond. He did. "Virginia, that would make sense. Proteins or whatever - something with an asymmetric electronic field - released into the region could cause distortions of charge that disrupt or misfire the somatic and dendritic circuits."

Cortland nodded. "Have either of you talked to the CDC people about this?"

Charles said, "In general terms, I did. But I read Bea's recent analysis only this morning. I'll get with Jeff Stanton soon. Will meet him for lunch today." He spoke of one of the major CDC team members, an immunologist from the Atlanta office.

Cortland said, "That's a good ..." Then her cell phone rang. The physician-scientist rescued it from her purse - there beside the chair - and answered. "Cortland."

There was a pause in the room. Bea and Professor Charles waited, watching the other face. The phone conversation was mostly one sided, Cortland nodding and saying, "I see," several times. Then she said, "Thank you," and hung up.

"Important?" Charles asked her.

Virginia Cortland let out a sigh. She suddenly seemed a little older. "Yes. Unfortunately. It seems we have another victim."

Bea's eyes widened but she restrained herself from comment. Charles, however, said, "One of the boys from the party?"

"Actually no." Cortland leaned down and wrote something on a note pad, apparently to make sure she didn't forget it. "It *is* a young man, from UT, but not from our famous party. His name is Letherage. Simon Letherage. Do you happen to know him, Bea?"

Bea shook her head. "No, doctor. But I suppose he must know some of the others infected or exposed."

"We can't say yet," Cortland said. "He was just admitted. Here. His apartment mate brought him in."

"Symptoms?" Charles asked.

"Serious. Like Mr. Pendergast, or so they think. They've just gotten him in. About ten minutes ago."

"I can talk to Melissa," Bea said. "She may know who this Letherage is."

"We'll find out," Charles said.

Cortland said, "Miss Thomas, I believe, is still here at the hospital. Maybe it would be a good idea, Bea, if you spoke with her. I'll find out where she is."

"I'll be glad to," Bea said. Her mind was racing. Who could have passed it on to this fellow? One of the four girls, probably. Melissa again? Bea wouldn't put it past her, but thought maybe not, this time.

—

Melissa Thomas sat in a waiting area of the cardiac wing of the UT Hospital. She was there because the isolation wing and others nearby were full of activity at the moment and had no room or schedule time for her. The young woman had just completed a third battery of examinations, including an MRI and CT scan of the brain. She was wearing a hospital gown and robe, with fuzzy slippers from home on her feet. Bea saw her at a distance and sensed a more subdued Melissa as she approached.

"Hello, Melissa."

Melissa had a paperback book in hand, reading. She looked up. "Oh hi, Bea!" There followed a genuine smile, but the pretty face didn't light up in its usual bright way.

"Is that a good book?" Bea asked, and sat down beside her.

Melissa, surprising the smaller student, leaned over and gave her a hug, then a kiss on the cheek. "Not so good, really, but ... it's something to do."

Bea saw that the book was some kind of romance novel and made no further comment about it. Instead, she asked, "Are they done with you for awhile, I hope?"

"One more thing." Melissa laid down the book. "Some kind of sample they're taking."

"Spinal fluid, I suspect."

"That's it. I hope it won't hurt."

"They'll be careful," Bea assured her, then got quickly to the point. "Listen, Melissa, there's been another virus victim, just brought here today."

"Oh?" Melissa looked suddenly very sad. Something of her own involvement in this unfortunate set of events had sunk in and constantly disturbed her.

"A student named Simon Letherage. Do you know him?"

Melissa closed her eyes. "I ... yes, I know him, but ... listen Bea, I never slept with him. I wouldn't lie about that!"

Bea looked away for a couple of seconds. She couldn't make herself be totally analytical about her dorm mate. There was no way to dismiss her feelings as unimportant. Quietly, Bea continued, saying, "Tell me how you know Simon Letherage. I'm no judge. And, if you don't want me to use your name about something, I'll try not to."

Melissa's eyes had formed a few tears, which she set about to wipe with tissue from a nearby box. "It's ... actually it's Maria," she said, as if that explained everything. Then, realizing it didn't, she continued. "Simon is ... he's pretty cool and Maria always liked him. She ... and I both saw him - Simon - oh, I don't know, maybe two or three days after the party. We were over at the Spot, and I think Maria had maybe had a few too many - that kind of a thing - and he came in - Simon did - with Jack. She told me - Maria did - that she wanted to, you know, do something with Simon. So I ... sort of kept Jack busy - talking, you know - and Maria went off in Simon's car."

"Did she have sex with him?" Bea wanted to get to the bottom line.

"Prob'ly," Melissa nodded. "I started to ask her about it once, but ..."

"And you're confident she had sex with Simon Letherage."

Melissa closed her eyes and nodded.

"Okay," Bea said, with a nod. "I'm sorry to nag at you about it, but it is important, don't you see?"

Melissa nodded morosely. "I know it is. It's so ... I'm such a slut! Don't think I don't know it. I can't blame anybody for ... for staying away from me."

"Don't be so hard on yourself."

Melissa looked about to cry again. "Wish more people were like you."

"We're all unique, Melissa," Bea said, sounding suddenly very philosophical. "But listen, now that you understand the real situation better, you need to think about everybody you knew at the party. Okay? If you know of any other ... uh, sex going on, or possible sex, you need to tell us. Okay?"

"Okay."

"This is really important."

"Is it? I don't think I really understand why. Not exactly. I didn't ... do it with Jack and he got sick. I don't think Maria did, either. I think she'd have told me, or ... or somebody. Or the other girls - they hardly knew him. So ... so why isn't it just something at the party?"

"Because you're a carrier, Melissa. We explained that. Or tried to."

"But, are we all ... all the girls there, are we all carriers?"

"Probably," Bea replied, a little too firmly.

"Oh, shit, shit, shit!" Melissa's eyes were red and she squinted through them. "So ... so this thing - this virus thing - it's ... I don't see how it could stop. It'll just keep getting worse! Bea, you know ... or maybe you don't, I don't know ... but people don't stop ... people don't stop fucking."

Bea nodded, sighing a little. "I think that sums it up perfectly, Melissa. Whether the virus is affecting the people it ought to or not, it's on its way. We have to face that."

"What?" Melissa looked confused. "What do you mean, 'people it ought to'?"

"Never mind, I shouldn't have said that." Bea patted her friend's shoulder. "Look, thanks for telling me about Maria and Simon."

"She's going to hate me like everybody else does anyway. Or maybe she already does." Melissa's eyes were shining and enlarged by the suspended tears. "Don't you hate me, Bea, please."

"I won't, Melissa. You can depend on that."

"Thanks a lot, really!" With that, Melissa hugged Bea to her again. The hug recipient felt heavy trembling vibrate through her. Thus it was that Bea's eyes closed in a brief surge of suppressed guilt. It took her several seconds to purge it from her system.

30. Revelation

BEA WAS SITTING IN HER PAJAMAS AT THE LAPTOP in her dorm room. It was after eight. The grad student's concentration was not what she wanted it to be. So much had happened so quickly. She felt a strange remoteness from what she was doing. How unlike herself. It was like working on automatic pilot. Mixed messages were passing back and forth through her thoughts. She stood up and went to her mirror.

"Magdalene," she muttered, barely audibly, "what's going on with you?"

"I'm just fine," said her other voice, almost angrily. "You know full well where the problem is!"

Bea sighed and looked intently at herself for a long time. She seemed to be taking in something she saw in her own eyes. Finally, she spoke again. There was a gritty but sad determination in her words. "Magdalene, it's time for you to go away!"

The silence in the room was palpable.

After standing unmoving long enough to take ten or twelve deep breaths, Bea went over to rummage around for a crossword puzzle to work on. Finding one, she fixed herself a glass of peach juice from a can she had chilling in the refrigerator, then dropped into her most comfortable chair. Having time on her hands was difficult duty for Bea de Winter. Then the phone rang.

"Hello."

"Hi Bea, it's Mike. How're you?"

Bea caught her breath. It was good to hear from him, though she'd made herself refrain from calling.

"Okay."

"So, what's goin' on? Are you busy doing something genius-like?" The tone was the typical Mike Baylor friendly.

"Hardly, Mike. How are you? Have they finished all the tests with you?"

"They have. And I guess no news is good news. Nobody told me anything."

"The CDC is having to come up to speed, I suppose," Bea said.

"You interested in a cup of coffee this evening, Bea?"

The pajama-clad girl expelled a breath. "I'm already ready for bed," she replied.

"Oops, sorry! I had just thought ..."

"But give me half an hour, okay, then meet me downstairs."

"Deal!" Mike sounded delighted.

Bea had come to the decision suddenly. But she knew it was what she had to do. She closed her eyes, then opened them again. "Then I'll see you in half a hour."

Mike, as usual, was right on time, pulling up as Bea exited the dorm entrance. He didn't get out to let her in - that would have been much too overt for Bea - but leaned over to push the passenger side door out for her. She slid in, gave him a pleasant look - though short of a smile - and buckled the seat belt before speaking.

"Thanks for coming over to get me."

"My pleasure. You know that, Bea."

"Let's go to the Sunspot, okay?"

"Sure."

They drove over in what might have been an uncomfortable silence for Mike some weeks earlier. But, with Bea, he had gotten used to long periods of quiet. It was her way, and he understood it now. They found a parking place, walked a short distance, and entered. A young waitress met them and escorted them to one of two or three tables available. The place was still busy but not completely packed.

Settled facing each other in a booth, Mike ordered them some chips and salsa to go with the pair of coffees. When the waitress went away with the order, he said, "Lot happening, isn't there?"

She nodded. "Mike, let me ask you something. Do you mind? It's a little personal."

He was clearly surprised at the question, but said, "Sure, that's okay."

"If you could make the world over into anything you wanted, what would you choose?"

The dark, bright-eyed face turned suddenly thoughtful. He rubbed his chin and let out a "Whew!" before saying, "That's quite a question, Bea. Let me think a minute."

Bea gave him a smile. She may not have known what impact her smiles had, but it nonetheless warmed him from head to toes. There could have been no stronger encouragement. Mike glanced to see the waitress returning with coffee. They both waited patiently as she poured, then left.

Finally, he spoke. "I don't think I'm the right guy to make a choice like that, Bea. Not smart enough."

Bea smiled again. "It's a game, Mike. You have to answer, okay? What would you choose?"

"Okay, let's see. Well, I'd sure like to get rid of crime and poverty, for starters."

"Fair enough. And how would you go about doing that?"

"Get rid of crime and poverty?"

"Yes."

"I suppose I'd start with education."

Bea nodded. "Go on."

"Wow, you're trying to make me think, Bea. Remember, I'm not into deep thinkin'. It hurts too much." He put his hand symbolically on his forehead. "If we could get almost everyone educated then maybe most people would have enough skills to get a reasonable job. But maybe more important, maybe we'd be more generous with poor people who are that way because of something they couldn't help. That kind of thing."

"Then you're saying that more education on the average improves the economic situation, with fewer poor or forgotten people, therefore less crime?"

"You said it a lot better than I could." He smiled back.

"So you think education, in effect, makes people less likely to abuse or hurt other people?"

"I think so," he nodded. "Maybe not because we are any better, really, but because we have more to lose."

"Interesting, Mike. Thank you."

"You're welcome, I guess. It's your turn, now."

"My turn?" Bea took a long sip of coffee.

"To say what you would choose to make the world like."

Bea eyed him carefully, but without intensity. "I'd fight cruelty at its roots," she said.

"Its roots? We all have those roots growin' in us," Mike observed.

"Even you, Mike?"

"Me 'specially, Bea."

"I can't see you as a cruel person," she said, shaking her head for emphasis.

"You just see the good, Bea. I'm ... well, I have to make myself count to ten a lot to keep from doing something stupid. And a lot of times that doesn't work and I still do it."

"You're underrating yourself like always." Another drink. She was watching him be embarrassed.

"How can you keep people from being mean, Bea? It just sometimes happens. Where are these roots you're talkin' about?"

"In your genes."

"My genes, huh? I thought you said you couldn't see me as a mean person."

"You have control of your genes. Not all men do."

"We talked about this before," he nodded. "Guys cause all the trouble, right?"

"Right."

"And women try to find non-violent ways out." There was no sarcasm in his voice.

"Something like that."

"So the genes are the roots. Is that what you mean?"

"Exactly."

"And, in your new world," he continued, with an accompanying smile, "the genes will be fixed. No cruelty."

Bea gave him another warm look, verging on a smile, as she drank the last of her coffee. "I wish I knew how to fix the genes, as you put it."

"Well, as you say, it's a game. You have to tell how to fix them."

"Mike, you got me there." And she smiled again, for one glowing moment, then went immediately somber. "I don't know how to fix them."

"Not even any ideas?"

"Would I bore you if I talked about it a little? I mean, not like in the game. You won the game."

"I could never win a game with you, Bea."

"You did. But, I'd like to talk about it. About "fixing" genes. Do you mind?"

"No, of course not. It's ..." He looked at her.

"It's something I've thought about a long time," she said, "but have never shared it with anybody before." Bea sounded almost vulnerable as she spoke. It was very touching to him.

"You sure I'm ... well, the right person to tell?"

"Quite sure, as a matter of fact." She looked at her empty cup. "Do you drink wine?"

"Wine?" He was openly surprised. "I ... sure, sometimes."

"Let's order wine then."

"Damn," he muttered. "But I guess you're legal now, right?" Then he grinned.

"Right."

The waitress didn't actually have to be signaled. She was bringing their chips and salsa and the coffee pot. Bea ordered two glasses of wine, dug out her student ID, and handed it over.

The waitress smiled oddly, and left to get the wine.

Mike said, as the server left, "I'm not askin' why you're so sure about me. Shouldn't question good luck, I say. But I can't help feeling honored."

"I've not been very honest with you, Mike," she said, shifting directions unexpectedly. "I intend to remedy that tonight, if you'll let me."

Mike showed a little concern in his face, not sure where she was going. "Okay," he said simply.

"Let's wait for the wine, then, if you don't mind."

"Sure."

The wait was only a couple of minutes. The waitress returned with two glasses of Chardonnay. Bea took hers with more confidence than she felt, lifted it, and said, "To truth and friendship."

Mike nodded, watched the waitress walk away, then raised his glass. "To truth and friendship. Can't beat those two." Then he smiled.

"A few years ago," she said, launching directly into what she wanted to say, "I thought about what it would be like to change human genes. Especially male genes."

"This is because of our evolution, like you said before?"

"Right. Have you heard about evolutionary learning, Mike?"

"Don't think so."

"Well, the way our genes were programmed, during evolution, was that various changes occurred, usually randomly from mutations, for example, and the results of the change were tried out in real life, so to speak. The beneficial changes helped survival and eventually became encoded in the genes. This kept going on for a very long time. Eventually, we arrived at where we are today, but the route we took was, in a certain way, a random one. The result was determined – in most ways – more by the environment than the route."

"I can see that," he nodded.

"Well, as it turns out, with modern computational power and with careful programming, it's possible to simulate a lot of what happened randomly in nature. And, in a computer simulation, you have the advantage of deciding what the answer to the question is ahead of time."

Mike wrinkled his nose at her. "You'll have to explain that a little more." He tapped his forehead again. "Pretty thick bone here over the frontal lobe."

Bea explained. "In nature, whatever we are like had to contribute to survival of primitive tribes. That's what we were living in for thousands of generations, as we evolved from one kind of primate to another. But in an imagined nature –

programmed into a computer - we would evolve into different kinds of creatures if nature were different. Do you see?"

"I think so." He sat down his wine glass, picked up a chip then held it for a moment, munching it tiny bit by bit. "As you said before, we became killers - we males - because it helped us survive. And you females - being sharper - got better at compromising and working together, that sort of thing."

"Approximately, yes." Bea's eyes were focused now on something far away. They returned to normal suddenly as she took another sip of wine. "Nature today is, in some important ways, quite different than the nature we evolved to survive in."

Again he nodded. "As you said before."

"Yes. And our behavior, especially when it comes to violence, hasn't had time to change its genetic basis. Nor is it clear that we, as a species, will be able to make such an evolutionary step again, in the random manner of natural selection."

"Why do you say that?"

"Because we live in such a fragile equilibrium today. All over the world there are small explosions of violence going on all the time. Any small genetic change - imposed randomly - would be as likely to take us toward more instability. More violence. And even if several small improvements occurred randomly, a single random step in the wrong direction might still introduce enough instability to induce catastrophe. Add to that our growing technical abilities to do more and more damage when we lose control."

"You're saying we won't evolve out of our situation?"

"Right. We won't. It's up to us to step in and move ourselves in the right direction. But the more I thought about that the more I realized how hopeless such an effort would be."

"You don't think we can figure out what genetic changes need to be made?"

"That's right. Because nature imposed our natures through a set of interrelated, random genetic changes. When we modify a single gene we may - are likely to, actually - modify thousands of different things about ourselves. And to move us away from much of our violent past would require action on a lot of genes. Yes, we can try to set up an imagined reality and try to let random processes move us toward it genetically - by these learning algorithms I mentioned - but we won't get it right. The odds are enormously against us, both in coming up with a finite number of simulation parameters that could make any sense whatsoever - in other words, in any realistic correlation with some possible future reality - and in finding a random route to this supposed future that could allow us to remain sociologically stable long enough for it to take effect."

"Wow," Mike muttered. "Unfortunately, I followed your logic, Bea. Sounds like we're better off not tampering with our genes - at least when it comes to behavioral traits."

Bea looked at him a few seconds, idly rubbing a finger along the rim of her wine glass. Her other hand lay flat on the table beside it. "So, I decided we couldn't reprogram ourselves safely. Or at least not quickly. We would have to hope that civilization remained more or less intact for a long time while we were trying very small things. You can imagine that I was pretty depressed about it."

"I can see that. But, Bea, we all have to work on this. No one expects you, by yourself, to get it solved for us. Not that you wouldn't be the best one to try it." He put a hand out to cover hers a moment. She didn't resist, but did look away. After about fifteen seconds Mike lifted up his hand and picked up his glass.

"But Mike, it finally dawned on me." Her eyes went back to his. "Tell me, what is a very characteristic and necessary aspect of all species?"

"The same genes, right?"

"Right. And wrong." Bea smiled. Mike felt like they'd turned on extra lights in the Sunspot.

She continued, "In our human species we all have the same genes - almost. It's those differences, of course, that allow us to do genetic typing, to find out who a person is kin to, that sort of thing.

"Okay."

"And since our genes vary a little from person to person, our genetic traits also vary a little from person to person." Bea touched her upper lip for a moment with her tongue, then took a sip of wine. "Finally I realized that some human beings were naturally more stable and less violent than other human beings."

"You're saying that females are less violent than males."

"Yes, but some males are less violent than other males. Genetically."

"I guess I believe that. But what about learned behavior? Isn't that just as important, where violence is concerned anyway?"

"In some ways, yes. When you mentioned education being the way to make your ideal world it made sense, in that context. The best way to keep our world civilized is to give everybody a maximum stake in keeping us safe. That does come through education and economic improvement for more and more people. But it's not likely to really solve the problem, in my view."

"Why not?"

"Because we haven't changed our average genetic makeup. There's always someone or some group that can disrupt the balance because of their primitive traits rising to the surface."

"Like, for example, the Nazis or some such group?"

"Yes, you remember the Nazis arose primarily because of depressed economic conditions, but in a culture that was perhaps the most educated in the world."

He nodded.

She continued, eyes brilliant with excitement. "We are inevitably going to have ups and downs economically. Maybe through resource allocation problems, mismanagement – whether intentional or not – natural disasters, whatever. During economic downturns we're especially vulnerable – like the Germans were in the 1930s. It's basically unrealistic to believe we can avoid large scale violence on and on into the future. The world hasn't avoided it up to now, after all. And the stakes get higher and higher. Do you understand, Mike?"

"All too well." He gave her a wan smile, a little awed at the intensity of her tone.

Bea was looking at him and through him at the same time. "Statistical variations among genes give us hope," she said. "And the most important thing we can do to insure a better future for our species is to emphasize variations that are more pacifistic from those that are more violent. We can't hope to be able to figure out soon what detail changes we have to make, but we don't have to. Mother Nature has already made them, in those less violent members of the statistical distribution."

"So," Mike said, nodding, "if we could talk the least violent of us out of reproducing we'd be heading in the right direction?"

"Exactly. But we know we can't do that. Part of nature's programming has been to make it pretty successful for violent males to reproduce. That's why they are still among us."

Mike sighed. "You're not advocating laws based on genetic typing, that sort of thing? Laws preventing violent people from having children, or maybe requiring sterilization?"

Bea shook her head. "Like the old eugenics arguments? No. Not that I can't see their point. But, they were trying to infer genetic distributions from race, very different from reality. No, we can't force compliance of this sort. For a long time it seemed to me that we were at a practical dead end."

"So, what's the answer, Bea?" He and she had both forgotten the chips and salsa, almost completely untouched so far.

"We can't do anything much about our situation unless we can identify specific gene-induced traits by some sort of physical or chemical quantity. We need a test parameter, a marker that corresponds to genetic predisposition for violence."

The young man's eyes widened. "Bea, are you ... are you talking about testosterone?"

"That's it."

Mike shook his head slightly, as if trying to clear something out of it. "High testosterone correlates with violent tendencies, doesn't it?"

"Very closely."

"But it doesn't follow that everyone with high testosterone is violent."

"No, it doesn't. That's what makes the problem as hard as it is."

"The problem?"

"The problem of knowing what exactly to do. There is the capability that some people have to overcome natural tendencies. And there must also be other chemical indicators that modify the testosterone effect."

"Well, you said it was a complicated problem." Mike cocked his chin a little to one side, looking at Bea a little oddly.

"Yes. I've been working on it steadily for nearly a year."

"Working on it? In what way?"

"That's why I agreed to get together tonight, Mike. I want to tell you."

The background noise of the restaurant seemed to recede into the walls. For Mike Baylor nothing was in his awareness at this moment except the girl that had mystified and fascinated him since first they'd met.

"You want to tell me something about ... about what, exactly?" He hadn't raised his voice and had not changed his respectful tone, but Bea could see he was very disturbed.

"I know this will upset you, Mike, but ... you are the finest person I know! Truly. And I have to tell you."

Bea de Winter was actually on the verge of tears. Mike felt a tightness in his own throat. He felt a distinct speeding up of his heart. "I'm not that fine, Bea, honestly. But ... but I am your friend. What do you want to tell me?"

She brought her glistening eyes to his. "The virus that we have been studying, and that you saw the effects of in Oak Ridge, that virus is something I ..." Bea closed her eyes. Tears ran down her cheeks. "I made it."

31. Advice

AT JUST AFTER EIGHT THE NEXT MORNING Bea's dorm room phone rang. She arose from her computer and went to answer it. There was a worried look on her pale face. She was guessing Mike was calling her. It had probably been a long night for him, as it had been for her.

"Bea, sorry to call so early."

"Hello, Dr. Charles," Relief quickly washed over her. "How are you, sir?"

"Bea, I'm pooped, if you must know. Been up most of the night."

"The virus work, I suppose," she said.

"Yes. I have a favor to ask of you, Bea."

"What is that, sir?"

"We need to be more efficient at testing for the new virus. Would you be willing to run a few samples? The lab here at UT Hospital hasn't gotten very good, yet, with your recipe. I'd hoped not to have to ask you, but ..."

Bea took a long breath. "I thought the CDC was handling all of that, Dr. Charles."

"Technically, yes. What do you say?"

"I'll be glad to help."

"Thank you so much."

"It would be easier, sir, to use my lab at UT. Is that possible?"

"I made the effort for you there, but I'm sorry, it's not," he answered. "The CDC can assemble what you need in one of their trailers over here at the hospital. Have you seen the entourage over here?"

"No, sir."

"Do you mind coming over and discussing the test right away, this morning?"

"I'll need transportation, sir."

"Dr. Cortland is on her way to your dorm now. We were counting on your support. She'll be there in about ten minutes, I'd say. Is that too soon?"

Bea looked at her mirror across the room. "No, I'll be downstairs in ten minutes."

"Excellent! Thank you so much, Bea."

After hanging up, Bea went to the mirror. She looked at her form a moment. But she said nothing to Magdalene, spoke no words at all. There was nothing more to say.

Right on time, the sedan pulled up and Bea, in her usual khakis and blue shirt, got in. They were nearly halfway to the hospital - the conversation having been nothing but polite comments to that point - before Cortland began speaking about things related to the virus.

"Bea," the driver said, looking over, "there are three new virus cases from Texas."

Bea was frankly surprised. "The same symptoms, Dr. Cortland?"

"Yes. We have blood samples coming to us. Bill - Dr. Charles - and I hoped you would test them. In the interest of time. But the CDC will pay you. I know it's an imposition on your work, but I'm sure your major professor will be understanding." She added a pleasant look.

"I'm happy to do it, doctor. Do you know more about these cases?"

"A little. I happened to be the one reachable by phone and took the call. The CDC lines were diverted to me because their people had gone home for the evening. The call came from Hillcrest Hospital in Waco. Three young men, students at Baylor - there in Waco."

"Hmm," Bea mused. She was trying to imagine the process of getting the virus a thousand miles west.

Cortland added, "The symptoms are very familiar ones to us. It must be the same bug."

Bea looked out the car window as she evaluated this piece of information. If this was her virus - and she had to assume that for the moment - someone from here in Tennessee would have had to take it to Texas. As far as she knew, the students at Melissa's party (as Bea thought of it) were all either in medical treatment or being observed at the UT Hospital. But the virus could have been transported by others they had contacted. Or by them before they knew about Reggie Pendergast or the other early victims. But she still remained uncertain about the transmission factors. Blood contact was certainly the most likely - or at least the most straightforward - but the aerosol process might continue under various potential scenarios. She cursed herself inwardly for not doing more work in that area. Then she forgave herself, knowing that the parameters associated with designing the virus did not allow for many options associated with the spread mechanism.

To Cortland she said, "Doctor, how do you think the virus could have gotten to Texas?"

"From previous contact, I suppose, with someone here who went to Texas for some reason. Or someone from Texas came here. Those are the obvious answers, of course, but there's also the possibility the virus had already gotten there - or here - from its origin. We may be looking at a disease agent that's been around awhile. Whatever the case, it is very disturbing. We have to be prepared for a major outbreak." Her eyes showed the seriousness of her points.

"Then we may have a number of cases soon," Bea said quietly.

"Yes we may." Cortland turned a corner then looked over at the student. "Bea, I have a confession to make to you."

"A confession?" Bea's brow furrowed.

"Yes. I confess to have had a little suspicion about you. And I passed on that suspicion to Dr. Charles."

"Something about the virus? Is that your meaning, doctor?"

"I wondered if you might have been responsible for it." The older woman turned her head forward again, concentrating on driving.

"For the virus?" Bea asked, trying not to sound too ignorant, though her heart rate ramped up nearly instantly. Cortland would have picked up on phony naïveté.

"Yes. But my suspicions seem to have been unfounded."

"Why would you have suspected me in this, Dr. Cortland?" Bea's voice did sound a little aggrieved, but in its usual iron control.

"Because of the comments I heard you had made during a presentation on women and our place in society."

Bea understood. "I see."

"I gathered you believe that we can only solve the problem of violence in the world by getting rid of men." The scientist-physician tacked on another smile.

Bea started to mention testosterone, but thought better of it. She said, "Not men, doctor, actually. It's male violence that is our major social problem, at least as I see it."

The older woman changed tack suddenly. "Could a virus like you've found be made, Bea? Bill didn't seem to think so."

Bea put both hands in her lap. "By forced mutations, if you knew what you wanted it to look like, yes."

"Forced mutations?"

"It's where you take a virus as a template and change it – usually its surface characteristics and of course in the RNA – by introduction of various tailoring chemicals, usually proteins."

"What about the genetic material?"

"You'd have to modify the genome. It would require sequencing the whole system of the template virus, but it can be done. Viruses are much simpler than other structures."

"So, could you have done this, Bea? Could you have made this virus we're dealing with?" Cortland's question came with stunning frankness.

Bea kept her face turned to look out. "If I could determine in advance the proper action of the modified virus, yes, doctor. Otherwise, it would be hit and miss, much like evolution would do it, and could take millions of tries or might never happen."

"I see." Cortland was crossing the Tennessee River, nearly to the hospital. "So it's possible in principle, but difficult in practice."

Bea turned to look at her. "Yes."

—

Mike Baylor entered the mouse lab by the back entrance and settled himself at the desk. His eyes showed lack of sleep, and his slightly shabby appearance was in marked contrast to his usual neat self. After making sure the mouse inventory was in order on the computer, he went back to the cages, checking the water and food. It had never been his job to feed and water the mice, but he'd always taken on the responsibility of seeing that biology students assigned the task had in fact performed it.

The mice were okay, except for a few water containers he filled. Then Mike went back to the computer and sat, looking at the phone. After awhile he picked it up and called Bea. It was a relief to him not to hear her directly, but to get her answering machine.

"Bea, it's Mike. We should talk some more, okay. Let me know when, will you? Bye."

Once again he stared at the phone, trying to think out his situation. He was mired in it. Mike got up and went to the counter where he'd first met Bea. How different his world had been then. All the way up to last night! He stood there a moment, as if waiting on someone who'd come to order mice. Then again he turned and again sat down at the computer desk. This was a quiet place. Rarely did more than a handful of students or faculty enter.

After a nearly motionless ten minutes, the young man took the cell phone off his belt and punched in a speed dial number - his number one. His eyes were closed when Aunt Jacie answered.

"That you, Mikey? You doin' okay, boy?"

"Not good, Aunt Jacie. I need some advice."

"Advice? What's this old woman gonna tell you, college boy? 'Spec you need to talk to a professor, don't cha think?"

"I need some wisdom, Auntie. Good Jacie wisdom."

"What's on your mind, boy?"

Aunt Jacie's accent wasn't strong, but it was distinct. Her vocal power, however, was weak. She'd never spoken loudly. In person, she could be very hard to understand unless you were very close to her when she spoke.

"You remember I told you about Bea?"

"Indeed so. The genius girl, right? The one you jumped in 'n saved?"

"She's done something terrible, Aunt Jacie."

"Don't say she's givin' up on you, boy."

"Not that, auntie. A lot worse than that."

"How can there be, Mikey? You can't fool me 'bout these things. Never heard you talk 'bout a girl that way before, ever."

"There can be," he said. "Yes, there can be." His eyes had formed tears.

"What's she done?"

"It's a little hard to tell you. Remember when we talked about Bea, about what she said about men and violence?"

"Yep. She's right there, and you know it, boy."

"Bea ... well ... ... well, maybe anyway, just fixed the problem."

"Good luck to 'er, boy!" Jacie laughed lightly. "Tell me somethin' reasonable, now."

"I mean it," he said. "I mean she thinks she fixed the problem. She's made a virus, Aunt Jacie. A virus that ... that infects males. Only males."

"She's *made* a virus?" The disbelief was dripping from the words.

"She has. I've seen what it does. And she told me. Prob'ly I'm the only one – except you, now – who knows. I don't know what to do about it. What should I do, auntie?"

Aunt Jacie was quiet for a few seconds. "Well, well, well," she muttered. "Say, I heard about this virus on the news. Mus' be. Guess you saw the news 'bout it?"

"Yes. The CDC is here in Knoxville."

"CDC?"

"Centers for Disease Control. They're the ones that're now doin' the investigation."

"They did sound worried. What does this virus do?" The motherly tone was still there, but a businesslike edge had been suddenly burnished onto it.

"It turns guys into ... well, like they have Alzheimer's. They're ... like gone."

"I heard that part. But what does it do?"

"Affects the brain. Turns stuff off up there. Bea told me something about how it works. Pretty ... complicated."

"An' she made the thing? Your genius girl, Bea? You're serious, ain't you, Michael Jamison Baylor?"

"Dead serious."

"Can this girl do such a thing? Tell me the truth here."

"If anyone could, Bea can. And she says she did it."

"An' you b'lieve 'er?"

"I have to," he answered. "What else can I do?"

There was sudden quiet. Mike could hear his aunt's breathing. The woman continued, finally, with, "An' you 'spec me to tell you what to do, do you?"

"Yes, ma'am."

"God alone could tell you a thing like that, son."

"I know," he muttered. "But ... well, God didn't answer me."

Aunt Jacie took a few seconds longer to think. "Tell me, what does your Miss Bea think this virus is gonna do? What's it for?"

Mike swallowed. Hearing what he was about to say had a ring of unreality to it, because it was so bizarre. "To get rid of males with lots of testosterone, auntie. That's the goal."

"Where, boy? There in Tennessee?"

"Everywhere, that's where."

"Come on, that won't happen, will it? How c'n that happen? Even AIDS didn't do that, am I right?"

"If nobody can stop the virus, it'll get us, auntie. Least I think so."

"Get us? You got too much testosterone, huh? Did your Bea tell you that?"

"She didn't say, but prob'ly."

"When's all this gonna happen? Tell me."

"Don't know," he said with a sigh. "It's already spread to some people around here, like you heard."

"How do they git it, these testosterone boys you're talkin' 'bout?"

"Sex, I guess. Maybe kissin'. Not really sure, auntie."

"Sex, huh?" The old woman seemed to be moving something around. "I'm sittin' down now," she said. "Sex, huh? Can't keep people from doin' it, boy. You know that."

"I know it."

"You haven't been messin' around with this Bea, have you?"

Mike actually made a laughing sound. It wasn't a real laugh, but it got the job done. "No way, auntie."

"Zero and null, right?"

"Zero and null. Bea's not ..." He stopped, not wanting to go farther with it.

"Tell me the truth here, boy," she continued, respecting his hesitation, "is this thing gonna really happen? Are testosterone carriers like you gonna get this thing? Everywhere?"

"I don't know, auntie. How could I know?"

"What's your Bea say?"

"She doesn't just say it like that, but she thinks it will happen. Eventually, I guess."

"Can't they jus' round up the folks with it and keep 'em away from everybody else?"

"I keep thinkin' that," he said. "I hope so. But I don't know."

Aunt Jacie was quiet a moment. He heard her breathing. "I 'pologize to you, boy. I kep' tryin' to think you're wrong about it. But you really do have a big problem. We all have, maybe."

"I can't talk Bea out of it, auntie. But even if I could, the virus is loose. Whatever that might mean."

"Why'd she really do it, son? Does she hate men, maybe? Bad things when she was little. Could that be it?"

Mike sighed. "Don't think so. But I don't really know. She says she did it to save us. To save human society. It sounds so ... so damn logical from her, but I know it's crazy, really."

"Is it, Mikey? You know it is, huh?"

"Killing millions, even billions of people has to be crazy, Aunt Jacie."

"So this thing kills 'em, huh?"

"It's killed one anyway. The others we've seen are ... like I said, they're gone. Same as dead in a way. Nothin' but shells. Or almost nothin'."

"Is it gonna kill you, son? Or make you gone. Is that what you're thinkin'?"

"I don't ... believe me when I say this, auntie. I don't know. But it might. Can't be sure how the thing spreads, really. If Bea's right, it ... it may very well get me."

"If she's right. Is she okay with killin' you, Mikey? Tell me."

"I hope she isn't."

"Is she? Tell me."

"No, I don't think she is. That's ... that's what's made her worry. And prob'ly why she told me."

"So she likes you?"

"Yes. But ... but I'm not sure what that means, for Bea."

"What's this testosterone thing you were sayin'? Tell me 'bout that agin."

"The virus - Bea says, and it makes sense since only men have gotten infected from it - the virus won't do whatever it does except when there's enough testosterone. She calls it 'free' testosterone."

"Free?"

"Loose in the blood, auntie."

"So ... listen here, is this right? If your testosterone was low enough, you'd be okay, huh. Tell me."

"I think so. But auntie, this whole thing is so crazy. I don't know what to think or do about it."

"An' you think I do?"

"I hope you do."

"Why didn't she make her virus lower men's testosterone instead? Wouldn't that 've been smarter?"

"I didn't ask."

"Why do you think? You're a smart boy."

"Because it wouldn't change the genes."

"Say what?"

"Aunt Jacie, we talked about genes, remember. If you crank down a guy's testosterone, his genes still have it in 'em to make his son's testosterone high. See?"

"I see, yep. So you wipe out the guys that are 'high-test' an' they won't have any kids."

"Or many anyway. I suppose the infected guys still have sperm. Don't know if Bea thought of that."

"Can't see many of 'em gittin' married, boy, kin you?"

Mike sighed. "What would you do, auntie, if you were me?"

"Guess I'd call me, like you did. It's a tough one, Mikey, a really tough one. What if Miss Bea is right? Did you think about that?"

"I did, yes. But there has to be a better answer than wipin' out so many people."

"Did you tell her that?"

"I told her. She said yes it was terrible to have to do it. But she had to."

"Goshen! That's ... that's I don't know what, boy!"

"I don't either."

"Listen, Mikey, this virus ... is there any other way to stop it, 'cep roundin' up the people an' keepin' them away from everybody else?"

"I don't know."

"Can you talk to anybody without causin' lots of trouble?"

"What's that mean, auntie?"

"You don't know enough, boy. That's the problem. Maybe this thing will go away on its own, as far as you know. Or maybe not, sure. Or maybe your Bea is ... has a little too big an imagination, an' thinks she's doin' somethin' she ain't. Or maybe somebody can cure the thing. These CD whatevers are on it, after all. Findin' a cure's purdy likely, I'd say. Maybe not too soon, but ... think about AIDS. It's not 'xactly cured but it didn't do everybody in like some people thought, did it? Tell me."

"Maybe," he admitted.

"So find out some more if you kin."

"So I shouldn't talk to anybody yet?"

"Didn't say that, boy. You have to talk to somebody, but it has to be the right somebody. Know what I'm sayin'? The wrong somebody could make a bad mess worse."

He nodded, then realized he had done that, voicelessly, and answered, "I know."

"Mikey," Aunt Jacie said, almost too quietly to hear, "what do you really know about your Miss Bea? Tell me the truth."

He swallowed before answering, "Not much, actually. She's ... she's pretty much on her own, you know. No parents or anybody she talks about that are friends or whatever."

"So she's maybe livin' in a real dream world, boy. But you know that."

"I know that. But she's so ... I wish you knew her. That's what I wish. She's good, in her way anyway, and acts like she really wants good things for me. And for the whole world, really. It's ... well, see why I'm not sure what to think."

"Son, I'm not sure what to think, either. But I know you, Mikey. You're as good as people git. When you figure what to do, go 'head and do it."

"Okay, Aunt Jacie," he said.

32. Looking Outward and Inward

VIRGINIA CORTLAND, BEFORE LEAVING THE HOSPITAL, was called to a telephone. She was told it was from Regan Jorgenson, who introduced himself as a vice president of Cable News Network.

"Dr. Cortland, CNN would like to record an interview with you this evening, if you'll permit."

"This relates to the virus outbreak, I presume," she answered.

"We understand you're one of the first to know about the virus, doctor. Is that correct?"

"I suppose so."

"May we speak with you there at the hospital, if that is convenient?" Mr. Jorgenson asked.

"Has this been cleared with the CDC?"

"We'd hoped you'd make those arrangements, doctor. Our plan is to offer you fifty thousand dollars for an exclusive. Would that be of interest to you, perhaps?"

"Wouldn't someone from the CDC be more appropriate for you?"

"No, Dr. Cortland. We're interested in the early history of the outbreak, and how it was discovered."

"If I get clearance to do so, I'll agree to the interview," she said. "But I suggest you also speak to Bea de Winter."

Jorgenson was taken a little by surprise. "I'm not certain who you mean, doctor."

"She's the student who isolated the virus, Mr. Jorgenson."

"A student? That is very interesting, indeed!" he admitted with an elevation in his tone. "Let me speak to my people. Where might we find her?"

"Here, as well. She's working with the blood samples."

"Do you think it might be possible to interview her as well as yourself?"

"I'll ask her major professor, if you like. He's a colleague of mine."

"You're speaking of Dr. William Charles, I suppose."

"Yes, have you spoken with him?"

"We've already interviewed him and a colleague, Dr. Sonja Masterson."

"I see. Perhaps I should hear that interview first."

"If you wish. It will be aired at eleven tonight. Or we can send you the recording."

Cortland said, "That would be kind of you, sir."

—

Mike met Bea just outside the analysis trailer. At first glance she was like she always was, in khakis and blue shirt. But as they approached he saw her face was tired and less resolute than usual. How he looked to her he didn't even want to guess.

"Hello, Mike," she said, hesitating and stopping a little closer to him than he expected. "Did you get your release? Your blood is clear."

"I got it," he said, trying to sound less confused and angry than he was.

"Good." A pause, then, "I'm grateful to you for driving me home." Her eyes had found his and transmitted something he couldn't quite fathom.

"It's no problem, really. Do you mind talkin' to me some more? I'm pretty smashed up, as I guess you can tell."

"We can talk if you wish. Or not if you wish. It's just nice to be with you, honestly."

They were well away from the trailer by this point. Mike's car was something of a hike around the hospital to a hastily prepared parking area on a formerly wild area next to the hospital grounds. "Why is it you like me, Bea?" he asked suddenly. "At least I think you like me, at least a little."

Bea, her usual half step ahead, stopped. She said, "How can I know exactly, Mike? You're ... well, you're the finest person I know. That's reason enough, but it's not the reason. It's a selfish thing. My feelings for you are ... I'm not good at saying such things, but I feel so much better about myself when I'm with you. It's so inwardly focused that I'm ashamed to say it, but it's the truth." She didn't smile, but her face, only barely discernible in the dim illumination, transmitted a look he sensed was not given to anyone else.

"Thanks, Bea," he said. "They worked you late tonight, didn't they? You're tired. Don't see how you can keep going."

"It wasn't all that late," she said. "I was late because of an interview, along with Dr. Cortland. I'm sorry to have made you wait longer than necessary."

"An interview?"

"With CNN."

"Pretty impressive. About the virus, I suppose."

"Yes." .

They had resumed walking "Were you tempted to tell the truth, Bea?"

She didn't answer for several steps. "No, I wasn't. Does that disturb you?"

"What do you think?"

"Sorry. I believe I understand your position, Mike. But I did what I thought was right."

"You still think so?"

"Yes."

"I was afraid of that. What did you talk about, during the interview?"

"I was introduced as the student who'd discovered the virus."

"Well that's right, isn't it?" he said, a little bitterly. "What did you say about it?"

"I spoke about its structure, that kind of thing. Dr. Cortland answered most questions."

"What's she like, anyway? Dr. Cortland."

"She's ... deceptively intelligent. She told me she had suspected me of constructing the virus."

Mike's attention perked up. "She suspected you? But she doesn't any more?"

"She says she doesn't."

"How about Dr. Charles? What does he feel about it?"

"I'm not certain. He's very difficult to read."

"So what will you do next, Bea?"

"I don't know."

The rest of the walk to the car was silent, except for crunching of shoes on freshly spread cinders. This time, Mike opened the door on Bea's side and held it for her. She slid in and let him close it, then waited until he came around and got in before she put on her seat belt.

A block or two into the drive she spoke again. "There are three cases in Texas, Mike."

He turned his head in response. "Your virus?"

"Probably. I need to find out how it got there."

"How could it have?"

"Through blood contact or possibly air borne and breathed in."

"Probably sex, though, huh?"

"Probably."

"That sex gets us guys in trouble, doesn't it?"

"I understand you're bitter, Mike. I truly wish there could have been another way."

"You ever think about sex, Bea? For yourself, I mean."

She looked straight ahead, not seeming to register his question for a while. Then she surprised him by moving a knee up and turning sideways, then reaching over to rest her right hand on his shoulder. "I never thought sex was something for me," she said quietly. "But I didn't understand much about feelings, either. In truth, I still don't. Maybe this organizing principle we talked about - or God, if you like - is making me pay for what I've done."

Mike put his left hand across to his right shoulder to cover hers. "It's not fair of me to ask you that. I'm sorry."

"No, it was completely fair. And I didn't answer you as honestly as you asked me. But I can't yet."

She resumed her former position, but if anything, seemed to be riding closer to Mike. They didn't speak again until reaching the dorm. Mike left the car running but got out and quickly came around to open her door. As she slid out and stood up, he stepped back, not noticing there were tears in her eyes. Bea, without warning, brought herself forward and put her arms around him, pulling herself to his solid chest. Her head was turned sideways against him as she said, "Thank you, Mike Baylor. Quit worrying about my feelings. Take your Aunt Jacie's advice." Then she released herself, stood on tiptoes and kissed him on the mouth. It was then he saw the tears.

"I'll call you soon," she said, and walked briskly into the dorm.

33. The Evening Before Revelation

THE YOUNG-LOOKING RESEARCHER WITH HER OFFICIAL badge made her way into the hospital building and straight to Melissa Thomas' room. She'd called ahead. Melissa was very happy to see her, something Bea couldn't quite understand, but received the hug with as much grace as she could muster.

Melissa's concern and confusion boiled over immediately into a rapid burst. "Bea, it's a madhouse, isn't it? I heard you were doing testing or something. What's going to happen? Any ideas? They haven't told us anything, you know. It's a fucking nightmare! How can they just keep us here anyway? My parents are so goddamned calm, did you know that! I'm still poison - probably, but they won't tell me anything! Bea, you have to know a lot more than we do. It's ..."

"Melissa, please sit down. We can talk. There's no hurry."

Melissa sat. She was wearing pale green hospital scrubs consisting of elastic waist oversized pants and a similarly too large button shirt with elbow length sleeves. With a badge and proper cap she could have been mistaken for a scrub nurse or orderly. The movement of the young woman's upper torso as she sat told Bea there was no brassiere under the shirt. At least she'd gotten comfortable. The mop of thick hair was mussy, as it often was, but only added a more natural allure to her pretty appearance.

"Bea, it's like a fucking jail here. Really. And those CDC people! God, there was some bitch woman in here a little while ago. They're always nosing around and being real asses."

"It's for your own protection, Melissa. But you knew that. Be patient." Bea had settled onto the only other chair in the room. Neither was especially comfortable.

"I keep hearing things, you know," Melissa continued. "Like people keep getting this ... this whatever thing. And they won't tell me whether I'm still ... you know, if I'm still a carrier or whatever."

Bea was close enough to touch the other's knee, and leaned forward to show a sympathy she actually felt. "I looked at a blood sample of yours this morning. Still no sign of the virus."

Melissa brightened a little, then darkened again. "That's the way it's always been."

"I know, but it's still good news." Bea added a thin but genuine smile.

Melissa leaned forward and took Bea's hand. "Thanks for trying to make me feel good. But you don't have to lie to me, okay?"

Bea returned the squeeze. "I'll try to convince the CDC to ease up on you a little. But as long as the virus keeps spreading they'll have you on a short leash. You're going to have to deal with that, Melissa. I'm sorry."

Melissa nodded bravely. "Hey, listen, you want some juice? I have a little frig - see? Mom brought it."

"Sure," Bea smiled. "That would be very nice."

The hostess bounded over, got out some orange juice and poured two hospital-issue tumblers full, and bought them back. Bea drank gratefully, knowing this would be her lunch.

"Melissa," Bea said, after the long drink, "have they told you there are three new cases in Texas?"

"I heard."

"I'm being a nag, I know. What about some of the other girls at the party? Could any of them have gone to Texas?"

Melissa shrugged, meaning she didn't know. "What are you going to do about it anyway? No one can ... well, treat this thing yet."

"Not yet, no."

"Can't they come up with a vaccine or something like that?" Melissa was back in the chair and nearly through with her juice.

"You can bet they'll try," Bea said.

"You think it can be done, huh?"

"Not likely. The virus is hard for the immune system to neutralize."

"Why's that? Why can't antibiotics or something like that kill it?"

Bea took the questions seriously, though she was aware that Melissa didn't really pretend to understand any of the science involved. "Antibiotics would have trouble doing it but might bind to the virus and make it slow going through the blood-brain barrier, but wouldn't stop it. The actual viral structure would be hard to crack, especially when it can reassemble later even if partially broken up."

"Huh?" Melissa grinned at her. "You don't expect me to know what you're saying, I hope."

"No, I was just thinking out loud."

"Being a nerd, as usual, huh? Bea, you are something else, you know that?"

Bea was still thinking. "This virus can hide in the marrow, like AIDS, for example. As long as the blood chemistry is adequate. And the precursors are even harder to identify. No, it'll be difficult to fight this one. And, since it is likely to mutate - not something I guess anything can be done about - a consistent immune response will be all the harder to develop."

Melissa had picked out a few words from the flow of mostly meaningless prose. "What's a precursor?" she asked.

Bea turned her attention back to the other person in the room, reminding herself she was being impolite and not a little bit arrogant. "Oh, a stage of development of the virus, actually. Just a detail."

"How about 'mutate'? What's that mean? I thought 'mutate' was something like ... well, like radiation could cause."

"It can, yes. A mutation is a change in the form of some living structure. In this case, the virus."

"Really? Is that bad or good?"

Bea ran a hand through her own short hair and looked at Melissa. "It's both, probably. It's bad because we can't be sure what the virus will do to the next person. It's good because if it keeps on changing the virus will ..." She stopped.

Melissa looked at her oddly, then smiled. "So?" Melissa said, sounding very cute indeed. "So, I don't understand a damn thing you're saying."

Bea felt a need to complete her thought. "So, the mutations so far haven't done much to the surface fields, but some eventually will. Down the road, and who knows how long – I'd guess several months to several years – mutations will end the virus's career."

"Bea, that sounds pretty hopeful, doesn't it?"

The was a pause while Bea finished her juice. "Hopeful is maybe the right word, Melissa. But if we can guess a doubling time of, say about a week, then more than ten to the fifteenth people would be affected in the next year."

"God damn, Bea! How many is that? It's more than there are of us."

"Right. But let's call the doubling time a month. It may be a better guess anyway. There'd be only around four thousand cases the first year, but in three years everyone who could get the disease would get it."

"So the mutation thing might be too late anyway?" Melissa scowled at the thought. "Bea, this is really scary! How can you be so ... so cool about it?"

"Nothing is that predictable, Melissa. The CDC or some group will find out more about the virus, and those infected will be isolated as much as possible. We really don't know what things will be like in, say, a year."

"I don't want to know, I'll tell you that! How about some more juice?"

"Thanks, no. I have to go actually. Thanks for the conversation." Bea smiled again. "You're really a very tough person, Melissa."

"Hell if I am. But it's great to see you, Bea. Come back, okay? It's as dull as ... it's like jail, really, or worse, a convent!"

As Bea left, she smiled at Melissa's assessment. For that young woman, a convent would, indeed, be the closest thing to hell.

–

It was from Maria Santos that Bea discovered the link to Texas. But someone from the CDC had beaten her to the information. While Bea was in the lab that morning all four girls from the party had been interviewed. Maria had told them – albeit reluctantly – of a long weekend trip to the Baylor Homecoming celebration. It had taken place the weekend after the party, and long before anyone had become ill. Like Melissa, she'd presumed the campus party link there in Knoxville was the only concern, and wasn't about to volunteer other, rather compromising, information. Where the virus had gone from there – in Texas – was anyone's guess, but it would be under investigation quickly enough. The first Texas blood samples had arrived that morning, and were undergoing general screening at the moment. She hoped to get at least one of them herself to do the virus testing on.

Bea worked until nearly midnight that evening. But even when she finally left the analysis trailer was still busy. One of the CDC technicians, a man in his thirties with a pleasant, though unreadable, demeanor, drove Bea to her dorm. Inside, she took the time to look at some of her simulation runs, set up other cases, and finally to settle down for a glass of peach juice. Sitting there drinking, she noticed her phone message light was on. She'd not gotten into the habit of checking it yet and was a little surprised to see it. The message was from Mike.

"Bea, I know you're gettin' in late probably. But give me a call. Whenever, okay? It's ... well, I need to talk to you."

A little quiver of alarm passed through the young woman. She wasn't sure what alarmed her, but she knew her feelings for Mike Baylor were genuine and good. She dialed his number slowly.

"Hello Mike, it's Bea. I'm so sorry to wake you up."

"Hi Bea," he said, sounding sleepy but reasonably alert. "I wasn't really asleep. Thanks for callin' me back."

"What's up?" she asked, trying to be casual without being flippant.

"Bea, I'm going to ... well, I have to tell somebody."

She held the phone to her ear and listened, but didn't speak immediately. When she did, it was in a slower pace than her usual use of words. "I guessed you would, Mike, and I honestly understand."

"Bea, I know you ... you are convinced you're doin' the right thing. I know that. And I can see your perspective. Honestly, I can. But ... but maybe if the right people know soon something can be done to stop this thing. You don't want that, I know, but ... I hope you won't hate me for it."

"I could never hate you, Mike." She spoke these words quickly and with absolute assurance. "And I knew when I told you that you would pass it on. It's your nature, actually. And it's a ... a wonderful, loving nature, Mike!" Her voice broke a little, despite her efforts to control it.

"I wanted to tell you first," he continued. "They're sure to ... to come after you. And I wanted to give you a chance to ... to do whatever you need to. Prob'ly you won't run, though. It's your nature, too, Bea."

"Thank you, Mike," she said. "No, I won't run. But I will have to lie. Forgive me for that."

"I feel like hell about this, you know," he said.

"It's what your Aunt Jacie would expect," Bea reminded him. "She'll expect you to do the ... well, the right thing."

"I know."

"So do it."

He took a few seconds to compose himself. "Will you ... I hope you won't have to ... reject me."

"I couldn't do that. I never want to ... never want to lose you as a friend."

"You're a ... a great person, Bea. You're ... I better not say anything more, but how can you not know how I feel about you?" A brief pause, then, "How long do you need before I ... before I speak?"

"I'm ready anytime. I planned for it."

"So I guess you would. I'll call you ... well, after I've done it."

Bea surprised him with, "Don't, Mike. They'll be tracking your every movement and word immediately. I'll know soon enough. Just don't forget - whatever happens - that I will always have you close to me, in ... in my heart. Okay?"

"Okay. That's more than I have a right to ask for."

"They'll probably have monitored this call, too," Bea continued. "Let me deal with it."

"Okay."

"Good night, Mike."

"Good night, Bea."

34. Dealing with the News

WILLIAM CHARLES LISTENED TO HIS ANSWERING machine as he sipped coffee the next morning in his kitchen. He'd acquired the habit recently, screening out calls he didn't want to take. When Mike Baylor's voice came over the speaker he didn't recognize it, but when the young man identified himself he went quickly over to the phone to pick it up.

"Yes, Mike, this is Dr. Charles. I'm sorry I didn't pick up right away. I get so many calls, you know."

"Yes, sir, I understand."

"What can I do for you?" Charles asked. He was sipping as he spoke.

"I'd like to see you right away, Dr. Charles. It's extremely important."

The professor was somewhat taken aback by the request. "Is it? Well, yes. When are you thinking about?"

"Now, sir. I can come wherever you choose."

"That important. Do you mind telling me something about what this is about?"

"It's only right to speak to you directly, sir. But ... well, it's about the virus."

"The virus?" He hadn't expected that, though he told himself promptly that it only made sense. The virus was on everyone's mind.

"Yes, sir. Where should I come?"

"Do you mind coming here, to my home?"

"No, sir."

Charles gave him the address, then after a polite sequence, hung up. He went to the window and looked out. The leaves were gone on the trees, leaving their silhouettes as artistic patterns against the sky. It was just after eight. Picking his phone back up, the professor called his colleague. She answered after three rings.

"Virginia, this is Bill. Sorry to ring so early. But I just got a call from Mike Baylor."

"Yes, Bea's friend," she nodded at her end. "And?"

"He's coming to talk to me here at home. Says it's very important, and about the virus."

"About the virus. It must ... well, I guess I don't know what it might mean."

"We'll know soon, I suspect. I'll call you after talking with him."

"Alright. I'll stand by here at home."

After hanging up, Charles prepared a fresh pot of coffee and straightened up a few things in his den, all the while trying to imagine what had inspired the young man. He guessed it had something to do with Bea de Winter, but didn't want to speculate further.

Mike rang the door bell only fourteen minutes after his phone call.

"Hello, Mike," said the professor at the door, offering a handshake. "Please come in. I have a fresh pot of coffee, if you're interested."

Leading him to the back and into the den, Charles offered a mug of the brew, which was accepted, and sat in a leather chair, indicating another.

"Sit down and tell me what this is about," was the pleasant suggestion.

The young man wore gray slacks and a deep green sweater. His dark face, however, was clearly troubled. Mike took a drink of the coffee before speaking, setting the mug on the small table next to him.

"Dr. Charles, this is very difficult for me to do. It is about Bea de Winter, as maybe you might guess. And she knows I'm telling you, because I discussed it with her before."

Charles nodded, not interrupting.

"The virus outbreak, sir, is ..." He looked away then back at his host. It was clearly difficult for him. "I'll just say it straight out, that's the best way, I think. Bea ... Bea made the virus, sir."

William Charles put his hands up and rubbed both cheeks and eyes. He watched the young man a few seconds before cocking his head and replying. "Bea made the virus?"

"Yes, sir."

"Did she tell you this, or did you ... did you discover it some other way?"

"She told me."

"Mike, I'm sorry to be ... well, to be so ... well, maybe skeptical, but I want to get this straight. She actually told you she made the virus?"

"Exactly, Dr. Charles."

"This is ... is really amazing, you know." Charles rubbed his cheek again with one hand. "Did she say ... well, why?"

"Yes, she did." Mike shifted a little uncomfortably, then reached for the coffee. "And like I said, she knows I'm telling."

The professor asked, "Did you tell her you were coming to me about this?"

"I didn't tell her who, no. Possibly she thinks I'll go to the CDC people. But I thought it was best to tell you first, sir, since you're her major professor."

The major professor nodded. "Thank you for approaching it like that, Mike. Listen, I don't want to ... to upset you in any way, but would you mind if I call Dr. Virginia Cortland to join us? She's very important to this problem and very trustworthy."

Mike was surprised at the request, and said, "If you ... well, sir, I just need to get it said. I'm not comfortable with waiting too long. I hope you don't mind."

"It'll take her only a few minutes to get here. I alerted her to the possibility. She lives in Sequoia Hills, too."

"Okay, then," Mike nodded. His nervousness had only increased, and he looked very uncomfortable.

"Thanks," Charles said and went to the phone. He called quickly and spoke quietly for a few moments, then hung up and came back to sit down. "She'll be here in less than ten minutes. Let me refresh your coffee."

Mike nodded and handed over the nearly empty mug.

Until Cortland arrived there were only a few additional words spoken. Mike sensed that it was best to say his piece once, to both of them. He concentrated on the coffee and his host got up to do a few meaningless things around the room, hoping to ease the tension. When the doorbell rang, however, Mike jumped a little in his seat.

"Just stay there, Mike," Charles said, moving quickly toward the door. "I'll bring her back."

Dr. Cortland was in a simple dark business suit and had a little morning puffiness around her eyes. But she greeted the student pleasantly and took his offered hand as he stood. Coffee was served the newcomer, and soon they all three were seated, facing each other in a rough triangle of chairs.

"Mr. Baylor has said," Charles began, "that his friend Bea de Winter fabricated the virus of our constant concern."

Cortland, who'd already been told that much on the phone, nodded. "Yes, I see. And she explained why, I take it?" Those words were directed at the young man.

"Yes, she did, Dr. Cortland," he said quietly, in somewhat better control himself now. "To deal directly with the problem of ... well, of male violence."

Cortland concentrated on the student's eyes. "Because," she said, "men are the source of most of our society's problems and potential problems. Is that it?"

"Yes, that's it."

Cortland looked over at her colleague, then continued. "And I suppose she also released the virus to infect the young men so far infected?"

"I think so, yes," Mike nodded. "Though she didn't explain anything about how it was done."

Charles interjected politely. "Suppose, Mike, you begin at the beginning, if you don't mind. And tell us everything you know about this."

Mike said, "Okay," released a long breath, and began to recount his story.

—

It was after eleven when Mike Baylor left the Charles house. He'd spoken a good while, then answered numerous questions, always polite and open in his responses. The young man made no effort either to defend or condemn Bea, but made it clear that, despite what was likely to happen, he wished her no ill.

Cortland's carefully worded suggestion that Mike and Bea might have had some romantic conflict was rejected and politely refuted. That he had come to them simply to do the "right thing" was explicitly stated and found to be consistent with everything he said. By the time the conversation ended, both professors were completely convinced he'd been motivated by a sense of decency, not by anger or for revenge. They told Mike they'd appreciate it if he spoke about this to no one else. Their tone quickly convinced him that the two were trying to come up with the fairest and most effective response they could, so he agreed.

"Your suspicions were right, Virginia," Charles said. They were still in his den, now into a third pot of coffee. "And I've been racking my brain to figure out how she could have done it."

"Any thoughts?"

"Not yet. But I'll be looking at that notebook again, I'll tell you that. She's bound to have left clues. And I know most of the approaches she could have taken. One of those is what she did."

"Any chance the boy is mistaken, Bill?"

"I kept hoping so, as we asked him about it, and yes, I suppose it's possible. But I believe him."

"I do, too," Cortland nodded. "This is a very bad business."

"What's your guess, Virginia, about what the CDC will do?"

"Somebody will call in the FBI," she said. "They can't do anything else, really. At least about Bea, I mean."

"I suppose so," he said in return. "I can't help but feel the whole thing will become a media feeding frenzy and huge nightmare."

She gave a hard humorless laugh. "You have to admit it's a great story. And it'll be bigger than 9-11 very soon, if that virus continues to do what it's doing."

"How could Bea have imagined such a thing?" he asked, shaking his head.

"We know some of it," Cortland replied. "But remember, Bill, Bea is the key to this thing. Our chances against the virus are greatly reduced if we have to deal with it without her."

"But she won't cooperate, if we've heard the truth this morning."

"Maybe not. But remember, she was willing to tell Mr. Baylor about it. And, according to him, she expected him to tell on her. I think the girl wanted it to come out. Maybe she's been having some second thoughts."

Charles let this idea sink in. "I agree that Bea is the key, but maybe Mike Baylor is the best one to turn the key. She apparently has deep admiration for the guy. Maybe she loves him."

His colleague nodded agreement. She said, "It's a very special relationship, I'd say, particularly with regard to Bea. And this young man is as solid as they come. From what I can tell. But I'm not sure he has any real control over her."

Charles said, thoughtfully, "I'm not sure anyone has any real control over Bea. But she's felt strongly enough to tell him."

"How can we use what we know, Bill?"

"She had some reason for telling him," was the indirect reply. "If we understood that, maybe we'd know how to take advantage of it."

Cortland asked, "Do you think Bea believes nothing can be done about the virus? In that case, it wouldn't matter whether she told – at least as far as her objective is concerned."

"And," he added, taking up the thought, "she could be doing a kind of penance for her deed, willing to suffer the consequences, convinced she'll succeed anyhow."

"Right. That's my guess, actually. Probably Bea knows what she's done is outrageous, at some level she is willing to admit. Or maybe she guesses we'll eventually find out anyway."

Charles said, "She's thought about these things for sure. Maybe what you describe is in fact just what she did."

"But can we stop it, the virus? Even assuming we get Bea's cooperation."

The man raised his head as if consulting the ceiling.

Cortland broke into his reverie and added, "Can this virus be killed, Bill? Wouldn't that be the best approach, to try to kill it?"

"Not like a bacterium, it can't," he answered. "The immune system doesn't seem to notice it. We know antibiotics don't work, since we've tried them. It would take a tailored drug or cocktail of drugs, like used in AIDS, for example. I'm sure CDC people are looking at available candidates and probably have started trying them with mice. But right now we don't have a large supply of the virus yet available for testing. Nothing any of the CDC people have told me indicates any success in these areas."

"What about hypothermic or radiation treatment?"

"Hypothermic may have a chance, but it would require a brain catheter to get the heat source close to the problem zone. Very difficult and very expensive. The CDC is looking into temperature effects on the virus, so that could be a lead. Radiation might be similarly effective if we could find a way to get radioactive attachments to the virus. But direct radiation into the brain would be risky at best."

Cortland changed tack a little. "Tell me, Bill, what's the word on the Texas cases?"

We're looking at the blood right now, probably. In fact, Bea - weird as it now seems - has been doing a lot of the blood studies. But we have learned that the virus is like ours, though with a couple of slightly different surface proteins. It has to be the same one."

"Damn," Cortland muttered. "But maybe that's a good sign, actually. If the source is here we have a better chance of stopping it."

"Maybe," he shrugged. "But who knows who else has it but hasn't yet shown symptoms?"

"And it's still strictly affecting males still?" she asked.

"Yes. Females apparently can't host the virus, or at least we haven't found any virus in any female sample yet."

"Yet they can be carriers, or it seems that way."

He nodded. "If so, the virus is maybe in the marrow or some such place, but doesn't affect females for some unknown reason. But when it gets into male blood streams it can. That part is very peculiar."

"How about marrow samples?"

"They're being extracted today from Miss Thomas and the other three girls in the ward."

Cortland formed a wan smile. "The girls'll love that, getting needles stuck into their bones."

"Right," Charles said, sympathetically. "The other thing is that they may have the virus in their lungs and it doesn't, for some crazy reason, get into their blood, but can be transferred as an aerosol and is able to get into male blood."

"Lots of questions," Cortland said. "And your wunderkind Bea has all the answers, I bet. We have to get the info out of her. If we are to have a chance to kill the thing we have to know everything we can."

Charles had a sudden look of concern. "Would the FBI torture her, you think? Assuming they believed she could help them."

"They'd use drugs on her, probably," the woman said, "if they thought that was necessary. They'd never admit to such a thing, of course, but we're looking at a potential crisis of the first magnitude. They'd do anything deemed helpful. I wonder if Bea is aware of the treatment she might receive?"

"Knowing Bea," he said, "she's thought of it. Yet still she told Mike."

"Sodium pentothal, some other drug cocktail, or some kind of clever torture may the only ways to get the information out of her, however."

"Could be. But Bea would know information could be extracted from her and would have taken that into consideration."

"You mean," Cortland said, "she thinks nothing can be done anyway, so she'll take her lumps, or maybe even talk before they apply the thumbscrews?"

"That would be like Bea," he admitted. "But we can't assume she's right - even though she probably is. We have to consider possible approaches."

"If the hormone thing is correct," Cortland said, "we can reduce those levels. Including testosterone, for example. If the girls are indicative, then we could keep the boys from getting sick."

"Yes, maybe, but at a price many guys wouldn't be willing to pay."

"Even for their lives?" she asked.

"Only if there were no other alternative."

"But how long might be necessary? You pointed out those mutations, after all. Maybe the virulence will mutate away eventually."

"And you'd want men to be emasculated for, what, years? Doesn't seem likely, Virginia."

"Hmm," she mused. "So what do we do immediately? I'm reluctant to tell the CDC right now. Especially since it's only hearsay, from a good source, yes, but hearsay. If Bea denies it there'll have to be some sort of due process. Time will work against us. Besides, the CDC will leak it, sooner or later, and our troubles up to now will seem like joy and light by comparison."

"But if we wait too long," he cautioned, "the authorities will be all over us for obstruction of justice."

She nodded. "It's a risk we take, I say. We can claim we weren't really sure and wanted to have a higher degree of certainty, given the volatility of the situation."

"You're right." He looked at his friend a moment. "So, we talk to Bea, right? That's the only logical next step - except for my digging into her data."

"I think that's it," Cortland agreed. "And I think we should call young Mr. Baylor back, too, and explain what we're doing. We don't want to take any chances on his talking to the CDC, or heaven forbid, the media."

"Good idea. I'll talk to him, since I know him a little bit, and since he chose to come to me."

"Then we have the semblance of a plan," she said. "I'll call Bea and arrange a meeting. But I'll wait till in the morning. We should spend some more time on this, in the afternoon. Let our minds have to time to wrap around it."

He nodded. "That sounds reasonable. But if she turns you down?"

"We'll deal with that if we have to." Cortland stood up. "Bill, thanks for calling me. But I don't know when we'll ever get these lumps out of our throats."

Charles shook his head. "It's hard to believe she would do it," he said. "Or even that she could do it."

35. Confrontation and Conversation

THE FOLLOWING MORNING WAS GRAY AT DAWN, then rainy. It was the kind of rainy day that made East Tennessee so green and full of life. This day was certain to be a drizzly one, with serious though short downpours mixed in. Bea received the call from Virginia Cortland just after seven thirty. Cortland had been driving the student to the university hospital, so Bea first assumed the call had something to do with scheduling on that chilly, nasty morning.

"Hello, Bea," said the professor. If her tone of voice was a little different, Bea didn't seem to notice.

"Good morning, doctor."

"Bea, would you be so kind as to spend a few minutes with me and Dr. Charles before going into the hospital this morning? It's quite important."

That statement did get Bea's attention. She quickly realized the professors knew. Mike had probably spoken to them first? It was his way. But did the CDC know yet?

"Yes, if you wish," Bea answered evenly.

"I'll pick you up at our usual eight o'clock, if that's suitable," Cortland continued. There was severe formality in her voice now.

"Fine, doctor. I'll be outside the dorm, as usual."

When Cortland arrived she looked very tired, Bea thought. But maybe, the student reminded herself, she was drawing an unwarranted conclusion. It was important to not make snap judgments. The conversation in the car was about the ghastly weather around them, slowing traffic, obscuring vision, and creating an image of the city that contrasted dramatically with the often bright days of fall.

They didn't go to the hospital, but up the Hill at the university to Hess Hall. Cortland and Charles thought the university setting better for their purposes, especially in that no CDC personnel were likely to interrupt or overhear them. The two women entered the building through a heavy drizzle, one middle aged, a little on the heavy side and somewhat frumpy that morning, the other very young, petite and quick on her feet. When they reached William Charles' office he was already there, and had prepared a pot of coffee. When their umbrellas were set aside to drip and jackets removed, Charles poured each a mug of coffee. Then the two professors faced the student across the little round table where they'd met before.

"Bea," Charles said, with no preamble other than a sip of black steaming brew, "your friend Mike Baylor spoke with us yesterday morning. He gave us some very chilling news."

Bea, mentally prepared for the confrontation, didn't answer, but lifted her gaze politely to her major professor.

"Mr. Baylor," Charles continued, "informed us that you developed the 'party' virus (as it was often called informally now), then intentionally exposed it to the public."

"That's a very serious charge, sir," she responded evenly.

"Is it true, Bea?" Charles asked, pointedly.

"Sir," Bea said, "would you expect me to admit to such a thing, especially if it were true?"

Cortland, watching the young woman, interjected, "It is a brutal way to approach a perceived problem, Miss de Winter."

The petite one turned to speak to Cortland. "Doctor, I assume you're referring to the discussion we had about Dr. Greinert's lecture." The young face was unreadable.

"Yes," said Cortland, revealing by her eyes that she was struggling to control her anger.

Bea said nothing further, waiting.

Charles then said, "We understand you told Mike Baylor of your actions and explained it was something you were compelled to do. Did we understand this correctly?"

Bea suddenly stood up. "Dr. Charles, are you actually accusing me of these actions you describe?"

"We're trying to understand what happened," Charles said, staying seated.

Bea looked calmly at both seated professors. She could see that Dr. Cortland was not taking this well at all. "As I see it," the student said, "we are dealing with a viral epidemic of potentially enormous proportions. There is a great deal of work to do, for all of us. In particular for me, there is a backlog of analysis. Unless you have more to tell me except what my friend has told you, I would like to request that I be allowed to get on with my job."

Virginia Cortland's face darkened. She didn't stand, but her voice shifted up in pitch. "Young woman," she said, a little too loudly, "do you realize the enormity of your behavior? Please sit back down!"

Bea stood her ground. "Doctor, please excuse me. But I need to arrange transportation to the hospital unless you are willing to take me."

Cortland, a little awkwardly in the process, also got to her feet. Then the Infection Committee chairman spoke, using every ounce of control and forcing out an authoritative tone that avoided shrillness. "Bea, there is no work for you to do at the hospital. Please sit back down and try to talk about this as calmly as possible."

"No work for me?" Bea asked, openly surprised. But she remained standing.

It was Professor Charles who answered. "Under the circumstances, Bea - and I'm sure you understand - I contacted the CDC and removed you from the viral team." Cortland sat back down as he spoke. Charles continued, "You're right, of course, that we have only your friend's word, but all of us here know he was telling the truth. But we don't want to attract any attention to this situation by taking any precipitative action. I explained to the CDC that we had unfairly taken you away from your research for too long."

Cortland, saying the words carefully, added, "But we can promise you, Bea, that you will be under constant scrutiny. That, too, I'm sure you understand."

Bea hesitated, seemed to consider sitting, then took a couple of steps toward the door. She spoke to her professor. "Dr. Charles, will I then have access to my lab?"

"No, Bea," he said, eyes showing a certain sadness that disturbed her more than Cortland's anger. "It will be off limits to you. But I've arranged some space for you in the corner lab on the third floor. It won't be exactly what you need, but it will maintain the necessary .... pretense."

The student let her eyes close for a moment. She hoped they didn't know how hard it was for her to appear calm. "Thank you, sir," she said simply. "I suppose I'll be on my way then. To see the new space."

"And you have nothing more to say?" Cortland asked, looking very hard at the young woman.

"No, doctor. Not at the moment. But thank you both for being frank with me."

Cortland glanced at her colleague, then said, "Anything you can tell us to help us beat this thing will be appreciated. And will make things much easier for you later."

Bea took a couple more steps, and turned around at the closed door to face them both. She put her left hand behind her because it was trembling slightly. "The virus mutates, it seems," she said, amazingly seeming to return to a scientific discussion that hadn't been occurring. "Its virulence may only continue for some months, though we don't have very good statistics yet. My guess is that standard treatments will make little difference. Aerosol transmission is still possible, and will be - to some degree - for some time, probably. But my guess is that blood transmission remains the most dangerous. As the winter season progresses, there will be concern about coughing and sneezing. These are important concerns, despite the fact that few transmissions are likely by this mechanism.

"It seems," Bea continued, "that male hormones - especially testosterone - are major factors in the virus survival in the blood stream. I've verified this in the latest mice studies we've recently completed. My notes are in the CDC trailer. Testosterone reduction, I predict, will be the most straightforward protection against the spread of the virus."

Bea picked up her umbrella and jacket then opened the office door. "I hope these ideas will be useful," she said. "And if you choose to reinstate me I'll continue my work as before. Have a good day, doctors." With that, she walked briskly away.

Virginia Cortland sat, in an angry trance, for a long minute. Her friend got up and closed the door again, then sat down as before. They both nursed their coffees idly. Then he said, words carrying a lot of irony, "Virginia, didn't that go so well?"

Cortland came out of her spell with a thin laugh. "Didn't it, though? I must say, she is an incredible human being!"

"And probably knew full well we were recording this meeting."

"Undoubtedly." The woman sighed. "I'm not sure what to do next."

"I know my drill," Charles said. "I started it yesterday, in earnest, and will get back on it. Bea's notes will be our best hope, I think."

"Possibly," Cortland said. "But if she's right, there's only two things we can do. Isolate people, and lower their testosterone. Just how well do you think that will be received?"

"About as well as the idea that a graduate student has hung the Sword of Damocles over every male on earth."

Cortland looked at him with bitter friendship showing. "Yes. And as the Bible says, 'Be sure your sins will find you out.' It's a hell of a deal for all of you."

"Tell me about it," Charles said.

36. Taking Advantage of Opportunity

WHEN BEA GOT BACK TO HER DORM, this time via taxi, she received another unexpected setback. There on the little table where she worked at her laptop computer was a note. Nothing else, at a quick glance, was out of place, but a sudden discomfort sank into the young woman's stomach. The note, written in a hand she recognized as Dr. Charles', said, "Bea, we've confiscated your laptop for a few days. Sorry for the inconvenience. We'll get it back to you. Don't worry about your work for a while. I'm sure you understand."

Being out of the loop, Bea didn't hear about two more cases of the "party virus," announced that same rainy day, one from Texas and another in Oak Ridge. Nor was she informed about several calls into the CDC, now that the virus was known about everywhere, concerning cases in the general East Tennessee area that were destined eventually to be tested and found to be the virus. The CDC, with huge resources fully brought to bear, was now able to test quickly for and isolate it. Their scientists were seeing the trend of mutations and had categorized three different variants so far - a number, however, smaller than Bea had expected. No other patients had died, and several of the cases had been characterized as "mild." This characterization, however, was unfortunately a relative one.

Research teams were now meeting regularly, sometimes twice a day. The fact of the young women carriers with no trace of the actual virus had registered in a number of minds the possibility of some kind of association between other complex structures in their blood. While nothing definitive had been determined and no clear insight established, the wheels were definitely turning in the direction of discovery of the viral precursors.

The news media were escalating the story precipitously, hour by hour. Rumors of the party virus all over the country and, indeed, in a couple of foreign countries, were rampant. Every reasonably close relative of every identified case was undergoing near constant attention bordering on harassment.

Reggie Pendergast and several other victims appeared in their dull emptiness over and over again on television, internet news sites, and every imaginable kind of social media. Attorneys came almost literally out of the woodwork to interview victims' families, searching for places to bring multi-million dollar suits. Medical facilities all over the American southeast and beyond were gearing up to treat party virus cases. In the central Texas area, the CDC had arrived in force. There, the concern was - as it had been, though more understandably, in Knoxville - that the viral spread was already well underway before any identified cases surfaced.

It had taken a few days for the full impact of the association of the party virus to male hormones to be felt, but once it was, the media frenzy took on a far more hysterical aspect. Pundits on various news programs began suggesting testosterone reduction as a possible preventative and soon the idea of "chemical castration" was being bandied about around the country. Foreign governments had already started conversations with the U.S. State Department as well as the CDC, but the odds were good - given the mobility of modern society - that some exposure beyond the American border had already occurred. To say that the American public was in some kind of panic was an overstatement, especially because very few people had seen or been kin to one of the victims, but there was a growing level of uneasiness, comparable - some historians pointed out - to the reaction in the 1940s and 1950s to outbreaks of polio, or the first years of the AIDS virus, in the 1980s. The new disease, like those in the relatively recent past, once contracted, could not really be treated. Treatments were commonly discussed, both in medical professional conclaves and by experts of many stripes for the benefit of news programs, but nothing that had thus far been attempted had made any headway. Every day that went by left the hope for a quick cure more and more remote.

Out at the edges of the swirling media current, Bea thought herself far enough removed to be relatively free from being sucked into it. As it turned out, however, her appearance in one interview on CNN and her image used regularly in accounts of the party virus, made Bea an ideal candidate for follow up interrogation by reporters of many kinds. Especially since the big players were making themselves ever more scarce and refusing many interviews, sending substitutes instead who came with carefully worded statements they stuck rigidly to. Because Bea was a student and because she downplayed her involvement in the "discovery" of the virus, it was true that most the media attention remained directed at higher level adults associated with the outbreak, in particular, Cortland, Charles and the CDC authorities, plus the experts they had thus far brought in. Bea's home address had been kept from the questioners, made possible by her being housed in a dormitory, and promises had been extracted that she - as a busy student - was not to be contacted directly in the future. Those promises, of course, were only likely to be kept as long as no special benefit could be associated with contacting her; consequently, the same rainy day she was confronted by Cortland and Charles, Bea was surprised at home by a reporter.

The knock came an hour or so after she'd returned to the dorm. She went to the peep hole in the door and looked out onto the face of a woman in her thirties, pretty and elegantly dressed in a Navy blue business suit. Bea had no idea who this could be, and asked aloud who was there.

"My name is Rosalind Vittorio, Miss de Winter. I'm with Reuters News Agency and would appreciate just a few minutes of your time."

"How did you know where to find me?" Bea said, getting to the basic question she had.

"I promise not to give away your address, my dear. Don't worry please. And it's only a very few minutes, if you don't mind. I hope you're not too busy to talk."

Bea considered this new situation with the same clearness of thought she used in every situation. After a couple of seconds, she responded. "Then please come in, Ms Vittorio. Do you mind if I see your credentials?"

The woman nodded, regarding the petite student with more respect, and took a photo ID out of her purse, showing her face, name, and the official language of Reuters International News Agency.

"Thank you," Bea said, returning the plastic clad item to her. "Please have a seat. May I offer you a cup of coffee."

The fresh pot in her little kitchenette was essentially all the definable progress she'd made since discovering her laptop had been taken away.

"Why, that would be marvelous! Thank you." Vittorio had a slight trace of Italian accent, that and her looks guaranteed to make her more appealing than the average woman, especially than the average reporter.

Bea poured two coffees without further conversation, then they settled into chairs facing each other across a little coffee table.

"This is wonderful coffee, Miss de Winter. Thank you."

"You're welcome. Please tell me what brings you here, Ms Vittorio."

"Please call me Rosalind. Let's not be formal. My purpose is very informal indeed."

"Fine. Tell me your purpose, Rosalind, if you don't mind." Bea attached a slight smile to keep from sounding too harsh.

"I understand you're the one who isolated the famous party virus."

"You must have seen the interview on CNN. I'm afraid I told the reporter there all I know."

"I'm sure you did, Miss de Winter. I'm really focusing on the human interest side of this story. I'd like to feature you, if you don't object."

Bea, who'd certainly have objected the day before or any time earlier, said, "No, of course not. If you wish. But I'm afraid it will be a very boring story."

"Oh, I'm sure it won't! First of all, do you mind if I record our conversation?"

Bea was confident they were already being recorded, probably by some gadget in the reporter's small purse, now removed from her shoulder and occupying a space on the floor beside the chair. "That's fine," Bea said.

The reporter made a point of reaching down into her purse and moving or activating something, leaving the purse open. "Thank you so much," she said affably. "I promise not to take too long."

"Fine," Bea repeated, and waited.

"Okay, first of all, tell me about yourself, Miss de Winter. I understand you have no family."

"That's correct," said Bea, then waited again.

"How do you feel about having discovered this terrible virus? Especially being someone basically alone in the world, with no family to act as emotional support?"

Bea had expected a question like this but had something else entirely in mind for the interview. She answered, surprisingly, "Have you considered, Rosalind, what motives might be lurking behind this party virus, as some are calling it?"

"Motives? Do you mind explaining, please?" The woman's eyes had brightened.

"Of course not. We have all heard the discussions about its affecting only males of our species. I wonder if you have considered the possibility that this virus was released by someone who has some reason to bring illness and grief to men?"

The other's eyes went round. "Well, of course there are many kinds of speculation, Miss de Winter. Is that what you are referring to?"

"No, my concern arises from some fairly close association with the study done thus far on the virus."

"Indeed! What do you mean in particular?" Ms Vittorio was leaning forward in her new enthusiasm.

"The work done to date has made me question whether a disease agent of this kind could come about by random mutation-driven chance. While I won't venture to say how, indeed, such a thing could be achieved, it certainly appears to be something more than a simple accident. Consider a moment. When the AIDS virus was first discovered it was thought of as a kind of special disease of homosexual males - because of the method of transmission. However, it soon became clear that the virus was easily as deadly for females as males. Such is the case with every known major disease agent in history. Isn't it curious, Rosalind, that this particular agent not only affects only males but can be transmitted, in some special way not fully understood, by females. If this isn't some kind of vendetta against men, then what, pray tell, can it be?" Bea's tone was far more emotional than she had ever used in the past. She hoped she wasn't overdoing it.

Rosalind Vittorio was fairly glowing with excitement. Bea, of course, was not expressing a completely new idea. The idea of some special attack on males - among dozens of other conspiracy theories - had been discussed many times, but never by anyone with any legitimate association with the virus team. Much less the very person who had first discovered it! Ms Vittorio said, "So, you are saying you are convinced that such a thing has been done? Is this correct, Miss de Winter?"

"Yes, I'm convinced of it, Rosalind. Of course I have no direct proof, but cannot accept the idea of a coincidence."

"But wouldn't such a thing be very difficult to achieve scientifically? Many authorities seem to be saying it is impossible to simply create a virus of this type."

Bea, looking amazingly authoritative for one so young and slight, said, "So I have heard, as well. But consider. The major biomedical research institutions of the world have made enormous progress in the last few decades. The ability to do gene splicing and other micro-miniature mechanical action at the cellular level should not be underestimated, in my opinion. While it may be difficult in concept, or even for a small group to achieve, it may very well be achievable by a dedicated team. And if the will is there, many research facilities around the world have the required instrumentation and laboratory conditions. There are fully thirty or thirty-five bio-medical complexes on earth that have such capability."

"The virus appeared first here in East Tennessee, Miss de Winter. Are you implying it could have been ... well, formulated here?"

"It could have been, yes," Bea replied without hesitation. "We certainly have the laboratory resources at hand. Such a conclusion, however, I would question. Were such a team to do this thing, it would be far wiser to release their product in some location that would not call attention to them. We can say, however - and indeed fortunately - that if a release in East Tennessee might have been hoped to remain unnoticed for a long time, that hope was dashed. Our excellent Infection Committee, headed by the famous scientist/physician Dr. Virginia Cortland, was very rapid, anyone would say, in discovering the problem and beginning to deal with it."

"And you, of course, Miss de Winter, were instrumental in helping make that discovery so quickly."

Bea ignored the compliment, continuing, "My thought is that two possible kinds of backgrounds are possible for a program of this kind. One would arise from leadership who had some grievance against society. The other possibility - and the one that strikes me as more compelling - would be a desire for power or money or both."

"Would you care to explain this second idea, Miss de Winter?"

Bea, glancing briefly at the purse where the conversation was being recorded, nodded and said, "Where can a person strike Western Civilization harder than the males within the society? Especially the males exclusively. Power resides, Rosalind, for the most part, in the hands of the males of our species. A disease of this kind, then, could be thought of as a kind of hostage situation. If, for example, there is an antidote to this viral menace, what could it be worth? And are there not many biomedical research institutions, profit making and non-profit alike, struggling daily to keep ahead of the competition in their rapidly expanding fields? Were a certain organization, for example, to release this virus somewhere, then later, when terrible damage had been done, suddenly came up with a cure, how much indeed would that cure be worth?"

"Amazing!" the reporter said, nearly gasping. "Could such a thing truly happen, then?"

Bea shrugged. "Who understands the corruption produced by the struggle for power and money?"

"Miss de Winter, this is an astounding accusation you have made. Do you mind saying how you came up with it?"

"Rosalind, let me make myself clear." Bea took a drink of coffee, far more relaxed now than her interviewer. "I'm not making any accusations. I'm simply stating my own opinions and speculations. Let me restate that this virus is the only major disease agent ever known to be sex specific. Our recent work has shown that male hormones are required for survival of the virus. The odds of such a dependence arising randomly and spontaneously are extremely long, as I see them. So, putting two and two together seems to me to imply four, not five or three. I hope I have made myself clear, Rosalind."

"This is remarkable news, Miss de Winter. I hope you realize that."

"Perhaps I am wrong in my speculations," Bea said pleasantly.

"But if not, what a terrible thought," said the reporter. She seemed very anxious now to end the interview. Standing suddenly and holding her purse, Ms Vittorio said, "Miss de Winter, this has certainly been a remarkable conversation. I hope you have no objection to my attributing these statements to you."

"No of course not," Bea said, standing as well. "But you must promise to not put words in my mouth, Rosalind. What I have said is only speculation, not backed by any proof whatsoever."

"Naturally, Miss de Winter. I will quote you exactly, as you request, and will be sure to make the point that this is strictly opinion. But your opinion, under the circumstances, will carry considerable weight, it seems to me."

"Thank you for your integrity, Rosalind. Are you sure you wouldn't like more coffee?"

"No thank you. I really must be going. Again, I am so appreciative."

"It's been my pleasure," Bea said, and extended a hand.

When the door closed, Bea went to the side window and watched until she saw the reporter - already talking animatedly on a cell phone - enter a car and pull away. Coming back to her seat, the young woman opened a drawer in the table next to it and withdrew a crossword puzzle. For a little while at least, she knew she'd have time to work on them.

37. Reaction

THE STORY BROKE ON CNN ON THE FIVE O'CLOCK afternoon news, Eastern Standard Time. As fate would have it, Randall Jackson, the CNN anchor who first announced the discovery of the virus, was the same one to proclaim the possibility of an insidious conspiracy. His fatherly, well-known face was somber as he said, "This just in from Reuters. The brilliant young graduate student who discovered the incurable party virus, Miss Beatrice de Winter, in an interview today, suggested that the terrible virus may have been intentionally produced and released, possibly in a cruel play for power and riches by some large bio-medical organization who would have much to gain by coming up with a cure. With more on the story, we take you to Erica Rotherford, who has remained on site at the University of Tennessee hospital in Knoxville since the virus story first broke. Erica?"

The scene switched, as it often had in recent days, to the facade of the UT Hospital, then to the sharply dressed blond reporter, who went into some detail on Bea's interview. The story concluded with CNN promising to quickly look further into this fascinating and horrifying possibility. In the major evening newspapers the story was longer and contained a lot of background information on Bea, citing again her outstanding early career and quoting words of praise from William Charles and Virginia Cortland. Several newspapers used the headline: "Party Virus Manufactured?" or something similar. The reverberation was powerful and quickly dominated every news report in the United States, Western Europe, Japan, and Australia. Other countries, too, gave it major coverage. Few informed people anywhere didn't know something about the interview in Bea's dorm room only hours earlier.

Reuters had released the story before following up with any other authority associated with the virus project. This was done to get the scoop, but all the news agencies knew that CDC and UT personnel needed to be contacted quickly. Even as Rosalind Vittorio was finishing dictating her breaking story via cell phone, she was on her way to Dr. William Charles' office in Hess Hall. Interestingly, he was there, at his computer, studying Bea's laboratory notebook. The knock on his door took him completely by surprise.

"Dr. Charles, sorry to disturb you. May I have a few moments of your time?" Vittorio said, presenting her Reuters credentials. "We've just released a story from an interview with your student, Miss de Winter, and we'd like to get your take on it."

Charles had opened his mouth to send the reporter away, vaguely wondering how she'd managed to get to his office past the university policeman assigned to prevent any unauthorized entry. But when he heard the words "interview" and "Miss de Winter" he changed his mind. He asked her to sit down, then closed the door. Charles' heart was racing.

"Dr. Charles, your outstanding student has suggested that the party virus was possibly manufactured intentionally and possibly released near Knoxville as a kind of cruel joke especially on you and Dr. Cortland."

"Did Bea say that?" He was truly stunned.

"She did say there was no proof of her idea, but pointed out that the virus' specific action only on males was unique in history and seemed to her to be more than a simple accident of nature."

"Oh my God," he muttered. "She said that, did she?"

"Absolutely, Dr. Charles. Do you share her opinion, sir, if I may ask?"

"I guess I didn't know about her ... her opinion. Is that all she said?"

"No, indeed. She pointed out that a number of large biomedical complexes around the world might be capable of developing a virus of this type, possibly with a cure for its action already developed as well. Then after it was released they could charge a very high price for stopping it."

"Incredible!" he said. One side of him was angry at Bea; the other was awed at her cleverness. "And she spoke of a possible cure, then?"

"She only speculated, Dr. Charles, but claimed to understand the science involved and believed what she described was possible."

"Very interesting," he said, thinking rapidly and knowing full well he had to be very careful in what he would say.

"What's your opinion, sir, of Miss de Winter's hypothesis, if you don't mind saying?"

"Well, I must admit, Ms Vittorio, it's a frightening idea. And I don't know of any scientific or research organization that would be so unethical as to do such a thing."

"Do you say then, Dr. Charles, that a scenario of this type is not to be taken seriously?"

"Well ..." He felt himself be boxed in, even as he spoke. "I think it's highly unlikely for any biomedical research team to intentionally produce a virus as dangerous as this one, then release it to the outside world."

Ms Vittorio wouldn't let him off that easily. "Tell me, sir, are you saying such a thing is unlikely or such a thing is impossible?"

"I think it's highly unlikely, Ms Vittorio.

"And given the peculiar action of the virus only on males, is Miss de Winter's theory strengthened or weakened, in your opinion?"

"I guess I don't have a well formulated opinion on this point."

"So, I take it, Dr. Charles, it is possible, in your view, for such a virus to be manufactured, but you don't know who might have done such a thing. Have I stated this correctly?"

"I'm saying," he said, feeling slightly panicky, "that while I don't know if it's impossible I also don't know who might have been motivated to do it - even if it could be done."

"So you or Dr. Cortland don't have any enemies or jealous colleagues who would consider it ironically appropriate to release this party virus right in your backyard?"

"I don't know of any such people, no."

"So you have only cordial working relationships with all your colleagues around the world, sir?"

"I don't really know how my colleagues feel about me, but none has ... well, threatened any behavior that could lead to something like this."

"Did you and your student, Miss de Winter discuss these possibilities before, sir? Or are these ideas strictly hers?"

"I would say these are Bea's opinions, Ms Vittorio."

"And are they farfetched, would you say, or could they be true?"

"If I had to choose one answer, I'd say farfetched."

"But possible."

"I ... suppose so."

"Do you have another other explanation, Dr. Charles - even a speculation - on why the virus acts only on males?"

"I had always supposed it was some sort of genetic mutation and happened to have those traits."

"Then you disagree with Miss de Winter that the probability of such a thing happening is essentially zero?"

"I haven't really tried to calculate the probabilities of such a thing. In fact, I don't know how to make such a calculation."

"Yet your student, whom you are mentoring, is willing to make such a comment. How can you explain, sir, why the party virus is the only major disease agent ever to act strictly on one sex?"

Charles made himself slow down, counting inwardly to ten. "Let me say this as well as I can, Ms Vittorio. We have been so busy working on trying to find out how this virus works and looking into what might stop it that I haven't had time to think about exactly where it came from. It's here and we must deal with it."

"So you don't think that knowing about its origins would help you deal with it? That seems odd to me, sir, if you don't mind my saying so."

"We didn't take an intentional creation of the virus into account as a possibility of its origin, that's true."

"So will you now - thanks to the insights of your student - take such an origin into consideration?"

"I suppose we must, yes."

"So if someone, some research team, created the virus who might these people be? Who are the most likely ones?"

"I have no idea."

"So you think Miss de Winter is completely wrong in her assessment? Are you repudiating her ideas?"

Charles hesitated. Did he want to go on record not believing someone like Bea herself could have made this virus? "Bea de Winter," he said, "is a a very bright student. Whatever point of view she has is worth considering. But she hadn't discussed this idea with me before."

"So you'll begin to take the possibility into account, then? Is that what you're saying?"

"I suppose that's right."

"And will you begin to consider which institution might be capable of manufacturing the virus?"

"I'm not sure we'll take it that far. We've been involved in the biomedical aspects of this virus outbreak, Ms Vittorio. We have only recently learned about its male specificity, for example. We are certainly not sweeping anything at all under the rug. Every day is a learning experience."

"Ah, so Miss de Winter has come up with this idea before any of the senior research team. Is that what you are admitting to me, sir?"

"I'm not admitting anything of the sort," he replied, a little irritation showing in his tone. "We certainly will take her opinions into consideration, as we have with any of the team."

"So Miss de Winter is an important part of the CDC/UT team, Dr. Charles? As the discoverer of the virus, I would think you'd have her very much involved."

"She's been very active, yes," he nodded. "I'm sure you understand the magnitude of an effort like this, Ms Vittorio. There are many very capable people hard at work on it."

"So you'd say Miss de Winter is more or less important than other members of the team?"

"I wouldn't make such a judgment actually. We're all working together."

"And she has been a major contributor, I take it."

"Yes."

"Dr. Charles, thank you very much for your time."

"Thank you, Ms Vittorio, for coming to me. This has been a ... quite a surprising direction taken."

"Sir, I'm assuming you won't object to my quoting you on this subject. I guarantee not to quote you inaccurately or out of context."

"I'd like to review what you submit, if you don't mind."

"I'll send a draft to your email, Dr. Charles, right away. If I don't hear from you about it we'll assume it meets with your approval."

"Thank you." He stood as she'd stood. The interview was quickly over.

–

About five thirty that afternoon, Bea's crossword puzzle concentration was broken by the ringing of her room phone. She fully expected someone to call, but was pleased to hear it was Mike Baylor.

"Hi, Bea. I guess you know you're now famous."

"Am I?" she asked, ingenuous enough. "Must have to do with the Reuters woman I spoke with."

She listened carefully to the tone of his voice. How Mike reacted was important to her - too much so, she realized, but knew it was still so. He said, "I don't quite understand what you're doin', Bea."

"I'm only doing what I have to, Mike."

"I know you think that. I was hopin' you'd maybe try to ... maybe not be as strong minded about this thing as you've been. But I was wrong, I guess."

"Mike, what if I buy you dinner? Would you be willing to join me?"

"Bea, the media will be all over you, you know that. I bet they're waiting outside your building right now. Only the door key is keepin' them out now, unless I miss my guess."

"Could be. But I can buzz you in. We can have dinner here. If you like."

"Didn't know you wanted me to come into your dorm, Bea. It's a private world of yours, I know."

"My world won't be private anymore," she said, sounding a little forlorn. "And I don't really know what will happen next. This is a chance to see you."

"And that's important to you?"

"The most important thing to me right now."

There was a hesitation before he said, "Then I'll come."

"When?"

"I can be there in a little while. But should I bring some groceries or something?"

"Maybe you can bring some wine. I have food."

"Okay. I could use something to eat."

"Haven't you been eating?"

"Haven't been very hungry."

"I'm sorry, truly," she said. "And trouble sleeping, too, I suspect. Like me."

"I suppose so."

"Listen, see you in a few minutes, Mike. And thank you."

38. Events on a Rainy Evening

"SO WHAT'S OUR NEXT STEP?" WILLIAM CHARLES asked. He was sitting in the UT office of his colleague. It was dark outside, with a slow cold drizzle falling. The illuminated clock on the wall opposite the window read 8:08.

Virginia Cortland, standing now with her back to the darkness outside shook her head. "Somehow I feel like we've let it get away from us. It's like there's nothing really we can do to make a difference."

"Damn hell of mess, actually," Charles said. "What's going on with Bea?"

"She's defending herself, of course."

"And the best defense is a good offense, right?"

"Right." Cortland looked even more tired than earlier in the day, if possible. And her clothing was even more rumpled, and her hair would have been considered a catastrophe by most women."So, Bill, when are we going to say Bea did it?"

"I was hoping we'd have proof."

"What if we don't get proof?"

"I don't know. She's already called our bluff."

"Will the CDC investigate her - if we don't alert them to her?"

Charles considered, rubbing the side of his head. "They're more likely to investigate us."

"I wondered about that," Cortland said. "Now that the idea is circulating they'll start being suspicious. And with what the media will do, they'll have to make a real effort."

"Do you think they'll buy the idea of someone inventing this for the money and releasing it here to get at us?"

It was Cortland's turn to consider. "If they'll accept a manufactured virus, they'll certainly take such a thing into consideration."

"Will the CDC accept a manufactured virus?"

"Not easily or readily. But they'll have to keep it in mind. Bea's made sure of that."

"And they may not take Bea seriously at first," Charles said, "but the more they dig into it the more they'll appreciate her so-called suspicions. Eventually they'll accept it."

Cortland came back around and sat down at her desk. "In the meantime," she said, almost to herself, "we keep getting cases."

"We do indeed." Charles turned his chair a little to accommodate her new position. "We'll know tomorrow how much free testosterone in the blood is required. In conversations today, we came up with a protocol. We'll use some of the party girls' blood, ramp up its testosterone and see what happens. That should be a clincher."

"Will it be just that simple?"

"Hopefully. We'll use a full male hormone mix, just to be sure."

"So you think testosterone is the trigger?"

"Probably."

Cortland shook her head in a kind of expression of regret. "Makes perfect sense, unfortunately." She looked at her friend. "How fast is this thing going to spread, Bill? Have we slowed it enough by isolating these people?"

Charles sighed. "We've slowed it some, because the original set of carriers is isolated, but it had already made the jump to the secondary set - like Dr. Forrest and the boys in Texas. Somewhere there are some third generation infections that we haven't found. Maybe even fourth. We didn't clamp down on the females at first. Who knows how many they could have infected? And since we know it takes a few weeks, on average, to show symptoms, the explosion could be just around the corner."

"And I suspect Bea knows that, too," Cortland said.

"You can bet she does."

"Could she herself - Bea - be a carrier?"

Charles wrinkled his nose as he responded. "She probably checked her own blood. And she knows what to look for there. Doubt it."

"If she did check herself, would there be any record of what she did?"

He nodded a moment. "It's a thought. But knowing Bea, she'd never leave that kind of evidence. But we'll look, sure."

"How about aerosol transmission, Bill? Has the CDC come up with any opinions?"

"The CDC thinks - as of the conversation today - that aerosol transmission is quite possible from a victim, someone with the virus intact in their bloodstream. This is because the virus seems to cross membranes pretty effectively. Not that the probability is high, like for blood transmission, but they figure the virus can't be completely stopped by isolation. Coughing and intimate contact like kissing, of course, would provide the most probable avenues."

"What about children?" Cortland asked.

"Children, naturally, wouldn't catch the disease - with low testosterone - but could be carriers like women. More importantly, of course, as I'm guessing you're thinking, children getting hugged and kissed could send these precursors off in many directions."

"Yes," she nodded, looking rather put out and openly disgusted. "So even if we find what the precursors are and figure out what to do about them, we'd have to consider the whole population at risk - at least in this area. Has the CDC thought about a testosterone-lowering protocol?"

"Have they ever?" Charles indulged in a humorless laugh. "That's the last ditch procedure."

"So as you asked, Bill, what's our next step? You and I. The CDC is moving in all the right areas at the moment."

"I wish we could get something out of Bea," he said. "But we won't. I'll keep going through her notes, but I suspect we'll find nothing specific enough to be useful. I'll also help with the covalent ion structure work - though the CDC has a couple of bright young things already on it. Bea'll have some data and codes stored somewhere, but we'll never get at it. It would take a warrant to go into her room again."

"Nothing on her laptop, I gather."

"Nothing yet. The CDC computer experts might do more, but we can't alert them. I've gotten some friends here in computational science to scour it."

"And Bea didn't react to having it taken, did she?"

"No," he said, "and that's a clue that we'll find nothing. She used it to run codes, that's for sure, but since the fast memory is volatile, nothing processed remains after it turns off. She'd have sent the relevant stuff to memory sticks probably. And the computer guys say she's likely to have used an overwrite program in disk areas where data or software might have been temporarily stored. To get rid of any evidence."

"Whew!" Cortland said. Then she looked at him more intently, suddenly. "Bill, what about you? Did you get your blood tested?"

Charles looked at her oddly. "Actually, yes I did. Yesterday, as a matter of fact. The test is now routine enough that my sample wouldn't waste much time. No virus."

"But we don't know about precursors yet, do we? You've certainly been around me and Bea a lot. I know you've taken precautions with the patients, but ... well, see my point?"

"Too well, Virginia."

–

Mike entered Bea's room nearly an hour after their phone conversation. He wore dark trousers, gray shirt and lined jacket.

"Come in!" she said, moved up to him, rose to her tiptoes, and kissed his cheek.

"Thanks," Mike said, then suddenly snapped his fingers. "Oh, Fitz! I forgot the wine."

"Oh, don't worry about it." Bea gave him a pleasant look and led him into the room. Her own khakis and blue shirt were perfectly pressed and clean. She'd even spent some time on her hair. Her appearance combined with that warm demeanor, she was charmingly pretty. "Is 'Fitz' what Aunt Jacie would say?" she asked over her shoulder, almost teasingly.

Mike rubbed his eyes a moment, then smiled. "I guess so. Did I say that?" He handed her his jacket.

"You did, sir." She simply laid it over a chair, smoothing the fabric briefly.

Looking around the room, the visitor said, "So this is where the famous interview took place?"

"Yes," she said, and led him further into the room.

Bea had been busy and had prepared a simple but interesting meal of chicken breasts stuffed with sun dried tomatoes and cheese, brown rice, and a nice salad of greens, walnuts and grapefruit. She'd had everything she needed, something she hadn't expected, and had enjoyed doing it, the chicken breasts and rice now cooking covered on the surface burner of her little stove. She fussed around with the preparation a little, then got some peach juice out and poured them each a small glass, bringing it over to him.

Mike had sat next to a little coffee table and across from where Bea would sit. It was set with two plates, napkins, utensils and two wine glasses.

"So Mike," she said, placing the juice by him, "I know you're ... well, I won't bring up anything unpleasant. It will just be good to visit. Hearing more about Aunt Jacie, for example, would be wonderful."

"I talked to her today," he said, and drank a little.

"And she's well, I hope."

"Fine, yes. We talked about ..." He stopped and looked at Bea more carefully. "Yes, she's fine."

"How did she get to be such a wonderful person? Did you know her parents, too?"

"Yes, well yes, sure. They were my mother's parents, too." He stopped again. "Something really smells good."

Bea smiled, more deeply this time. "I hope you'll like it. I'm not really a cook."

"Oh, I bet you are, Bea. Everything you do is ... pretty cool, I mean it's done well."

She turned him away from her cooking. "Tell me about your grandparents, if you don't mind."

Mike went along with her request and spoke about his family for a few minutes, then suddenly stood up. "I need to smell that good food," he said, then walked across the few steps to the stove, sniffed, and lifted both lids. Bea waited, seated, for him to return. Something about the action pleased and confused her.

"Are you just trying to be nice to me, Mike?" she asked, quietly and with as much gentleness as she could muster.

"What, no. Or I mean, yes, I'm trying to be nice to you. What do you mean?"

Bea shook her head, as if at herself. "Oh, nothing, I'm just paranoid, I suppose."

He sat down and finished his juice, not commenting to her statement. A few minutes later, they were seated at the other table and Bea served the food. They ate mostly in silence for a few minutes.

"I hope you'll eat well tonight," she said pleasantly. "I'm sorry your appetite hasn't been ..."

"It's good," he interrupted. "I'm okay."

"Mike, it's ... well, I know you're distracted this evening. Are you ... is there something specific on your mind. You don't have to just be nice to me, you know." She'd put sparkling water into their wine glasses, along with slices of lime, and sipped after she spoke.

The dark young man looked at her. "I'm a little distracted, yes. I guess I am. I'm sorry."

"Is seeing me disturbing to you? Be honest."

The young man's eyes became more intense. "You have to know it is, Bea."

"Because of what I've done."

"You have to know that, too," he said. "And because you know I care about you."

Bea stood up to clear the table. This seemed like a good time to break the spell. She realized she was putting him on the spot. She'd asked him to come, basically as favor to her. How could he be anything but bitter toward her? And, he'd done as he said he would and passed on the information she shared with him. She wanted his approval or at least his acceptance and knew she had no right to expect either. As she picked up the dishes she told herself to allow him a graceful exit if he chose one. Why had she done this anyway? It had been very selfish of her.

They went back to their former chairs, this time with coffee cups from a pot she'd started when they sat down to eat.

"So," she said, "how's your research going these days? You haven't said much about it lately."

Mike shrugged. "Good coffee," he commented. "Don't ask me about that, will you? I know why you asked me over."

Bea nearly blushed. "Because you know I want your ... acceptance for what I've done."

"You don't have it, and you know it, Bea. All I can say is that I believe you thought you were doing something good. It's a damn weird way to do good, however."

"I know you think that," she said, and rubbed her eyes a moment.

Both were quiet now, each drinking and looking at the other. Finally Bea spoke again. "I suppose I knew you'd never agree with what I did, but really I asked you over here because ... because I feel very isolated right now. And because I know you care."

His brow furrowed at the words, and his eyes seemed to cloud over with sadness. "I have get out of your life, Bea. As little as I'm in it, and I know that, I still have to go away. I'm being pulled apart at the seams. Can you understand that?"

She got her feet suddenly, and knelt beside his chair. "Mr. Baylor," she said quietly, "you are the one flaw in my plan. When you go away most of my doubts will go with you. But I ..." Bea turned her head aside. He could see tears there, tears that had surprised her. She continued, "I can't bear the thought of your leaving. Don't you see?"

Mike closed his eyes, unable to hold them on the face that bewildered, thrilled, and frightened him beyond description. "I have to," he said. "But, I do it because I ... because I love you."

She swallowed, rubbed at a tear, and nodded. Leaning over she kissed his cheek, then stood. "You are far too fine a human being to waste love on me, you know. But I ... I will always be grateful to you for being so foolish!" Then she smiled. The brilliance of that look hit him like a flash of light.

Bea walked several steps away. There she was, petite, almost demure, and totally out of his emotional reach, but he knew she felt as deeply for him as she was able. For a moment she seemed about to say something, but didn't. He knew the time had come, and stood.

"I'll be going now," he said. "Thank you for the wonderful meal, and for the chance to see your place. And for the talk."

Bea nodded slightly, then stepped forward. "Please don't forget me," she said quietly. "And keep forgiving me, will you?"

"I won't," he said, with a kind of bitter smile, "and I will."

Walking toward the door, she stayed with him, now a half step back. Taking a short detour, she got his jacket and helped him into it, in a gesture so domestic as to seem completely natural. Then he turned and looked down at her. Bea stood again on tiptoes and kissed him once more, this time gently on the lips. When he began to say something she raised a finger to those lips to stop him. The look in her eyes said everything either of them needed to hear.

39. Telling the CDC

BY MORNING A COLD FRONT HAD MOVED THROUGH East Tennessee. The weather was hovering near twenty. Gray clouds that looked like possible snow sources were looming above. The bitter change in the weather was busy harassing anyone unfortunate enough to be outdoors. It was especially hard on the huge media corps that had gathered around UT Hospital, because many of them were lying in wait for university and CDC officials who were constantly entering and exiting the hospital complex and the several trailers parked in a kind of ad hoc community near the entrance. William Charles, his coat buttoned all the way to the neck, was moving faster than normal that morning, hurrying to get out of the bitter chill in a long trek from the remote parking area. He carried his briefcase in one gloved hand and had the other stuck in a coat pocket. The professor stamped his feet a little while waiting for credentials to be checked by the entrance guard, then expelled a breath of relief when stepping into the warm lobby. Several reporters had tried to stop him on the way in, but - probably because of his heavy coat and ski cap - he'd not been very recognizable and was able to ignore them effectively enough.

On the third floor, there were more reporters, of course, but Charles managed to not be noticed before he reached the locked ward entrance there. He showed his ID and was allowed in. He entered the conference room immediately to the right. There, Dr. Stafford Fellows and Dr. Marjorie Devault stood to greet him. Already standing, just behind them, was Virginia Cortland. Dr. Fellows was the chief of the CDC staff assigned to the virus case and Dr. Devault was his deputy. The CDC chief was a tall, stern looking man around sixty, with gray hair around a bald pate. He was athletic looking for his age and wore his suit well. His deputy was only in her forties, attractive with short dark hair, good figure, and an intense aspect about her. Both looked extremely neat and well kempt in comparison to Dr. Cortland, who was dowdy and grandmother-like, shabbier than usual, in fact, in a gray suit.

Fellows spoke quickly and in a midwestern accent. "Thank you, doctors, for meeting with us so early. Please, let's get right down to it. There's coffee here, tea, and various pastries." He pointed to the service arranged on a side table.

Charles got some coffee and a Danish, then sat down by Cortland. She had already taken her seat, also with coffee, but no food. Across from him was Dr. Devault, also skipping the nourishment but steeping a tea bag, moving it up and down in the hot water as she took her seat. Dr. Fellows lowered himself into a chair, with his coffee and sweet roll, across from Cortland.

"Our topic, as you've probably guessed, doctors," Fellows said, making eye contact with all three others at the table, "is the interview Ms Bea de Winter gave yesterday. I don't need to tell you how shocked we were to hear of it. We'd appreciate it if you could shed more light on this whole thing for us." This last sentence was aimed directly at the two university professors.

Virginia Cortland said, "Bill and I talked about this briefly. Neither of us intimated any of these ideas to her."

Marjorie Devault said, in a cultured Georgia accent, "Dr. Fellows, I took the opportunity, sir, to discuss the student's ideas with several of our staff last evening. There had already been discussion among our people. In fact, some consideration had already been given to a possible intentional introduction of the virus, but none that I spoke with believed it likely that the virus could be manufactured."

Fellows nodded but said nothing and looked at Charles.

Charles said, "Ford, have your people looked into the testosterone dependence?"

"Yes, indeed. The mice studies confirm it completely. When the free testosterone falls below a threshold level, the virus loses viability and dies - though not immediately."

Charles asked, "And have you looked at the brain chemistry?"

"To some extent, yes. My latest report is that there is some difficulty in estimating the human rates across the blood-brain barrier from the mice studies. But they're guessing it takes several days to get sufficient virus from the bloodstream into the brain."

Devault got them back on topic. "Dr. Cortland," she asked, "if you don't mind saying, what's your opinion of this young woman, Bea de Winter?"

"Opinion, in what regard, Dr. Devault?"Cortland responded. Then she added, "Please call me Virginia, everyone. This really isn't a time for formality, I'd say." Then she smiled.

Devault returned the smile. "Virginia, then. And I'm Marjorie." She looked across at her boss, not sure she had been given the same leave of informality with him. Then to Cortland: "Virginia, is this student the kind of person to ... well, to like attention and to offer conspiracy type theories?"

"Actually, no." Cortland looked pensive. "She's very much the opposite, I'd say. Bill, what's your opinion here?" She and Charles exchanged glances.

Charles nodded. "Bea's a loner, very much so. And never has looked for publicity."

Fellows was tapping a pen as he listened. He interjected, "So she said what she really thought then, and in your opinion she wasn't grandstanding."

Charles looked at Cortland a moment, and got a discernible nod from her. Then he said, "Virginia and I actually know why Bea gave that interview. And probably why she said what she said. Or at least we are convinced we know. But before we get into it, we'd like to ask you both to consider keeping what we have to say in confidence, at least for a time." He added a look toward Devault to include her directly.

"This sounds very mysterious, Bill," Fellows said, a slight smile.

Devault said, "Are you speaking, Dr. Charles ... or, yes, Bill, about something directly pertinent to the virus?"

"Yes, I am," he said, "but what we have learned is not something that can be readily proven."

Fellows had stopped tapping his pen. "Please continue."

Charles gave Cortland one more look, then nodded. "We believe it was Bea de Winter herself who created and released the virus."

There followed a screaming silence. Devault looked at her boss then back at Cortland and Charles. It was she who broke the spell, though easily fifteen seconds had passed. "You're saying, sir, that your student ... that she was able to - in effect - create a living organism with planned characteristics?"

Charles nodded. They could see his hands were trembling a little. "Bea is ... well, in my opinion, the only person I know who could actually have done it. And, we have it on the authority of someone who claims she admitted it to him, that she in fact did it."

Fellows shook his head slowly in a show of either disbelief, amazement, or both. "I can see now, doctors, why ... well, why you cautioned confidentiality. This is an incredible charge, as you know!"

"How well we know," Cortland said. "Bill was approached by someone we believe is trustworthy. So, unless Bill's student is lying about herself - and, as already said, a lie is totally inconsistent with her nature as we've observed it - this virus is her brainchild."

Before the two CDC people could speak further, Charles added, "We've investigated as much as we reasonably can - Virginia and I - and it's likely Bea has covered her tracks well."

"I don't quite understand," Fellows blurted out. "She's admitted it and ... but only to this one person? Has the girl denied it, too?" His brow was wrinkled and eyes narrowed.

"Effectively, yes," Cortland said. "Naturally, after we heard from her friend, we confronted her. Bill and I both talked to her. Bill even got some expert help from the Computer Science department in trying to find traces in computers she had access to. But she's been one step or more ahead of us."

"This is astounding!" Fellows said, raising his voice a little. He brought a hand up to rub against the side of his head. "So you're saying she's admitted it - informally - to someone, but won't admit it to you or anyone else you know of?"

"Exactly," Cortland said.

"But why," Fellows continued, "did she admit it to anyone at all? It makes so little sense."

"Possibly," Charles admitted. "But the one she confided in is probably her closest friend here at UT. We don't know exactly what motivated her to tell him, but it ..."

Cortland interrupted, "She may, in fact, have admitted it as a part of some further plan she has. This young woman is beyond figuring out, I'd say."

Charles shook his head slowly. "I don't think ... well at least it doesn't seem to me that Bea would have either lied about making the virus or confessed that she'd done it for some strategic purpose."

Cortland said, "I'm not sure I'm with Bill there, but for the life of me I can't imagine what could have motivated her to tell."

Devault asked, looking at Cortland, "Do you agree that this student has the ability to do such a thing? To develop and tailor a virus like this?"

Cortland replied, "I guess I'd defer to Bill on Bea de Winter's abilities. At least, her detailed abilities. But, from my contact with her, there can be no question she is a remarkable thinker. My sense is it that she really did do it. And probably because she wants to cause some impact on the negative effects - as she sees them - of testosterone on the human race."

Fellows heard this last with a clear expression of suspicion. "This sounds extremely melodramatic to me, friends. So this is the reason you think this young woman did what you think she did?"

"That's right, melodramatic as it may be," Cortland said.

"Commenting and doing are very different things," Fellows said. He looked at Charles and Cortland. "And you both believe we'll not be able to come up with any evidence relating her to the virus? Is that what you're saying?"

Cortland nodded. "We're saying we haven't found anything definitive. Yet. Bill is working through her notes, as I understand."

Charles nodded. "Yes, and the only clues I've seen so far are strictly inferential. There's nothing direct I've been able to find so far."

Fellows said, "Our CDC resources, however, are quite extensive, Dr. Charles. It seems very important, I'd say on first consideration, for us to bring everything to bear that is needed to find out if the student has been telling the truth."

"I suppose so," Cortland agreed. "But my chief concern, I have to say - given that the virus is already spreading - is not whether Bea actually did what she said she did, but what useful thing can we get from her now that may help us lick this virus. If she's responsible, what better source than she? Her knowledge would give us the best chance of finding out how to kill or prevent the viral action."

"Makes sense," Fellows agreed, "if she really made it, of course. So how can we get this student to help us?"

"I'm worried," Charles said, "that confronting her officially might do us more harm than good - especially if we can't find anything definitive to pin on her."

"So," Fellows interpreted, "Bill, you favor investigating her first and confronting her later?"

Charles nodded, then said, "What do you think, Marjorie?"

Devault was a little surprised at being asked, and hesitated. "What do I think? Well, I'm not sure. If I understand you correctly, this young woman has - at least so far - done this thing in a way that doesn't trace back to her, at least legally. Yet, she's admitted it to a friend. She had to guess he might tell - or at least had to consider the possibility. Especially since he actually did tell. And, remember, she's given this interview that got us together in the first place. From the background you've given, I'd say the interview was definitely for the purpose of throwing us off the scent, or at least distributing the attention around to other possible sources."

"A good summary," Cortland nodded. "Young Miss de Winter had to figure that suggesting other culprits would be a confusing tactic."

"Yes," Charles agreed. "Now if we accuse her without much evidence, she can say or at least suggest that we're protecting powerful interests of some kind. It's ... well, that's the kind of thing Bea would figure out."

"Bill, you have high regard for this student, don't you? Fellows noted. "But if you're right about her, she's committing first degree murder, and on a grand scale. Whatever else is real or is not, this virus is damn real!"

Charles looked suddenly somber. "I keep forgetting, I admit, what a terrible thing we're dealing with - because we're caught up - Virginia and I - in the details, and especially in my case, in tracking the process Bea probably went through to make the damned thing."

Cortland said, "Ford, we know this is not an academic exercise, if that's what you're implying. But it is a very bizarre situation. After all, we've had Miss de Winter working with us until recently. She, as you remember, came up with the definitive test to find the virus. Her measurements, some of which have been recently checked, have been accurate. She's made no attempt to falsify anything - as far as we can tell, anyway - except her own involvement in the matter. And that involvement she's only falsified by omission. She didn't directly deny her involvement when we spoke to her. She simply asked why we would possibly think she did or could do such a thing?"

"Could you be wrong about her, Bill?" Fellows asked.

Charles paused to think, then shook his head slowly. "Possible but ... no, she did it."

"Why are you so convinced? Tell me again."

The professor took a long breath. "Because everything I know about Bea de Winter tells me she could really do this. That, combined with the male-specific nature of the action and the comments Virginia found out Bea had made about men, add up to more than just odd coincidences. This is not to mention that Bea lives very close to one of the students closely connected to the first cases."

Devault reacted to the last fact. "I haven't followed that aspect very closely, I guess. It never was clear to me about those early cases. And this party that the virus has its popular name from."

Charles said, "Melissa Thomas lived two doors down from Bea in the dorm. And it was Melissa's boyfriend, the Pendergast boy, who contracted the first case."

Devault nodded. "In the same dorm. I see. What about this party?"

Virginia Cortland responded to that question. "It took place some days later. Miss Thomas and Mr. Pendergast were there. They are the main link to the other young men at the party, all but one of whom have since been infected."

"And there's no other route," Fellows asked, "that could have exposed the young men? Why could not some other person at the party be the carrier?"

Cortland said, "It's of course possible, Ford, but Pendergast, being the first victim, has been assumed the first exposed. We know, however, that the viral propagation process is not very well understood, and could be different for different people."

"So it's possible that all the students were exposed at the same time, at this party," Fellows continued. "And the virus was actually brought there by someone else."

"Possible," Charles admitted. "But what are the odds of a new disease of that type occurring randomly for the first time so near a research facility where researchers - namely Bea and myself - have been studying brain chemistry and physics, including the kinds of mechanisms that the virus is affecting?"

"Good point," Fellows nodded. He paused to drink some coffee, obviously considering what to do next. He knew very well that the ball had been bounced into his court, and he alone would have take some kind of swing at it. But he certainly was wise enough to seek out council before he did it. He continued, "So, let's make the assumption that Miss de Winter is the perpetrator. Any suggestions about the next step?"

Cortland ran a finger around the rim of her cup, then looked up to say, "Possibly, if our Miss de Winter knows the word on her has been gotten to the CDC, she'll react in some different way, or even make some mistake that we could take advantage of."

Charles shook his head. "I don't think so, Virginia. If she learns that but also isn't questioned or accosted by the authorities, she'll immediately know that no real evidence has been unearthed. Bea wouldn't be intimidated by such a situation. Not unless I've seriously misjudged her coolness."

"If we investigate her," Fellows said, "and we damned well have to, it's going to be difficult to keep from a number of people in the CDC from knowing. And I suspect it's going to be necessary for me also to go to the FBI."

Cortland sighed. "As we supposed, too. But some strategy to get her to help us, I say again, would be the best possible thing we could do."

Majorie Devault released a sigh. "How about the FBI? Would they have the freedom to question her? I'm thinking about pentothal or some other similar drug."

Charles looked at the deputy chief. "You mean get information from her whether she volunteered it or not?"

"Yes," Devault said. "As distasteful as it is, we're not dealing with something trivial here. As we all know."

"But," Charles pointed out, "would the law allow such action? Especially if there is not compelling evidence. And we don't have it yet, and may never get it."

Fellows said, "Marjorie is right. Unfortunately. We may have to take dire action in the public interest. That's why I feel like it's necessary for me to speak to the FBI."

Cortland slowly nodded her head. "I really doubt Bea would help us voluntarily."

Charles shook his head. "But she's already helped us. What I'd hoped is that we could ask for even more help. Not that Virginia or I would pretend we didn't think she'd done it. But by not seeming to have told anyone else, Bea might remain confident about her situation. Then she might do or say something that would help me and others figure out more about her design and how she implemented it. That's what would truly help us, after all."

Fellows regarded Charles a long moment, then shook his head. "We can't put too much hope in that idea, Bill. Unfortunately. Besides, unless we've falsely accused her - and I'm convinced, from what you say, we haven't - this student of yours is a criminal. Plain and simple. We can't simply ignore that truth and pretend she's okay."

Devault basically agreed. "If the girl is ... well, she certainly seems the likely designer at this point - I for one wouldn't trust any help she might give. Maybe she'd be pretending something that would lead us off track even more."

"But," Charles insisted, "she's not done that up to now."

Cortland looked at her friend and colleague. "I know Bill thinks Miss de Winter has a certain kind of integrity. But ... my reading is that she's been playing us all like a violin, choosing the tune, so to speak. I don't trust the girl, in all honesty. Maybe if she were scared a little, in fact, she might begin to realize what kind of the terrible reality she has been responsible for."

Charles bit his lower lip. "You can't scare Bea. You can make her clam up, sure. You can even throw her in jail, or whatever. But you won't scare her."

"Whatever we do," Fellows offered, "it would be disgusting to just let her think she's gotten by with it."

"But she has," Charles said. "That's exactly what she's done. And knew it before she confessed to her friend."

"Damn it!" Fellows muttered. "Let's hope you're wrong, Bill."

"Yeah, let's hope," Charles nodded with a shrug. Then he looked at Cortland. "Virginia is probably more honest about Bea than I am. Maybe I know Bea too well, or maybe I don't know her at all."

Cortland gave Charles a warm look. "You're not a woman, Bill. You can't understand Bea de Winter unless you are. She thinks you are the enemy, you know. You and all your testosterone-poisoned brothers."

"I suppose you're right," Charles sighed. "Keep reminding me, will you?"

Fellows suddenly stood up. "Let's get back together tomorrow, shall we? I have some thinking to do. Marjorie, will you hang around a few more minutes?" Then he said, "Thanks so much, Bill and Virginia. We'll talk soon."

On the way out of the hospital the two friends were silent, each in his or her own thoughts. Then the swarm of the reporters in the lobby below brought each back to the reality that would not go away.

40. Response

EARLY THE NEXT MORNING, DR. STAFFORD FELLOWS put in a call to the Federal Bureau of Investigation in Washington, D.C. The telephone conversation lasted more than an hour.

It was mid-morning when a pair of FBI agents found Mike Baylor at the mouse repository. He'd been reading at the desk, back to the two approaching.

"Mr. Baylor?" said the quiet but commanding voice behind him.

He turned and looked back, then quickly got to his feet. "Yes," he said, "I'm Mike Baylor."

The agent who spoke was a woman in her thirties, looking very professional and competent in a dark suit. She held out an FBI ID card for him. "I'm Agent Saunders," the woman said. "This is Agent McMasters." She indicated the man beside her, who reached out to shake Mike's hand. He was a little younger than she, with a freshly scrubbed look.

At the agents' suggestion, Mike closed and locked the repository doors to allow a private interview. He knew full well what it would be about. And the two wasted no time in getting down to business. "You are a friend of Miss Bea de Winter, we understand," Saunders asked. She and her colleague each had a small note pad in sight, making it clear they were taking notes.

"Yes," he said simply.

"Do you know her location?" Saunders continued.

"I saw her last night," he said, "but haven't seen her today."

"Did she give you any clue as to where she might be today?"

"No," he replied, shaking his head. "Has she gone somewhere, then?"

"She's not in her dormitory, her laboratory space at the university, or the university hospital. Are there other places she might go in the area, from your knowledge, Mr. Baylor?"

Again he shook his head. "No. Bea doesn't have time for much but her work."

"It was you, we understand, Mr. Baylor," said by the man McMasters, speaking for the first time since introducing himself, "who Ms de Winter told about inventing and releasing the party virus. Is that correct?"

"Yes," he nodded. "Yes, she told me."

"Why did she tell you," the man continued, "if you don't mind my asking?" He tacked on a pleasant, non-threatening look.

"I think she wanted me to ... well, accept what she did."

"But you didn't?" interposed Agent Saunders. She, too, gave him a pleasant expression.

"No," he said.

"Was she angry at you because of this?" the woman asked.

"No, Bea wasn't angry at me. Disappointed maybe, but not angry." Mike looked at the two agents a second or two, then added, "Actually, she didn't really need me to ... to accept what she did. All she wanted was to be straight with me." Then he looked away. "But I guess that doesn't really matter to you, does it?"

"Mr. Baylor," Saunders said, "it's your word alone - as you well know, of course - that your friend did this heinous thing. "Is there ..."

Mike interrupted her with, "No, there's no way Bea would have made it up. And yes, I'm willing to testify to what she told me. And yes, Bea knows I will." He closed his eyes a moment, then reopened them.

"I see," Saunders said. "She must be very angry with you."

Mike shook his head. "No. As I said, she wasn't."

"She sounds like a remarkable person to me," McMasters ventured, glancing at his colleague.

Mike didn't take the bait, nor did he know what the agent was fishing for. "Bea is my friend," was all he said. "I think she did a terrible thing, but she did it for a reason ... she did it because she thought she had to."

"She had to?" Saunders asked. "I don't quite understand."

"I'm sure you've been told about this," Mike said quietly. "She knew she could do what she did and felt it had to be done. She'll ... she'll take the consequences. That's Bea."

Saunders said, "So she knew she was committing a crime against humanity?" The words came out in a kind of brittle coldness.

Mike shook his head. "She believed ... believes, still, she was doing the best she could for humanity. If it broke the law - and she knew it did, sure - so be it."

"And you think she's misguided in this?" Saunders continued.

"Yes, I do."

"Why, if I may ask?"

"Because of the suffering. But Bea thinks it will be confined to one generation, then things will get better."

"Does that make sense to you, Mr. Baylor, that things will get better?"

"I don't know," he said.

Saunders stood, indicating they were done with him. "We thank you very much for your time. We may have to get back to you. Hope you understand." Then she extended a hand.

Then they were gone. Mike rubbed his chin a while, staring at the door they'd used, then unlocked the doors and made the mouse repository available again.

–

Bea de Winter dropped the small package into the mailbox just outside her dorm. Then, bundled up in her winter coat, she stood nearby until the cab arrived about five minutes later. After the short ride over to the Strip, she got out just outside The Sunspot. The breakfast crowd had thinned out and the lunch crowd had not arrived yet. When Bea entered the place she had her choice of tables, opting for one far from the front windows but not far from an overhead light. She had a book with her and was reading it when coffee was brought. She ordered an English muffin and some flavored yogurt. She put down her book and opened the Metropulse - a local weekly paper she'd picked up from a stack near the door. Bea read a story about the "Party Virus," written by a student who knew several of the victims and several of the girls who were at the now-famous party, including Melissa Thomas. Bea had brought her backpack, as usual, but it only contained a few items, omitting several books, the confiscated laptop, and other odds and ends she normally carried around on the campus. But on that morning she knew she wouldn't go to the campus or to the hospital complex.

After the food came, Bea ate most of it, then stood, signaling the waiter, who was nearby.

"I'm going to the women's room a minute," Bea said to him. "Would you please watch my backpack for me?"

The long haired one smiled pleasantly and assured her he would. Bea entered the restroom to find it empty. She looked at the two closed stalls, peering under their doors to verify no one was there, and went into one of them. The restroom had a drop ceiling, put in to cover pipes and other protrusions in the ceiling area. Bea stood on the closed toilet and was able to extend her arms and lift up one of ceiling panels. Sliding it aside a little, she reached up so as to be able to touch the top surface of the Styrofoam-like material. Satisfied with how it felt, she got out three memory sticks from her pocket and pushed their metal connectors, one at a time, into the soft ceiling panel surface. The memory sticks, side by side, were projecting up from the upper surface of the ceiling panel, pushed in far enough to hold them firmly in place. Bea then repositioned the panel, leaving the stuck objects out of sight on top of it. Completing the charade, Bea washed her hands, dried them on paper towels, and exited the restroom. Back in her seat she read while waiting for the waiter to return with her bill.

As the waiter approached, about five minutes later, Bea saw two nicely dressed people, a man and a woman, enter the front of the restaurant. The hostess met them, and they showed her something. Then the young hostess pointed toward Bea. Bea saw the gesture, but pretended not to. She was busy reading her book when the FBI agents stopped at her table.

The ride to the police station took less than fifteen minutes. Bea sat quietly in the back seat, bundled up in her winter coat, continuing to read. The two agents, Saunders and McMasters spoke in low tones in the front. When they arrived at the station, the young woman was led down a hallway to an interrogation room. The room was not far from where she and Mike had reported the campus attack. It hadn't been that long ago, but now it seemed ages.

Agent Saunders sat with Bea at the table. There was a mirror in the room, and Bea figured McMasters and possibly others were observing them from the other side of it.

Saunders said, "Miss de Winter, thank you for agreeing to come. It's certainly a better place to talk than the restaurant, don't you agree?" She gave Bea an encouraging smile.

"How can I help you, Agent Saunders?" Bea asked.

"As you probably know, we're investigating the party virus outbreak, and are quite interested in the ideas you recently shared with the Reuters News Agency. I suppose you must have seen your interview printed in a number of papers."

"Actually I didn't read it," Bea said. "And I'm a little surprised it got so much attention."

"Surprised?" Saunders smiled politely. "The idea of a possible conspiracy behind the virus has stirred a lot of interest. You can certainly see that the Bureau wants to find out if a conspiracy is indeed what is going on."

"Yes, I can certainly appreciate that," Bea nodded.

"We're particularly interested, Miss de Winter, in whether some bio-medical facility might want to produce the party virus for financial gain, or even for some sort of political blackmail. Perhaps you could expand on your thoughts about this possibility."

Bea seemed very small and young at the table, looking across at the imposing female agent. The student, however, met the other's eyes easily as she replied. "The truth is, Agent Saunders, I have no experience with large profit-making biomedical organizations. My speculation to the reporter was simply that: a speculation. It was only an effort to find a plausible reason why the virus had come into being. It would have been logical to assume the virus was strictly a random mutation except for the specificity of its action."

"So you, then, Miss de Winter, think the virus couldn't have come about naturally?"

"I think it's possible it could have happened from a mutation, yes, but unlikely."

"Could you explain that a little more, if you don't mind?"

Bea thought for a moment, attempting to decide what and how much to tell. "As I mentioned to the reporter, the viral action is sex specific. I don't know of any other neuro-active virus like that."

"Neuro-active? You mean acting on the brain?"

"Yes."

"So, the viral action only affects males? Are you and the others on the biomedical team sure of that, Miss de Winter?"

"There seems to be a correlation with free testosterone levels in the blood. That's the basis of our belief."

"There's nothing else in males that could account for them getting infected?"

"You mean some other chemical condition unique to males?"

"I'm not sure what I'm asking, Miss de Winter," Saunders said. "We're just trying to get some handle on this conspiracy idea. You mentioned in the Reuters interview that since power in the society resides for the most part in the hands of the males of our species, that a disease of this kind could be thought of as a kind of hostage situation. Could you go into this a little more? It would be helpful."

Bea lowered her eyes, then gave the other full concentration a moment. She looked aside just before she spoke. "When I spoke about hostages my thoughts were that possibly some group might demand something in return for a cure or a vaccine. But our understanding of the virus and its environment continues to improve, Agent Saunders. Right now at least a cure is not in sight. As for a vaccine, the only likelihood, at least until even more is learned about the virus, is to lower male testosterone levels. This isn't exactly the answer you requested, I understand, but ..."

"No, continue, Miss de Winter, if you would." The agent had an encouraging expression on her face.

Bea continued. "As you probably know, shifting male free testosterone concentrations downward has direct effects on male behavior. So, such a 'vaccine' would not be satisfactory to most people, especially males. I suppose my suggestion for the FBI would be to investigate biomedical groups with enough resources to go a step beyond testosterone reduction."

"You mean a real vaccine or a real cure?" Saunders took an instinctive glance at the window.

"Yes," Bea nodded.

"But this doesn't speak to the motives for these groups, Miss de Winter. What is your feeling here?"

Bea shrugged. "I'm wouldn't say my feeling has any special significance, to tell you the truth. Surely the FBI can consult with sociologists, psychologists and the like. My expertise is limited to bio-physical and chemical systems."

"But how do you respond personally, if you don't mind saying, to the idea of large numbers of men succumbing to this viral disease?"

Bea had been expecting this question, or some variant, and answered with no hesitation. "It's sad to see innocent people suffer, Agent Saunders."

"So there's no upside to a male-specific disease of this sort, in your opinion?"

"Upside?"

"Benefit that comes despite the downsides. Kind of like a rainbow from a thunderstorm."

Bea again spoke with no pause. "It's not my place to speculate about such things. But disease agents, in both animals and plants, tend to disproportionately infect the weaker members of the species. It's a natural purging effect and one of the ways natural selection drives the process of evolution."

"So males, in your view, are weaker members of our species?" Saunders kept her expression light, even slightly frivolous.

"Weaker when it comes to resistance to this virus. That we have evidence for."

Agent Saunders, in the next blink, changed her demeanor. Her eyes were cool steel now. "We have reports, Miss de Winter, that you yourself are the one responsible for the virus. Are these reports true?"

Bea narrowed her eyes and wrinkled her brow. "Responsible?" she asked. "I have no responsibility at all at the moment, Agent Saunders. My major professor has released me from the virus team work so I can get back to my graduate research."

"You know I don't mean that kind of responsibility, Miss de Winter. I mean you designed and released the virus yourself. Is this true?"

"My involvement with the virus team came after the first cases were reported," Bea said, her calm remarkably evident.

"The first cases, Miss de Winter, were among students you had direct access to, through your friend in the dormitory, Miss Melissa Thomas. Tell me, did you design and release the virus?"

"Agent Saunders, should we question your personal involvement in criminal cases simply because you were part of the investigation? After all you were very close to the parties involved."

"I simply asked you, Miss de Winter, if you designed and released the virus. It's not a complicated question."

"It's a peculiar question, actually," Bea said, eyes as hard as her interrogator's. "I was led to believe you wanted scientific information to help your investigation."

"I want the truth," Saunders retorted, but calmly. "We have reports that you did this thing. Did you?"

"Do you really believe a single student could design such a virus?"

"What I believe is not an issue, Miss de Winter. I ask you again, did you design and release the virus?"

"This question doesn't deserve an answer, Agent Saunders. Were I to say yes it would be admitting something for which there is no evidence. Or it might simply be a grandstand play by a student to get some undeserved recognition. There's no reason for you to believe me since there is no direct evidence of any involvement on my part except to help identify the virus and correlate data associated with it, as part of the early investigation. All of that involvement is fully documented in the laboratory records. Were I to say no you'll continue to investigate me, I suppose. We may as well ask you if you were the designer. Your yes or no would carry the same lack of meaning."

"If you say yes, Miss de Winter," Saunders said, unruffled, "we would also expect you to give us corroborative evidence. In that case a positive answer carries significance, wouldn't you say?"

Bea shrugged, looking suddenly very student-like. "There is no corroborative evidence of the kind you suggest. So my answer to your original question is unnecessary. It could only prejudice any further investigation."

"So you refuse to answer that question? You refuse to say yes or no to the question of whether you designed and released the virus?"

"I'll be happy to answer relevant questions, Agent Saunders."

Agent Saunders stood up. "Miss de Winter, I am arresting you on suspicion of the federal crime of terrorism. You have a right to remain silent. Anything you say now can and will be used against you. You have a right to request legal council, though granting council requires specific agreement of federal authorities in the United States Department of Justice."

With that said, she withdrew handcuffs from the table drawer, indicated for Bea to stand and turn around, then cuffed the student's hands behind her back. As this was happening a uniformed police woman entered the room. Bea said no further word as she was led away.

41. Continuing Questions

CHRISTMAS VACATION AT THE UNIVERSITY of Tennessee had been scheduled on the school calendar to begin on December 10th, fifteen days after Bea's arrest. As events actually unfolded, however, the university closed early, December 3rd marking the last full day of classes. With Knoxville the epicenter of the party virus, university officials had no real choice. Normal life had been disrupted in any place where new cases had been identified. For Knoxville, normal life had little residual meaning. The great struggle for those in positions of leadership in East Tennessee, in fact, was to avoid total chaos. What the members of the virus team had speculated about, discussed, planned for, and had understood in a conceptual, theoretical way, had - almost overnight, it seemed - actually come to pass. The gravity of the situation struck home everywhere in the United States on the evening of December 8th when the President addressed the nation on virtually all radio and television outlets, with simultaneous streaming on dozens of official and unofficial internet web sites.

"My fellow Americans," were the first words of the Chief Executive, spoken from the Oval Office, followed by, "it saddens me to inform you that our nation, and indeed the whole world, is under siege. We are under attack by an insidious enemy, an invisible foe that strikes down our young men, our most vital men, without warning. All of you have heard of the virus - known to most of us as 'the party virus' - and are aware of its devastating effects on the human brain. Perhaps many of you, like myself, were not fully capable of understanding the enormity of the danger it presented, and not having seen any cases yourself, couldn't fully perceive that the danger posed included those near and dear to you. My friends, let me say - and it is a bitter pill for me and all Americans to swallow - that the terrible time has arrived for us as a great people, as a nation under God, to directly face the reality of this threat."

The President paused, took a drink from a water glass next to the podium, and continued. "As of this morning, there are fifteen regions of the United States that have been placed under total quarantine. All airports in these areas will be closed until further notice. All highways and rails into and out of these areas will be closed at the quarantine region boundaries. No one will exit these areas for any reason whatsoever unless released by the authority I have designated to the Centers for Disease Control. No one will enter these regions, again except for the CDC's concurrence. I have placed our American Military under round-the-clock alert and will make our service men and women available throughout the nation to support law enforcement in maintaining civil order and to support medical teams as needed. The quarantine zones are shown on this map." The view switched to a map of the United States with fifteen regions outlined in bold red. "These regions, for the moment, will remain under normal state and local administration, but if conditions worsen I will not hesitate to place them under military jurisdiction."

The President's face returned to center screen, showing deep concern and a noticeable aspect of fatigue. "As reported by the CDC one hour ago, there are now more than sixteen thousand confirmed cases of the party virus. The number has doubled in just six days. Ten of the infected regions have been identified only in the last week. I cannot stress strongly enough, fellow citizens, how dire this threat is to our American society, its economy and its well being. I plan to address you as a nation at this same time day after tomorrow to keep you informed about this terrible menace and our combined efforts to combat it. Now is a time for prayer, a time for a cooperative spirit, and heroic effort in a common cause. It is not a time for selfish or greedy behavior, or for despicable criminal acts. Be certain that our response to maintain order and decency within the nation will be swift and sure. I trust that all of us will pull together in a common cause and, under the will of Almighty God, will prevail against our common enemy. Goodnight, and God Bless America!"

Stafford Fellows punched the video remote to turn off the television mounted on the wall of the conference room in the third floor isolation wing of the UT Hospital. Seated with him around the table were the eight senior members of the CDC Virus team, including his deputy Marjorie Devault, Virginia Cortland and William Charles. Fellows looked around the assortment of faces and said, "There was some reluctance in Washington three days ago, but the six thousand new cases since Monday changed a lot of minds."

An austere looking man in his fifties, Dr. Werner Compton, looked over at Fellows and said, "Ford, are you going to bring us up to date on the latest on the virus?

Fellows nodded thoughtfully. "We moved fifty cases from here to Methodist Medical Center in Oak Ridge yesterday." Then he looked around the table. "Let's see, what else is new? Maybe Bill should talk about the precursor work. Bill?"

Charles had his notes piled in front of him. The professor looked thinner and a little more haggard every day, it seemed. "We've run into a number of problems, as you probably have heard," he said, almost sighing. "To remind you, we're reasonably certain the virus assembles from a group of precursors, but nothing like we've modeled has shown up yet. As you know, the number of chemical species in the blood is large. We have a dozen people watching for possible formation sequences, but haven't found them yet. But we will, eventually. The worse problem though, in a nutshell, is that even when and if we identify specific precursors we have to find a way to isolate and kill or break them down without killing the patient. The models so far have not been encouraging in this regard. And without getting rid of all of the precursors, the chances are still significant to form the virus."

Majorie Devault asked,"I heard you had begun a vaccine study, Bill. How's that going?"

Charles didn't have an encouraging tone when he answered. "We have begun, that's about all I can say. The challenge is great since we have never worked with a virus structure like this before."

"What about the hypothermic treatment study?" another of the group, Dr. Ivy Cho, an Asian-heritage woman of slight build, asked.

"No good," Charles said. "We can't kill the virus - in the blood or brain - by heating it or cooling it - except of course at extremes that we can't use in living patients. We're looking into passing blood through different wavelengths of laser light, hoping we can get some specificity that doesn't do too much other damage. But that's just started."

"How about viral variants?" the original questioner, Dr. Compton, asked.

Charles sighed. "There are five more identified so far. That's added to the nightmare in the precursor study. We don't know what could cause the variants - at least in the modeling phase."

Fellows said, speaking to everyone, "the testosterone threshold levels also vary a little from variant to variant, but we've established what we think is a safe level. And that, of course, works, as Miss de Winter planned." There was a detectable bitterness in his last words.

Cortland raised a hand, then spoke. "As a matter of interest, I can give you a little more about Bea's case. I spoke with Agent Saunders yesterday afternoon."

Fellows nodded, "Please."

"It's important to remind you all," Cortland said, "that Bea de Winter is not officially identified or arrested. So far we've managed to hold the media off to everything but rumors. They can't find her and we can't find her, either - that's our stand. Remember, only we in this room and a few others in Washington have this information. It's vital that nothing gets out. If there are leaks, the FBI will come after us here at the table. The situation has already gone to hell." She looked intently at everyone.

Fellows said, "Yes, so far, so good. And Virginia's caution is important to never forget, any of us. Do not speak anything of it! Any glimmer the media get and God knows what the consequences will be."

The murmurs around the table told him they'd gotten the point.

Cortland then continued. "Bea – as we said last meeting – has given no information to the FBI. We don't even know where she is now. Saunders said they've done all the 'standard' things they can do. From the context and tone of what the agent said, we can expect they'll be giving her drugs soon."

William Charles looked away, making an effort at composure. He didn't speak. But Fellows said, "It's a matter of vital national interest." He was directing his words at Charles. "Bill, when she talks, we'll have the precursors, or at least we can hope so."

Werner Compton said, "We're certain about this student, I suppose? I know, I've heard the whole tale, but ..."

Cortland interrupted him. "Werner, if Bea's not guilty the drug treatment should show it. If she doesn't know anything she can't reveal anything."

Charles said, "She's twenty-one years old. How can we know they're treating her with ... with dignity?"

"We can't," Cortland said. "I didn't ask what the 'standard' things were that they'd done. But this situation is a lot bigger than this young woman. Don't forget the horror she's already caused."

"Bea is not a particularly healthy person," Charles said. "She has a chronic asthmatic condition."

Cortland had not heard this before. "There's no reason to believe they'll threaten her health, Bill."

Charles nodded, then closed his eyes before speaking again, opening them as he began. "From the rate of increase of cases, we know a huge number of men already have the virus in their system. It's clear now that aerosol transmission occurs, despite being less likely than blood borne infection. All us men on the team – I don't need to remind you – are being tested every other day now. This Damoclean sword is about to hang over the whole country. This is not to mention the cases in Europe and Asia. The testosterone reduction protocol looks like our only near-term hope and no one has dared to impose it ... yet. The quarantine regions are probably too little too late. We pushed the feds for this two weeks ago, and even then it may have been too late. We have well over three hundred known cases outside the U.S. already. At the present rate of increase - being optimistic - we're seeing, based on the sixteen thousand confirmed cases here, about a six percent increase per day now. That's nearly 100,000 cases this month, and around three million by March. But the realistic scenario, that the rate will go up for a while, means it'll be even worse."

Fellows looked at Charles. "So, Bill, what else can we do?"

"Nothing," Charles admitted. "We're doing all we know. Bea has done something like pushing Humpty Dumpty off the wall and we're finding ourselves in the role of all the King's horses and all the King's men."

—

Mike Baylor's Aunt Jacie, in her dark green housecoat and felt-lined house shoes, came downstairs in the old tenement building in Detroit where she lived, and where Mike had grown up. Jacie's thick, mostly gray hair had two rollers in it, the extent of her beauty preparations for the day. She was a heavy woman, but not excessively so, and made her way downward with some of the grace she'd had thirty years earlier when she'd moved into that building. The package had been thin enough to push through the one-inch width of the mail slot near the top of the mailbox. Jacie was immediately curious about it. She rarely got packages in the mail.

Climbing the stairs to the third floor - though not quickly anymore - Jacie went back into her neat apartment. The place had two bedrooms, hers and Mike's - when he was home - a small kitchen, living room-dining room combination, and a single bath. There was also a narrow balcony outside the living room on which she grew - during the growing season - an assortment of flowers and vegetables. It was on that balcony that Mike had told her about his graduate fellowship to the University of Tennessee. Jacie put the other mail on the old wooden kitchen table and sat down there with the package. It was easy to open, having a tear tab near the sealed end.

Inside were three USB memory sticks, each sixteen gigabytes in capacity, and a folded note. Jacie sat the memory sticks aside and opened the note. It was handwritten in a small, precise script, and read:

"Dear Aunt Jacie, I'm being presumptuous to call you that, but Mike has spoken so warmly about you that I have come to think of you as my aunt, too. You've noticed the memory sticks in the package. I want to ask you a favor involving them. Would you please store them somewhere safe for me? It might be months before I ask you about them. The files they contain are encrypted, so they'll make no sense to anyone else, but they're very important to me.

"Aunt Jacie, I know you may be less than pleased to hear from me. But I want to tell you thank you for raising Mike. He is the finest person I've ever known. I'm sure you are as proud of him as he is of you.

"Again thank you very much for keeping these memory sticks for me. I hope I'll have the honor some day of meeting you and thanking you personally.

Sincerely, Bea de Winter."

The big woman reread the note, a certain awe having come over her. What had Bea put into her safekeeping? It had to be something about that virus. And why send the memory sticks to her? It had to be because this youngster figured someone would find them otherwise. Suddenly, Jacie realized, she'd been drawn into the web of influence of this very odd and wonderful - or so Mike definitely felt - girl.

Jacie went to her phone and dialed Mike's number. The young man answered after the third ring.

"Dear boy, how are you today?" Jacie asked him, trying to sound less disturbed than she was.

"Fine, Aunt Jacie. Don't need to tell you not much is goin' on here."

"The truth is I got a package in the mail today from your Bea."

"From Bea? Really. I haven't seen or heard from her in ... well, it's been two weeks. Don't have to tell you I've been concerned, even if it is my own fault."

"This package was mailed ... let's see ..." Jacie looked at the front of the package. "Looks like two weeks ago alright. Sure took its sweet time gettin' to me."

"Mail's always slow there, Auntie, you know that. What's in it?"

"Three of those memory sticks for computers."

Mike was silent on the phone a moment. "Oh damn, it's ..." He paused.

"Somethin' to do with that virus, idn't it, boy?"

"Probably, yes."

"Truth is that's why I called. What should I do with them?"

"Was that all she sent?" Mike sounded concerned.

"A note, too. Asked me to keep 'em for her."

Another pause, then he said, "I don't know what to do about them. Let me think about it, okay?"

"Okay. Figured you'd say that. Tell me, boy, where is Miss Bea? Any idea? Think she's runnin' away?"

"Hard to believe she would, Auntie, but ... well, maybe she is. But no one can run far, as you know. I have no idea where she might go. She doesn't have any family, and doesn't know many people. I can't imagine her professor - Dr. Charles - helping her out."

"What about the cops, son? Have they got her?"

Jacie could hear his heavy sigh before he spoke. "That's what I'm afraid of. But ... well, I guess they won't hurt her or anything."

It was Jacie's turn to hesitate. Then she said, "Try not to worry about her, Mike. Nothin' you c'n do about it anyway. Hope you're stayin' busy."

"Tryin' to, Aunt Jacie. Lot to read about the Smoky Mountains and its flora."

"Spec so, son. Love you, you know. Call me when you've done your thinkin'."

"I will. Promise."

"Bye for now." Jacie hung up.

Outside the weather was its usual December bleak. A little snow had begun to fall. Jacie went to the window to watch the weather a moment. She spoke aloud to herself after a few minutes of silence. "The boy's caught in the middle of his own Winter."

42. Words That Needed to be Said

THE ROOM'S SHADES WERE DRAWN, leaving the space around the bed in nearly total darkness. Bea's awareness of the room was vague, but gradually increasing. She was waking up but taking a long time in the process. At first she only sensed that she was lying down and that air around her was cool, a little too cool. Eventually, however, she began to piece together recollections, snatches of memories. A remembered image of Mike formed, then broke up, dissolving. Bea shivered as another, more shadowy image formed: the creatures that had tried to kidnap her. It, too, faded quickly, however, replaced by the face she had seen so often in recent days. Those eyes that were so deceptive in their aspect. Bea closed hers, thinking to blot out the visage. Then she heard the voice. That same voice. Would that voice never cease?

"Bea, wake up."

A light came on. It was a lamp beside the bed, but focused directly on Bea's face. The young woman turned her head aside, eyes tightly shut. A dull throb formed a rhythm between her temples.

"Bea, wake up," the voice repeated.

The lamp beam was diverted away from Bea's face, and she turned her head back and opened her eyes. "Is it morning?" the reclining one asked, the words barely audible. The throb was a little worse as she grew more awake.

"It's time to speak again," Agent Saunders said, firmly.

Bea instinctively moved to rub her eyes, but couldn't, then remembered her arms were restrained. Each wrist was attached at her side by a padded cuff on a steel bar that ran parallel to the side of the bed, holding her firmly, but comfortably - except when it would be nice to use her hands. Bea's ankles were similarly held at the bottom of the bed, but she hardly felt the restraints there.

Bea's eyes found the agent's and Bea said, "I suppose it is, Agent Saunders. I'll say good morning, though I don't know that it is applicable, in either sense of the term." The headache was growing worse.

"I'd like to speak with you, Bea, before the nurse comes with your injection."

Bea looked away from her. "I'm hardly in a position to refuse."

The agent sat in a chair next to the bed. "I'll remind you, Bea, that we had a court order for the drug administration you received. And we have recorded all you said. Due process and proper decorum have been followed. We have given you far more respect than we believe you deserve." The last line was icy off the woman's lips.

Bea returned her eyes to the questioner. "Since I'm to receive another injection, I suppose that means, then, that you've not gotten the information you wanted."

"Not all, no. But you did provide important facts. Do you remember speaking with us, Bea, after the injection?"

"No," Bea answered.

"You admitted you fabricated the virus, Bea, just as we had been told."

"I suspect," Bea replied, her voice slightly stronger now, even if the throbbing was worse, "if you had asked me if I could fly I would have admitted that, too."

"You are a very evil person, Bea. How can you make light of such behavior?"

Bea's countenance changed noticeably. Her eyes seemed almost liquid as she looked at the other. "Agent Saunders, how can you live with yourself after what you have put me through?"

"How can I indeed?" Saunders retorted. "Easily. Simply by reminding myself that my goal is to save the lives of countless people, and that maybe we can do that when we get the needed information from you."

"What you think you want, you won't get, Agent Saunders." Bea shook her head back and forth briskly, indicative of clearing her thoughts. The headache was pushing her almost to tears, and tears were the last thing she wanted to shed. Biting at her lip a moment, Bea continued, "I've researched the drugs you are using. They are effective only in general ways. Yes, you can ask me to admit something and I'll – at the reduced level of awareness the chemicals have put me in – be able to respond to that. But anything complex will be beyond my ability to recite, much less recall. You will be working with a person who's barely functional even for simple mental tasks."

"How appropriate, Bea, that you think you have everything so well figured out," came the frigid retort.

"These are things I've already explained to you a number of times, Agent Saunders," Bea said, eyes now closed. "When will I be allowed to speak with an attorney?"

"You are being held, as you know, Bea, as a terrorist. The law is clear on this point. You have no right to an attorney."

"Because you don't want the truth of what you have done to me to come out, Agent Saunders. You and your associates prefer to remain in your state of delusion."

"You're one to speak of delusion," the woman replied. "But I want to give you another opportunity to speak voluntarily before we administer more drugs."

Bea kept her eyes closed. "May I ask for a physician to examine me first? The injections are ... are not kind to me."

"And you were kind to all those men you have destroyed?" Saunders maintained her cool demeanor but anger was always just below the surface.

"You're diverting the subject away from the relevant point," Bea said, closed eyes turned toward the other. "Your goal is to get me to recount certain things to you. To reach that goal requires that I am alive and mentally functional."

"There are physicians available if needed," Saunders said. "The nurse is coming in five minutes, unless you choose to speak to us voluntarily."

Bea turned her head aside. A tear had leaked out of her closed eye and she didn't want it seen. "I'd like to make another request, Agent Saunders. May I speak on the phone with Mike Baylor?"

"To what purpose, Bea?" There was no sympathy in the tone.

"He is my friend. It would be very ... good to hear his voice."

Saunders considered the request. "How can we trust you, Bea, not to call attention to what we are doing here?"

Bea, as usual, had already anticipated the question. "Put me on a two-second delay. If I say something untoward you can block its transmission."

The FBI agent stood. "That might be possible, Bea. Does that mean you will speak to us voluntarily afterward?"

"Every word I've spoken, Agent Saunders, except those under a drugged state - and words I can't remember nor vouch for - every word has been voluntary."

"Bea, you never waver, do you?" The tall woman in her neatly pressed business suit looked down at the restrained Bea de Winter, there under a sheet and light blanket, only her head visible. After a long silence, Saunders said, "I can do that for you, Bea. I'll arrange it. If necessary the nurse will come in afterwards."

"Thank you very much," Bea said earnestly. "That is very kind of you, truly."

Saunders turned to leave, but Bea's voice stopped her. "Agent Saunders."

"Yes?" The woman turned back, a trace of irritation showing.

Bea opened her eyes and took the other completely in. "I know this whole thing has been very difficult for you," Bea said. "I know you followed your sense of duty and conscience, and I know you hold my motives in disdain. In your place, I would have very probably felt the same." Bea swallowed, fighting back another tear. "I want you to know I deeply respect you and admire you. Nothing you have said or done has been intentionally cruel or done with anything but a motive to do the right thing. I should ... I apologize for not saying this sooner. And I don't want you to think I'm saying it now because you're acceding to my request."

Saunders didn't reply. After a few seconds, she formed a grave smile on her face. "I'm not sure what to say," she finally said. "But I take your words at face value, Bea." Then she left the room.

Bea tried to make herself relax. The pounding in her head was worse, now that she was completely awake. She made herself concentrate on things she could see: the window with the opaque gray shade and dark red drape, partly closed; the off-white ceiling tiles above her; and the stand next to the bed with a saline bag hanging on it. The back of Bea's left hand near the wrist had an IV port in it, taped over now. It was the first time she'd noticed it. Could her memory of having it put in have been purged by the medications they'd used? She was well aware of the so-called "amnesia" drugs - she guessed a cyclohexylamine - used for many surgeries, designed to erase any memory of the surgery, including some period of time before it began. A trace of panic set in, and she breathed through her mouth a few breaths, trying to regain calm. There was no sound except the quiet purr of air circulation. She picked out two ceiling vents, equally spaced along the center line. By concentrating she could feel the actual motion of the circulated air on her cheeks. All the while the headache kept up its rhythmic throbbing.

After a long ten minutes Agent Saunders came back in, carrying a phone. It was some kind of cell phone. A uniformed nurse followed her. Bea hadn't seen the nurse before - or didn't remember her, in any case. The nurse, without a word, came to the bed, lifted the covers on the side and released Bea's right wrist from the strap. After the nurse left, Saunders gave Bea the phone.

"Mr. Baylor is on the line, Bea," she said. "I'll give you five minutes."

"Thank you," Bea said, suddenly feeling a lump in her throat. She watched as the agent left the room.

"Hello, Mike?" Bea said, her voice a little quavery.

"Bea, are you alright?" Mike's tone was worried.

"I'm ... really pleased to hear your voice," she answered.

"Where are you? What's going on with you?"

Bea smiled a wry smile. They'd let the question get through the filters. And she knew they were hoping she'd say something they could use - otherwise why let her speak to Mike. She fought back against the pounding in her head, and said, "I don't really know, Mike, but I'm ... well, I haven't had much time to talk before."

"I've missed you, Bea. Are you really safe?"

"I'm safe enough. How are you doing? Have you talked to Aunt Jacie?"

"Oh, sure. She's like always. And says to say hello."

"So she got my note?"

"She did. Commented about your handwriting."

A tear came out of Bea's eye. She dabbed it away with one of the fingers of her free hand. "Give her my best next time you call her, okay?"

"Okay." Mike was struggling for composure.

"Mike, I can't talk long. Have something coming up. But I just wanted to ... well, to tell you something."

"It's so great you called," he said. "What do you want to tell me."

"I'm sorry you can't see my face, Mike. I'm smiling at you. Can you remember that?"

"I could never forget your smile."

"Good. What I wanted to say is ... Mike, even though I don't really understand what it means, I ... well, I love you."

The young man was silent. Then she heard what she knew was a sob. He wanted to answer but couldn't. Bea smiled at the ceiling. "You don't have to say anything," she said gently. "I just had to tell you."

"You ... you've known a long time ... Bea, that I love you, too."

"I guessed you were that foolish, yes."

"You know, Bea, why ... why I had to leave?"

"Of course I do! Listen, Mike, I need you to promise me something."

"Sure." His voice broke on the single syllable.

"Take good care of yourself. Don't forget the virus is out there."

"Bea, I will."

"I have to go now, but ... I think about you a lot. Thank you for ... being who you are."

"It's ..." Again his voice broke. "Are you going to be okay, Bea?"

"Don't worry about me."

"You know I can't help doin' that."

"Goodbye, Mike."

"You take care, Bea ..." Then he heard the connection break.

Bea held the phone out for Agent Saunders when she returned, seconds later.

Saunders, standing by the bed, looking down, said, "What's your decision, Bea?"

"I guess I've done all I can," Bea said, apparently not answering the question.

"Shall I call the nurse, then?"

Bea looked up at her. "If you wish."

43. Final Truths

A HEAVY SNOW WAS FALLING ON CHRISTMAS morning. Out in the backyard of William Charles' home several little birds were sheltered under the big hemlock tree near his patio, making occasional chattering jaunts through the flakes to the fresh stock of seeds in the bird feeder. Knoxville was quiet that morning. No children were outside yet, fresh from opening gifts from Santa. The grayness of dawn had still not given away to the brighter cloudiness that would make the snowflakes flash against the drab background of houses, streets, trees, parked cars, and wooden fences that were plentiful in his neighborhood. Charles awoke when a hemlock frond from that big tree tapped roughly against his bedroom window, driven not by wind on that still morning but by heavy snowflakes that accumulated on the green collector, then fell away in a clump that released the springy branch.

The professor crawled out of bed and went to the window. He stood and watched the snow for a long time. Eventually, the scent of fresh coffee worked its way into his awareness and he went into the kitchen where his automatic coffee maker had done its morning task. After pouring himself a cup, he went to the kitchen window to continue watching the snow. It was a kind of mesmerizing experience for him. When his phone rang suddenly, Charles jumped, drawn unwillingly back into reality.

"Hello."

"Merry Christmas, Bill."

"Hello, Virginia. Yes, merry Christmas. Beautiful snow."

"Isn't it? I took a chance you were already awake."

"Is there some news?" His voice gave away a surge of concern.

"Yes. We missed you at the meeting yesterday."

"I can't say I actually missed going," he said. "But – I hope they knew I was in the middle of a run."

"They knew. Bill, do you mind if I drop by? I know it's a mess out there, but ... well, it's important."

"If you want to. I have fresh coffee. Virginia, you know this is pretty somber for a Christmas morning."

"I suppose it is. I'll be there in about half an hour."

Charles waited, though not patiently, for his colleague, diverting his attention by listening to NPR news. That was about the only news outlet where he could hope to hear any story other than something related to the virus epidemic.

Cortland arrived about when she'd said, and entered with overcoat dusted over with snow.

"It's really coming down out there," she said.

"Come on back in the den. I poured the coffee when I saw your car."

"Thanks, Bill."

They settled down across from each other in his two most comfortable chairs.

"Good coffee," she said after a drink. He could see she was as haggard looking as he felt.

"Go ahead, Virginia, let's get it over with."

"There are several things, Bill. All have to do with Bea."

"I guess I'm not surprised at that." He looked down at his cup as he spoke.

"First, there was a report on the memory sticks sent to Mike Baylor's aunt."

"Yes. From your tone, it doesn't sound like good news."

"It's not, as far as the virus is concerned. They were the accumulated data and analysis of her dissertation work. In perfect order, and with an essentially a complete final paper. But nothing that anyone's found yet that even remotely relates to the virus."

"Strange. Why would she hide that?"

Cortland sounded flat, with very little life in her tone. "It's something she would do, Bill. It's very much like her."

"I guess so. What's the second thing?"

"The three memory sticks found in The Sunspot ceiling. Guess what was on them?"

"Another wild goose chase?"

"Exactly. Random bits, forty-eight gigabytes worth."

"Not the encryption?"

"No. They're still looking at them, but the computer guys say she encrypted random numbers."

"To lead us astray, obviously."

"She succeeded," Cortland said.

"The situation is certainly not getting any better. I suppose they'll continue grilling her then."

"No they won't, Bill." Her eyes seemed peculiar.

"Won't? So they've given up? Don't they realize how little we've managed to come up with so far?" His tone had gotten energetic. "Everyone's blaming everyone else. The damned CDC is about to drive me up the wall. I've asked thirty times to get to talk to her!"

"That's not going to happen."

"She's our only real chance, Virginia. Damn it! Those precursors are ... well, I'm sure they were talked about at the meeting."

"Extensively." After a pause, Cortland added, "By the way, the case count went over a hundred thousand two days ago. Her Christmas present to us. Had you heard?"

"No," he said. "I guess I don't even want to hear anymore. Why won't they let me talk to her?"

"Because, Bill, because she's ... I'm so sorry I have to tell you." Cortland paused, then reached out to cover his hand. The silence was ominous. "Bill, Bea is dead."

"What?" He barely uttered the word. "Oh, God no!"

"I'm so sorry, Bill. For you, for everyone."

"What happened?" Charles' face was contorted.

"Officially, nothing." Cortland took a heavy breath. "Officially, she has disappeared. No one has heard from her. It's very convenient, actually, because she has no close relative to make any waves."

"What happened, Virginia?"

"The story I got - and of course in absolute total secrecy. That's why I had to come over here. It seems she had an allergic reaction to the drugs they were giving her. You were right, she was more fragile than we ... they wanted to admit. The first times it was only - only! - a severe headache. After the third injection, she ... well, she didn't come out of it. It could very well have been a mistake. Or even ... I hate to say it, intentional. But no one will ever know, you can be sure."

"But they got the ... the information out of her?"

"The whereabouts of the memory sticks, yes, and admission that she was responsible for the virus. But little else. It's not surprising, Bill. With those drugs, the person is barely functional when most susceptible to suggestion. She probably couldn't have explained her procedures even if she'd tried."

William Charles shook his head in dismay and sudden deep sadness. "Bea would have known that. And would likely have told them." He rubbed an unbidden tear away. "What a ... a horrible waste!"

"Yes. She could have done so much good for the world."

The silence between the colleagues hung heavy. Then Charles said, "She ... Virginia, you know she did what she sincerely believed *was* good for the world."

"I know. But the horror has just begun. It's a very bad time to be a normal male human being."

Charles shifted in his seat. "That I know full well. My FT has been tweaked down and I plan to keep it there. But I'm not burdened with siring children and don't have much of a social life anyway."

Cortland said, "Bill, I've been told we absolutely cannot inform Bea's friend, Mike Baylor."

"Not a surprise, I guess." He looked completely dejected.

"Only the committee and a few FBI people know about Bea. We were only told as a courtesy, and because we are trusted."

Charles was not handling the news very well. "What will they do with her body?"

"If I had to guess, I'd say it has already been cremated. All trace of Bea de Winter will be erased. Even if we were to tell the media what happened, besides whatever repercussions we'd have to suffer, they'd deny everything, and with no data refuting it, the issue would fade quickly."

"All trace erased," he mused, then smiled bitterly at his colleague. William Charles shook his head ruefully. "Bea would have guessed the tactic, Virginia. But what the CDC and FBI want really hasn't happened. And she knew that, too."

He looked away for a moment, regarding the snow falling outside the windows. Then he said, quietly, "All trace of Bea de Winter can never be erased."

The End

About the author

M R Cates is a physicist-turned-writer. He lives with his wife, two happy cats, and a happy-but-sometimes-worried dog in a house in the woods. He and his wife have a daughter, a son, a daughter-in-law, and a granddaughter who have made them tremendously proud and optimistic about the future. In addition to writing, Cates loves music, conversation with friends, wine and chicken wings in front of a burning fireplace, being groomed by Rufus the cat, encouraged in his craft by Guy Noir the other cat, and trying to let the dog Pogo know that all is well. He is grateful, too, for all the lovely friends in his life, knowing full well that there is no way anyone could deserve them. To his readers, he offers this tale with the hope that each will relate to it in his or her own uniquely meaningful way, processed through the wonders of individual lives and experiences.

www.ingramcontent.com/pod-product-compliance
Lightning Source LLC
Chambersburg PA
CBHW072054020726
47501CB00003B/582
* 9 7 8 0 6 1 5 8 4 1 0 1 4 *